DENIS HIRSON, born in 1951, left South Africa with his family in 1973 when his father, who had been a political prisoner for nine years, was released and went into exile. He has lived in France since 1975, working as an actor, and as an English teacher with the French Ministry of Foreign Affairs. Hirson's first novel, *The House Next Door to Africa*, was published in 1986 and subsequently translated into French and Italian. He has also translated a selection of Breyten Breytenbach's poetry, *In Africa Even the Flies are Happy*, published in 1977.

MARTIN TRUMP lived until recently in Johannesburg with his wife and two children. He worked in the English Department at the University of South Africa, teaching and publishing in the field of South African literary studies. He held degrees in English and Comparative Literature from the Universities of Witwatersrand, East Anglia and London. He was the editor of *Armed Vision: Afrikaans Writers in English*, an anthology of Afrikaans stories (Ad. Donker, 1987) and *Rendering Things Visible*, a collection of essays on South African literary culture (Ravan Press/Ohio University Press, 1990). He also taught at universities in North America and Israel. After a prolonged illness, he died of cancer in December 1993.

THE HEINEMANN BOOK OF
SOUTH AFRICAN SHORT STORIES

Edited by Denis Hirson, with Martin Trump

Heinemann Educational/UNESCO Publishing

Heinemann Educational Publishers
A Division of Heinemann Publishers (Oxford) Ltd
Halley Court, Jordan Hill, Oxford OX2 8EJ

Heinemann: A Division of Reed Publishing (USA) Inc.
361 Hanover Street, Portsmouth, NH 03801-3912, USA

Heinemann Educational Books (Nigeria) Ltd
PMB 5205, Ibadan
Heinemann Educational Boleswa
PO Box 10103, Village Post Office, Gaborone, Botswana

FLORENCE   PRAGUE   PARIS   MADRID
ATHENS   MELBOURNE   JOHANNESBURG
AUCKLAND   SINGAPORE   TOKYO
CHICAGO   SAO PAULO

UNESCO COLLECTION OF REPRESENTATIVE WORKS
African Series

Introduction, notes and selection
© Denis Hirson and Martin Trump 1994

First published by Heinemann Educational Publishers in 1994
Series Editor: Adewale Maja-Pearce

British Library Cataloguing in Publication Data
A catalogue record for this book is available from the British Library.

AFRICAN WRITERS SERIES and CARIBBEAN WRITERS SERIES and their
accompanying logos are trademarks in the United States of America of
Heinemann: A Division of Reed Publishing (USA) Inc.

Cover design by Stafford and Stafford
Cover painting by Lyn Gilbert
by kind permission of Francois de Kok

ISBN 0435 90672 0
UNESCO ISBN 92-3-102944-4

Phototypeset by Wilmaset, Birkenhead, Wirral
Printed and bound in Great Britain by
Cox & Wyman Ltd, Reading, Berkshire

94 95 96 97 10 9 8 7 6 5 4 3 2

CONTENTS

ACKNOWLEDGEMENTS

The first people we have to thank are those who involved themselves wholeheartedly in the long, even if finally unfruitful search for African language stories. These include Mollie Bill, Rosalie Finlayson, Nhlanhla Maake, Bheki Ntuli and Noleen Turner.

Thanks are due to Catherine Knox for her collaboration as a translator (see note below), and to Dawie Malan of the UNISA library who collected together wads of information for the biographical notes on page 242.

We would also like to mention the help given to us on one aspect or another of this anthology by Robert Berold, Kate Trump, Baruch Hirson, Allen Hirson and Craig Mackenzie. A special word of appreciation for Adine Sagalyn whose sense of implacable judgement while roving these pages has been invaluable from beginning to end. And lastly, thanks to Vicky Unwin and Ruth Hamilton-Jones of Heinemann Publishers for their patience and warm encouragement.

The publishers would like to thank the following for permission to use copyright material:

Faber & Faber Ltd. and Farrar, Straus and Giroux, Inc. for 'The Double Dying of an Ordinary Criminal' from *Mouroir* by Breyten Breytenbach. Copyright © 1984 by Breyten Breytenbach; Blake Friedmann Literary Agency on behalf of the author for 'Mad Dog' from *Leigfabriek* by Etienne van Heerden; A. M. Heath & Company Ltd. on behalf of the author for 'The Zulu and the Zeide' from *Inklings* by Dan Jacobson, 1973, Weidenfeld & Nicholson; Human & Rousseau (PTY) Ltd. for 'A Bekkersdal Marathon' from *A Bekkersdal Marathon* by Herman Charles Bosman, 1951; John Johnson Ltd. on behalf of the Estate of the author for 'The Prisoner Who Wore Glasses' from *Tales of Tenderness and Power* by Bessie Head, Heinemann, 1990; London Magazine for 'Familiarity is the Kingdom of the Lost' by Dugmore Boetie, *London Magazine*, October 1966; Penguin

Books Ltd. and Houghton Mifflin Company for 'Bloodsong' from *Bloodsong and Other Stories of South Africa* by Ernst Havemann, Hamish Hamilton, 1988. Copyright © 1987 Ernst Havemann; Shelley Power Literary Agency on behalf of the author for 'The Prophetess' by Njabulo Ndebele, *Tri-Quarterly*, 69, Spring/Summer, 1987. Copyright © 1987 Njabulo S. Ndebele; Random Century Group, with Macmillan Publishing Company for 'Life for a Life' from *Debbie, Go Home* by Alan Paton, Jonathan Cape, 1965, and from *Tales From a Troubled Land* by Alan Paton, Charles Scribner's Sons. Copyright © 1961 Alan Paton; and with A. P. Watt Ltd. on behalf of the author for 'Six Feet of the Country' from *Six Feet of the Country* by Nadine Gordimer, Jonathan Cape, 1956; Ravan Press Pty Ltd. for 'The Hajji' from *The Hajji and Other Stories* by Ahmed Essop, 1978; Rogers, Coleridge and White on behalf of the author for 'Learning to Fly: An African Fairy Tale' from *Private Parts and Other Tales* by Christopher Hope, Routledge and Kegan Paul, 1982; Tafelberg Publishers Ltd. for 'Night at the Ford' from *Storyflight* by Elise Muller, 1986, trs. for this volume by Catherine Knox; 'I Take Back My Country' by Bartho Smit, published in Afrikaans as '*Ek vat my land*' in *Bolder*, 1973; and for 'For four Voices' from *House Visits* by Hennie Aucamp, 1983; Mango Tshabangu for 'Thoughts in a Train', included in *Forced Landing*, ed. Mothobi Mutloatse, 1980. Copyright © Mango Tshabangu; Virago Press Ltd. and Pantheon Books, a division of Random House, Inc, for 'A Trip to the Gifberge' from *You Can't Get Lost in Capetown* by Zoë Wicomb. Copyright © 1987 by Zoë Wicomb;

Every effort has been made to trace all the copyright holders, but if any have been inadvertently overlooked the publishers will be pleased to make the necessary arrangement at the first opportunity.

Editors' Note

Several previously published translations have been reworked by Catherine Knox for this anthology. These are: 'Night at the Ford' by Elise Muller; 'I Take Back My Country' by Bartho Smit (originally entitled 'I Reclaim My Country'), and 'Mad Dog' by Etienne van Heerden. In addition, there are minor changes to the previously published version of Mango Tshabangu's 'Thoughts in a Train'. 'Familiarity is the Kingdom of the Lost' by Dugmore Boetie was originally published in *London Magazine* in 1966, and later integrated into a book of the same name. We have chosen to reproduce the story using the more satisfactory punctuation of the book version.

Introduction

'South Africa' is a deceptive name, one that reveals the country's geographical location while hinting only vaguely at the specific identity which might separate it from the rest of the continent. Yet South Africa is very definitely a place apart. Its frontiers have always, quite literally, bristled: as early as 1659, a hedge of wild almonds was planted around the new Cape Colony;[1] as recently as 1986, an electrified fence with a 20,000 volt charge was erected along the Zimbabwe border, aimed at preventing guerilla incursions.[2]

Few other countries of the mainland have been made to mascarade as an island for such a long period of time; and few islands have found themselves so geographically isolated. But it is within South Africa itself that the harshest frontiers have been drawn. Over the past forty-five years the National Party has devoted itself to dividing the land up into narrowly restrictive areas of habitation, classifying them according to colours (not always outrightly named) from an official colour chart. There have been, among other things: black homelands; black and 'coloured' locations and townships; white cities – declared by one rather hopeful prime minister to be 'white by night';[3] white towns, dorps and farmlands; black compounds; one 'coloured' district, immortalised as 'District 6', which buzzed on a blue mountainside above a white metropolis before it was razed to the ground; black spots, grey areas, black closer-settlement camps, black resettlement areas and squatter camps, and so on.

The country, pigmented according to this chart, would seem from the air to be suffering from a rampant skin disease. It did, and still does.

Today, with the lifting of influx control, there is a large-scale movement of impoverished people to the towns and cities, and the disease, kept in check for so long by a massive deployment of police, military and bureaucratic forces, is in full eruption.

This is not to infer that South Africans have never shifted about before. They have, under vastly differing circumstances and despite the various obstacles placed in their way, a long history of trekking, marauding,

migrating, prospecting, squatting, marching, setting off on punitive
expeditions or desperately trying to avoid them, crossing rivers and
dongas, koppies, baked Karroo sand and bundu, often neglecting to
return to where they came from in the first place.

The record of their meetings reads like a seismograph; yet only
intermittently has this seismograph shivered across the pages of South
African literature with the terrible momentum spoken of in the history
books. It is as if those same forces breaking the country into fragments
have also interrupted the span of the creative imagination. Both writers
and their fictional characters have often found themselves poised on a
strip of territory as thin and jaggedly defined as a glass shard.

Es'kia Mphahlele, discussing the black condition in South Africa,
states that:

> . . . as long as the white man's politics continue to impose on us a
> ghetto existence, so long shall the culture and therefore literature of
> South Africa continue to shrivel up, to sink lower and lower; and for
> so long shall we in our writing continue to reflect only a minute
> fraction of life.[4]

It would seem that writers bounded by such a 'minute fraction of life'
often turn to shorter literary forms, and elsewhere Mphahlele is more
specific about this:

> It is impossible for a writer who lives in oppression to organise his
> whole personality into creating a novel. The short story is used as a
> short cut to prose meaning and one gets some things off one's chest in
> quick time.[5]

Stories committed to paper under such conditions – usually, in the South
African context, by black writers – give the impression of a train hurtling
through a half-lit landscape, with scenes and visions flashing by too fast,
characters glimpsed but not filled out, emotion pounding but rarely
transcended. Whatever is described looms too close to be clearly visible,
only to disappear before its full significance can be grasped. In between,
in the dark, there is too often an excess of explanatory and didactic
language.

Njabulo Ndebele, discussing the spectacular yet short-lived
impression such writing leaves behind, comments that 'it is the literature
of the powerless identifying the key factor responsible for their powerlessness. Nothing beyond this can be expected of it.'[6]

If in black South African writing there is frequently a collapse of the
distance between the writer and his or her subject matter, much white
South African writing may leave the reader with an equal yet opposite
effect: that of remoteness from the raw nerve of the black condition in
particular, and human oppression in general. As if the writer was not

really there: 'I live on the periphery of an existence I do not understand,' says a white woman of the blacks who come and go from her own back yard, in a story by Elsa Joubert.[7] Or as if the blacks themselves weren't there. J. M. Coetzee speaks of

> . . . a certain historical will to see as silent and empty a land that has been, if not full of human figures, not empty of them either . . .[8]

This (to transpose the terms used by Njabulo Ndebele above), is the literature of the powerful denying, however equivocally, the presence of those upon whom their power rests.[9]

These general statements concerning black and white writing in South Africa are fortunately no more than generalisations; at best they give some idea of the limits which writers must radically transform if they are to create a work of any enduring interest.

Martin Trump and I have selected those stories in which the language is finely crafted and which give shape to the raw stuff of experience, yet reach towards the core of the human condition in South Africa; those which flare with love or laughter, rage or despair, but do not burn up before they come to an end; those which seem to be pitched at the right distance between the writer and the reader[10] and whose content we have found to be both striking and memorable.

Perhaps you will discover, as I have, that some of these stories lodge themselves in your memory, and expand there, so that on going back to them you are surprised to see how few pages they actually fill. This ability of a story to expand, like a Japanese paper flower opening from its shell in water, is compelling at the best of times. In the fragmented context of South Africa, where human relations have been defined in such a cramped, feudal fashion, a story which appears to move outwards beyond its own brief boundaries is a breath of miraculous air.

We hope that, side by side, these stories might have the effect of a mosaic, giving you some sense of the very different realities which go to make up the country known as South Africa; and yet we are aware of just how partial the picture will be, given the present disparate state of South African literature.

As Lewis Nkosi points out:

> Until apartheid has been abolished there is no such thing as a South African *national* culture but only a patchwork of *national group* cultures . . . there is . . . no such thing as a *national* literature of South Africa but only the literatures of various national groups.[11]

The pig-iron machinery of apartheid has officially been dismantled and yet the cogs continue to turn. Nkosi's statement, made in 1987 and still largely true today, underscores the need to define precisely what is and is not included in an anthology of South African short stories.

In this anthology, you will find stories all of which originally appeared either in English or in Afrikaans. I should add that all the writers represented here spent their formative years in South Africa – hence the exclusion, for example, of work by Doris Lessing. However, to my knowledge, six stories – almost a third of the total number in this anthology – were written outside the country, while one was written in prison.[12]

Though literary translation from Afrikaans into English is not always what it should be, and perhaps inevitably so in a country where linguistic apartheid is still very much alive and well, the passage between these two languages is a wide gleaming highway when compared with the thickset long-thorned bush that continues to separate both of them from the African languages of South Africa.

There are, regrettably, no stories here translated from an African language. I will save you a blow-by-blow account of the full saga of letters, phone calls, faxes, meetings, pleas slipped on to tables and under doors, which lead to the production of many seemingly bland and predictable African-language stories in summary form; and a few full translations, lifeless if quirky, with the exception of one which almost made its appearance here but turned out to have been originally written in siSwati by a Swazi national, and was translated into Zulu, and from Zulu into English.

Perhaps there are no contemporary South African stories in an African language which, given their literary strength, would stand against the best in this anthology. I suspect that at least a handful must have appeared somewhere between the late 1940s and late 1950s with the same fresh cutting edge as stories such as those by Herman Charles Bosman, Nadine Gordimer, Jack Cope, Dan Jacobson, Elise Muller and Bartho Smit reprinted here, all of them written before South Africa seized up in the political winter of the 1960s and 70s.

Then again, perhaps I am wrong, and the dead-end street of Bantu education, the monopolistic sway of Afrikaans and missionary publishing houses over African-language writing, combined with the attraction of an English-speaking readership, enticed most black prose writers of any worth to write in English. Es'kia Mphahlele, writing in the early 1960s, adds a political dimension to this decision:

> Now because the government is using institutions of a fragmented and almost unrecognisable Bantu culture as an instrument of expression, we dare not look back. We have got to wrench the tools of power from the white man's hand: one of these is literacy – the sophistication that goes with it. We have got to speak the language that all can understand – English . . .[13]

Mphahlele appears to be choosing here not only the English language over any other, but also the quest for power over an exploration of ancestry and tradition; many South African writers have, in different ways and at different times, made a similar choice. Yet a close reading of the stories in this anthology might reveal to you a change in the relative importance of these far from mutually exclusive domains of interest over the past decades.

The stories we have chosen were all written between 1945 and 1992; to our minds, they contribute towards this being a comtemporary anthology, in that they throw light on the human condition in South Africa today. We were tempted to include certain stories written before 1945; stories which might well be termed contemporary, speaking as they do in an essential and undated manner of life in South Africa – irrespective of the historical period they happen to be clothed in. (I am thinking here particularly of work by Pauline Smith and William Plomer.) We have, nonetheless, decided to limit ourselves to the period between the end of the Second World War – when the National Party, which was to take power in 1948, was already on the upsurge – and the early 1990s, with the abolition of the legal framework of apartheid, the legalisation of various opposition parties including the African National Congress and the Pan Africanist Congress, and the release of Nelson Mandela.

Few events in recent years in South Africa have had as potent a symbolic effect as this release. It was as if the door of a gigantic freezer had swung open, and the history of an entire country could make its slow dazed way outwards, shaking the ice from its limbs.

As if, for decades on end, the National Party had managed, in the face of revolt and rage, to maintain the illusion of absolute power not only over the space of an entire country, but also over time. As if a government could by its actions gel the social perception of time, and have people believe that there was no history but state history, no real past but only official myth and generalised amnesia.

In February 1990, at the very moment when they were being publicly accused of crimes against humanity, National Party officials appeared on television appealing to viewers to forget the past and build a new society in their beautiful country.[14] One might as well shove a piece of driftwood in the ground and expect it to bear paw-paws.

But perhaps their request was in fact a sign of recognition that the past, or rather many varied and contradictory versions of the past, had already become a vital issue for people in South Africa seeking to re-situate their political struggle and cultural vision. Amongst these people are some of the writers whose work appears in the following pages; writers engaged in opening the box which Mphahlele, in the quote above, labeled 'We Dare Not Look Back'. Among the riches in this deep box are myths, tales and legends from the various oral traditions in South Africa, which give expression to elemental forces of rare strength and strangeness.

Here is a somewhat macabre example of what I mean:

The Zombie Labourers

There were once two brothers, Umlilo and Umlango. One day, Umlango felt tired and lay down, although he had always been healthy. In a few days, he grew so weak and exhausted that he died. So his brother buried him, although he noticed that Umlango's body remained soft. Normally, a dead body will grow stiff after a few hours. Umlilo suspected that witchcraft was the cause of his brother's fatal illness, and he decided to discover the evil-doer. He was right: when he came back to inspect the grave on the day after the funeral, the open pit stared at him, and his brother's body had disappeared.

Umlilo was now certain that an evil sorcerer had bewitched his brother, so that he fell ill and died, after which the sorcerer could dig him up and make him into an *umkovu*, a zombie-slave. What could Umlilo do to save his brother? He decided to go out in search of him first. After travelling for many days, he heard people talking in whispers. They were discussing a powerful and dangerous man who was rumoured to have a large farm in the hills.

This made Umlilo suspicious and he decided to find out what happened there. At dusk, he reached the hills and there he saw a strange sight: a silent army of workers labouring the fields, hoeing all night, planting maize, clearing fields. But were they alive? Did their hearts beat? Did their blood flow, or were they pale shadows of men?

Suddenly, Umlilo saw his own brother among them. His skin looked grey in the darkness; his face was sad, for the *umkovus* remember their families. Umlilo called his brother, but he could not answer, only babble, for his tongue had been cut out. He was completely in the power of the sorcerer.

Umlilo took his brother in his arms (how light he was!) and ran with him to safety. At home, Umlango died again, this time a real death that made the body stiff.[15]

I am glad to have been able to include the full version of this story here. The person who related it, believed it to be a report 'about historical facts that had taken place within living memory'.[16] This in itself would in some way make 'The Zombie Labourers' a contemporary story. And since an estimated 8.3 million black adult South Africans are illiterate,[17] perhaps stories of this kind might inform the world of their experience and imagination when written stories would, by definition, escape their notice.

If we had found a sufficient number of transcribed texts which read as well as 'The Zombie Labourers' does, we might have considered interweaving them with the more literary short stories we have chosen. But many of the myths, tales and legends originally meant to be recounted in the theatrically vibrant ambit of the fireside, seemed to be in exile on the dry white page; in this respect it is worth heeding Ruth Finnegan's judgement that:

> . . . in the case of oral literature . . . the bare words can *not* be left to speak for themselves for the simple reason that . . . so much else is necessarily and intimately involved.[18]

If the oral tradition is not directly represented in this anthology, traces of it can certainly be found in stories as diverse as those by Bheki Maseko and Herman Charles Bosman (who drew on the tales of the rural Afrikaans community where he worked as a teacher).

More generally, though, some writers in South Africa today are turning more overtly to the resources of history, personal and ancestral memory. (See, for example, the stories in this book by Njabulo Ndebele, Zoë Wicomb and Bheki Maseko.)

What is at stake here is not only the cross-fertilisation of traditional and contemporary, oral and literary perspectives. Writers are slowly beginning to free themselves of the culturally desiccated and historically distorted environment that is a legacy of white rule in general and National Party apartheid in particular.

As they find access to multiple, often previously hidden currents welling out of the past, they are participating in the growth of new, hybrid forms of culture,[19] a process that began almost three and a half centuries ago, in the shadow of the same walls originally meant to keep those cultures apart.

Just how far this process has evolved you will perhaps begin to evaluate for yourself after dipping into the pages that follow.

Denis Hirson, 1994

Postscript

While working on the proofs of this book, I received a letter from Martin Trump's wife, Kate, informing me of his untimely death. Martin will be missed by many, not only family and friends, but also those with whom he shared his passion for South African fiction. It is small consolation that he helped bring life to the following pages.

Notes

1 Eric Walker, *A History of Southern Africa*, Longman, London, 1959, pp. 40–41. The hedge, along with fencing and blockhouses, was designed to keep the Khoi women and children out of the Cape settlement, the men being allowed to barter cattle. It was planted by the settlers in 1659–60, after they had defeated the Khoi in a war for land.

2 *The Guardian*, 13 January 1986. According to this report, the fence was described by the Afrikaans Sunday newspaper *Rapport* as an impenetrable 'wall of death'. By 1989, the fence had already claimed seventy human victims (not to mention animals whose natural paths it cut across). *Institute of Race Relations Survey*, Johannesburg 1989–90, p. 142.

3 According to the 'white by night' policy, announced by Prime Minister J. B. Vorster in the 1960s, blacks were supposed to leave the white urban areas at nightfall.

4 Es'kia Mphahlele, *The African Image*, Faber, London, 1962, p. 109. cf. also Stephen Clingman's fine essay 'Writing in a Fractured Society, the case of Nadine Gordimer' in *Literature and Society in South Africa*, eds Landeg White and Tim Couzens, Maskew Miller Longman, Cape, 1984.

5 Es'kia Mphahlele, 'Black and White', *The New Statesman*, 10 September 1960, p. 343.

6 Njabulo S. Ndebele, 'The Rediscovery of the Ordinary: some new writings in South Africa', in *Rediscovery of the Ordinary*, COSAW, Johannesburg, 1991, p. 46.

7 Elsa Joubert, 'Back Yard', in *A Land Apart*, eds André Brink and J. M. Coetzee, Faber, London, 1986, p. 219.

8 J. M. Coetzee, *White Writing*, Yale University Press, New Haven, 1988, p. 177.

9 cf. Chinua Achebe, 'African Literature as Celebration', *Dissent*, Summer 1992: '. . . I want to suggest that in the colonial situation *presence* was the critical question, the crucial word. Its denial was the keynote of colonialist ideology,' p. 346. (Achebe's italics.)

10 '. . . every experience basically defies description as long as we try to express it through the actual example that has impressed us. I can express what I want to say only by means of an example that is as remote from me as it is from the listener, that is to say, an invented one. Essentially only fiction – things altered, transformed, shaped – can convey impressions . . .' Max Frisch, *Sketchbook 1946–1949*, Harcourt Brace Jovanovich, New York, 1977, p. 259.

11 Lewis Nkosi, 'Resistance and the Crisis of Representation' in *From Popular Culture to the Written Artefact*, Evangelische Akademie, Bad Boll, 1987, p. 43. (Nkosi's italics.)

12 'The Double Dying of an Ordinary Criminal' was written in prison by Breyten Breytenbach. The stories by Ernst Havemann, Bessie Head, Christopher Hope, Dan Jacobson, Njabulo Ndebele and Zoë Wicomb were all, to my knowledge, written outside South Africa. In some cases

there are specific political reasons for this; but, more generally, South Africans have often found it easier to write when away from the stifling pressures of their own country.

13 Es'kia Mphahlele, *The African Image, op. cit.*, p. 193.

14 I don't know how widespread this kind of appeal was, but it did occur – along with the accusation of crimes against humanity – on French television, during the hours following Nelson Mandela's release on 11 February 1990.

15 *Bantu Myths and Other Tales*, translated and annotated by Jan Knappert, E. J. Brill, Leiden, 1977, pp. 174–5. The story is of Zulu origin.

16 *Ibid.* p. 170.

17 1990 Census. According to B. Stewart, managing director of the KwaZulu Training Trust, 78% of blacks, 55% of coloureds, 23% of Indians and 2% of whites are illiterate (*African Business*, March 1991). Source in both cases: *Institute of Race Relations Survey*, Johannesburg, 1991–1992, p. 213.

18 Ruth Finnegan, *Oral Literature in Africa*, Oxford University Press, London, 1970, p. 15. (Finnegan's italics.) A similar argument is pursued by Harold Scheub in *The Xhosa Ntsomi*, Oxford University Press, London, 1975, pp. 44–5.

19 'In the future, perhaps, the very pluralism of the influences upon [South African writers with a multicultural background], and their metaphysical ability to synthesise, will be accounted their greatest strengths'. Stephen Gray, 'A Sense of Place in the New Literatures in English, Particularly South African' in *A Sense of Place in the New Literatures in English*, ed. P. Nightingale, University of Queensland Press, St Lucia, 1986.

Publisher's note

The story 'The Prophetess' also appears in *The Heinemann Book of African Short Stories*. We decided not to replace it with another story in this anthology because it seemed particularly appropriate to this volume.

NJABULO NDEBELE

The Prophetess

The boy knocked timidly on the door, while a big fluffy dog sniffed at his ankles. That dog made him uneasy; he was afraid of strange dogs and this fear made him anxious to go into the house as soon as possible. But there was no answer to his knock. Should he simply turn the doorknob and get in? What would the prophetess say? Would she curse him? He was not sure now which he feared more: the prophetess or the dog. If he stood longer there at the door, the dog might soon decide that he was up to some mischief after all. If he left, the dog might decide he was running away. And the prophetess! What would she say when she eventually opened the door to find no one there? She might decide someone had been fooling, and would surely send lightning after the boy. But then, leaving would also bring the boy another problem: he would have to leave without the holy water for which his sick mother had sent him to the prophetess.

There was something strangely intriguing about the prophetess and holy water. All that one was to do, the boy had so many times heard in the streets of the township, was fill a bottle with water and take it to the prophetess. She would then lay her hands on the bottle and pray. And the water would be holy. And the water would have curing powers. That's what his mother had said too.

The boy knocked again, this time with more urgency. But he had to be careful not to annoy the prophetess. It was getting darker and the dog continued to sniff at his ankles. The boy tightened his grip round the neck of the bottle he had just filled with water from the street tap on the other side of the street, just opposite the prophetess's house. He would hit the dog with this bottle. What's more, if the bottle broke he would stab the dog with the sharp glass. But what would the prophetess say? She would probably curse him. The boy knocked again, but this time he heard the faint voice of a woman.

'*Kena*!' the voice said.

The boy quickly turned the knob and pushed. The door did not yield. And the dog growled. The boy turned the knob again and pushed. This time the dog gave a sharp bark, and the boy knocked frantically. Then he heard the bolt shoot back, and saw the door open to reveal darkness. Half the door seemed to have disappeared into the dark. The boy felt fur brush past his leg as the dog scurried into the house.

'*Voetsek*!' the woman cursed suddenly.

The boy wondered whether the woman was the prophetess. But as he was wondering, the dog brushed past him again, slowly this time. In spite of himself, the boy felt a pleasant, tickling sensation and a slight warmth where the fur of the dog had touched him. The warmth did not last, but the tickling sensation lingered, going up to the back of his neck and seeming to caress it. Then he shivered and the sensation disappeared, shaken off in the brief involuntary tremor.

'Dogs stay out!' shouted the woman, adding, 'This is not at the white man's.'

The boy heard a slow shuffle of soft leather shoes receding into the dark room. The woman must be moving away from the door, the boy thought. He followed into the house.

'Close the door,' ordered the woman who was still moving somewhere in the dark. But the boy had already done so.

Although it was getting dark outside, the room was much darker and the fading day threw some of its waning light into the room through the windows. The curtains had not yet been drawn. Was it an effort to save candles, the boy wondered. His mother had scolded him many times for lighting up before it was completely dark.

The boy looked instinctively towards the dull light coming in through the window. He was anxious, though, about where the woman was now, in the dark. Would she think he was afraid when she caught him looking out to the light? But the thick, dark green leaves of vine outside, lapping lazily against the window, attracted and held him like a spell. There was no comfort in that light; it merely reminded the boy of his fear, only a few minutes ago, when he walked under that dark tunnel of vine which arched over the path from the gate to the door. He had dared not touch that vine and its countless velvety, black, and juicy grapes that hung temptingly within reach, or rested lusciously on forked branches. Silhouetted against the darkening summer sky, the bunches of grapes had each looked like a cluster of small cones narrowing down to a point.

'Don't touch that vine!' was the warning almost everyone in Charterston township knew. It was said that the vine was all coated with thick, invisible glue. And that was how the prophetess caught all those who stole out in the night to steal her grapes. They would be glued there to the vine, and would be moaning for forgiveness throughout the cold night, until the morning, when the prophetess would come out of the house with the first rays of the sun, raise her arms into the sky, and say: 'Away, away, sinful man; go and sin no more!' Suddenly, the thief would be free, and would walk away feeling a great release that turned him into a new man. That vine; it was on the lips of everyone in the township every summer.

One day when the boy had played truant with three of his friends, and they were coming back from town by bus, some grown-ups in the bus were arguing about the prophetess's vine. The bus was so full that it was hard for anyone to move. The three truant friends, having given their seats to grown-ups, pressed against each other in a line in the middle of the bus and could see most of the passengers.

'Not even a cow can tear away from that glue,' said a tall, dark man who had high cheek-bones. His balaclava was a careless heap on his head. His moustache, which had been finely rolled into two semi-circular horns, made him look fierce. And when he gesticulated with his tin lunch box, he looked fiercer still.

'My question is only one,' said a big woman whose big arms rested thickly on a bundle of washing on her lap. 'Have you ever seen a person caught there? Just answer that one question.' She spoke with finality, and threw her defiant scepticism outside at the receding scene of men cycling home from work in single file. The bus moved so close to them that the boy had feared the men might get hit.

'I have heard of one silly chap that got caught!' declared a young man. He was sitting with others on the long seat at the rear of the bus. They had all along been laughing and exchanging ribald jokes. The young man had thick lips and red eyes. As he spoke he applied the final touches of saliva with his tongue to brown paper rolled up with tobacco.

'When?' asked the big woman. 'Exactly when, I say? Who was that person?'

'These things really happen!' said a general chorus of women.

'That's what I know,' endorsed the man with the balaclava, and then added, 'You see, the problem with some women is that they will not listen; they have to oppose a man. They just have to.'

'What is that man saying now?' asked another woman. 'This matter started off very well, but this road you are now taking will get us lost.'

'That's what I'm saying too,' said the big woman, adjusting her bundle of washing somewhat unnecessarily. She continued: 'A person shouldn't look this way or that, or take a corner here or there. Just face me straight: I asked a question.'

'These things really happen,' said the chorus again.

'That's it, good ladies, make your point; push very strongly,' shouted the young man at the back. 'Love is having women like you,' he added, much to the enjoyment of his friends. He was now smoking, and his rolled up cigarette looked small between his thick fingers.

'Although you have no respect,' said the big woman, 'I will let you know that this matter is no joke.'

'Of course this is not a joke!' shouted a new contributor. He spoke firmly and in English. His eyes seemed to burn with anger. He was young and immaculately dressed, his white shirt collar resting neatly on the collar of his jacket. A young nurse in a white uniform sat next to him. 'The mother there,' he continued, 'asks you very clearly whether you have ever seen a person caught by the supposed prophetess's supposed trap. Have you?'

'She didn't say that, man,' said the young man at the back, passing the roll to one of his friends. 'She only asked when this person was caught and who it was.' The boys at the back laughed. There was a lot of smoke now at the back of the bus.

'My question was,' said the big woman turning her head to glare at the young man, 'have you ever seen a person caught there? That's all.' Then she looked outside. She seemed angry now.

'Don't be angry, mother,' said the young man at the back. There was more laughter. 'I was only trying to understand,' he added.

'And that's our problem,' said the immaculately dressed man, addressing the bus. His voice was sure and strong. 'We laugh at everything; just stopping short of seriousness. Is it any wonder that the white man is still sitting on us? The mother there asked a very straightforward question, but she is answered vaguely about things happening. Then there is disrespectful laughter at the back there.

The truth is you have no proof. None of you. Have you ever seen anybody caught by this prophetess? Never. It's all superstition. And so much about this prophetess also. Some of us are tired of her stories.'

There was a stunned silence in the bus. Only the heavy drone of an engine struggling with an overloaded bus could be heard. It was the man with the balaclava who broke the silence.

'Young man,' he said, 'by the look of things you must be a clever, educated person, but you just note one thing. The prophetess might just be hearing all this, so don't be surprised when a bolt of lightning strikes you on a hot sunny day. And we shall be there at your funeral, young man, to say how you brought misfortune upon your head.'

Thus had the discussion ended. But the boy had remembered how, every summer, bottles of all sizes filled with liquids of all kinds of colours would dangle from vines and peach and apricot trees in many yards in the township. No one dared steal fruit from those trees. Who wanted to be glued in shame to a fruit tree? Strangely, though, only the prophetess's trees had no bottles hanging from their branches.

The boy turned his eyes away from the window and focused into the dark room. His eyes had adjusted slowly to the darkness, and he saw the dark form of the woman shuffling away from him. She probably wore those slippers that had a fluff on top. Old women seem to love them. Then a white receding object came into focus. The woman wore a white *doek* on her head. The boy's eyes followed the *doek*. It took a right-angled turn – probably round the table. And then the dark form of the table came into focus. The *doek* stopped, and the boy heard the screech of a chair being pulled; and the *doek* descended somewhat and was still. There was silence in the room. The boy wondered what to do. Should he grope for a chair? Or should he squat on the floor respectfully? Should he greet or wait to be greeted? One never knew with the prophetess. Why did his mother have to send him to this place? The fascinating stories about the prophetess, to which the boy would add graphic details as if he had also met her, were one thing; but being in her actual presence was another. The boy then became conscious of the smell of camphor. His mother always used camphor whenever she complainted of pains in her joints. Was the prophetess ill then? Did she pray for her own water?

Suddenly, the boy felt at ease, as if the discovery that a prophetess could also feel pain somehow made her explainable.

'*Lumela 'me*,' he greeted. Then he cleared his throat.

'*Eea ngoanaka*,' she responded. After a little while she asked: 'Is there something you want, little man?' It was a very thin voice. It would have been completely detached had it not been for a hint of tiredness in it. She breathed somewhat heavily. Then she coughed, cleared her throat, and coughed again. A mixture of rough discordant sounds filled the dark room as if everything was coming out of her insides, for she seemed to breathe out her cough from deep within her. And the boy wondered: if she coughed too long, what would happen? Would something come out? A lung? The boy saw the form of the woman clearly now: she had bent forward somewhat. Did anything come out of her on to the floor? The cough subsided. The woman sat up and her hands fumbled with something around her breasts. A white cloth emerged. She leaned forward again, cupped her hands and spat into the cloth. Then she stood up and shuffled away into further darkness away from the boy. A door creaked, and the white *doek* disappeared. The boy wondered what to do because the prophetess had disappeared before he could say what he had come for. He waited.

More objects came into focus. Three white spots on the table emerged. They were placed diagonally across the table. Table mats. There was a small round black patch on the middle one. Because the prophetess was not in the room, the boy was bold enough to move near the table and touch the mats. They were crocheted mats. The boy remembered the huge lacing that his mother had crocheted for the church altar. ALL SAINTS CHURCH was crocheted all over the lacing. There were a number of designs of chalices that carried the Blood of Our Lord.

Then the boy heard the sound of a match being struck. There were many attempts before the match finally caught fire. Soon, the dull, orange light of a candle came into the living room where the boy was, through a half closed door. More light flushed the living room as the woman came in carrying a candle. She looked round as if she was wondering where to put the candle. Then she saw the ashtray on the middle mat, pulled it towards her, sat down and turned the candle over into the ashtray. Hot wax dropped on to the ashtray. Then the propetess turned the candle upright and pressed its bottom on to the wax. The candle held.

The prophetess now peered through the light of the candle at the boy. Her thick lips protruded, pulling the wrinkled skin and caving in the cheeks to form a kind of lip circle. She seemed always ready to kiss. There was a line tattooed from the forehead to the ridge of a nose that separated small eyes that were half closed by large, drooping eyelids. The white *doek* on her head was so huge that it made her face look small. She wore a green dress and a starched green cape that had many white crosses embroidered on it. Behind her, leaning against the wall, was a long bamboo cross.

The prophetess stood up again, and shuffled towards the window which was behind the boy. She closed the curtains and walked back to her chair. The boy saw another big cross embroidered on the back of her cape. Before she sat down she picked up the bamboo cross and held it in front of her.

'What did you say you wanted, little man?' she asked slowly.

'My mother sent me to ask for water,' said the boy putting the bottle of water on the table.

'To ask for water?' she asked with mild exclamation, looking up at the bamboo cross. 'That is very strange. You came all the way from home to ask for water?'

'I mean,' said the boy, 'holy water.'

'Ahh!' exclaimed the prophetess, 'you did not say what you meant, little man.' She coughed, just once. 'Sit down, little man,' she said, and continued, 'You see, you should learn to say what you mean. Words, little man, are a gift from the Almighty, the Eternal Wisdom. He gave us all a little pinch of his mind and called on us to think. That is why it is folly to misuse words or not to know how to use them well. Now, who is your mother?'

'My mother?' asked the boy, confused by the sudden transition. 'My mother is staff nurse Masemola.'

'Ao!' exclaimed the prophetess, 'you are the son of the nurse? Does she have such a big man now?' She smiled a little and the lip circle opened. She smiled like a pretty woman who did not want to expose her cavities.

The boy relaxed somewhat, vaguely feeling safe because the prophetess knew his mother. This made him look away from the prophetess for a while, and he saw that there was a huge mask on the wall just opposite her. It was shining and black. It grinned all the time showing two canine teeth pointing upwards. About ten feet away at the other side of the wall was a picture of Jesus in which His chest was open, revealing His heart which had many shafts of light radiating from it.

'Your mother has a heart of gold, my son,' continued the prophetess. 'You are very fortunate, indeed, to have such a parent. Remember, when she says, "My boy, take this message to that house," go. When she says, "My boy, let me send you to the shop," go. And when she says, "My boy, pick up a book and read," pick up a book and read. In all this she is actually saying to you, learn and serve. Those two things, little man, are the greatest inheritance.'

Then the prophetess looked up at the bamboo cross as if she saw something in it that the boy could not see. She seemed to lose her breath for a while. She coughed deeply again, after which she went silent, her cheeks moving as if she was chewing.

'Bring the bottle nearer,' she said finally. She put one hand on the bottle while with the other she held the bamboo cross. Her eyes closed, she turned her face towards the ceiling. The boy saw that her face seemed to have contracted into an intense concentration in such a way that the wrinkles seemed to have become deep gorges. Then she began to speak.

'You will not know this hymn, boy, so listen. Always listen to new things. Then try to create too. Just as I have learnt never to page through the dead leaves of hymn books.' And she began to sing.

> If the fish in a river
> boiled by the midday sun
> can wait for the coming of evening,
> we too can wait
> in this wind-frosted land,
> the spring will come,
> the spring will come.
> If the reeds in winter
> can dry up and seem dead
> and then rise
> in the spring,
> we too will survive the fire that is coming
> the fire that is coming,
> we too will survive the fire that is coming.

It was a long, slow song. Slowly, the prophetess began to pray.

'God, the All Powerful! When called upon, You always listen. We direct our hearts and thoughts to You. How else could it be? There is so much evil in the world; so much emptiness in our hearts; so much debasement of the mind. But You, God of all power, are the wind that sweeps away evil and fills our hearts and minds with renewed strength and hope. Remember Samson? Of course You do, O Lord. You created him, You, maker of all things. You brought him out of a barren woman's womb, and since then, we have known that out of the desert things will grow, and that what grows out of the barren wastes has a strength that can never be destroyed.'

Suddenly, the candle flame went down. The light seemed to have gone into retreat as the darkness loomed out, seemingly out of the very light itself, and bore down upon it, until there was a tiny blue flame on the table looking so vulnerable and so strong at the same time. The boy shuddered and felt the coldness of the floor going up his bare feet.

Then out of the dark, came the prophetess's laugh. It began as a giggle, the kind the girls would make when the boy and his friends chased them down the street for a little kiss. The giggle broke into the kind of laughter that produced tears when one was very happy. There was a kind of strange pleasurable rhythm to it that gave the boy a momentary enjoyment of the dark, but the laugh gave way to a long shriek. The boy wanted to rush out of the house. But something strong, yet intangible, held him fast to where he was. It was probably the shriek itself that had filled the dark room and now seemed to come out of the mask on the wall. The boy felt like throwing himself on the floor to wriggle and roll like a snake until he became tired and fell into a long sleep at the end of which would be the kind of bliss the boy would feel when he was happy and his mother was happy and she embraced him, so closely.

But the giggle, the laugh, the shriek, all ended as abruptly as they had started as the darkness swiftly receded from the candle like the way ripples run away from where a stone has been thrown in the water. And there was light. On the wall, the mask smiled silently, and the heart of Jesus sent out yellow light.

'Lord, Lord, Lord,' said the prophetess slowly in a quiet, surprisingly full voice which carried the same kind of contentment that had been in the voice of the boy's mother when one day he had come home from playing in the street, and she was seated on the chair close to the kitchen door, just opposite the warm stove. And as soon as she saw him come in, she embraced him all the while saying: 'I've been so ill;

for so long, but I've got you. You're my son. You're my son. You're my son.'

And the boy had smelled the faint smell of camphor on her, and he too embraced her, holding her firmly although his arms could not go beyond his mother's armpits. He remembered how warm his hands had become in her armpits.

'Lord, Lord, Lord,' continued the prophetess, 'have mercy on the desert in our hearts and in our thoughts. Have mercy. Bless this water; fill it with your power; and may it bring rebirth. Let her and all others who will drink of it feel the flower of newness spring alive in them; let those who drink it, break the chains of despair, and may they realise that the desert wastes are really not barren, but that the vast sands that stretch into the horizon are the measure of the seed in us.'

As the prophetess stopped speaking, she slowly lowered the bamboo cross until it rested on the floor. The boy wondered if it was all over now. Should he stand up and get the blessed water and leave? But the prophetess soon gave him direction.

'Come here, my son,' she said, 'and kneel before me here.' The boy stood up and walked slowly towards the prophetess. He knelt on the floor, his hands hanging at his sides. The prophetess placed her hands on his head. They were warm, and the warmth seemed to go through his hair, penetrating deep through his scalp into the very centre of his head. Perhaps, he thought, that was the soul of the prophetess going into him. Wasn't it said that when the prophetess placed her hands on a person's head, she was seeing with her soul deep into that person; that, as a result, the prophetess could never be deceived? And the boy wondered how his lungs looked to her. Did she see the water that he had drunk from the tap just across the street? Where was the water now? In the stomach? In the kidneys?

Then the hands of the prophetess moved all over the boy's head, seeming to feel for something. They went down the neck. They seemed cooler now, and the coolness seemed to tickle the boy for his neck was colder than those hands. Now they covered his face, and he saw, just before he closed his eyes, the skin folds on the hands so close to his eyes that they looked like many mountains. Those hands smelled of blue soap and candle wax. But there was no smell of snuff. The boy wondered. Perhaps the prophetess did not use snuff after all. But the boy's grandmother did, and her hands always smelled of snuff. Then the prophetess spoke.

'My son,' she said, 'we are made of all that is in the world. Go. Go and heal your mother.' When she removed her hands from the boy's face, he felt his face grow cold, and there was a slight sensation of his skin shrinking. He rose from the floor, lifted the bottle with its snout, and backed away from the prophetess. He then turned and walked towards the door. As he closed it, he saw the prophetess shuffling away to the bedroom carrying the candle with her. He wondered when she would return the ashtray to the table. When he finally closed the door, the living room was dark, and there was light in the bedroom.

It was night outside. The boy stood on the veranda for a while, wanting his eyes to adjust to the darkness. He wondered also about the dog. But it did not seem to be around. And there was that vine archway with its forbidden fruit and the multicoloured worms that always crawled all over the vine. As the boy walked under the tunnel of vine, he tensed his neck, lowering his head as people do when walking in the rain. He was anticipating the reflex action of shaking off a falling worm. Those worms were disgustingly huge, he thought. And there was also something terrifying about their bright colours.

In the middle of the tunnel, the boy broke into a run and was out of the gate: free. He thought of his mother waiting for the holy water; and he broke into a sprint, running west up Thipe Street towards home. As he got to the end of the street, he heard the hum of the noise that came from the ever-crowded barber shops and the huge beer hall just behind those shops. After the brief retreat in the house of the prophetess, the noise, the people, the shops, the street lights, the buses and the taxis all seemed new. Yet, somehow, he wanted to avoid any contact with all this activity. If he turned left at the corner, he would have to go past the shops into the lit Moshoeshoe Street and its Friday night crowds. If he went right, he would have to go past the now dark, ghostly Bantu-Batho post office, and then down through the huge gum trees behind the Charterston Clinic, and then past the quiet golf course. The latter way would be faster, but too dark and dangerous for a mere boy, even with the spirit of the prophetess in him. And were not dead bodies found there sometimes? The boy turned left.

At the shops, the boy slowed down to manoeuvre through the crowds. He lifted the bottle to his chest and supported it from below with the other hand. He must hold on to that bottle. He was going to heal his mother. He tightened the bottle cap. Not a drop was to be lost. The boy passed the shops.

Under a street lamp just a few feet from the gate into the beer hall was a gang of boys standing in a tight circle. The boy slowed down to an anxious stroll. Who were they? he wondered. He would have to run past them quickly. No, there would be no need. He recognised Timi and Bubu. They were with the rest of the gang from the boy's neighbourhood. Those were the bigger boys who were either in Standard Six or were already in secondary school or were now working in town.

Timi recognised the boy.

'Ja, sonny boy,'greeted Timi. 'What's a picaninny like you doing alone in the streets at night?'

'*Heit*, bra Timi,' said the boy, returning the greeting. 'Just from the shops, bra Timi,' he lied, not wanting to reveal his real mission. Somehow that would not have been appropriate.

'Come on, you!' yelled another member of the gang, glaring at Timi. It was Biza. Most of the times when the boy had seen Biza, the latter was stopping a girl and talking to her. Sometimes the girl would laugh. Sometimes Biza would twist her arm until she 'agreed'. In broad daylight!

'You don't believe me,' continued Biza to Timi, 'and when I try to show you some proof you turn away to greet an ant.'

'OK then,' said another, 'what proof do you have? Everybody knows that Sonto is a hard girl to get.'

'Come closer then,' said Biza, 'and I'll show you.' The boy was closed out of the circle as the gang closed in towards Biza, who was at the centre. The boy became curious and got closer. The wall was impenetrable. But he could clearly hear Biza.

'You see? You can all see. I've just come from that girl. Look! See? The liquid? See? When I touch it with my finger and then leave it, it follows like a spider's web.'

'Well, my man,' said someone, 'you can't deceive anybody with that. It's the usual trick. A fellow just blows his nose and then applies the mucus there, and then emerges out of the dark saying he has just had a girl.'

'Let's look again closely,' said another, 'before we decide one way or the other.' And the gang pressed close again.

'You see? You see?' Biza kept saying.

'I think Biza has had that girl,' said someone.

'It's mucus man, and nothing else,' said another.

'But you know Biza's record in these matters, gents.'

'Another thing, how do we know it's Sonto and not some other girl. Where is it written on Biza's cigar that he has just had Sonto? Show me where it's written "Sonto" there.'

'You're jealous, you guys, that's your problem,' said Biza. The circle went loose and there was just enough time for the boy to see Biza's penis disappear into his trousers. A thick little thing, thought the boy. It looked sad. It had first been squeezed in retreat against the fly like a concertina, before it finally disappeared. Then Biza, with a twitch of alarm across his face, saw the boy.

'What did you see, you?' screamed Biza. 'Fuck off!'

The boy took to his heels wondering what Biza could have been doing with his penis under the street lamp. It was funny, whatever it was. It was silly too. Sinful. The boy was glad that he had got the holy water away from those boys and that none of them had touched the bottle.

And the teachers were right, thought the boy. Silliness was all those boys knew. And then they would go to school and fail test after test. Silliness and school did not go together.

The boy felt strangely superior. He had the power of the prophetess in him. And he was going to pass that power to his mother, and heal her. Those boys were not healing their mothers. They just left their mothers alone at home. The boy increased his speed. He had to get home quickly. He turned right at the charge office and sped towards the clinic. He crossed the road that went to town and entered Mayaba Street. Mayaba Street was dark and the boy could not see. But he did not lower his speed. Home was near now, instinct would take him there. His eyes would adjust to the darkness as he raced along. He lowered the bottle from his chest and let it hang at his side, like a pendulum that was not moving. He looked up at the sky as if light would come from the stars high up to lead him home. But when he lowered his face, he saw something suddenly loom before him, and, almost simultaneously, felt a dull yet painful impact against his thigh. Then there was a grating of metal seeming to scoop up sand from the street. The boy did not remember how he fell but, on the ground, he lay clutching at his painful thigh. A few feet away, a man groaned and cursed.

'Blasted child!' he shouted. 'Shouldn't I kick you? Just running in the street as if you owned it. Shit of a child, you don't even pay tax.

Fuck off home before I do more damage to you!' The man lifted his bicycle, and the boy saw him straightening the handles. And the man rode away.

The boy raised himself from the ground and began to limp home, conscious of nothing but the pain in his thigh. But it was not long before he felt a jab of pain at the centre of his chest and his heart beating faster. He was thinking of the broken bottle and the spilt holy water and his mother waiting for him and the water that would help to cure her. What would his mother say? If only he had not stopped to see those silly boys he might not have been run over by a bicycle. Should he go back to the prophetess? No. There was the dog, there was the vine, there were the worms. There was the prophetess herself. She would not let anyone who wasted her prayers get away without punishment. Would it be lightning? Would it be the fire of hell? What would it be? The boy limped home to face his mother. He would walk in to his doom. He would walk into his mother's bedroom, carrying no cure, and face the pain in her sad eyes.

But as the boy entered the yard of his home, he heard the sound of bottles coming from where his dog had its kennel. Rex had jumped over the bottles, knocking some stones against them in his rush to meet the boy. And the boy remembered the pile of bottles next to the kennel. He felt grateful as he embraced the dog. He selected a bottle from the heap. Calmly, as if he had known all the time what he would do in such a situation, the boy walked out of the yard again, towards the street tap on Mayaba Street. And there, almost mechanically, he cleaned the bottle, shaking it many times with clean water. Finally, he filled it with water and wiped its outside clean against his trousers. He tightened the cap, and limped home.

As soon as he opened the door, he heard his mother's voice in the bedroom. It seemed some visitors had come while he was away.

'I'm telling you, *Sisi*,' his mother was saying, 'and take it from me, a trained nurse. Pills, medicines, and all those injections, are not enough. I take herbs too, and then think of the wonders of the universe as our people have always done. Son, is that you?'

'Yes, Ma,' said the boy who had just closed the door with a deliberate bang.

'And did you bring the water?'

'Yes, Ma.'

'Good. I knew you would. Bring the water and three cups. MaShange and MaMokoena are here.'

The boy's eyes misted with tears. His mother's trust in him: would he repay it with such dishonesty? He would have to be calm. He wiped his eyes with the back of his hand, and then put the bottle and three cups on a tray. He would have to walk straight. He would have to hide the pain in his thigh. He would have to smile at his mother. He would have to smile at the visitors. He picked up the tray; but just before he entered the passage leading to the bedroom, he stopped, trying to muster courage. The voices of the women in the bedroom reached him clearly.

'I hear you very well, Nurse,' said one of the women. 'It is that kind of sense I was trying to spread before the minds of these people. You see, the two children are first cousins. The same blood runs through them.'

'That close!' exclaimed the boy's mother.

'Yes, that close. MaMokoena here can bear me out; I told them in her presence. Tell the nurse, you were there.'

'I have never seen such people in all my life,' affirmed MaMokoena.

'So I say to them, my voice reaching up to the ceiling, "Hey, you people, I have seen many years. If these two children really want to marry each other, then a beast *has* to be slaughtered to cancel the ties of blood . . ." '

'And do you want to hear what they said?' interrupted MaMokoena.

'I'm listening with both ears,' said the boy's mother.

'Tell her, child of Shange,' said MaMokoena.

'They said that was old, crusted foolishness. So I said to myself, "Daughter of Shange, shut your mouth, sit back, open your eyes, and watch." And that's what I did.'

'Two weeks before the marriage, the ancestors struck. Just as I had thought. The girl had to be rushed to hospital, her legs swollen like trousers full of air on the washing line. Then I got my chance, and opened my mouth, pointing my finger at them, and said, "Did you ask the ancestors' permission for this unacceptable marriage?" You should have seen their necks becoming as flexible as a goose's. They looked this way, and looked that way, but never at me. But my words had sunk. And before the sun went down, we were eating the insides of a goat. A week later, the children walked up to the altar. And the priest said to them, "You are such beautiful children!" '

'Isn't it terrible that some people just let misfortune fall upon them?' remarked the boy's mother.

'Only those who ignore the words of the world speaking to them,' said MaShange.

'Where is this boy now?' said the boy's mother. 'Son! Is the water coming?'

Instinctively the boy looked down at his legs. Would the pain in his thigh lead to the swelling of his legs? Or would it be because of his deception? A tremor of fear went through him; but he had to control it, and be steady, or the bottle of water would topple over. He stepped forward into the passage. There was his mother! Her bed faced the passage, and he had seen her as soon as he turned into the passage. She had propped herself up with many pillows. Their eyes met, and she smiled, showing the gap in her upper front teeth that she liked to poke her tongue into. She wore a fawn chiffon *doek* which had slanted into a careless heap on one side of her head. This exposed her undone hair on the other side of her head.

As the boy entered the bedroom, he smelled camphor. He greeted the two visitors and noticed that, although it was warm in the bedroom, MaShange, whom he knew, wore her huge, heavy, black, and shining overcoat. MaMokoena had a blanket over her shoulders. Their *doeks* were more orderly than the boy's mother's. The boy placed the tray on the dressing chest close to his mother's bed. He stepped back and watched his mother, not sure whether he should go back to the kitchen, or wait to meet his doom.

'I don't know what I would do without this boy,' said the mother as she leaned on an elbow, lifted the bottle with the other hand, and turned the cap rather laboriously with the hand on whose elbow she was resting. The boy wanted to help, but he felt he couldn't move. The mother poured water into one cup, drank from it briefly, turned her face towards the ceiling, and closed her eyes. 'Such cool water!' she sighed deeply, and added, 'Now I can pour for you,' as she poured water into the other two cups.

There was such a glow of warmth in the boy as he watched his mother, so much gladness in him that he forgave himself. What had the prophetess seen in him? Did she still feel him in her hands? Did she know what he had just done? Did holy water taste any differently from ordinary water? His mother didn't seem to find any difference. Would she be healed?

'As we drink the prophetess's water,' said MaShange, 'we want to say how grateful we are that we came to see for ourselves how you are.'

'I think I feel better already. This water, and you . . . I can feel a soothing coolness deep down.'

As the boy slowly went out of the bedroom, he felt the pain in his leg, and felt grateful. He had healed his mother. He would heal her tomorrow, and always with all the water in the world. He had healed her.

DUGMORE BOETIE

Familiarity is the Kingdom of the Lost

When I was about nine, I got myself a job at the Good Street Bus Depot in Sophiatown. It was more voluntary than fixed.

I worked without asking permission from anybody. I busied myself sweeping stationary buses with an improvised rag broom.

At night, I would wait for the last bus to come in. It had to be the last bus because you never knew which one might pull out first. The last bus would come in between eleven thirty and twelve midnight and then I'd coil myself on the back seat and sleep.

When the first bus pulled out at four a.m. I would get up and stand at the corner of Good Street and Main Road to wait for the baker's horse-cart. Right on time I would hear the clop-clop echoes of the horses' hoofs on the tar road as they galloped towards Newlands. This was a daily routine. They were delivering fresh-baked bread to the white inhabitants of Newlands.

I would stand hidden behind one of the shop pillars and watch the driver till I was sure that all his attention was centred on the road before him, then I would dart swiftly out of my hiding place and without hesitation jump lightly on the back step of the van. Sometimes I would just sit there with my bare feet dangling while I enjoyed the ride.

One morning I was too hungry to brag. I pulled at the thick wire loop to swing the door open, but nothing happened. Then I noticed that the van was freshly painted. The paint made it difficult for me to lift the loop; it needed stronger hands. Hands that materialised right out of the tar road. Or so it seemed. One minute I was struggling with the wire loop and the next I knew, a different pair of hands appeared mysteriously and lifted the loop without effort.

'Jump!' was all he said.

I did. We retreated up Main Road with four loaves of fresh-baked bread under our armpits. When we came to the spot where he had so mysteriously appeared, he stopped and eyed me speculatively.

'Where's your home, boy?'

I shook my head. 'No home.'

'Where d'you sleep?'

'At the bus depot in Good Street, on the back seat of the last bus.'

He had a big dent in his forehead and it was throbbing violently as if it was inhaling and exhaling. He was very much undecided about something. What made him come to a quick decision was the shouting we heard from the still receding baker's cart.

We had forgotten to close the back door of the van. The door was flapping wildly in the wind and someone was hailing the driver, hoping to draw his attention.

'In here,' said my new-found father. He threw himself on to his stomach and, sliding crabwise, vanished into the gutter.

I was still undecided when I felt his fingers closing around my ankle in a powerful grip. That decided me. I went flat on my stomach and slid in after him.

I felt him crawl, and I followed. We had crawled for only a few yards when suddenly he wasn't in front of me any more. If he hadn't grabbed me, I would have blundered head-first into a larger tunnel.

Here it was blacker than the inside of a devil's horn. You couldn't see your own hand in front of you, but at least you could stand upright.

'Follow me, and trail with your hand against the wall,' he said.

I did. We travelled this way for about a mile, and then we stopped. He groped for my hand and led me up four steps. Up here, he was forced to stoop, while I still remained upright.

That was how I first met the man who was responsible for my future life. It was a dog's life, but nevertheless a life.

I heard him going through his pockets, then I heard the rattle of matches. He struck one. The flame nearly blinded me. He got a lamp from somewhere, and lit the wick.

I gasped. I was looking at the cavern of Ali Baba and the forty thieves. Only that was fiction and this was real.

The walls were plastered with pictures of Tom Mix the cowboy. Strewn on the floor was what must have come fresh from a washing line. There were bed-sheets, pillow-cases, ladies' bloomers, men's underwear – all were still damp. There was a wheelbarrow, a gramophone and records, a stale wedding cake, a police helmet, a pressure stove, pots, a red battered money-box, a guitar with three strings, and a horseshoe nailed to the entrance to keep away evil spirits.

But above all the prizes, my eyes kept straying towards the gramophone. He must have noticed this, because he went straight to it and started playing some records.

I looked around and saw that this part of the tunnel was V-shaped. Water couldn't come through here because he had placed a thick slab of cement to block the outlet that runs through to the main tunnel. One tunnel was then forced to share the water of the other. What really helped a great deal was that we were about three feet above the major tunnel.

After enjoying some of the records, we had our breakfast. Then my father started schooling me on the numerous small tunnels that start in and around Sophiatown and end up here in the big one.

I was taught when and how to take advantage of them, which one to use, and which one to avoid, where they led to, and what to do in case of rain. It was like a game of snakes and ladders with the ladders crossed out. We didn't need the ladders because they led up. All we needed was the snakes. The snakes swallowed us, and when we crawled out of their bowels we found ourselves back in our underground home with arms heavily laden with stolen goods. And no tail behind.

I looked with awe at my father when he was through explaining. He was an unusually short man. Because of this, it was difficult to determine his age. He could have been anything between twenty and forty.

He told me that his real name was Ga-ga, but because of his bandy legs, people referred to him as Kromie, 'Crooked' in Afrikaans. When I begged him for permission to refer to him as Ga-ga, which was his real name, meaning not to remind him of his bandy legs, he refused. He told me that in the American comic strips ga-ga means mad; he wasn't mad.

The dent in his forehead was frightening to look at. It was so big that you could fit a tennis ball into it. He told me that it was caused by the hoof of a farmer's horse. I started hating horses until this very day.

Kromie was bad through and through. He was more mischievous than troublesome. He could without effort cause a highly religious person to use vile words. Wherever he went he left grief and chaos behind. I honestly don't think that he could walk past a dry field of grass without setting fire to it. His pocket money came from children sent to the shops by their parents. My teaming up with him did not improve my relationship with the young population of Sophiatown nor the Main Road shop owners. There was a verbal prize hanging on our heads.

Take Honest Charley, for instance, from the Chinaman shop next to the bioscope. He was named Honest Charley instead of Black Market Charley. This Chinaman kept a big pocket-watch in one of his waistcoat pockets. The watch was attached to a chain.

I must have made a note of it unconsciously. One morning, after oversleeping and missing my usual bread supply on the road, I went into the shop to buy myself a tickey's worth of bread. I was suddenly struck by a mischievous brainwave.

'Charley,' I said, leaving out the Honest part of his name, and holding out the bread in my hand, 'will you please push this bread down the back of my neck? I'm afraid the other boys will snatch it and run into the bioscope with it.' Charley grinned, showing a row of golden teeth.

While Charley was busy pushing the bread down the back of my neck, I lifted the watch.

It was more through fate than anything else that I bumped into Ga-ga, my gutter father, as I was leaving the shop. Outside, I showed my father the watch. He whispered fiercely into my ear, then he dragged me back to the shop's entrance. He called to Charley who was busy scaling sugar into sixpenny bags.

When Honest Charley looked up, Ga-ga said, 'Look, he's got your watch.' Honest Charley dropped what he was doing and grabbed a meat cleaver. If I had known that the watch meant so much to him, I wouldn't have pinched it. Maybe he had come all the way from Chinaland with it.

I wanted to run for my life, but Ga-ga held me fast. The cleaver was being brandished with murderous intent. I tried to pull free from Ga-ga, but he held on. It was only when the cleaver was lifted for the fatal blow that Ga-ga let go. I ran down Main Road as if the Devil was after me. Maybe he was, at that.

Then Ga-ga went into action. He darted into the empty shop, jumped over the counter, and emptied the till . . .

I was lying flat on my stomach, another morning, with my cheeks resting on the palms of my dirty little hands. A gramophone record was playing.

The voice in the record belonged to Jimmy Rodgers. He was singing a song called 'Waiting for the Train' with guitar accompaniment. The first time I heard that record, I took to it like a drunkard takes to drink.

I must have been really dreaming. Of what? Only my ancestors know. But what I do know is that I was dreaming, because Kromie had looked up from his comic strip and said:

'I'm talking to you!'

'What?' I asked.

He pointed a fat jam-stained finger at the comic strip. 'Do you think the Red Indians will catch him?'

To shut him up I said, 'Yes, he doesn't stand a chance.'

My Daddy chuckled gleefully at the plight of the pony express rider. As long as you agreed with him, nothing went wrong. I didn't want anything to go wrong. Not while I was listening to that record.

But something did. Good things don't last. My father trampled on my favourite record by accident.

A nightmare search for the record started. Every time I stole a record, it would turn out to be the wrong one. You see, I couldn't read. If I could, I would have saved myself a lot of trouble and the Jew a lot of grief.

It went on so long, that I was beginning to think that the old Jew at the bicycle shop didn't have that record.

But my will was as obstinate as the cracks on my mud-caked feet. I was in and out that Jew's shop as if I owned it. At last I got the right record and six months in the reformatory. The youngest convict there.

When I came out, I was bitterly reprimanded by my father for stealing records instead of food.

One morning I went out as usual for our daily bread. When I came back, the gramophone was missing. My father had sold it during my absence. He claimed that it was spoiling me.

I felt as though my back was broken. My bowels wanted to work. I packed my guitar and left the tunnel for good to wander again in a world of uncertainty.

I didn't wander long. I soon found myself working for a circus, washing elephants' feet. Sometimes I wondered which feet needed to be washed most, mine or the elephants'. But seeing that I wasn't getting paid to wash mine, I didn't bother with them.

I travelled with the circus to Cape Town where for the first time I saw the sea.

In Cape Town I was mostly with a Coon Carnival group known as The Jesters. There was a guitar player that I greatly admired. He played almost like my Jimmy Rodgers. We were inseparable; I trailed behind him like a devoted young pup.

He sent me everywhere. I went daily to town for him to pick up cigarette stubs and empty wine bottles. Eight empty wine bottles landed him a full one at the liquor store. In turn he taught me a few chords on the guitar.

I was so busy running errands for my friend that the circus left without me. I didn't care much. I was fed-up with the elephants' feet and getting tips instead of wages. I felt that if I kept on washing elephants' feet I'd never get around to washing my own.

I liked Cape Town because sleeping accommodation was no problem. I just slept where I felt sleepy. In corridors. On stairs. Balconies. Anywhere. I just lived, and lived, and lived.

My life was so free that I was just beginning to be convinced that this nice town had no reformatory. Then they arrested me for trying to steal a bus conductor's money bag.

My knife was too blunt, otherwise I would have gotten away with it. I had his money bag, which was hanging from a leather strap, with my left hand, while my right was slashing at the leather strap which was buckled to the bag. The damn-fool knife wouldn't cut the strap in one stroke. The white conductor tried to grab my knife hand. That made me forget the leather strap. Instead, I sank my knife through his hand. It's funny, the knife wouldn't cut the strap but it sank through his hand as if it was made of reformatory soap. That got me two years in Tokai, the Cape Town reformatory. The kind of work they gave me in the reformatory got me out of the reformatory. We were weaving fishing nets. My nimble fingers were so good at it that in a year they gave me a 'hat' as promotion. I was now a monitor.

It was while I was a monitor that I learned about the fish train.

The fastest train on the track. It travels non-stop from Cape Town docks to Johannesburg, with one water break at Bloemfontein so that the fish it carries shouldn't get rotten. The non-stop journey plus the chunks of ice with which they line the coaches keep the fish still fresh all the way to Johannesburg.

Maybe the fishing net business was beginning to bore me. Or perhaps it was the fish train knowledge. I don't know. All I know is that I found my hands manufacturing a rope ladder instead of a fishing net, while the corner of my right eye kept straying towards the prison walls. It's a long time ago, but I can still hear the echoes of police whistles in my ears whenever I recall what I now refer to as the Tokai Break. They behaved as if I was forty instead of eleven.

Seven days after my escape from Tokai, a policeman was saying:

'Jump over his head and get to the other side, then work on the fingers of his left hand while I work on the right.'

A crowd of onlookers had gathered on both sides of the fish train. I was perched between two coaches. The white policeman on my right was grumbling and swearing as he struggled to release my frozen fingers from the wire cage of the coach. He was hurting me. The other policeman on my left was more gentle.

'Can't we light a fire and melt the ice around the little devil's fingers?'

'No, he'll get frostbite.'

'I wonder how the devil the little bastard got himself into such a mess.'

He gave one quick unexpected pull and my right hand was jerked free. Blood dripped from my fingers and tears spurted from my eyes as I examined my bleeding hand. The nail on my little finger was missing.

'Better do the same with that left hand, we can't afford to waste any more time with this little brat.'

'Hold on, I'm only left with the thumb.'

Pulling the baton from his belt, he knocked it several times against the wire cage. The ice cracked and fell away, and my thumb was free.

They hauled me off the train. At first, my knees wouldn't let me stand upright, but after the police gave them a good rub I was able to stand unaided.

'Pikannin!'

'Yes, baas.'

I looked up at the policeman with a dirty, tear-stained face.

'What on earth were you doing on that train?'

'I was trying to get loose, baas.'

'Yes, yes. I know. What I don't know is how the hell you found yourself hemmed in between two coaches and half-frozen to death?'

'I was coming home, baas.'

'Coming home from where?'

'From Cape Town, baas.'

'You mean,' spluttered the other policeman, 'you travelled a thousand miles from Cape Town like that?'

'I come from Cape Town with this train, baas.'

'Where do you stay, boy?'

'Sophiatown, baas.'

'What street, boy?'

'Good Street, baas.'

'What number?'

'No number, baas.'

'You mean there is no number at your house?'

'No number, baas.'

'Why?'

'Is not a house, is a bus garage, baas.'

'You mean, you sleep in a bus depot?'

'Yes, baas. On the back seat of the last bus.'

'The back seat of the last bus, heh?'

'Yes, baas.'

'This is a case for the social workers . . .'

'Not social workers, please, baas.'

'Why not social workers?'

'Long time ago, they say I'm a head sore.'

'A what?'

'A head sore, baas.'

'You mean a headache?'

'Yes, baas.'

'How old are you?'

'Leben.'

'Eleven!' they echoed in unison.

As I was led through the gaping crowd, I fished out a half loaf of stale bread from inside my shirt and started biting into it.

I didn't care what they were going to do with me as long as I was back home. Familiarity is the kingdom of the lost.

They locked me up and only released me when they felt that I was old enough to look after myself. I could, too, if the police would only stop interfering.

ERNST HAVEMANN

Bloodsong

The Path of the Ancients started somewhere on the tableland, where the clan chief, Insimbi, had his kraal, and it ran through the valley to the east hills, where many of the clansmen lived.

Our farm was part of the white settlement that lay in the valley dividing the clan's land. Natives crossing from one side to the other usually went by government road, but occasionally someone would use the Path of the Ancients. If my father saw him, or her, he would scold, pointing crossly to the sign NO TRESPASSERS. NO RIGHT OF WAY. He had had it translated into Zulu, but since the trespassers could not read, this made little difference, except that the place where the sign stood came to be called the Place of Scolding.

Sometimes a man, though more often an obstinate old woman, would insist on proceeding. My father fumed but did not otherwise interfere. 'I suppose they have a right-of-way by immemorial usage,' he said, in extenuation of his weakness. The path was not in fact immemorial. All members of the clan knew exactly when it had been established. It had come into use nine generations ago, when Duma of the Battleaxe had led the clan's ancestors down from the mountains to occupy this piece of thornveld. Every man, and almost every boy, could recite his own pedigree step by step back to Duma or one of his band. When you wanted to thank someone, or show respect, you called him Duma or Child of Duma.

I knew about the Path and Duma and Insimbi because Ngumbane, the foreman, was my friend. When things had gone wrong with my birth, Ngumbane had run fifteen miles to fetch a doctor. The doctor arrived too late to save my mother, and the desperate run left Ngumbane with a permanent limp. My father gave him a Friesian cow in recompense. The affair also left Ngumbane with a permanent stake in my development. As soon as I could toddle, he began taking me on his rounds with him. He talked to me about animals and insects, the clan's history, farm activities, and the private lives of the farm labourers. For a long time I was more fluent in Zulu than in English, but when I learned to read I would translate bits of the newspapers to him. My father was happy about the relationship. He knew I was in safe and affectionate hands, and that left him free to go away on his hunting trips.

When I was fifteen, my father went off on an extended trip during my school holidays. I stayed on the farm, as usual. One Saturday afternoon, shortly before work stopped, Ngumbane said, 'Nkosane, there is something we must talk about.' When no other people were present, Ngumbane called me 'my little boy' or Child of Duma or perhaps by a fanciful praise-name describing my alleged feats or character traits: Mastiff That Breaks the Dog Chain, Exterminator of Locusts, Shield That Protects Ngumbane from Wrath. His addressing me respectfully as Nkosane signaled something weighty. I sat down, to show I recognised that he wanted a serious discussion.

'Nkosane,' he said, 'you know that the Paramount Chief, whom we call the Lion, the chief of all our nation, comes next month to visit Insimbi. All the clans around here will meet to give him a royal greeting.' I knew, of course; it was a major topic of local news.

Ngumbane went on, 'There will be war dances, as in the old days. But the young men do not know all the dances. They have never performed together in regiments, only in little bands. So there will be a gathering tomorrow at Insimbi's place for them to practise together. They do not want to be clumsy when they greet the Lion. Many will come from over there.' He pointed to the east hills and paused, as if the implication were clear.

I said, 'I am listening, my father.'

He resumed, patiently. 'Exterminator of Locusts, those people who live over there must cross the valley to get to Insimbi's place. They say that because it is for the honour of the Lion, they will use the Path of the Ancients, as in the old days, before there were white farms here.'

I said, 'That does not matter. I will give permission to all who ask.'

Ngumbane looked at his feet. 'They will not ask, Johnny. Some of the older men think they should, but not the young ones. The youngsters say this day will be as in the days of our grandfathers, when the clan could pass freely over their own land. They are full of insolence.'

'What do you want me to do?' I asked.

'Why do you not go and visit the white village tonight?' he suggested. 'If you are not here, the people will cross over tomorrow morning and return tomorrow night. If you are not here, their offence will not be seen, and there will be no trouble.'

I had no intention of going to spend a boring Sunday in the village. 'The people will be on the Path,' I said. 'I shall stay here at the house. They will not see me, and so they will not be uncomfortable, and I will pretend not to know that they are there. After all, one cannot see the Path from the house.'

Ngumbane sighed and then nodded reluctantly. 'That will be good. Stay well, Johnny.' He went off to join the labourers, who had already lined up, ready to leave for the African reserve where they had their homes.

I always enjoyed Sundays alone on the farm. On weekdays the dawn was full of the noises of oxen and mule teams, carts creaking and drivers shouting. On Sundays, in the quiet, one could hear successive waves of chirps and singing from awakening birds and other small creatures. But this Sunday morning the bird sounds were overlaid by something else – a pervasive hum, like that of large, distant beehives. I could see nothing around the house, so I took binoculars and climbed a tall lookout tree that gave a view across the farmlands to the river and the hills.

The Path of the Ancients, hardly noticeable in the normal course of events, was now thronged with an almost unbroken line of people: men carrying oxhide shields and fighting sticks and capped with widow bird and ostrich plumes, and parties of women and girls in beads and ochre, carrying beer pots and food trays on their heads. All the way to the east hills little tributary trails fed more people into the thickening stream on the Path itself.

I had never seen such a sight. It would, of course, be even more spectacular when they and scores of other streams of people met at Insimbi's kraal. Why shouldn't I go there and see?

I quickly saddled a horse. I thought of wearing my riding breeches but decided against it: they would make me look like an official. Better to go in ordinary khaki pants. I stuffed some sandwiches into one saddlebag, and a few sticks of tobacco and boxes of matches into the other, for use as gifts. My eye fell on a large grey pebble; I added it, to throw on the cairn that flanked the Path. I set off along the farm road, which ran from the farmhouse over a little ridge. Beyond the ridge it briefly joined the Path.

The Path itself, usually no more than overgrown track obliterated in parts by ploughing, was now sharply defined by the passage of many feet. It meandered to avoid obstacles that no longer existed, curved wide round a marsh long since drained, and twisted between circular patches marking places where trees had once stood.

The marchers resolutely followed the Path's original route, never taking a shortcut, even where the Path ran across a ploughed field or sown pasture.

I waited for a break in the line. Several times people obligingly stopped, saying, 'So you're coming with us,' but I waved them on, because I knew the horse would be an embarrassment in the middle of a group. Some marchers greeted me, or saluted, or remarked on the horse. Twice a woman called, 'Ha, Sea-eyes!' whereupon her companions all looked at me, saying, 'Truly, eyes like the sea.' Blue eyes never failed to amaze the Zulus.

The parties of older men marched stolidly, merely muttering a repetitive song phrase to keep time – 'The strength of the antbear,' 'The bees of the mountain,' 'Kindle fire, my lads, kindle fire.' The young men sang more elaborate part-songs or solemnly recited an old war song: 'Shame on the man who is burned in his hut. Come out and fight.'

Eventually a break in the line allowed me to get on to the Path. I intended to leave it farther on, where it diverged from the straighter farm road, but when I made to turn off, the man ahead of me put out his arm to stop the horse. 'That is not the way,' he said reprovingly. When we reached the NO TRESPASSERS sign at the Place of Scolding, a number of people turned round and looked at me, smiling, but no one said anything.

The line halted when we reached the stone cairn. It is very bad to pass one of these cairns without adding another stone to it; consequently, all stones for hundreds of yards around had been picked up. Prudent people avoided bad luck by bringing small stones with them if they were to pass this way. Most of the people ahead of me had remembered to bring pebbles, and duly threw them on to the pile, sometimes spitting on them first, but some had forgotten, and were now having to search the veld. When I reached the stopping place and took my pebble out of my saddlebag, I heard congratulatory shouting and laughter. A girl cried, 'Did you bring a stone for me, too?' An old woman reprimanded her for being pert to a white man.

From here onward the Path climbed an escarpment, winding round many bends. I had to dismount and lead the horse. About halfway up, the marchers ahead stopped. When we got moving again, I saw the cause. In a little enclave beside the trail sat a skinny old man, with his leg stretched out and a very twisted ankle. Some young men were comforting him and lashing together sticks to make a crutch. I said, 'Can you ride a horse, grandfather?'

The old man grinned through his pain. 'I have never ridden a horse, Nkosane. Surely your white man's horse will resent an old black man and throw me off?'

'No,' I said reassuringly, 'he is tame. He and I both respect old age.'

The old man laughed. The youths carefully lifted him to put him on the saddle. Before scrambling over he motioned for them to wait. He took off his leopardskin cape and spread it meticulously over the saddle so that he would not touch the leather with his bare legs. He said quietly, apologetically, 'We old folks smell,' and then settled on the saddle, gripped the pommel with one hand, and waved with the other. 'Look,' he declared grandly. 'I am a mounted policeman. Salute the servant of the government!' The crowd laughed and cursed happily, enjoying the opportunity to jeer with impunity at a policeman, especially a mounted one.

A boy came forward to take the reins, but I waved him aside. 'Never let a stranger touch your reins' was one of my father's rules. I led the horse up the hill, feeling very foolish. No white person was likely to see me, leading a horse like a servant, with a crowing old Zulu in the saddle; but you never know, so I kept my head down.

When we reached the top of the hill, the young men pointed out a kraal close by. We took the old man there. He praised me excessively. 'Duma!' he shouted. 'Chief of Chiefs! May you grow like a mountain!' I wished him well and headed for Insimbi's place.

Outside the kraal, on the level tableland, I saw hundreds of men. They were forming into companies, most of them with matching shields – black, or black and white, or white, or brown and white. Some companies were in single or double files, stamping to the rhythm of their own chants. Greybeards with long sticks demonstrated songs and steps, shouted orders, and whacked the shins of men who stepped out of line.

I gave the main crowd a wide berth and rode round to the back of the kraal. I halted twenty yards or so from the stockade and waited. A small boy playing there leapt to his feet, shouting, 'White man! There is a white man!' Some women peered curiously. Presently a man appeared. He was obviously someone of importance. I dismounted and saluted him. He acknowledged my greeting and then asked, anxiously, 'What is the matter, child of a white man? Is there trouble? Why have you come?'

I explained that I wanted to see the dancing. Would the chief please allow me? I presented the twists of tobacco.

He took the tobacco and smelled it approvingly. 'You have a great liver,' he said, 'to come into our country, black people's country, on a day like this. But you know how to show respect. Where did you learn Zulu?'

I told him about Ngumbane. 'The limping one,' he said. 'He used to be a fine dancer. I will tell the chief you are here. Take your horse over there.' He pointed to a tree beyond a little ravine. 'It will be a safe place, but do not offsaddle.'

I dismounted under the tree and gave the horse his nosebag. Presently two little girls appeared, one carrying a small pot of beer, the other a grass mat with a lump of meat. I gave them sandwiches in exchange.

As the day wore on, the drilling on the tableland grew more and more orderly. The smaller companies were amalgamating into regiments, performing manoeuvres in long waves. They advanced slowly; charged, beating their shields; retreated; advanced again; repeating the exercises until their elderly instructors were satisfied or exhausted.

By early afternoon the exercises were breaking up. Women had for some time been carrying out food and beer, and most of the dancers now sat down, quiet except for an occasional showoff who leapt about, slashing and stabbing at an imaginary enemy. A few real fights had also broken out, and some spectators were trying to stop them; others were excitedly urging on the combatants or joining in. The chief and other older men were having to intervene, shouting and laying about them with clubs and whips.

Glancing at the group around Insimbi, I saw several arms pointing to me. Soon afterwards a youth of about my age appeared. He was bleeding from a head wound and had a weal where a whip had got him. He stood provocatively in front of me and said, 'Little white man' – he used an insulting diminutive – 'little white man, hear the words of the chief. Insimbi says you must go now. He says in the dusk a white man looks like any other wild creature.'

I mounted quickly. 'I thank the chief,' I said. 'I send him respects.' I added, condescendingly, 'Stay well, little lad,' and cantered off.

Many of the women and girls had already left, together with older men who were anxious to reach home before dark. They started off in big groups, which shed fragments as family or neighbourhood parties broke off to go their separate ways. No one made way for me. A group of men stood in front of the horse and demanded that I take one of them to ride with me; I had to make a wide detour to get past them. Several times someone said, 'What are you doing here, white man?' Once or twice a man deliberately tried to frighten the horse.

I decided not to risk the Path of the Ancients down the escarpment; there were too many little danger points. Instead, I went a long way round on the government road and did not get home until after sunset. A few stragglers were still on the Path, but the main traffic had apparently passed.

I finished supper and was getting ready for bed when my horse became restless. I had tethered him for the night in a little cornfield near the house. The dead cornstalks had been gathered into bundles, which stood like rows of ghostly men in the moonlight. The horse was so disturbed that I feared a predator might be around. Then I heard what had been disturbing him. It was far away but unmistakable: a war song, sung by a great many men. It sounded like a whole regiment.

I had already undone the tether and let the horse canter off before I realised that I now had no means of getting away if I needed to.

The sound came and then went faint. It was an antiphonal song, the leading voices clear and high, the responses muffled but strong. It grew suddenly louder. By visualising the Path of the Ancients, I could tell how the sound would alter. As the singers went down through the old riverbed, it faded; it grew louder as they emerged, and faded again as they went around the hillock at the Place of Scolding. When they reached the ridge opposite the farmhouse, the sound should almost disappear.

After a moment's silence, too soon for them to have reached the ridge, a new song started, a different sound. I could not hear words, and indeed the song had no words: just *Eee yoh haa haa haa*, starting quiet, rising high almost to a scream, and then falling to the deepest guttural that the singers could reach in their throats and chests. High again, then down, down, *haa! haa!* High, then down low, repeated over and over.

I knew the song, because a gang of labourers on the farm had once started singing it. Ngumbane had intervened, very angry, shouting, 'We will have no songs like that here!' He told me it was a song that had been sung in the old days when warriors anticipated a great killing. 'When you sing it, your blood wants blood,' he said. In my mind I called it the Bloodsong.

The sound receded when the singers got to where the Path ran behind the ridge, and grew faint as they went down into the old stone quarry. I went indoors with much relief: they were on their way to the hills. Then a great burst of the Bloodsong hit me. A large company of warriors had silently climbed the ridge and was now massing at the head of the clearing that ran down to the house. Obviously the others, on the Path, had gone on singing to provide a cover so that this party could get close to the farmhouse without being detected.

As fast as I could, I shuttered the windows and locked all the doors except the top half of the kitchen door. I put the pressure lamp to shine out through the door, dragged sacks of meal and seeds to form a little barricade, and loaded both barrels of the shotgun. I put in birdshot, because that was what I mostly used, but then I remembered that when the farmers had formed a commando to get the madman who shot his wife and kids, they all loaded up with slugs or buckshot, so I quickly slipped in buckshot instead.

In the moonlight I could see the great shields of the warriors gleam when they turned. They were now singing the battle challenge: 'Shame on the man who is burned in his hut. Come out and fight!' As they sang, they shuffled into some kind of formation. I knew what they would do: they would split into three lots to form the bull, the classical Zulu attack formation. The two horns of the bull advance to harass the enemy's flanks while the main body, the bull's chest, awaits the right moment for a frontal charge. My father's friends had not been in the Zulu wars, but they often talked about them; their theory was that if you managed to crumple one of the bull's horns, the whole force was thereby confounded. One had therefore to concentrate on one horn and bring down as many men in it as possible.

Presently two files of men, rather fewer than I had expected, began creeping down the clearing. I tried to gauge the distance – not easy in the moonlight – and desperately wished I could remember what the *Sportsman's Handbook* said about the range, penetration, and scatter pattern of buckshot. As one horn moved diagonally across the clearing, I cocked both hammers and kept my bead on the leader, wondering whether I should aim at his legs or at his chest. If I only wounded him, perhaps the others would not be deterred. But what if I killed him?

I was puzzled, because the two horns were not advancing to surround the house but were moving obliquely towards the cornfield. The singing of the main body suddenly stopped. After a thin scream of command they all charged, shouting and hissing the clan battle cry. I scrambled out of the kitchen into the storeroom, which gave a view of that side of the clearing. I doubted whether I could get set up in there before they had me. I tore open the window shutter and pushed the gun barrels out, ready for the first man who came within range.

No one was there. But in the cornfield the whole company was stabbing and slashing at the upright bundles of stalks, crying, 'Die! Die!' or leaping about in shadow combat with unseen enemies. I felt a great warm wetness down my trousers as I shakily put the gun down.

The display in the cornfield lasted only a few minutes. Soon most of the warriors sat down, breathing heavily. I counted only a dozen or fifteen of them. One man walked to the house, deliberately standing in the lamplight. He leaned his shield and sticks against the wall and stood waiting, making a knocking click with his tongue.

I shouted, 'What do you want?' immensely relieved that my voice was rough and harsh, not fearful and squeaky. The man saluted in the direction of my voice. I saw that he was a boy, not much older than I was. 'Nkosane, we ask for water. We are dying of thirst,' he said.

I replied gruffly, 'Wait, I am coming,' and frantically looked for a pair of trousers to replace my wet ones. I unloaded the shotgun, alarmed to see how shaky my hands were. Then I went out, unlocked the water tank, and gave the youth a tin mug.

He waved to the others. They carefully stacked shields and sticks against the wall and respectfully greeted me. They were all teenagers. Each one drank in turn, taking care not to spill. The last one rinsed the mug and held it over his head, looking at me for permission. I said, 'You would not do that if it were beer.' They recognised my weak joke as a gesture and laughed uproariously, boasting about their drinking capacities.

I waited for them to go, but they sat down, obviously intending to rest and talk. One youth said, 'Nkosane, did you know that old man with the broken ankle?' I recognised the speaker and two of the others as having been among those assisting the old man. I shook my head. He turned to the group and related what had happened. They appeared to know already, for two of them were miming the old man putting down his cape to protect the saddle. Everyone laughed, and someone said, 'He smells like a polecat's backside now, but they say he was a great fighter when he was young.' Someone else said, 'You did a kind thing, Nkosane. Our little band has come to thank you. That old man is greatly honoured in our family. He was the guardian uncle of my father and of this boy's father.' He indicated another youth, who seemed to be the leader. The leader said, 'Johnny, you took a thorn from the foot of a stranger. So we give you this praise-name: You Pull Out Thorns for Strangers.' The rest applauded, drummed on their shields, and cried 'Thorn Puller', 'You Pull Out Thorns.' We discussed praise-names and the uncomplimentary nicknames of some of the white farmers. My father was called the Dancer, because he stamped his feet when he was angry.

I went into the house and brought out a big tin of rusks and some tobacco. They demolished the food and made rough cigarettes. They asked if I was courting. I fetched a picture of my girlfriend. They stared at it, carefully not touching with their fingers but holding it on open palms, and exclaimed admiringly at her plumpness.

They showed me a big stone axe they had found in a cliff in the hills. They had had it ritually purified in case it had been used to kill a man; the old women said that small yellow cannibals used to live in those cliffs. They asked whether I had not been scared up at Insimbi's, being the only white person there. The boys who had been with the old man said, 'We kept an eye on you where you sat under the tree. If any trouble had started, we would have protected you.' The leader assented. 'With brave men like us you would have been safe. Did you see us attack that enemy in the cornfield? They outnumbered us many times, but we slew them without mercy. We were heroes, were we not?' There was much laughter as various members of the band enacted their own past or future exploits. I fetched the shield Ngumbane had given me. They examined and admired it, and I had a mock stick fight with one of them; several gave me advice or demonstrated cunning blows and feints.

The moon was sinking towards the western tableland before they left. As they went by, each one said, 'Stay well, brother,' and clasped me by the forearm. Then they all turned round and cried, 'Puller of Thorns! You are one of us,' and raised their shields in salute. For the next half hour I could hear their voices, clear and soaring *Eee yoh*, then falling low, deep and ominous, *haa haa haa*. The Bloodsong faded, rose, faded, and finally died in the valleys of the east hills.

I often saw members of the band subsequently, loafing around trading stores, working on farms, or trotting down the highway to the music of a mouth organ. They always greeted me with the greatest friendliness, but none of them ever again called me brother or said, 'You are one of us.'

JACK COPE

Escape from Love

Franz fumbled a little tying the reins of his horse to the post under the great cypress tree and stood then with both hands on the saddle. He gazed up at his home. Close around him was the hot scented shade. A small stain of shade very dark as if the great and whispering height of the tree made up in sheer density against the sun what it lacked in the leafage of more generous trees. His legs were stiff, unused to riding, and there was a sharp edge of weariness, not unpleasant, in his back. Franz de la Rey liked the steaming smell of the horse and the creaking of stirrup leathers in the saddle. They called up a sentimental picture he cherished to balance his present smallness against a more heroic past. His forebears were pioneers, men of the smooth-bore rifle, the covered trek-wagon and laager; men welded in the saddle, welded and tempered in fire; conquerors. As he looked across the horse's rump at his home the thoughts rose and burst faintly like bubbles behind his eyes leaving his mind empty, a blank, and only a heavy mood stayed to darken his homely open face.

He was more used to the driving seat and the simple plastic controls of his maroon and biscuit-coloured Studebaker. The car fatigued him stealthily with insidious comfort. But the hard old saddle of his father took punishment out of him for his softness. The living, uncompromising curve of the horse's bulk shaped out against his untrained legs, straining joints, chafing up skin. Where he had been he could not go in a car. He had ridden because he had no other way of getting there and it had been no pleasure ride; no heroics, no gold-splashed dreams of his ancestors long ago. The horse was blown and foam-flecked, but it had lapsed out of his consciousness and he did not think to loosen the girth or rub down the saddle marks. He was young, ruddy-skinned and had brown curly hair with a shine in it under the sun and his eyes now were full of trouble, of anger and fear, a lost look, disillusioned, resentful.

Franz saw his dog, a tan setter beautiful in every point, get up from the stoep and come into the hot sun. Lazily it stretched and yawned and its clean pink tongue curved upwards as if on a spring. The setter was a dignified dog, almost insolent. It made no show of being too excited over Franz's comings and goings and now came trotting down the path in the dust swinging the long feather of its tail like a stately fan. Franz pushed aside the fine head of the dog and it took the snub calmly, going on to have a familiar sniff at the horse's nose. Satisfied, it turned to follow its master back to the house. But half-way to the homestead the setter stopped in the path. An unusual manner about the man made him stop, the way he walked, quick and jerky. A hint of danger in a man walking like that with turmoil enough inside him to be picked up by the alert senses of the hunting dog.

Three new concrete steps took Franz up to the new stoep of painted woodwork, glass screens and a floor of green plastic tiles. Green for coolness! How could a colour make any cooler the shimmering white-heat of January noon in the thornveld? She thought it could. Aletta thought so and she had modern ideas. Aletta did everything about the house; she had changed everything until there remained no recognisable feature of the old home of his father and grandfather and great-grandfather. The poky little voorkamer had gone, heart of the boer-house with its dung-smeared clay floors, and with it the dark, small sitting-room. The sitting-room had always spoken to him of the mystery, the suppressed and unspoken things of his family. He remembered with awe the four black chairs and black table and a bible-desk inlaid with a star in ivory; the Brown Bess musket and an ox-horn powder-flask hung above the fireplace that had never been lit to his knowledge, just as the room had never been used, except once for his mother's funeral. The keyhole of the room used to moan softly with the draught, though mostly it was silent, charged with its musky animal smell, with secrecy and gloom. He had been excited and also disturbed far down in his feelings when Aletta had partitions knocked down, big windows, glass doors punched into the old thick outer walls, plaster and paint slapped over the shale and basalt stonework. And colours, colours to heighten her happiness, to make illusions of coolness or joy or love. While she had done these things he had worshipped her, followed her in everything with a primal ache in his heart of terrible possession. With her near, his old feeling of awe for the family past sank away to nothing.

This girl was his, his, in all her convolutions and inner strangeness solely his possession. But not always. She could stand apart from him, retreat into an exclusive self. He dreaded his own future then, the wonder of love, the agony of it was too overwhelming to last. Her separateness and her potency to move subtly out of his range held over his head a curious dismay filling him with inadequacy and powerlessness.

He came into the softly furnished lounge she had created out of the hard and uncompromising house of his fathers. And there she was. His heart stopped as she uncurled from a corner of the settee and stood to greet him. At first he saw the involuntary little dent of happiness in her smile that made him reel and his limbs grow weak. Then she must have caught the bitterness in his face and her eyes went dark and big as she came across the Persian carpet to him. Her eyes then looked to him deep, all pupil, containing in a single moment all his soul clung to, and yet able to shut him out as if by the mere closing of her lids.

'O Franz,' she said. That was all. And she put her hands on his shoulders and he smelt her breath sweet like ripe quinces, sweet, drugging. He backed a step. A moment later he had done something he did not know was in his power. He took her hands off him and let them drop and he brushed past her, going out at the glass door that led to the cool back of the house. He knew she would be watching him, stunned, and the dog would be standing in the doorway to the green-paved stoep watching him too.

How deliriously mad he had been in his surrender, a submission so profound that he could not take a breath, or speak to a stranger without her essence rising in him with a kind of bubbling confusion. People had laughed at him and he laughed with them because that was the limitless measure of his happiness. Now he was beginning to see things as though he had been blind and the light had struck a whiplash through his eyeballs. That green stoep – he had fancied in his daze that her work had been like the building of Solomon's chariot, 'the midst thereof being paved with love'. But it was a green plastic paving to create the silly illusion of coolness after she had cut down the old gum and juniper trees to open a view to the snow-topped mountains a hundred miles away. She had spared the single great cypress because he had told her his father's favourite dog was buried under it. And she loved dogs. She also loved his father and her curious assurance had won the old man to her side.

Franz went into the bedroom. He did not want her to come in and he stood listening for her steps while his heart in its darkness boomed at his throat. He was afraid because he had gone so far that he could not turn back. Not if he wished. The thing was clear and he had no choice but to go on the way he had started.

Four years after his mother's death his father had a heart attack and only by a miracle, so the doctors said, he had recovered. Christiaan de la Rey was one of the wealthiest farmers in the district and he could afford easily to follow the doctor's orders to retire and live at the sea-coast. He bought himself a house at Doonside Beach and there he lived a comfortable jovial sort of life with a housekeeper and three servants and any of the de la Rey relations, no matter how distant, who cared to accept Oom Christiaan's open hospitality. And many of them did. Christiaan was popular with the relatives and the neighbours and holiday-makers and especially with children. They thought the stout mahogany-faced old man with surprisingly blue eyes and a little white goatee beard was some kind of a friendly spirit whose purpose in life was to tell marvellously funny stories and produce surprises out of his baggy pockets. Christiaan turned over the running of his farms with four thousand sheep and a large beef herd to his only son – Franz. The same year Franz and Aletta were married. Franz had kept trusted headmen on the farms and mostly he left them to look after the sheep and cattle. Aletta had spent the time they were home rebuilding and redecorating the main farmstead, but that could not remain the driving purpose of her life. Her creative centre was somewhere else, and soon she would grow restless, sad. Franz knew her moods to a hair and so it became a joke with them to look at one another and say almost in one breath: 'Well – shall we go?' They went to the Victoria Falls and to the National Park. They took a trip up the coast to Portuguese East Africa and gambled in the casinos, not heavily, because they were beginners. They drove a thousand miles to Cape Town to watch a rugby test match against the British Lions team. Each trip had been to Franz like a honeymoon. Their real honeymoon had misfired; they had gone to Madagascar in a French ship and Aletta got a touch of fever in Tananarive. Still, they had made up for it. In between their longer expeditions they thought nothing of weekends in the city or a flying visit to have Sunday dinner with old Christiaan. The farms paid. The cattle bred and thrived and had to be sold to keep down their numbers. The wool clip paid handsomely. Making money was easy as falling in a dam.

Then Christiaan suggested a check-up and Franz found one flock of over a thousand sheep no less than six hundred short. Six hundred! More than half gone. He was so staggered he felt he had been punched on the jaw. 'Where are they? Where are they?' he kept saying. He sat on an ant-heap under the blazing sun and in his bewilderment and frustration he did not notice his eyes fill with tears.

'The jackals took many, my basie. Others died of blue-tongue, gall-sickness,' a headman said.

'Gall-sickness to hell!' he bawled, springing up. His face had turned livid. 'You lost them! You stole them, and you have the nerve to talk about gall. God damn you! Where are they?'

The headman lowered his eyes, dark, black slits, dark glinting holes, black with malice.

'My basie cannot say I took them. What have I done with them then?'

'Well, you know. You know where they went.'

'I told my basie.'

'It's a lie, curse you, filthy thing!'

There were losses in the other flocks, but not so heavy. All told, less than a thousand he could not account for. He was unable to hide it for one minute from Aletta. She came to meet him as he climbed out of the Studebaker.

'Franzie,' she said gravely. 'Something is wrong.'

The setting sun, he remembered, shone on her thick light hair but her eyes remained cool and deep like the darkness of a valley after sunset. And after he had faltered it out she said: 'But, my treasure, we still have three thousand.'

'How am I going to tell Father?'

'Tell him of course how bad the sickness and the jackals are.'

'No. He will not believe it. He couldn't. I myself don't believe it. No. He would have another heart attack.'

'Ah heaven! Franzie – that's true.'

'I have to find those sheep.'

'But where?'

'I have to find them.'

They had gone up to the house together and he had gripped her hand like a little boy, helpless, wanting to be consoled, wanting to cry.

In the night he had sat up suddenly in bed. The moon was in the window-panes and the sky like milk. Aletta woke with a little cry seeing him rigid, staring at the window. The setter came in at the bedroom door and flopped on the carpet to scratch.

'Somebody is outside,' Franz whispered.

She put her arms round him, alarmed. 'But there's Rooi; he is not barking. He would bark if there was somebody.'

The dog went on scratching, tapping its hock on the floor with a steady, muffled knock, knock, knock.

'There – it's only Rooi scratching. But what made you think there was someone? My darling, you were dreaming.'

'Yes, I must have been dreaming. I – I was sure, somehow, it was Dismata the witch-doctor.'

He turned to her with a face made much paler in the dimness of the night and his pupils looked dilated, enormous.

'But does not Dismata live far away down in the Bushman Ravine? He would surely never come here. At night.'

'No.'

'Kiss me and go to sleep.'

Still he sat up, staring past her. 'I was thinking of going to see him, to find my sheep. Then I suddenly thought he was outside. Do you think he knew? There's nothing they don't smell out, and I have heard Dismata has often found lost stock for the farmers.'

'Ah,' she whispered with an instinctive shudder. 'Franz, don't think of going to Dismata. Such things come of it. Promise me, Franzie. Those witch-doctors are evil to us, evil. He could do nothing but lead your feet on an evil path.'

'I don't care, if he finds my sheep.'

'And if he does not?'

'He will point to the thief.'

'Franzie, Franzie, you scare me so. Promise me not to think of it.'

He stretched on his back and pulled the sheet up to his chin. The night was too hot for a blanket. Then his eyes closed and the moon made his face gaunt, bony, bloodless. She thought with a sudden horror of how he would look if she had to lay him out, dead.

Franz afterward had a recollection before falling asleep again of her fingers softly touching his face, round the curve of his cheeks and along his lips, softly in the near-dark. His heart had squeezed with a strange tenderness. He did not know what she had seen as he lay there with closed eyes.

Am I going to lose her now? he thought, standing in the bedroom and listening for her. There was no sound. He went across and opened a drawer of her dressing-table and took out a garment from among her underclothes, a thing of translucent machine fibre, machine-made lace, machine-patterned – modern, as he thought of it. She was a modern girl and had worked in Johannesburg. He had met her on a holiday at Doonside Beach where his father lived and her town smartness and shine had appealed to his own restlessness, his discontent. But now for the first time he was thrown back on himself; he felt her sympathy and love were not there beyond question for him to lean on. Angrily he stuffed the garment in his pocket, seeing himself fragmented in the three-angled mirrors. Deeper in the glass he caught sight of Aletta standing at the door.

'Franz, what have you taken – what do you need that for?'

He stood with his back to her, shoulders hunching. When he turned, his face was deeply flushed and the veins stood out on his neck and temples. She was in the door, quite still and tense with the big dog Rooi at her side and her fingers twined in his silky coat, the crimson of her varnished nails like blood-drops against the iron-red of him. Franz took the garment from his pocket and it unfolded in his outstretched hand.

'That is what I took,' he jerked out with a bitter twist to his mouth.

'But what for, why?'

'You would not understand.'

'No, it's true, I do not understand. You are so strange, Franz.'

They stared across a great distance, over a terrifying depth in this first crisis of their life together. He glanced from her to the dog and back.

'Franz,' she said. 'You have been to Dismata.'

He nodded.

'And it was he who told you to take my bra?'

'He needed certain things.'

She understood, but not as he thought. In the hidden core of her heart was an awareness that she was facing not Dismata the witch-doctor nor Franz's shock and his will to recover the lost sheep. Her instinct went at once to the centre and saw the man in him rising against her – not even against her, but against absorption, domination by her sex. Against love. It took a great heart to endure love and a great spirit to be free. Against the fear of the darkening of his life Franz was groping not into light but into a hell, back into the nightmare of her people, the terror that crept in the small hours of the night when life was weakest and the soul grew small on its lonely flight. She recognized the nightmare; as a woman she knew better than Franz ever could. She knew the awful attraction of it like a dreamer drawn nearer and nearer the brink of a bottomless dream-fall. She had to go softly with him not to wake him violently.

Aletta ordered the dog out in a low voice and it went reluctantly, hanging its head and turning up its eyes at her. Then she closed the door and sat on the bed.

'Franz, you rode all that way. Are you not tired?'

'Tired? No.'

'And hungry?'

'Well – '

'I have never seen Dismata, but of course everyone talks about him. Is he awful?'

'You can say that again,' he slanged, feeling easier. He was surprised at her, taking this so calmly, smiling.

'He does strange things, they say.'

'That's just what is so – so queer. He did nothing. Only sat there looking, looking at me like a devil. Hai! But strange things happened.'

She was silent, round-eyed, waiting for him to go on. He knew as surely as anyone could know without putting it into words that he was being mastered. His resoluteness, his independence, were being sapped away. But it was so much more delightful to hold her interest. He drew up the dressing-stool and sat astride it to tell her, and he could always tell a story better with his slim pliant body relaxed and hands free for the full play of gesture.

'Ai Hemel!' He shook his head incredulously. 'But you should have been there. You will never believe it.'

He told her about the witch-doctor. He had been terribly impressed, appalled, and now it came rolling out and he almost lost himself in the telling. Dismata used the talking and whistling spirits. Franz had come into his hut and crouched in the semi-dark until he saw the face of the medicine-man solid black, heavy, shining like polished stone. Then voices shrieked in the soot-blackened roof of the hut and the hair rose on Franz's neck. Behind him an old, wicked voice said with a laugh: 'You have lost your sheep!' He turned and found nobody there. So it had gone on. The 'voices' knew exactly why he had come. They chattered among themselves, jeered. Sometimes he picked out clear words, at others only a shrill yell. He was wildly confused by it and unnerved, and he found it difficult to tell her all he had heard, what Dismata had said and what came from the spirits. Difficult – because they had talked about her, about Aletta, not plainly but in a way he grasped quite well. They spoke about a 'lioness with a yellow mane and red claws.' That was her, and he glanced uneasily again at her soft hands and varnished nails. His substance was being wasted away, they had jibed. And they meant, by her.

He skipped that bit of the story and went back to Dismata. The medicine-man had dropped a single stick on the fire which flared like a torch. By its light he seemed to shrink. He was no more a heavy menacing demon, but small, withered. He was naked to the waist and wore a girdle of monkey tails. In ordinary bad guttural Afrikaans he had told Franz he would see the trail of his sheep, but he must bring four things to guide the *totolo*, the whistling spirits.

'Four things,' Franz repeated.

'Haai, Franz,' she whispered, entering in the awe and mystery of his experience. 'They know so much, surely these spirits do not need to be guided. O surely, surely it is better to keep clear of them.'

'So you do believe there are the spirits?'

'I don't know what to believe, only I feel, I still feel it is a path of evil that Dismata will find. Not the trail of your sheep, Franz, but a path of terrible evil. We should never sink down to that, our people. If we sink down to witchcraft in some way a fearful punishment will surely fall on us.'

'Ag! But that is nothing else than superstition. What sort of punishment?'

'That is in God's will, but I think the same that has fallen on the Kafirs. They are in darkness, a thousand years behind us, because they are sunk in witchcraft. They have powers, oh, I know, but turned back into darkness. It stops them from thinking as we do. Franz, let Dismata be a warning to you.'

'You haven't been long enough in the countryside and you don't understand, Aletta. The farmers often go to Dismata, and where's the punishment?'

'Franz, I love you and I am only saying what comes from my heart.'

'Ja, ja.' He stood up impatiently and went to stare out of the window. A gay-striped canvas awning threw a square of shade and beyond it was the white quivering heat and the shrill of cicadas coming up sharp as if a part with the vibration of the sun itself. He was sorry now he had told her, and he waited tensely for her to ask about the four things Dismata wanted. How would he get over that difficulty? Rather than face up to it he thought of dropping the scheme altogether. He was afraid of Dismata, in a way; the medicine-man had found a chink in his soul, a feeling of paralysis that halted his will. Aletta had warned him and the warning went closer than she could suspect. He found it uncanny that she said nothing now, and left him to struggle with himself. The setter dog came in sight trotting through Aletta's parched little north garden among lines of marigolds and zinnias. He turned from the window.

'What if I don't go back to Dismata? I can make another plan, and I need not pay him.'

'Did he ask for payment?'

'An ox to make the spirits talk.'

She knew he must have agreed to the payment, but still she said nothing, running a ribbon slowly through her fingers. It was torture to him.

'I did not tell you what that witch-doctor wanted, and you don't ask,' he said sharply. 'Why are you putting on this act? Is it to shame me out of something you are scared about, or don't you want to know?'

'One of the things I know already – my underclothes. How insulting, Franz, that he makes such conditions. What the others are I don't like to guess.'

'So little you know, and you say it in a way to put me in the wrong.'

'I just felt hurt that you could take that man something so personal as my bra.'

Franz was in a position where he knew explanations could only make matters worse. But there was still more to come, and he persisted doggedly.

'You understand, that Kafir did not ask for this or that – how can he know what a white woman wears? He just said bring something of yours, I mean something you wear – against your skin.' His face had darkened.

'Why something of mine? – I have not lost the sheep.'

'Mine too, don't worry. A part from my car and a part from a plough.'

'Weird . . . what ideas! And what else?'

He still kept her fixed with that dark stubborn look. 'Weird, yes. The other thing he wants is the fat from my dog's body.'

She caught her breath and silence thickened between them. At last he said: 'That is the other thing you wanted to know.'

'How awful.' She ignored his tone. 'The fat from poor Rooi's body. He tells you to kill Rooi.'

'Blood always comes into these things. I believe it once used to be human blood,' he added, with a harsh laugh.

'How can you make a joke when you were ready to kill Rooi – for witchcraft?'

'Who says I would kill him? I could take some sheep's fat.'

'And cheat the spirits?'

'Ag, this kind of talk makes me sick!' He flung open the door and stamped out. Once he had started he rushed on and in a moment was striding down the path he had walked up so full of trouble and foreboding a while back. The stable-boy had taken his horse from under the cypress and there was only the enormous dark green pinnacle of the tree rearing up from the density of its shade. He stopped in the shade, smelling the resinous scent that oozed subtly from the presence of the tree like myrrh. It reminded him of his childhood and the strong all-embracing being of his father. The tree was all he had left to cling to that sky-clear past. She had cut the others down, cut everything from under his feet. She had even won over his father, and he could see how the old man's face came to life in Aletta's presence. It had been a shock to him to find his father looking at her unawares, as a young man looks at a girl with a quiet speechless satisfaction. Now the tree reminded him of his father, not the funny old idler uprooted and cast adrift on the ocean shore, but the Boer with his flat felt hat down tight on his brow, astride his black horse with a fine plaited whip trailing behind him and his dog following, a liver-and-white pointer. The dog lay buried under a smooth square flagstone at the foot of the cypress. That was why Aletta had spared the tree.

Franz sat on the stone, his eyes narrowed and the vision turned inwards on his memories, trying not to lose the picture of his father as he had been in all his strength. Enough for the whole family; not that his mother lacked a kind of tenacious strength, but she was dazzled, withered by the constant heat of Christiaan's energy, like a small old flower. There was no doubt he would have to account for the sheep to Christiaan. If he did not find them. The one really difficult term Dismata had made was the stipulation for the fat of his dog. He was sure, from their uncanny insight, that the medicine-man and his *totolos* would trace the sheep. He was quite sure. And it would be a triumph his father would appreciate when he told how he had done it. If Rooi had to die, he could be buried there under the same stone at the foot of the tree. He was not going to be sentimental about that. Except for Aletta. He had known right from the first moment what this would mean. It was the acid test of himself, of his whole character, his self-possession and his will.

He had not eaten and it seemed hours since his return. The shadow was moving away and the sun came burning on him. He must go through the repugnant business with Rooi, though it would be better if he were alone and could get Aletta away on a visit. Strange how his thoughts separated them now – him and her. Two beings, opposite poles, individual, and between them an unsuspected, unmeasured gulf. Never since they were married had he thought of either going anywhere without the other. Now he wanted her out of the way.

When he stood up at last he was surprised to see a woman and a small boy waiting some way off, patiently squatting in the dust. They were black and both were thin and tired, dressed in a few shapeless and filthy tatters.

'Yes?' he demanded. 'What is it?'

'My basie, I have come for the ox.'

'The ox . . . I don't know what you are talking about.'

'For Dismata, my basie.'

'What! He has not found my sheep.'

'The spirits talked, the ox is his . . .'

'Verdom!' Franz swore.

'He said the basie was afraid, he said you would not come again because you did not have enough liver. Thus he sent me after you to fetch his ox. I am his woman.'

'Lord God!' Franz murmured in an agony to himself. And he shouted to the hag: 'Go back. You can tell him I am coming again. You can tell him that – you understand!'

He strode up to the house, and from the green-paved stoep he could see Aletta moving about in the dining-room. There was a bowl of red and gold nasturtiums and a starched white cloth on the table and everything set out pleasantly with a kind of dew freshness for the midday meal. Aletta made things feel that way.

'Here you are at last,' she called. 'What a long time you have been, Franz.'

'I shall eat later. Crows are worrying the lambs and I am going after them.'

He went through the lounge and was taking down his rifle from the gun-rack in the passage when she came from the dining-room. Rooi was at her heels.

He slipped a clip of soft-nosed bullets in his pocket. 'Damn those crows. They would trouble me just now!' he muttered, glancing down his cheek at her.

'Franz, what are you doing?'

'I told you I was going after the crows!' He was already half-way out to the stoep and shouted back at her. And he hurried on and whistled to the dog. Rooi looked up once at Aletta and then raced out. But on the path he stopped and raised one front paw in hesitation.

'Come, Rooi! Sa, sa, sa! Hasies!' Franz called.

Aletta took the things off the table and put the meat dish with a lid over it in the warming oven to keep for Franz. She had a queer feeling all the while going about the house and arranging things. The maid watched her aslant.

'Ai, my nonna, what is the basie doing?' the girl suddenly asked.

Aletta was bending over a camphor chest sorting and putting away the newly-ironed linen. And she remained quite still. So the Kafir maid knew there was something wrong. Her heart was gripped, seared with a jet of anger. What right had this girl to ask, what right to interpose one spoken word between her and Franz? She was black, a thing of instincts, and she had guessed somewhere in her dark soul that the white people were walking in fear. A crack had opened under their feet.

'Go out, Beta.' She had a husk in her throat trying to control her voice and did not turn. 'Go out and clean the chicken-hokkie.'

The girl went and Aletta was alone in the house. She walked to the window and looked out. Beyond the near-black column of the cypress was the slope of the bush-dotted valley, close and hot, dropping away in haze. And then far off were the hills, crest behind crest of deepening blues to the peaks on the skyline, without snow but looking unattainable and cold under the pulsing ash-blue sky. It was unsettling to see so far – she knew that now. The distance stole like a restless wind into one's heart and gave one no peace. She had made a mistake hacking through the old shaggy trees of the Boer homestead, bursting out a window on the outside. Better for one's peace to build the walls up higher, let the woods grow denser, thicker, closing round the loneliness of a single spirit, shutting out the unbearable winds of the great world. She and Franz had failed to find any firm centre; the farm provided them, but could not contain nor hold them in its essential rhythm of work; and now that they were tested there seemed nothing left, no escape. They could get away if they were together, like truants, for a time. But they had to come back, to reality. Better if Franz had been strong, stronger than she like his father Christiaan, though his gentleness and good nature, his lack of ambition or greed had been so attractive. He was so generous, trusting.

She went back to the kitchen and walked about the house seeing nothing, but automatically shifting a vase of flowers and pushing back a curtain. Then she deliberately changed into rubber-soled walking-shoes and put on a neat little hat and dark glasses. She was going to find Franz.

Aletta heard a noise on the stoep, shuffling, a chair being moved. She thought with a new flicker of anger it was the maid come back to pry into her secrets. She walked out firmly, through the lounge and out at the glass doors. It was not the maid on the stoep, it was Rooi. He was lying on the green paving, one foreleg had been shattered above the elbow joint by a bullet and he was slowly licking the wound while the blood welled gradually out in a puddle near him. Franz had shot him – she saw at a glance – and failed to kill him.

She stood in the doorway, her heart bursting, and her tears came in a rush.

'Rooi, Rooi, oh, Rooi!' she sobbed, going forward to him. 'What am I going to do?'

The dog growled.

She was shaken with crying now, bitter within her, and knelt by him trembling. He let her stroke his head, but when she tried to touch the shattered leg, to stanch the blood with her handkerchief, he showed his teeth red with his own blood in a snarl. 'What am I to do?' she cried, and she was thinking of Franz.

She had no medical knowledge and could think of nothing but to stroke the dog's head while it went on stoically licking that awful wound.

She heard Franz coming, his footsteps rapid on the path, and her heart died in her. He was up the steps in a bound; she remained kneeling over the dog and felt him behind her, his presence like a weight on her.

'Aletta, it was an accident,' were his first words. He had to lie to her, now, of all times; he was so craven and weak. 'I shot at a crow on the koppie and the ricochet hit him. Ag, it was terrible, he went straight for home on three legs . . . Speak to me, Aletta, for God's sake. You don't believe me!'

She shook her head.

He slammed down the rifle and dropped on one knee at her side. 'Why don't you talk to me, Aletta? God, God say something. You must believe me.'

The dog had stopped licking its wound, raised its head balefully and growled as it had done when she first approached it. To Franz the growl came as a fearful shock. He stared open-mouthed and deadly white into the pain-deadened eyes of the animal. It was accusing him, as she was. She had turned against him as if she herself had been struck and the bullet was flying on . . . on . . . mowing down every dream and hope of his life. He found he was staring at the shattered leg, the wound and the blood pool on the tiles. Sickened, he stood up, and without thinking stretched out and took the gun. Aletta saw him, and in a moment was on her feet.

'Franz, are you mad? Put that gun down!'

He faced her woodenly, and it seemed his brain had grown benumbed and refused to grasp the position he was in.

'Why do you speak to me like that?' he demanded stubbornly.

'Give me the gun, Franz – you have done enough harm already.'

'No, I won't then,' he answered.

She reached forward slowly for the rifle, expecting that after a moment of hesitation he would surrender it to her. But he made no move, and she in her pain and grief and pity failed to see how shattered he was inside. She grasped the gun and he let it go. But her action had sparked off a sudden rage in him and he snatched the muzzle with one hand. She struggled to keep hold, her fingers slipping cruelly over the sharp metalwork as he jerked. Then there was a momentary pause as they faced one another in flaring anger, oblivious of all else. And she shifted her hold and the gun went off in her hands. Franz's fingers relaxed quite slowly and he went over to the wall and slid down it in a heap.

In the night she went back to where he was lying and put out the lamp and sat beside him. The neighbours had come and some were moving about the house and others talked low in her lounge. One of the farmers had put Rooi out of his suffering and they buried him under the flagstone at the foot of the cypress. The older women had laid Franz out and dressed him in his best suit and crossed his hands over his breast. She was weeping subduedly as she sat near him seeing his face in the dimness of their room. But there was a strange quiet acceptance far down in her soul. There had been no escape for them, no escape, no escape. And she had lost him at the moment they had found it out.

'My darling, my darling,' she whispered. 'Why did it have to be you?' And she remembered how dead he had looked last night as if in a grim, unread wish, while now he seemed merely in a deep and unutterably peaceful sleep.

ELISE MULLER

Night at the Ford

One moment the road was a white ribbon in the headlights, the next everything was plunged into darkness. The scraping of branches on metal . . . A thud . . . The car swerved violently and screeched to a standstill. Silence reigned for a long moment. Then the young man at the wheel gave a slow relieved whistle and his left hand dropped to his knee.

'That was close,' he said, turning the key in the ignition.

'What's wrong with the lights?' The woman beside him betrayed no anxiety whatsoever.

'The road, of course – this wretched gravel road. I imagine something has shaken loose.'

'Well then get out and have a look.'

Smiling as he groped in the cubby-hole for a torch, he cast her a sideways glance. The yellow light from the dashboard lit her face, making her full, painted lips look almost black against the mask-like complexion that matched her emotionless tone. He got out, shone the torch back down the road and exclaimed in a voice still unsteadied by shock: 'Good heavens, you should see the tracks. Come and look at our skid-marks.'

She said with a touch of impatience, 'The only thing that interests me now is the road ahead.'

At this remark he turned to lift the bonnet. While he stooped under it to investigate, she estimated when they'd reach their destination. It was already nearly eight, more than half an hour after sunset. Jerry would have to drive cautiously from here on: you couldn't tell when the lights were going to fail again and the road was rough and tortuous. She smiled when she thought of how deftly he'd brought the vehicle to a halt, but it never occurred to her to congratulate him on his dexterity. Her smile was one of pure self-satisfaction. She knew how to organise things to her own advantage. She'd hired him as a driver and within a few months he had proved to be good behind the wheel and a help with the bookkeeping, too. Pursuing this train of thought, she mechanically obeyed his instructions to turn the lights on and off. But in less than five minutes she had lit a cigarette, frowning.

'For heaven's sake,' she snapped. 'You've been at it for at least a quarter of an hour.'

'Come and hold the torch,' was his only rejoinder.

She threw back the travelling rug and got out. 'It's freezing!' Shivering, she took the torch and leaned against the vehicle to direct the beam of light on to the engine.

Half an hour after they'd stopped, he looked at her with an apologetic shrug.

'And now?' she asked.

'We could wait until it gets light,' he suggested, taking out a cigarette.

'Spend the whole night here?' Her voice had lost its earlier control. 'Can't you fix it?'

He too was beginning to sound irritated now. 'I'm employed as your driver and part-time bookkeeper – that's all. I never pretended I had a degree in engineering.'

Ignoring his indignation, she said icily. 'It can't be far to the ford and they said there were people living there, didn't they?'

He nodded. 'Fine, it's your car. If you think it's possible to get to the ford in the dark, you drive. Just don't ask me to get in, that's all.'

She paused before speaking again. Her eyes swept from the clear starry sky to the dark thicket of proteas that edged the road. 'I'll walk,' she said.

'And the car?' he asked, half-joking because he never dreamed that she was serious about walking.

'I'll go. You stay with the car.'

'Afraid of public opinion?' he mocked.

'To hell with public opinion,' she snapped. 'Do you imagine I want to spend a cold night sitting bolt upright in your company?'

'You could do worse,' he suggested, but when she opened the back door and he realised she actually intended to go, he added quickly, 'We could make a bed for you on the back seat.'

She pulled an overnight bag out from among the heavy cases stacked in the back of the car and then slammed the door shut. 'I've been on the go since six this morning. I intend to sleep in a bed tonight no matter what I have to pay for it.' Winding a scarf round her head, she slung her handbag over her shoulder and picked up the other bag. 'The torch please, Jerry.'

'I could try to drive with it,' he ventured tentatively.

She laughed, shaking her head. 'Not on these bends. There's nothing to worry about. You know what I carry in my handbag, don't you? Just don't get a fright if you hear a shot fired.'

Thirty seconds later the sound of her footsteps had faded into the night.

In the kitchen of the house above the ford, silent flames licked at the protea logs in the grate. A woman stood pensively before the range, her hands clasped together under her gingham apron. In the firelight that flickered over her narrow face, she looked older than her sixty years. But the minute she heard the sound of footsteps at the back door, her weary expression vanished. She pulled the black iron pot to one side and banged the fire hatch shut over the grate. The burly farmer brought a draught of cold air into the kitchen with him.

The woman threw a worried glance at the guttering candle and then looked questioningly at her husband. Above the sparse beard his mouth was stern.

'Not a breath of wind,' was his terse answer to her unspoken question.

Hopefully she said, 'Perhaps later tonight . . .'

He shook his large head and slumped down at the table with an elbow on each side of his plate. 'Not a breath,' he sighed more to himself than to her. 'And not a cloud in the sky. It's a night for frost if ever I saw one.'

Once she'd served bean soup from the cast-iron pot into deep plates, he continued, 'A fortnight ago, when it was so warm, I reckoned we hadn't seen the last of the frost.' He broke off to say grace and his voice trembled over the simple words because he was certain that this sudden biting wind boded ill for his daily bread. They ate in silence. Conversation was impossible in the face of disaster. They were defenceless; this was the ultimate test of their faith. Oh, for just a breath of wind, a couple of clouds – *anything* to keep the cold white fire from the tender young wheat!

Throwing his head up suddenly, the old man broke the tense silence. Through the stillness of the night they clearly heard the sound of footsteps coming across the farmyard and up to the homestead. A knock at the front door . . . Taking the candle, the old man went through the front room towards the door. A woman stood outside, so he automatically looked behind her for someone else.

But she was alone. 'Good evening,' she said and her voice told him at once that she was not as young as her make-up had led him to believe. 'I've had car trouble. I'm looking for a bed for the night.'

Noticing the overnight bag she carried, he invited her in. 'Went off the road?' The words were brief but the tone was friendly.

'The lights failed suddenly just up there,' she explained. After the sharp night air, the unfamiliar smell of dung-smeared floors turned her stomach. 'Yours is the only house I came across.'

The old woman appeared in the kitchen door. 'There's a farm just under half a mile further on,' she said. 'Across the ford. Are you alone?'

'My . . . my friend stayed with the car.'

The old people's eyes met as though they were conferring. Peevishly, she wondered if they were weighing up the pros and cons of taking her in. But almost immediately, the woman said, 'All we can offer is the best we have. We could also put your husband up.'

She smiled as she answered 'We aren't married,' noticing how the old man's eyes narrowed under his beetling brows. *Of course they'd frown on people like Jerry and me driving around together after dark*. But why should she care what they thought? There was no apology in her tone as she explained that she worked as a travelling representative, selling household linen for a city firm. There was so much valuable merchandise in the car that they couldn't leave it unattended. 'Jerry is my driver. We called at the farms along the river until after sunset. The people there told us to take this road to Cedarville.'

The woman nodded. 'Put your bag down here on the bench. I'm sure you'd like something to eat, wouldn't you?'

Sitting at the kitchen table, she leaned against the low back of her chair. Her eyes wandered round the small room, over the old-fashioned range where the odd flame from the smouldering fire sent a flash of light through the broken grate on to the casseroles, over to the little window she'd seen light shining through as she came down the road. A small, uncurtained window without a sill. Primitive, she thought. She'd realised this as the torchlight played over it; but right then she didn't care what sort of house or shack it was or who lived there. It was inhabited, that was enough. She was not normally nervous, but the long walk in the dark with a tangle of proteas on either side, her footsteps the only sound on the unknown road that twisted and rose and fell in the torchlight until she thought it would go on for ever . . . She shuddered and pulled herself upright. Thank heaven the walk was over; it was crazy to get so worked up over nothing.

'There's some bread to have with your soup,' the woman said.

Smiling gratefully, she wondered whether they always dined in such Spartan style. But she was hungry and the smell of the soup sharpened her appetite. What would Jerry say at the sight of her eating unstrained bean soup and coarse bread? Oh well, it could have been worse. Every now and then she caught the two old folks exchanging glances which made her uneasy because she knew it must have something to do with her. Naturally they'd find her appearance odd. Had her make-up put them off? Perhaps her scarlet enamelled nails? In this wilderness things like that probably didn't go down very well. Perhaps they were wondering why she hadn't spent the night with the young man seeing she was driving around with him unchaperoned. They could guess their guesses and exchange all the glances they cared to, as long as they gave her a bed warm enough to compensate for all the hotel luxuries she'd have to do without. In the morning she'd pay them more than their roof over her head was worth. *Just how much would you pay in a hotel for bean soup and dry bread?* she wondered with a wry smile she couldn't quite conceal.

The old woman stood up – 'to get the room ready,' she said – and went off through the front room. So she was left alone in the kitchen with the old farmer. Sipping his coffee and periodically sucking a stray drop off his beard, he attempted a conversation.

'You sell linen, you said?'

'Yes. Linen, embroidered goods and some women's clothing . . ' Out of habit, she smiled the cool but friendly smile she always wore when talking business.

He didn't appear to notice. 'You said you were up there along the river. Did you perhaps hear how the wheat was doing there? Were the ears already forming?'

She gaped at him, completely at a loss. 'Ears forming?'

'That's what I said.'

She shook her head, laughing. 'Goodness knows. I'm not an agriculturist.'

Terse as ever, he countered, 'But you eat bread.'

Was this meant as a reprimand or should she simply put it down to his brusque manner?

Confused, she couldn't meet the eyes that challenged hers from his lined face. What right did he have to criticise her? She ate bread and she paid for it. Why should she be under any further obligation? If these old people chose to live from hand to mouth it was their business, but that didn't give them the right to point a finger at her. Awkwardly she unzipped her bag, took out a packet of cigarettes and offered him one. His eyes narrowed in distaste. 'No, thank you,' he said, more mildly than she'd expected.

'Do you mind if I do?' Without waiting for his dubious nod, she took one out, lit it and inhaled the smoke, leaning on an elbow. When she looked up again he was gazing over her shoulder. The old woman stood in the doorway. She quickly wiped the stunned surprise off her lean face, but not before her amused guest had noticed. *Have you never seen a woman smoking before?* she wondered. It was worth the trouble and expense just to arouse such naked disapproval.

She followed the woman and her candle through the front room. The light fell on the old-fashioned leather-thonged bench, on two armchairs whose shabbiness spoke eloquently of poverty. The room they entered was small and, like the front room, sparsely furnished. The brass double bedstead shone surprisingly brightly against the dingy wardrobe and time-worn washstand. *But beggars can't be choosers*, she told herself wearily.

'Would you like some hot water to wash with?'

'Thank you.'

When the woman had gone, she sat on the bed. The feather mattress gave way under her. Hmm . . . hot water and such a soft mattress! Jerry would never believe this. She opened her overnight bag which had been placed at the foot of the bed.

The woman reappeared with a steaming enamel jug. Placing it on the washstand, she said, 'I opened the window a little at the top. The wind hasn't picked up yet.'

'Are you expecting it to blow?'

'We're hoping it will. If it blows, there won't be frost.'

'And if there's frost?'

An indulgent smile played about the woman's mouth. 'We get a lot of frost round here,' she said, 'but the warm weather came so early this year the wheat is already forming ears. Frost could cause a lot of damage now. When would you like to get up in the morning?'

'Oh, just call me when you're up,' came the reply. 'My driver will arrive as soon as it's light. I don't eat breakfast so a cup of coffee will be plenty, thanks.'

She undressed quickly, slipped between the cold starched sheets and blew out the candle. Dozing, she relived the walk here – so scary and lonely in the dark! Then she smiled to think of Jerry spending the night shivering in the car. The muted sound of the old people's voices in the front room stirred her curiosity briefly. Were they sharing their bitter disgust for the uninvited guest and her cigarettes within their hallowed portals?

Then she fell asleep.

The old woman brought her coffee next morning while it was still dark. 'It's very early but now you can take your time dressing,' she said as she left. The other woman sipped her coffee, suddenly repelled by the poor furnishings and the absence of any luxury. *How on earth could anyone bear to live like this? Could people really make do with only the bare essentials?* She drained her cup. She had to get out of here. One night was more than enough – the less one saw of it all in daylight, the better. Heavens, the deprivation, the bleakness of everything!

She was still dressing when she heard the car hooter. Jerry, of course, and she wasn't at all put out that he'd come so early. At least she wouldn't have to wait for him. The old woman put her head round the door to say there was no need to hurry, her husband had gone to offer the driver a cup of coffee.

'Thank you,' she answered, but it didn't improve her mood. If Jerry saw the inside of the house, he would never believe she'd enjoyed a comfortable night. She could hear his voice in the front room. Would he make a better impression than she had? Snapping the overnight bag shut, she slung her handbag over her shoulder and went out. Jerry pushed his empty cup away and got up from the table. The old man nodded a greeting to her and the woman appeared from the kitchen with a brown paper bag. 'Sandwiches,' she said, 'just a little something for the road.'

Jerry took it, his other hand going to his trouser pocket.

'Don't worry, Jerry. You go ahead, I'll settle things here.' As he stepped out into the yard, she said to the old people, 'It was good of you to put me up. How much do I owe you?'

'Nothing,' answered the old man as though he didn't want to discuss it. She'd already unzipped her bag and taken out a banknote. She held it out to him but he ignored it. 'You don't owe us anything,' he repeated.

Looking past him to the old woman, she said, 'I want to pay.'

A kind smile lit the old woman's narrow face, but there was a hint of pride in the soft voice. 'One doesn't charge for hospitality, my dear.'

Momentarily at a loss, she stood holding the banknote. 'Please take it.' The old woman shook her grey head.

She put the money back in her purse, thanked them once again for the bed and said how good it was of them to offer her shelter on such a cold night, the words tumbling out clumsily over her embarrassment. Then she left.

It was only at the main road where Jerry waited for her that she noticed how hard the ground was underfoot. Frost? She couldn't tell for certain in the deceptive early light. For a moment she slowed down, surprised by the impulse to return and ask the old people if the frost had damaged their wheat. But the frustration of their parting proved stronger and she didn't even look back from the car.

The engine started up and they drove away. 'Did you have a comfortable night?' he mocked.

'Very pleasant, thank you,' she answered in the same sharp tone. 'And you?'

'Not bad. At least mine didn't cost anything.'

'Neither did mine,' she snapped.

'What? Didn't you pay them?'

She shook her head. 'I couldn't. What they had to give wasn't for sale. Don't you know one doesn't charge for hospitality?'

The car lost speed as he stared at her. 'You sound odd this morning. That bed wasn't bewitched, by any chance?'

She didn't answer, rummaging in her bag for a cigarette. He repeated the question, this time without the sarcasm. 'By the way, where *did* you sleep? On that leather-thonged bench?'

And in a flash of insight she saw through the walls of the little house – a simple three-roomed dwelling. Inside her bag, her fingers went limp and then clenched together. 'No,' she said at last. 'I slept in the bedroom on the only bed in the house.'

As she spoke the words, her lips trembled with regret, sharp as the frost of a winter's morning. And that night left her with a heavy burden of debt, not because of the loving kindness she had received, but because of the kindness her blind arrogance had withheld.

Translated by Catherine Knox

HERMAN CHARLES BOSMAN

A Bekkersdal Marathon

At Naudé, who had a wireless set, came into Jurie Steyn's voorkamer, where we were sitting waiting for the railway lorry from Bekkersdal, and gave us the latest news. He said that the newest thing in Europe was that young people there were going in for non-stop dancing. It was called marathon dancing, At Naudé told us, and those young people were trying to break the record for who could remain on their feet longest, dancing.

We listened for a while to what At Naudé had to say, and then we suddenly remembered a marathon event that had taken place in the little dorp of Bekkersdal – almost in our midst, you could say. What was more, there were quite a number of us sitting in Jurie Steyn's post office, who had actually taken part in that non-stop affair, and without knowing that we were breaking records, and without expecting any sort of a prize for it, either.

We discussed that affair at considerable length and from all angles, and we were still talking about it when the lorry came. And we agreed that it had been in several respects an unusual occurrence. We also agreed that it was questionable if we could have carried off things so successfully that day, if it had not been for Billy Robertse.

You see, our organist at Bekkersdal was Billy Robertse. He had once been a sailor and had come to the bushveld some years before, travelling on foot. His belongings, fastened in a red handkerchief, were slung over his shoulder on a stick. Billy Robertse was journeying in that fashion for the sake of his health. He suffered from an unfortunate complaint for which he had at regular intervals to drink something out of a black bottle that he always carried handy in his jacket pocket.

Billy Robertse would even keep that bottle beside him in the organist's gallery in case of a sudden attack. And if the hymn the predikant gave out had many verses, you could be sure that about halfway through Billy Robertse would bring the bottle up to his mouth, leaning sideways towards what was in it. And he would put several extra twirls into the second part of the hymn.

When he first applied for the position of organist in the Bekkersdal church, Billy Robertse told the meeting of deacons that he had learnt to play the organ in a cathedral in northern Europe. Several deacons felt, then, that they could not favour his application. They said that the cathedral sounded too Papist, the way Billy Robertse described it, with a dome three hundred feet high and with marble apostles. But it was lucky for Billy Robertse that he was able to mention, at the following combined meeting of elders and deacons, that he had also played the piano in a South American dance hall, of which the manager was a Presbyterian. He asked the meeting to overlook his unfortunate past, saying that he had had a hard life, and anybody could make mistakes. In any case, he had never cared much for the Romish atmosphere of the cathedral, he said, and had been happier in the dance hall.

In the end, Billy Robertse got the appointment. But in his sermons for several Sundays after that the predikant, Dominee Welthagen, spoke very strongly against the evils of dance halls. He described those places of awful sin in such burning words that at least one young man went to see Billy Robertse, privately, with a view to taking lessons in playing the piano.

But Billy Robertse was a good musician. And he took a deep interest in his work. And he said that when he sat down on the organist's stool behind the pulpit, and his fingers were flying over the keyboards, and he was pulling out the stops, and his feet were pressing down the notes that sent the deep bass tones through the pipes – then he felt that he could play all day, he said.

I don't suppose he guessed that he would one day be put to the test, however.

It all happened through Dominee Welthagen one Sunday morning going into a trance in the pulpit. And we did not realise that he was in a trance. It was an illness that overtook him in a strange and sudden fashion.

At each service the predikant, after reading a passage from the Bible, would lean forward with his hand on the pulpit rail and give out the number of the hymn we had to sing. For years his manner of conducting the service had been exactly the same. He would say, for instance: 'We will now sing Psalm 82, verses 1 to 4.' Then he would allow his head to sink forward on to his chest and he would remain rigid, as though in prayer, until the last notes of the hymn died away in the church.

Now, on that particular morning, just after he had announced the number of the psalm, without mentioning what verses, Dominee Welthagen again took a firm grip on the pulpit rail and allowed his head to sink forward on to his breast. We did not realise that he had fallen into a trance of a peculiar character that kept his body standing upright while his mind was a blank. We learnt that only later.

In the meantime, while the organ was playing over the opening bars, we began to realise that Dominee Welthagen had not indicated how many verses we had to sing. But he would discover his mistake, we thought, after we had been singing for a few minutes.

All the same, one or two of the younger members of the congregation did titter, slightly, when they took up their hymn books. For Dominee Welthagen had given out Psalm 119. And everybody knows that Psalm 119 has 176 verses.

This was a church service that will never be forgotten in Bekkersdal.

We sang the first verse and then the second and then the third. When we got to about the sixth verse and the minister still gave no sign that it would be the last, we assumed that he wished us to sing the first eight verses. For, if you open your hymn book, you'll see that Psalm 119 is divided into sets of eight verses, each ending with the word 'Pouse'.

We ended the last notes of verse eight with more than an ordinary number of turns and twirls, confident that at any moment Dominee Welthagen would raise his head and let us know that we could sing 'Amen'.

It was when the organ started up very slowly and solemnly with the music for verse nine that a real feeling of disquiet overcame the congregation. But, of course, we gave no sign of what went on in our minds. We held Dominee Welthagen in too much veneration.

Nevertheless, I would rather not say too much about our feelings, when verse followed verse and Pouse succeeded Pouse, and still Dominee Welthagen made no sign that we had sung long enough, or that there was anything unusual in what he was demanding of us.

After they had recovered from their first surprise, the members of the church council conducted themselves in a most exemplary manner. Elders and deacons tiptoed up and down the aisles, whispering words of reassurance to such members of the congregation, men as well as women, who gave signs of wanting to panic.

At one stage it looked as though we were going to have trouble from the organist. That was when Billy Robertse, at the end of the 34th verse, held up his black bottle and signalled quietly to the elders to indicate that his medicine was finished. At the end of the 35th verse he made signals of a less quiet character, and again at the end of the 36th verse. That was when Elder Landsman tiptoed out of the church and went round to the Konsistorie, where the Nagmaal wine was kept. When Elder Landsman came back into the church he had a long black bottle half-hidden under his manel. He took the bottle up to the organist's gallery, still walking on tiptoe.

At verse 61 there was almost a breakdown. That was when a message came from the back of the organ, where Koster Claassen and the assistant verger, whose task it was to turn the handle that kept the organ supplied with wind, were in a state near to exhaustion. So it was Deacon Cronjé's turn to go tiptoeing out of the church. Deacon Cronjé was head warder at the local gaol. When he came back it was with three burly Native convicts in striped jerseys, who also went through the church on tiptoe. They arrived just in time to take over the handle from Koster Claassen and the assistant verger.

At verse 98 the organist again started making signals about his medicine. Once more Elder Landsman went round to the Konsistorie. This time he was accompanied by another elder and a deacon, and they stayed away somewhat longer than the time when Elder Landsman had gone on his own. On their return the deacon bumped into a small hymn book table at the back of the church. Perhaps it was because the deacon was a fat, red-faced man, and not used to tiptoeing.

At verse 124 the organist signalled again, and the same three members of the church council filed out to the Konsistorie, the deacon walking in front this time.

It was about then that the pastor of the Full Gospel Apostolic Faith Church, about whom Dominee Welthagen had in the past used almost as strong language as about the Pope, came up to the front gate of the church to see what was afoot. He lived near our church and, having heard the same hymn tune being played over and over for about eight hours, he was a very amazed man. Then he saw the door of the Konsistorie open, and two elders and a deacon coming out, walking on tiptoe – they having apparently forgotten that they were not in church, then. When the pastor saw one of the elders hiding a black bottle under his manel, a look of understanding came over his features. The pastor walked off, shaking his head.

At verse 152 the organist signalled again. This time Elder Landsman and the other elder went out alone. The deacon stayed behind on the deacon's bench, apparently in deep thought. The organist signalled again, for the last time, at verse 169. So you can imagine how many visits the two elders made to the Konsistorie altogether.

The last verse came, and the last line of the last verse. This time it had to be 'Amen'. Nothing could stop it. I would rather not describe the state that the congregation was in. And by then the three Native convicts, red stripes and all, were, in the Bakhatla tongue, threatening mutiny. 'Aa-m-e-e-n' came from what sounded like less than a score of voices, hoarse with singing.

The organ music ceased.

Maybe it was the sudden silence that at last brought Dominee Welthagen out of his long trance. He raised his head and looked slowly about him. His gaze travelled over his congregation and then looking at the windows, he saw that it was night. We understood right away what was going on in Dominee Welthagen's mind. He thought he had just come into the pulpit, and that this was the beginning of the evening service. We realised that, during all the time we had been singing, the predikant had been in a state of unconsciousness.

Once again Dominee Welthagen took a firm grip of the pulpit rail. His head again started drooping forward on to his breast. But before he went into a trance for the second time, he gave out the hymn for the evening service. 'We will,' Dominee Welthagen announced, 'sing Psalm 119.'

BREYTEN BREYTENBACH

The Double Dying of an Ordinary Criminal

Carpe diem, quam minimum credula postero . . .

(i)

It is an unapproachable, ungrateful country. Along the coast, in an undulating green strip between the indigo sea and the ribbed, foaming mountain chain, the climate is tropical. There are sharks in the ocean and other fish large and small, dark coloured or of silver or ivory. On the land flamboyant trees grow, trees with shiny green fleshy leaves and violent outbursts of flowers: banana, palm, mango, the blossomy downpour of the bougainvillaea, the star-wounds of the poinsettia, the hibiscus with hairy dark ants most likely looking with sticky legs for sweetness in the calyx, canna, Ceylon rose. Nights the humid darkness is scented with the secretive magnolia, the camellia, the gardenia. The fruit are often fibrous, glutinous and soft. The trees – such as the guava – are enclosed by their particular smell, the heavy perfume of a full-bodied woman who has perspired a lot. The heat and the high humidity cause the milk to turn sour instantly, grow mould on the clothes strung on wires or kept in wardrobes, rot the wood while steel and iron are devoured by oxidation. To the North and West stretch the swelling sugar-cane plantations, the cane is cultivated and chopped by people of a dark race, people with large sombre eyes and smooth black hair. These people are sometimes called 'sea kaffirs'. Here and there among the rippling and sharply whispering sugar-cane they erected rudimentary single-roomed temples for their gods, the inner walls decorated with bright representations: often the swarthy mother god, Kali, she who also at times assumes the aspect of Parvati or Sarasvati on the winged throne of a swan, or that of Shakti – the bride, companion and *alter ego* of Shiva the destroyer. On these plantations as also in the cultivated forests further removed from the ocean, where lumberjacks cut and saw the yellow and red trees, and elsewhere too, there is the constant flashing of many kinds of birds, butterflies, large insects with shimmering black bodies. As well as snakes. The cities service the ships which come to trade here, and the holiday-makers and pleasure-seekers come to relax on the guava-coloured beaches and to bathe in the tepid waves within the protection of the shark nets. When the barriers are raised the stuck sharks are there like white torpedoes. In the streets one encounters the many fumes of decomposition and dismantling, of viscosity and dry rot and sweetness; occasionally also the harsher tang of spices and seasoning herbs. There are night clubs and taxis and rickshaws. People smoke or use in other ways a rank stupefier commonly called *dagga*; other names heard are *bhang*, 'real rice', *gunja, jane*, 'Maryjay', 'rooney', 'DP', 'green stuff', 'weed', 'grass', 'dope', 'popeye', 'wheat', 'Tree of Knowledge', *insangu*. It makes the eyes darker from within and red around the lids and it lies like a curly smokiness on the voice. It analyses the sense of time the way one would eat a fish morsel by morsel off the bone. It entices the appetite.

The Coast is separated from the Heartland by a chain of mountains which seem blue from afar, the mountains of the Dragon, hundreds of miles long, like the Great Wall of China with its watchtowers. The colours of the sun remain entangled mostly in the structure of the mountains. But some of this citadel's summits are so high that they've lost all colour; they are dusted with a sparkle which could be snow or ice.

Beyond the mountains the Heartland commences, an inhospitable region, a semi-desert which further and deeper will silt up in a true desert of brown and grey dunes; unresting dunes. It is a high plateau with hardly any diversity and little vegetation apart from the grass which grows tall and becomes white like a bleached photo during the winter. Now and then there are crevices or denser ravines in the folds of the high country, something which can be held darkly in the hollow of the hand, or more elevated ledges, ridges and mesas. When summer comes gigantic cloud constructions wash over the land, are piled up, unchain in thunderstorms of a prehistoric force with coiling swords of electricity and smoking arrows of light, until the clouds crack and tear, the bottom gives way and flood waters are poured over the ochre earth. The people of this land are hard and obtuse and doughty – but cunning – as the earth and its climate require of them. Their eyes lie waiting deep and unflinching in the heads, robed in wrinkles under thick eyebrows, and when they lose their teeth quite early on, as happens often, the jaw muscles are tough and bitter. They cultivate the topsoil. They sow and reap maize with big red-painted tractors, ploughs and other farm implements. They keep numerous herds and flocks, Brahmans with awkward humps, or earth-red oxen with white horns spread very wide on either side of the head – Nguni or Afrikaners by name. These beasts constitute practically the only heritage left by an ancient yellowish race of humans with Asiatic features who wandered over these wastes in days of yore. The real wealth of the Heartland is hoarded under the earth's crust where, when the earth still moved, layers and veins of gold were deposited, and copper, and further south also buried volcanoes, pipes and alluvial soil full of diamonds. Over these riches the people built their cities: glass, concrete, steel – rising from the desert to sometimes be split and obliterated again by fulminations from above. In the streets the long, flat automobiles crawl, flashing the sun like heliographs; inside the vehicles are people who have absorbed too much food, with fantastic *coiffures* or moustaches pearling perspiration, and with knees spread wide. The other people without means of transport are of a darker hue and they trot along the pavements with long rhythmically flapping coat-tails, passing by the enormous shop windows. From these cities are ruled and administered the Coast, the South, the Mountain Fastnesses, the Old-Land, the Gap, the Middle State, the Frontier, the Reserves, the Desert, and other colonies and possessions.

He was born in the country of Coast and grew up there. Little has been documented concerning his juvenile years and not much touching on his adult life. His mother became very old and started wearing a black dress with thick woollen stockings. Her back was bent high between the shoulder-blades. He was a tall and sturdy fellow with brown hair, slightly oily, falling straight over the forehead. His legs were hairy and when he deigned to smile only the left side of his mouth was tilted upwards with a minimal contraction of muscles. We don't know whether he was interested in any sport. There is talk of work he was supposed to have had, and of a wife; even children are mentioned. He was still young. Twenty-eight years old.

Hell doesn't exist. It *comes into being*, each moment it is created relentlessly, and then it is strictly personal and individual, that is, proper to each individual – which doesn't necessarily imply that others aren't touched or concerned by it. As tubes of light the hells burst in the heavens and illuminate, alter, the area within their reach. The act, the misdemeanour then, a fraction in time, causes a chain reaction, a mutation eventually flowering in the fated echo or the obverse of it; a clandestine bleeding. Each crime contains the hell befitting it. The snake's skin fits without any crease or pucker over the snake. When the felony is committed the hell opens up on the spot; when it at last – and often in public – bursts forth, it is redeemed. The one is an utterance of the other. The one eliminates the other.

He became a bum – nobody quite knows why or how. He met up with a woman, much older, a companion and an *alter ego*, a person like him dwelling in the dark mazes of the city. As much and as often as they could afford to they smoked and they drank. Nights they then slept in empty plots by smouldering rubbish heaps, or in condemned buildings due for demolition. Sometimes they lay in water furrows. They also danced.

The old woman tried to tempt drifters with her poor body – boozers, sailors, blokes ostensibly gentlemen with problems sneaking through the streets late at night (late in the blossoming of life, already in the dropping of death). She was the bait. He was the hook. Also the tackle, rod, gaff and cudgel. When she managed to seduce an unsuspecting customer with an obscene caricature of hip swaying and the slimy dark tongue as clotted bleeding between the more tropical red of the lips, the edges of the wound, leading him to a sheltered or deserted spot, then *he* jumped on the greedy or shaky one from behind. With a stick or a knife, sometimes with a length of piano wire twisted in a noose. Always the purpose was to break the subject open, to murder; three times at least it is known that he succeeded. Some victims were chopped up and chucked piecemeal in a sewer. Robbery, it would seem, was not the motive. Perhaps it was a perverse form of sexual satisfaction or the foreplay thereof. One night the prey was a blind jeweller, who could understand the facets of gems or the shivery internal working of watches with sensitive fingertips. It may also be that the jeweller's blindness is an injury resulting from the assault.

Without too much trouble they are trapped by the police. During the subsequent trial they are both found guilty and sentenced: she with tearing mouth to an insane asylum, he to the death cell. The expression is: he got the rope. They would top him. His life was to be reeled in with a cord.

He is transferred to a cell in a building of red bricks in one of the ruling cities of the Heartland. His appeal against the death sentence is rejected. The request for mercy likewise. The long wake has started. Altogether a year and a half passed.

The Monday the hangman came to inform him that the next Tuesday would be it – hardly a week then. Together with him in the pot there were five more 'condemns', Unwhites, people with sallow hides and of diverse crimes. They would go up together but were not to swing simultaneously. Maybe the Unlife up there would make them equal. A folded sheet of paper with a black border, where his dying day is announced, is handed to him. The hangman weighs him, measures his height and the circumference of his neck. With these data the length of the rope et cetera are calculated in an approximately scientific approximation. It was a Monday during the summer and each day of that season the clouds were a thundering sea battle above the hard, cracked earth.

Some people are dead before they even come to die. When the Unwhites are informed (when the countdown starts), they directly open up in song, they break and let the words erupt. There is a pulsating urgency about the singing, as if one can hear how scorchingly alive their voices are. All the other prisoners – in any event only awaiting their turn – help them from that instant on: the basses, the tenors, the harmonisers, the choir. Every flight of the prospective voyagers' voices is supported and sustained by those of the others. As if a stick is suddenly poked into an antheap. The sound of the voices is like that of cattle at the abattoir, the lowing of beasts smelling the blood and knowing that nothing can save them now. Perhaps the Jews too, had they been a singing people, would have hummed thus in the chambers where the gas was turned on. Maybe they did? This making of noises with the mouths continues day and night, erases night and day, till those who must depart go up in the morning, at seven o'clock. The best flying is done early in the morning. For that last stretch those who leave will sing alone. Day in day out it continues and in the early hours it is a low mumbling, the murmuring sound of the sea which never sleeps but only turns on to the other hip. In this fashion, during the final week, that which is fear and pain and anguish and life is gradually pushed out of the mouth. A narcotic. And so they move with the ultimate daybreak through the corridor as if in a mirror, rhythmic but in a trance, not as men alone but as a song in movement. They are no longer there; just the breaths flow unceasingly and warm and humid over the lips. (The opposite may be alleged too: that this delicious and fleeting life is purified and sharpened over the last week by song to a shriek of limpid knowing.)

For him there is no such grace because his like – the fellow condemns in his section, in his part of the prison, the pale ones, the Uncoloureds, people from the ruling class – don't sing easily. Nor can he, like the others in the pot, be put in a communal cell – of course there are far more Unwhite candidates than Uncoloured ones. *He* must pray death (or life) all the way out of himself. The pastor is there to assist and to show him the words, for words are holes in which you must stick death. He will die in another way before he is dead. He becomes his own ghost. The eyes are deep and bright in the sockets. It gives his head the appearance of a skull. His quiff falls lank over the forehead. He sneers without any fear of the warders. Like the other seasoned prisoners – those who know the ropes – he wears his shoes without socks.

> All hope is lost
> Of my reception into grace; what worse?
> For where no hope is left, is left no fear!
>   (blind Milton)

The minister. In fact a chaplain, and with a rank in the service. He is a small chap with an absolutely naked scalp, dressed in a modish tailored suit and shirted in flowers branching out over ribs, belly and the small of the back. He has red puffy bags under the eyes and, so one imagines, folds of white flesh around the midriff and in the groin. It is his task to prepare the soul, to make it robust, to extract the soul and wash and iron it, and then to let it be acquiescent. It requires a fine ingenuity because the soul is like smoke and so easily slips through the fingers. He spends much time on his knees and it is not good for the pants. He prays and emits suffocated sounds. Some vowels are stretched beyond measure, are pronounced in a placatory way as when a little child tries to make a big animal change its mind. When he prays he closes his eyes and holds the hand of the convicted. With eyes closed, when talking aloud, you move on another level. That which is there is not there. That which isn't there is there perchance. Heaven grows behind closed eyelids. His order is a tall one. During the last week something crystallises from the doomed, surreptitiously, and comes to cleave to the clergyman. It is the soul wishing to remain among the familiar living when the soma comes to nothing. Like a snail it is searching for a new shell. So the body becomes lighter . . .

The executioner (bailiff, hangman, topper, rope expert, death artist) is a tall man in the sombre weeds of pious neutrality and with a melancholy countenance. His post or position is private and part-time. When, through resignation or death, a vacancy occurs, anyone – a pensioner for instance, or the father of numerous sickly children who needs a little extra income – can submit his application to the magistrate. He then tenders for so much or so much per head (at present, before devaluation, it is seven rands) for he is remunerated by the head. He must see to it, together with his assistant (if any), that the gallows remain in good well-oiled working order, for they are often made use of. When the pot is pointed out it is his duty to be the announcer and to make the necessary preparations. He is the tailor who will fit you out in a new life. On the fateful morning he is there bright and early. He reposes his head on interlaced fingers against the bars as if he were praying or dozing off. When the candidates are brought in under escort he makes them take up their indicated positions – warders are keeping them upright – and adjusts the nooses around the necks below the ears until they fit just right. Then he closes the eye-flaps of their hoods and presses with a pale finger the button activating the trap-door. They then plunge twice their own height. The complete procedure seldom takes more than seven seconds. Up to seven persons can thus be served simultaneously, standing in line like bridegrooms before an altar. After the thrashing about the corpses remain hanging for ten minutes in the well. What has not snapped will be throttled. Thereafter the still warm and very heavy (because deadweight) corpses are pulleyed in, the handcuffs taken off, they are undressed, and lowered again. If the correct results were not obtained the whole process is repeated. When shudders and convulsions are no longer observed the limp cadavers are deposited in washing troughs and the doctor on duty makes an incision in the neck to establish which vertebra was broken – this information must be entered in duplicate. Bloodstains have penetrated the metal of the wash-basins. Blood-stains, crud, snot splotches also on the ropes and the hoods, and the cupboard where the coiled ropes are kept stinks of stale effluence.

The burial takes place within a few hours. The clothes of the deceased are brought back into circulation in the gaol. After all, it's state property. If for some or other reason a dead body must be preserved, there are modern, shiny ice-boxes for that purpose in the autopsy room. As all of this happens during the fresh and innocent hours, the vocation of hangman need not interfere with any other job; your executioner could be a teacher, a psychiatrist, a politician, a chicken farmer, publisher, or unemployed.

The gibbets. In other ages the pillory was erected prominently in a square or on a hilltop, and the complete ceremony was public and a joy for the birds, not so much for its deterrent effect but because it was such an intimate part of everyday life and death, and a rude form of amusement. We live in *these* days and no longer frequent or know one another. No longer are we animals with the snouts in the trough of death. Also, civilisation has come over us. In our time the place of execution is a privileged one, where it is dark, behind walls, through passages, in the heart of the labyrinth. Few people know when the seeker has found it. It is there like some bashful god, like the blind and deaf and self-satisfied idol of a tiny group of initiates, for the satisfaction of an obscure tradition. And that which is intimate, like defecation, must be kept hidden from prying eyes. The artificial gloss of an insouciant existence must be safeguarded. Usually there is no trouble or unpleasantness during the execution. But it has happened that some of the damned refuse to fit the pattern and that they then, that last morning when the cell door was unlocked, threw a blanket over the officer's head and tried to smash him against the wall, head first like a battering ram – so that he had to live for months afterwards with his neck in traction. And it has also happened that one flappie*, in that fraction of a second when the trap-door falls open, timed the moment exactly, and jumped on to the back of the man in front of him so that his fall was broken and he had to be hoisted back up, kicking, to die all over again. The blind shaft is as inevitable as the sunrise; the ritual leaves no room for any deflection or improvising. The last route is secure and actually no longer part of the personal hell.

*Flap – long-tailed widow-bird, sakabula; common name for black prisoner.

The pilgrim, the candidate, is accompanied to the preparation room by a spiritual comforter and the officers. This place is called 'the last room', the departure hall. The nauseating sweet smell of death is already all-pervasive. Here he is handcuffed and a white hood is placed over his head. The flap above the eyes remains open until he has taken up his position below the gallows. Exceptionally it may happen that the spine and neck break completely at the instant when the earth falls away below his feet and that the head becomes separated from the body, that the head alone remains suspended there. But that just happens in the case of candidates who are rotten with syphilis, and then mostly with female Unwhites. For this negligible probability, seen statistically, one can hardly provide in advance, in a scientific way, a solution. What occurs more frequently is that the male reprobate at the critical crossover reaches a benevolent, jetting orgasm. To beget a child is thus always a form of dying. What's more, this final poke in the dark is fulfilment, at last a total embrace of the mother god. An influx and an unfolding. It is said: to die by the neck is to sodomise the night . . . Precautionary measures are however taken with female executees. They get water-tight rubber bloomers and the dress is taken in around the knees and sewn up. Nor will she afterwards be undressed like the men to be hosed down, but she'll be buried just the way she is in her clothes. The reason being that the female parts – uterus, ovaries – are spilled with the shock of falling down the shaft.

At times a doomed one may attempt during the last days and nights to take his own death. He will for instance try to crush his head against the cell wall or to dive head first from the bed to the floor and thus be rid of his thoughts on the cement, as of a hard rain. But it is not allowed; after all, it's not a sacrifice which is demanded but an execution which concerns others too and in which each one must play his ascribed part. It is a matter of mutual responsibility. Steps are therefore taken to prevent the suicide of the weak-hearted. Those whose lives in reality ceased existing with the death sentence are kept alive in bright cells permanently lit and day and night a warder keeps watch through the barred aperture in the door. There are days and there are nights . . . Once the candidate has been chosen his person and his cell are frisked for any concealed weapon or means of release. But apart from that he lives his last days like a king. The meal of the convicted may be ordered to taste, even fried chicken.

He swore that they'll never string him up alive, that he will do himself in. His cell is searched. In the ink vein of his ballpoint pen they find a hidden needle. A dark needle, blue at present, which was to be introduced into the upper arm from where, theoretically, it could accomplish the short trip to the heart where with a flashing snake of pain it would perforate that organ-organism the way the god Krishna (an incarnation of Vishnu) long ago pinned down the snake Kaliya with his lance: a short ultimate journey. He doesn't know that his needle has been discovered so that he retains the illusion that he himself may freely decide when to abrogate his life during the fatal week. Perhaps it doesn't matter. He will die in another way before the final sunrise.

It would however have been better and more effective had he smuggled in a razorblade at the beginning. He could have done so with the pretence that he wanted to cut out pictures to stick them on a sheet of paper. He could then spend such an inordinately long time doing so that the guardian will end up forgetting about the blade. This little silver-fish he should then break in two, washing the one half down the toilet bowl; the other part he hides on his body at all times. The last evening he wishes all the warders a good night and lies down in his bunk with an extra blanket over him and his back to the door. He has one hand under his head on the pillow and pulls the blanket up to his chin. Then he would have to work quickly for the convicted is not allowed to sleep with his hands below the blankets during the last week. With the broken blade he slices through the large vein in the crook of the arm, in the valley of the shoulder, in the armpit; a clean cut several centimetres long. His hand stays under the ear; the arm thus remains flexed so that the wound, the bearded and sighing mouth, may peacefully continue bleeding under the blanket – like the mysterious, sweetish smell of a tropical flower in the night. He rests with his body to the wall so that the blood may gather on the floor between the bed and the wall. When they arrive then the next morning to wake him for the final exercise, the body is already all of marble . . . Or – an alternative – he could have pulled, with the fingers, his tongue as far as it would go, closed his teeth over it, and then have tapped lightly with one hand against the lower jaw. In this way the lower teeth break through the tongue close to its roots. Nothing can save you from that blooming. Or he might even have swallowed the tongue. Fool!

From the land of Coast his mother arrives with her grey hair and her black back. Together with the preacher she visits him daily – but she of course is behind a glass partition since contact visits are not permitted. Death is contagious. When she prays, her hands, the knuckles and the joints, are so tightly clasped that it must be a tiny god indeed who finds asylum in such hand-space, a god like an idea worn away over the years, rubbed small, like a seed.

He stands in his cell under the bulb-eye from the ceiling, talking to his warders. One warder expects him to make shit at the last because he caught him doing exercises that final night. The pointing day is a silver-fish in a big bowl of liquid as murky as blood, in a dark house where night yet resides.

Monday comes with a cold persistent drizzle, an unheard-of way of raining in the Heartland in the summer. But apparently, so it is speculated, strong winds were blowing over the ocean from the Coast and a penetrating rain fell there. This strange weather is brought to the Heartland by the wind from the East – from the Coast therefore.

His last wish is that his eyes should be donated to the blind jeweller. His eyes are of a shiny green colour, like the stones jewellers sometimes mount on silver for a bangle or a gorget. It is not known whether eyes too have memories – who can say for sure where sensory memories are situated? When one leaves one's eyes to someone, doesn't it in a way mean the grafting of one person on another? But an eye cannot be grafted – only the cornea under favourable circumstances. And, in any event, his last wish cannot be honoured since there is not sufficient time to comply with the required formalities in duplicate and triplicate.

When the day comes he is up early. He will not see the dawn because the forbidden place where fruit will be hung on the trees of knowledge of good and of evil is in the very same building. Neither the knife of day nor the cape of night are known there. Some detectives come to enquire whether he might not be amenable, for old time's sake, to admitting his culpability for a series of unsolved murders. He pretends to be exclusive – as if each man were an exception. He will take many dead with him to the rot-hole. It is suspected that he may have polished off up to fifteen victims . . . He is led down the tunnels by officers and a soul-stroker. The song has already taken the Unwhites up, through the same corridors, ahead of him. At last, after whiling away so many months in the waiting rooms and the outer sanctums, purified and prepared, he will now enter the secret and sacred circle. Another hell is to be wiped out; a new one may be opened. Cause and effect continue. But he is no longer the man he was eighteen months ago.

In the preparatory room he greets the warders one by one by hand. The lines in the hand-palms are laid over one another; there is a touching, a crossing, a knotting of fingers. Night-flies meeting, parting. He claims he will meet them all again 'up there'. Here there is the aroma of sweetness although the night is icy-cold. He is given his hood and his shackles. Now he is the minotaur.

The mother is already waiting on her knees in the undertaker's hall where the box with the rests, the shell of the sacrifice of atonement, will be brought: at her request the family will take care of the burial. What the gods don't wish to eat will be fed to the earth. There is no more room between her hands. From her body something like a bleeding bubbles up, the reminiscence of a foetus, and breaks in her throat like the dark cooing of a dove.

He stands underneath the tree. Upwards, higher than the ceiling and than the roof ridge, is heaven; peace blue; stars have been incinerated by the light. A fish mirrors. The hangman, who has been leaning his head on folded hands, comes to adjust the rope, the umbilical cord. Exactly behind the ear the knot must lie, where the marrow, consciousness, the wire of light, grows into the skull. He follows to the last the cool movements of the executioner. The eye-flap is turned down. It is dark.

It is dark.

The trapdoor opened with a shudder running through the entire building. A door closing. A flame of lightning through a cloud. A knife slipping into the fatty layer below the ribcage. One heartbeat through all the tentacles, nets of silence, equilibrium-sticks and vein-sides of the body when you are shaken awake from the dark.

Outside the day. The sky a deep blue, purple nearly, the way it looks when seen through the porthole of a high-altitude aircraft or above very high silver-clean mountain peaks. The sun is a blinding thing, so ardent that you daren't look at it to establish its shape. In the air nothing, no substance which may deflect the sword strokes. A sharp and clear cold, crumbly and yet glass hard. Breaths hang in limp tufty cloudlets from the lips. Somewhere snow or hail must have fallen, surely in the mountains, and that in summer.

(ii)

> Once upon a time
> not so long ago . . .

One is loath to write too soon about something like the foregoing. You let the days pass you by although you're aware of the fact that you'll have to open the thing sooner or later. You allow the days to go hard in your throat. For it is like a contusion around the neck: first too tender to the touch, swollen with blood compressed in the capillaries; later the swelling goes down and the injured region becomes bluish purple; still later a yellowish blue and then a lighter yellow when it starts itching. Afterwards it is for a while still a scratchy place in the memory. And yet the matter must be disembowelled because we are the mirrors and mirrors have their own lives. Mirrors have a life too and that which gets caught in them continues existing there. Reality is a version of the mirror image. It is a literary phenomenon I'd like to point out to my colleagues: the ritual must be completed in us also. Before death points? Does death depend on us?

> you hang the life
> tied to death
> until it dies
>
> you drop life
> gibbeted to death:
> until death is.

Even though something can be inserted easily enough into the mirror, none of us knows precisely how and when it can be taken out again. Do mirrors have looking-glasses too, deeper layers, echoes perhaps incessantly sounding the fathomless? This is the result: the eye and the hand (the description) embroider the version of an event, the anti-reality without which reality never could exist – description is experiencing – I am part of the ritual. The pen twists the rope. From the pen he is hanged . . . He hangs in the mirror. But where in reality he is separated – conceivably in spirit or vision and growth of flesh draped over humid bone – hanged, taken down, ploughed under – each of these steps remains preserved in the mirror. The mirror mummifies each consecutive instant, apparently never runs over, but ignores as far as we know all decay and knows for sure no time. (A mutation, yes . . .) He thus keeps on hanging and kicking in the remembrance. You only need to close the eyelids to see each detail before the eyes. And the writer just as the reader (because the reader is a mirror to the writer) can seemingly make nothing undone. He cannot reopen the earth, cannot set the snapped neck, cannot stuff the spirit back into the flesh and the light of life in the lustreless eyes full of sand, cannot straighten the mother's back, cannot raise the assassinated, cannot reduce the man to a seed in the woman's loins while a hot wind streams over the Coast.

Or can he?

Is that the second death?

(Shiva, as Nutaraya – King of the Dancers – has in his one right hand a drum which indicates sound as the first element of the unfolding/budding universe; the uppermost left hand holds a fire-tongue, element of the world's final destruction: the soil is fire devouring the body to ashes, and brings repose, till the next time. The other arms represent the eternal rhythmical balance between life and death. The one foot rests on the devil of 'Forgetfulness', the other treads in the void, as is usual when dancing, and depicts, according to Heinrich Zimmer, 'the never-ending flow of consciousness in and out of the state of ignorance'. Shiva, god of destruction, god of creation, et cetera. The heart is a mirror/The mirror is a heart.)

IVAN VLADISLAVIĆ

The Brothers

Once in High Hope Province there were two brothers called Blokjan and Oswald. They were farmers. They had a pig farm on the road to Nooitgedacht, not far from City Deep.

One Saturday afternoon the brothers were walking home from the City, chatting and making jokes, when Oswald tripped and kicked up a yam, as the saying goes. No amount of hopping up and down on his good foot would ease the pain he felt in the hurt one, so he sat down on a milestone and took off his shoe.

'I think it's broken,' he said, examining his swollen toe. 'If only I'd worn my boots.'

The brothers had spent the morning in the provincial capital, attending to business, which is why they were wearing their town shoes rather than their sturdy, shovel-nosed boots.

'What good is a shoe if it cannot keep a toe from stubbing?' Oswald asked, and lobbed the shoe into the bushes at the roadside.

'None whatsoever,' Blokjan agreed. 'Your toe looks bad. You won't be able to walk.'

'We are far from Vergenoeg.' This was the name they had given their farm. 'What are we going to do?'

'Don't worry, brother. I shall carry you.'

Blokjan was very strong. At the agricultural shows he was known for tossing the porker further than any other man in the district. Oswald decided to put himself in his brother's hands. He took off his other shoe and threw it into the bushes as well. What good is one shoe to a two-legged man?

Blokjan hefted Oswald over his shoulder like a pocket of soup-greens and set off with a long and steady stride.

Oswald's stomach began to hurt, because Blokjan's stony shoulder was pressing into it; his head began to ache, because it was hanging down behind Blokjan's back and filling up with blood; and his nose began to burn, because it was breathing clouds of fine dust the colour of chilli powder. But he didn't complain, because that would seem ungrateful. He bit his tongue and looked down at his brother's footprints on the dusty road.

After a while Oswald made an observation: the distance between one print and the next was getting smaller. And soon after that he made a deduction: Blokjan was slowing down. He got slower and slower. At last he was going so slowly that he was almost going backwards, as they say in High Hope Province. Then Oswald said, 'I can't help but notice that you're running out of steam, Blok. What's troubling you?'

'I've got plenty of steam – but I think I've skinned my peaches.'

'Well, there's only one way to find out. Let's stop and take a look.'

'I'll just go as far as the crossroads.'

There was a baobab at the crossroads, and the thought of resting in its shade gave Blokjan courage to go on. They soon reached the place. While Oswald was walking round the tree to see whether it had changed since he was last there, Blokjan sat down on one of its swollen roots to take off his shoes. Blokjan too was wearing his town shoes, which were very narrow and shiny, in the fashion of that time, and this must account for the size of the blisters on his soles. You couldn't have covered one of them with a silver slotsak.

'I told you not to wear socks,' said Oswald, reappearing from behind the trunk. 'It causes friction.'

'This is no time for jokes. I cannot walk on these feet, and we are still far from home. What are we going to do now?'

'Don't worry, brother. My toe is much better. I shall carry you.'

Oswald's toe had stopped throbbing. It had been pointing up at the sky and all the bad blood had drained out of it.

Now Oswald was not as strong as his brother, but he was no weakling either: he usually came second at tossing the porker. Some people said that farming with pigs gave the brothers an unfair advantage. In any case, Oswald heaved Blokjan over his shoulder and set off.

Before long Blokjan began to feel queasy. He was not used to being carried. Also, he had eaten a mixed grill at the New Butchery Eating House, one of City Deep's finest establishments, to sustain him on the journey, and now the different parts of it were flying around in his stomach and mixing themselves up disagreeably.

'Any second now he'll get tired and put me down,' Blokjan

thought. But on they went. What Oswald lacked in strength he made up for in determination.

At last Blokjan could contain himself no longer. 'I hate to say it, Os, but I've got to go into the bushes.'

On this stretch of the road to Nooitgedacht there was not a bush in sight, just stubbled mealie-fields and empty veld. But Oswald's ear was close to Blokjan's stomach, which was gurgling like a drain, and so he knew at once what his brother meant, and put him down smartly.

Blokjan climbed through the barbed-wire fence that ran next to the road and walked off into the distance. Oswald sat down and rested his back against a crooked fence post. Blokjan kept walking and looking back and walking again, until when he looked back he could no longer make out his brother's features. Then he judged that there was a decent distance between them, and he squatted down in the sand.

In fact, he needn't have bothered to go all that way, for Oswald had dozed off as soon as he sat down, and he only woke up again when Blokjan returned and prodded him in the side.

'Where's your shirt?' Oswald asked.

'I had to use it,' Blokjan said with a scowl.

'And your jacket?'

'I'm leaving it behind. What good is a jacket without a shirt?'

'So they say.'

'Come, brother, climb up on my back. I can see you are sleepy, but we must get going. We are still far from home.'

'But what about your blisters?'

'Don't worry about them, they are much better. All this sunshine has dried them out.' So they went on, enduring hardships by sharing them.

Every now and then one or the other would say, 'We still have so far to go. What will become of us?'

Without fail one or the other would reply, 'Don't fret, brother, it's just around the corner. I can carry you.'

And it is certain that by this means they would finally have come home to their farm.

But it happened that a stranger was passing through the district, and the road he was travelling by crossed the road to Nooitgedacht. At the crossroads the stranger stopped to rest in the shade of a baobab tree, and there, in the fork of a fat root, he found a pair of shoes.

The stranger licked his finger and wiped a film of dust from one of the pointed toes. Underneath he found very shiny patent leather. (His own shoes were down at heel and tied together with string.) He pulled a sock out of one of the shoes and stretched it over his hand. It was slightly damp, and it was green, like spinach, and covered in brightly-coloured windmills, but there was not a single hole in it. (His own socks had more potatoes in them than a High Hope stew.)

He was on the point of trying on the shoes when he noticed a set of footprints leading off along the road. 'Why would a man take off a good pair of shoes and socks, and go on in his bare feet?' he asked himself. 'I see: someone is playing a trick on me.'

He walked round the tree, but no one was hiding behind the trunk. He walked back the way he had come and looked up into the branches, but no one was concealed up there. He walked on towards his destination, but after a mile he turned round and sneaked back to the crossroads. The shoes were still there.

He tried them on.

He was a very small fellow and the found shoes were much too big for him, but he stuffed the socks into their toes and laced them tightly. They looked wonderful.

'What sort of man would leave behind such a splendid pair of shoes and go barefoot?' he asked himself. 'He must be a fool.' So he turned away from his destination and hurried after the footprints, and as he went he lifted his feet very high so that he would not scratch the leather of his new shoes or kick up yams with their sharp points.

He had not gone far before the footprints veered off the road. A perfectly good jacket was hanging there on a fence-post. He shrugged off his own threadbare blazer, which he had stolen from a truant schoolboy many years before, and tried on the found jacket. There was a bit of peppery sand in the pockets and pigskin patches on the elbows, but otherwise it was in excellent condition. With the sleeves rolled up, it fitted him like a greatcoat. 'He's a bigger fool than I thought,' the stranger muttered and hurried on in pursuit.

For many miles the road ran straight across a flat and barren plain. The stranger saw no trace of his quarry other than the footprints. Once a speck of white in the distance made him quicken his pace, hoping to find a silk handkerchief for his breast pocket, but the speck turned out to be a tattered shirt collar and a pair of cuffs.

At length the road came to a place riven by gorges and cracks and it began to weave in and out among outcrops of rock and boulders piled one on another. Scurrying around one of these piles, the stranger finally caught sight of the man he was chasing. He was just a short way ahead, surprisingly enough, but even more surprising was the monstrous shape of him. He had a huge hump on his back and four arms, two of them hanging down lifelessly behind and two waving wildly about him as he shambled along.

The stranger hurried on fearlessly. When he drew near to the monster he saw that it was in fact one man carrying another on his back.

'Two for the price of one!' the stranger squealed, hitching up the tails of his coat and breaking into a trot.

Blokjan was looking at the ground and counting his footsteps; Oswald, who was tied to Blokjan's back in a sling made from his own jacket, was dozing. The stranger had to dance around them twice and block the way to attract their attention.

'Where did you come from?' Blokjan asked, undoing the sling and letting Oswald slide to the ground.

'I've been following you for many a long mile,' the stranger replied. 'And now I've caught you at last.'

'Doesn't he look a sight?' said Oswald sleepily. They looked at the little man in his huge coat. His coat-tails were dragging in the dust and his long sleeves hung over his hands. You couldn't see his feet either, except for the ends of his shoes sticking out through the folds of his coat.

'Look who's talking,' said the stranger.

Blokjan and Oswald looked at one another. They did look frightful, with their dirty trousers rolled to their knees and their bloody feet bound in the rags they had torn from Oswald's shirt.

'Who are you?' asked the stranger. 'And where are you going?'

'We are brothers and farmers,' said Blokjan. 'And we are trying to get home. But we have been beset by misfortune every step of the way.'

'Who are you?' asked Oswald. 'And why are you following us?'

'I am a stranger in these parts. I have come to tell you that I have a plan, which I am willing to share with you.'

'Go ahead,' said the brothers.

'I can see that you are a burden to one another. My plan is simple: whoever is weaker should stay here and rest. The other should go on alone and fetch a wagon from the farm.'

'We don't have a wagon,' said Blokjan.

'We have a wagon,' Oswald corrected him, 'but no horses.'

'We had a bakkie once too –'

'A Toyota.'

' – but it was stolen.'

'Ah,' said the stranger. 'In that case I have another plan, a slightly more complicated one, which I am willing to share with you. My good friend Boemke lives near here, and he has wagons and horses aplenty. The weaker of you should stay here. The other should come on with me, to Boemke's, to make the arrangements.'

'We need time to discuss this plan,' said Oswald. 'Please leave us alone.'

The stranger went behind a rock.

'What do you think, Blok?'

'I think it is a good plan, but one thing about it bothers me: why can't he go on alone to Boemke's for the wagon?'

'Perhaps he wants company on the road.'

'You could be right, brother. What do you think of the plan, Os?'

'I think it is a good plan, but there is one thing that bothers me: if he's a stranger in these parts, as he says, how come he knows this fellow Boemke?'

'Perhaps he knows him from way back when.'

'You could be right, brother.'

They were both lost in thought for a few moments.

Then Blokjan said, 'We are still far away from home.'

And Oswald replied, 'Don't worry, I can carry you brother, if I have to . . . but it would surely be easier in Boemke's wagon.'

They called the little man out from behind the rock and gave him their decision.

'Let's shake on it,' said Blokjan. He clasped the stranger's sticky claw, Oswald wrapped their hands in both his own, and the brothers shook their hands slowly up and down and intoned, 'What's done is done.'

The stranger looked at them glumly.

'You must also say it,' said Oswald.

'Why?'

'That's how we do it around here.'

'Why?'

'I don't know!' Oswald looked helplessly at Blokjan.

'Because if you don't say it too, it doesn't count,' said Blokjan patiently.

'Very well.'

Their hands were still in a knot between them. They moved the knot up and down.

Oswald said, 'One . . . two . . . three.'

They all said, 'What's done is done.'

'Let's be going then,' the stranger continued at once, disentangling his fingers. 'Who is the weaker?'

'He is,' said Blokjan.

'He is,' said Oswald.

'Your concern for one another is commendable, brother-farmers. But one of you must be stronger than the other. It's only natural. If we had a porker with us, we could decide the issue in a jiffy.'

So it was agreed that Oswald would remain behind while Blokjan went on with the stranger.

It happened that they had stopped on the edge of the Valley of Disenchantment, through which they would have to pass to reach salvation. For most of its course the valley road was lost among boulders and bushes, but on the opposite cliff was one bright ribbon of sand through a clump of aloes. Blokjan pointed this spot out to his brother, and said, 'You'll see the two of us when we reach there, and then you'll know that we are through the worst, and we will soon be back for you.'

'You'll wave?'

'We'll wave.'

Oswald made himself comfortable on a shady ledge. Blokjan and the stranger went down the road into the valley and were lost to sight.

They had not gone far when the stranger, who was walking behind, called out, 'I hate to be a nuisance, fellow-traveller, but I've gone and skinned my plums.'

'You mean your peaches,' said Blokjan.

'Peaches, plums, what does it matter?' He sat down on the ground and took off the shoes. Then he pulled out the socks from the toes. 'These shoes are much too big for me. Why don't you try them on? They look about your size.'

Blokjan unwrapped the rags from his feet and put on the shoes. 'They're a little tight.'

'Better a tight shoe than no shoe at all,' the stranger said ruefully, sticking out his bare feet.

'So they say.'

The stranger's feet were small and pale. 'How will we go on?' he asked. 'My feet are much too soft to endure these sharp stones.'

'Don't worry, stranger. I'll carry you. There's not much of you, as far as I can see, and my shoulders are broad.'

'That's very kind of you. But you've sweated so much your muscles are like river-stones. What if I slip and fall? Put on this coat of mine, then I'll hold on tight to the cloth.'

Blokjan put on the jacket. 'It fits me well,' he said, 'but it does seem odd without a shirt.'

'Better half a suit than stark naked,' the stranger said, twisting his skinny body from side to side.

'So they say.'

Blokjan picked the little man up and laid him across his shoulders. He was surprised at how heavy he was and how sharp his bones were. The small body pressed into his flesh like an ill-made yoke. But Blokjan was proud of his strength. He began to walk.

The stranger curled his limbs and snuggled himself in. He shut his eyes, the better to feel the swaying of the body beneath him. The tang of its sweat tickled his nostrils, he even thought he heard the surging of its blood.

Blokjan went down into the valley. The little man grew heavier and heavier, but Blokjan kept walking. The little man grew heavier at every step. Blokjan wanted to speak. He wanted to say, 'I can go no further,' and hear the little man answer, 'Don't worry brother, we are nearly home. I can carry you.' But these words caught in his throat, which the stranger's arm encircled like a vine.

They came to the River of Tears in the depths of the valley. Blokjan wanted to stop, to shrug off his burden and plunge his tired body in the salty water. But the stranger was part of him now, cleaving like a lumpy callus to his neck and shoulders. A hot tongue licked at his back and drove him on across the drift. His shiny shoes rattled on the cool stones, the water swirled, then he was on the road again, climbing up between red rocks and dusty bushes.

Oswald looked out across the valley, to the ribbon of road on the opposite cliff, until his eyes ached. At last Blokjan appeared, dragging his feet and bent over double. The stranger was nowhere to be seen. Oswald started to his feet, calling his brother's name and waving, but all to no avail.

HENNIE AUCAMP

For Four Voices

A JOKE'S A JOKE

The whole business began as a joke (Oom Toon Lourens said); a practical joke. Without jokes life in Die Hoek would get one down. It was a time of drought and depression and we bachelors – Beimen Botes, together with the little Scot who had taken over the store and post office a short while before, and myself – couldn't go on the tiles every weekend. It was a question of money and transport. Besides, you needed to be on your farm to save what could be saved. Saturday evenings were a killer for everybody. Before you knew it, you were on your way to Oom Frik's place. He was better off than we were, but that wasn't the thing. He was a cheerful person and so was his fat wife, Tant Das. At their place you could forget your sorrows for an evening, laugh and eat *vetkoek*, drink coffee or orange syrup, and sometimes dance, for Oom Frik had a gramophone – and a daughter. Nobody had ever thought of his daughter, Let, as a life's companion: she didn't either, I guess, because of the disfiguring birthmark that covered half her face like a purple rag. But even she was jolly and was fun to dance with. Often, particularly in winter, we also played cards – nap and whist and *klabberjas*.

Freddy, the little Scotsman, must also have felt the loneliness in that world so full of sorrow, for every so often he would join us – although he could cope better than most, for he was a bookworm. He read big fat books, sometimes right through the night.

Good old Beimen, on the other hand, had probably never looked at a book since his catechism, except for the Bible – and even that, between friends, I doubt if he ever read. Not that he was stupid. He just wasn't that sort of person. He was a man for deeds, of action. Hunting, swimming and breaking in horses. He was also the keenest on girls. He was bored after work. It was that keenness that made

Oom Frik think of the plan. We were all gathered in the *voorhuis*, Freddy too, only Beimen hadn't yet arrived.

'Freddy,' said Oom Frik, 'you're almost too good-looking for a man. Let's pull Beimen's leg tonight and dress you up as a girl.' 'Go on, go on,' we all shouted, the women first. I've often noticed that women are mad about games and seldom think of the consequences. Freddy tried to resist us. 'What about my moustache,' he pleaded. 'You can grow another,' said Oom Frik, 'and next time fertilise it from the beginning to show the mangy bits what's what.'

The moustache was shaved and the women took Freddy off to the bedroom. In the meantime Oom Frik and I kept cavey to see when Beimen was coming; we were as excited as schoolboys.

When Oom Frik's cousin from Kimberley made her appearance, both Oom Frik and I caught our breath, for the picture was perfect. Years ago Tant Das had had a switch made of the long hair she had worn as a young girl, and she had worn it until her own hair had begun to go grey. The switch was exactly the same colour as Freddy's hair, straw blond, and almost golden when the sun shone on it. With that he wore an old dress of Let's which Beimen wouldn't recognise since nobody ever paid attention to what Let wore, lots of powder and scent, a blood-red mouth and earrings. Then Tant Das and Let coached him with a vengeance on how a woman walks and sits to be ladylike.

Never will I forget Beimen's face when he saw Freddy for the first time: wonderment and joy, as if his prayers were being answered. He could not keep away from Fifi, as the niece from Kimberley was called for short.

Every so often Oom Frik had to go outside to laugh. So did I. The old chap was doubled up with laughter, and to recover from our fits of laughter and coughing we had a quick nip behind the quince hedge.

Our long absence suited Beimen. When we returned, still flushed from laughing, he and Fifi were in each other's arms, dancing to *The Young Bullock Waltz*, and Beimen, gazing pop-eyed over Fifi's shoulder, was singing.

> 'My ma's milk is sent to the farmer's table,
> what's left I drink as fast as I am able.'

Tant Das and Let nudged each other in the corner. They so enjoyed the joke that they pretended not to notice the smell of brandy on our breath.

We danced until three o'clock that night. Oom Frik and I pretended to cut in for a dance with Fifi, but Beimen said flatly, 'Sorry, chaps, you dance with Let and Tant Das, this girl is booked by me.'

How Beimen could have been so easily deceived remains a riddle. Freddy spoke in his own voice, a tenor. (I can still hear him singing *Bonnie Prince Charlie*.) Perhaps he was taken in because Freddy acted so well. The way he looked up at Beimen and then batted his eyes and rested his head on Beimen's shoulder.

Beimen was persistent. He must have a date on the very next day, and when could he come and visit her in Kimberley?

Tant Das and Oom Frik had to make up excuses on the spot. They said that Genevieve was leaving the next morning at the crack of dawn.

Beimen's disappointment made one feel really weird. It wasn't just disappointment, it was as if he was afraid that he was being robbed of something precious. It was then that I thought: a joke's a joke. Oom Frik didn't feel that. Not yet. 'Write to her,' he urged.

'Naturally,' said Beimen, even though it wasn't at all natural for him who never read and hated to write even a short note.

Those letters must have taken him hours. Two letters a week, we learned in a round-about way. Freddy never said anything about them until he came self-consciously to borrow the whole get-up, switch and all, to have a photograph taken. Then he mentioned the letters, in fact he had to. 'Beimen insists on a photo,' he said.

Freddy could control the letter business easily since he was both shopkeeper and postmaster. What he did about the postmark I don't know. Perhaps he had a Kimberley stamp. As regularly as clockwork Beimen got his two letters a week and then waited, sick with anticipation, for the next.

Oom Frik went to talk it out with Freddy, and I, as an accomplice, went along as a witness.

'This nonsense must stop now, Freddy. I began it and I'm sorry I did now. We must call Beimen in and explain it all.'

Freddy didn't want to know. 'He'll kill you, he'll kill me.' (Did Freddy think then about that farewell kiss? That passionate kiss that Oom Frik and I had spied on from behind the lace curtain?)

'Beimen is a real brick and man enough to know when he's been made an ass of. He'll pay us back in his own way.' Freddy gave a strange laugh. 'I don't want to be around when it happens.' He stroked his upper lip, which was paler than the rest of his face. Suddenly I realised that he had not grown his moustache again.

'We dare not insult him. He must never know what happened. It would break him.' Freddy's voice got shriller.

Oom Frik and I looked at each other.

Freddy continued, growing more agitated.

'The niece must die. I'll see to it in a telegram.'

The niece did die. She killed herself.

That Saturday afternoon a young labourer walking past the post office saw something red seeping out from under the door. He thought it was paint, a pot of paint that had spilled. He walked nearer. Smelled the red. Tasted it. Then ran away to find help: blood.

Oh God, why did Freddy put on that bun and that dress before he . . . I mean it was terrible enough, so unnecessary . . . Why, why, why? Perhaps one of you educated people can explain to me. Sometimes after hunting we swam together, and I can assure you there was nothing wrong with Freddy. To be quite honest . . .

EVERYTHING HATH AN END

Shortly after coming to Die Hoek Freddy McTavish wrote to a close friend in Cape Town: 'The landscape is quite Brontë-esque, stark and desolate, but breathtakingly beautiful towards the evening, and the mountain air is invigorating, as Dr Sim promised me it would be. That, of course, is the whole purpose of my exile, for the mountain air is supposed to cure my asthma. But will I survive the Afrikaners? There is not a single English-speaking person in the whole of Die Hoek. Luckily for me I learnt the *Taal* at a very early stage, when my dear Mother, an Afrikaner by birth, was still alive. I can therefore converse with ease. But the Boers have so little to talk about, except the drought, which, by the way, *is* very severe. Basically they are kind, but naïve, the whole style of living nineteenth-centuryish. There is one character though who is fun, called Oom Frik. His wife, Tant Das, is rather corpulent; the daughter Let has no choice but to be virtuous, on account of a birthmark that disfigures her completely . . '

His letters remained in that strain: something about the landscape, the weather and something about the people. Sometimes he wrote a long letter about a jackal hunt or an open-air communion service.

There were regular references to individuals: Oom Frik and his family; a local philosopher called Toon Lourens; and increasingly to a young Samson, Beimen Botes, who could carry a sack of corn as easily as if it was a paper bag, but who shook like a leaf whenever he had to fill in a form.

Once Freddy sent a few snaps, but all were black and white and showed nothing of the soft sandy colour that can make the Stormberg seem so huge and desolate. They were depressing little snaps: one of the brick house in which he lived and worked (post office and shop) with two tamarisk trees in a bare yard. One was of himself, but out of focus, because Beimen, who took the photograph, shook. The friend in Cape Town never came to visit as he once or twice promised to do and later he stopped writing.

But that didn't bother Freddy. In fact it suited him, because he began to feel as if his letters had been treacherous. One doesn't gossip about one's friends. He had also discovered that the farmers did have something to say once you got past the façade of drought and Calvinism. They know the veld and the name of every indigenous plant and animal, from the resurrection bush to the river cat, and they tell wonderful stories set in the natural world, some of the stories chilling testimony of shadows that lurk in man. Of a boy of nineteen who fathered a child on his sister of thirteen, and, in despair, murdered her and hanged himself from the giant blue gum next to the toll-house. Oh yes, it is the selfsame tree that stands there at the entrance to Die Hoek, although of the toll-house no more than the foundations survive.

Freddy began drawing again, small precise drawings of plants and animals. He also kept a diary of the stories and sayings of the farmers. In the evenings he read Dickens, for he had promised himself that he would read the complete works during his exile. He spent his time in Die Hoek profitably, as it is called. But there were evenings, particularly over weekends, when they could not contain him, evenings when his emotions needed some focus other than books; evenings when he was desolate and needed people or, to put it better, a particular person. But that he only realised too late.

One Saturday afternoon when there was only an hour or two of the day left, driven by an indefinable restlessness, he climbed on his bicycle. First he rode in the direction of the town, that lay twenty-five miles away, but after a quarter of an hour he turned around and rode instead to Oom Frik's place, as he had often done recently.

In front of Oom Frik's house, with its high stoep decorated with the horns of buck, grew a hedge of sage bush, the kind with the red flowers that have sugar-sweet nectar. This was the only evidence of garden in all that drought.

Freddy sucked one flower after another of its juice, just as children always do. The sweet taste and the heat intoxicated him. Then Tant Das's voice broke the spell. She leaned over the half-door and beckoned him to her.

'Come in, Freddy, you'll get sunstroke – and be careful of those flowers, they are fading.'

Tant Das served orange syrup on the stoep. Toon Lourens had also arrived and came to the house with Oom Frik from the stable. Freddy could swear that he smelt drink, but Oom Frik and Toon were both decorous. Too decorous, according to Freddy; this was usually the prelude to banter and rowdiness. And then they wouldn't stop, not even when what had been funny was no longer funny.

'I wonder if Beimen will come over tonight. Old Streepsak tells me he's having trouble with his windmill,' said Oom Frik and squinted up at the sparse clouds as if there was a direct link between the arid heavens and the problem of the windmill pump.

'Oh, he'll come,' chuckled Toon Lourens. 'He's more scared of being alone than of buckshot. But only when the pump is fixed.'

A light breeze lifted on the stoep, but Tant Das from habit fanned herself with a handkerchief wet with sweat and eau-de-Cologne. Let came out on to the stoep with a jug of orange squash. 'Shoo!' she said. 'It's hot.'

'Give Freddy some more,' said Tant Das in a motherly way, 'he's looking very down-at-mouth. How are your family, my boy?' Let nudged her mother, who had once again forgotten that Freddy's mother had died very recently.

'Well,' said Freddy, smiling absently. Why was he so disappointed when Oom Frik speculated about Beimen? Beimen contributed nothing to conversation; he just laughed at everything and got in everybody's way with his great big body.

Later, when the breeze became a south wind, they all moved indoors to the living-room, where the gramophone stood on its own table and the family Bible lay on another table made of yellow-wood that was inlaid with bone and stinkwood.

Once more Beimen was the topic of conversation.

'Poor devil,' laughed Tant Das, 'he needs someone to look after him, what with his only sister away in Tzaneen.'

Oom Frik interrupted, somewhat abruptly, as it seemed. 'Let's lead the old boy a dance this evening,' he said mischievously and looked at Freddy expectantly. 'Will you play along with us, Freddy?'

Freddy felt threatened, but vaguely excited. 'It depends, Oom Frik.'

'Look,' said Oom Frik, 'you're almost too good-looking for a man, Freddy. If we were to make you up . . .'

'Go on,' shouted Toon Lourens, 'it'll be sports. We can forget for a while about our mortgages with the Land Bank and the drought.'

'Yes, go on, Freddy,' begged Let.

'I've still got my switch,' said Das. 'We can use one of Let's old dresses. Come on, man, a good laugh never hurt anyone.'

Freddy tried to fight his growing excitement. 'My moustache . . .' he hedged.

'Grow a new one. And this time make a good job of it. Every morning and evening spread a layer of chicken shit on it.' Oom Frik laughed uproariously at his own joke, and Toon Lourens joined in and they both neighed until they were thoroughly boring.

'OK,' said Freddy quietly.

Then and there Let shaved off Freddy's moustache, after she had fetched soap, water, a razor and a strop. Then the women took him off to the bedroom, where they worked on him for a full half-hour. He came out of the room nicely rounded out, with red lips and cheeks and his straw-coloured hair caught up in a bun; a slightly vulgar-looking woman, perhaps, but with a certain undeniable plus quality.

'Hot stuff! If only Beimen would come . . .' Oom Frik looked out of the window and then went out on to the stoep. Hurriedly he came back. 'He's on his way, chaps; now we must get our story straight. Look here, Freddy, you're my niece from Kimberley. We'll call you Genevieve.'

'That's too long,' said Tant Das. 'We'll call him Fifi.'

Let and Toon Lourens laughed fit to bust.

'Just don't stand and laugh like that in front of Beimen,' Oom Frik warned them. 'Go outside if you can't hold it in.'

Beimen's shirt was open across the chest. (No shirt ever remained fastened across his broad and muscular chest.) He seemed to grow even larger when he saw the almost fragile Genevieve standing before him. He crushed her hand too hard and held it too long. Welcome, he rejoiced, looking deep into her eyes and meaning: welcome into my life. And she signalled the same message to him.

Never had an evening passed so quickly in Die Hoek. After supper – whole-wheat bread, dripping and golden syrup – the gramophone was wound up. *Old Hessie's Tipple* and *The Young Bullock Waltz*. Sometimes Tant Das and sometimes Let disappeared to laugh helplessly in the kitchen or bedroom. Oom Frik and Toon Lourens celebrated the joke behind the quince hedge.

Coming back, they spied on Beimen and the niece through the window. Viewed from outside the dancing seemed more intimate, and on entering Oom Frik said, 'Ach no, Beimen, half-time, change partners.' But Beimen was adamant: 'Oom Frik has Tant Das and Toon can dance with Let, but this lady is booked by me.'

The later it grew, the more unreal it became for Freddy: was he playing a part or was he finally at home with himself? He took fright at his thoughts and tried literally to distance himself from Beimen, but Beimen, perspiring and jolly, quickly re-captured him. (Does he suspect nothing? thought Freddy. What about my hands and my skin? And what about the others giggling and suddenly disappearing?)

After one dance he excused himself and went and smoked a cigarette in the bedroom. Oom Frik peered through the doorway. 'You're sitting with your legs too far apart, Fifi,' he bellowed with laughter.

'How long are you going to keep it up, Oom Frik?' Freddy asked. 'I'm beginning to pity Beimen.'

'No, you mustn't spoil the sport, man! We must start up a correspondence. Think of the letters and all the trouble Beimen will have getting his words in order.'

But the letters weren't Beimen's cause for sorrowing. They were Freddy's. Beimen came to him at the post office, big and clumsy and lost, just as he had been on that Saturday night.

'It was love at first sight, Freddy,' he confessed. 'My letters must bring her back here, but I can't find the words. You must help me, old man . . .'

Twice a week Beimen received letters from Kimberley, and twice a week Beimen rode over to dictate his passion.

'Freddy,' he asked one day in the middle of a sentence, 'what is it? You seem different.'

'I've shaved off my moustache.'

'Is that what it is? I could have sworn . . .'

But what he could have sworn to even Beimen didn't rightly know. He felt restless when he was with Freddy. Freddy strengthened his yearning for Fifi, for there was something in Freddy's gestures, his appearance that for one tormenting moment brought Fifi back to him, and he knew he must have her with him, at any cost.

'A photograph,' he said, 'ask for a photo. I want a photo of her.'

After a long debate with himself, Freddy rode over to Oom Frik's to collect the get-up of the big night.

'Do you mean you're bloody well writing letters and have said nothing to us?' demanded Oom Frik angrily. 'After all, the whole plan was mine!'

And when Freddy rode away with a cardboard box full of clothes fastened to his carrier, Oom Frik was still offended and decided to tell Toon Lourens all about it.

The following day Oom Frik and Toon pitched up at the post office.

'Look here, Freddy, this nonsense has gone on long enough. I don't like to see two grown-up young fellows make a spectacle of themselves.'

'But it's precisely what Oom Frik wanted.'

'Yes – then, but not now. A joke's a joke, but everything has an end. We must tell Benjamin.' (It was only when he was serious about Beimen that Oom Frik called him Benjamin.)

Freddy went white. 'It will humiliate him terribly. He'll kill me. No no, it's better he should know nothing. The niece from Kimberley must vanish – have an accident, marry, or go abroad. Please leave it to me.'

Oom Frik walked off morosely. Toon looked as if he wanted to stay, his long face suddenly serious, but Oom Frik shouted: 'Well, come on, what are you waiting for?'

Freddy stared after them. The afternoon was not yet beautiful. It was too early. Later the mountains would turn purple and the bare ridges would be clothed in final light. But now it was still dry and everything was desolate and empty.

He walked up and down in his room, confused and tormented. Occasionally he looked out at the yard, but never registered the two tamarisk trees. He had left three choices to the cousin from Kimberley, each as impossible as the other. He recalled Beimen's rough kiss, his china-blue eyes that were clear even after a day in the dust and heat, and he knew that he was lost.

Perhaps he had one chance. One chance in a thousand.

Carefully, as if for a wedding, he put on Let's old dress. A bluish dress with delicate flowers. He struggled with his hair, but managed to pin the switch after a fashion. He collected cosmetics from the shop that led off from his room, powder and lipstick. His hands trembled so much that he smeared the lip line, so that his mouth looked wounded, smeared with blood.

Hours later Beimen found him. He was sitting, legs spread wide, his head between his knees as if he were vomiting. When he finally looked up his eyes were empty, without hope or recognition or love.

AND HATH LOVE 1

On the road home Beimen Botes thought with a rising sense of shame: I went too far. I should not have done it. I must turn back and see.

He allowed his horse to carry him deeper and deeper into the afternoon. For he did not want to see the smeared mouth, the crumpled flowered frock, the bun crooked across the neck. The drought-stricken sunlight pressed like hands against his shoulders, pressing him forward against the horse, that smelt of saltpetre. He pulled himself upright: the last gate before his house. The gate glittered and faded, glittered and faded. Beimen shook his big head violently: was this what sunstroke felt like? He dismounted, opened the gate, and let his horse into the yard.

In the bitter cool of the pepper trees he found respite. He let the horse drink at the trough and walked him until he was cold, but did not unsaddle him: who knew, perhaps later. He went indoors and fell into a heavy sleep on his double bed. A troubled sleep. He saw Genevieve before him, sitting in a garden or in the veld. He walked closer to her, but when he placed his hands on her shoulders it was Let who looked up at him with red eyes in her purple, disfigured face, an ugly laugh on her lips.

Toward milking-time he woke, soaked through with sweat and with a violent headache. Perhaps it would help if he bathed. So, taking a towel, he walked down to the stone dam. It was too narrow for swimming and in any case had too little water in it, but he could at least cool his feverish body. He let himself sink through the shreds of duckweed, pushing the slime away in disgust. He began to wash himself passionately, particularly his genitals. Briefly he lay flat on the dam floor, the water and slime a roof over him.

His bath refreshed him, but it did not resolve the anxieties in him. The pain and anger that fought for precedence; the emotions that were foreign to his nature and for which he had no counsel. Self-loathing, hate for his fellow man and for God, regret, compassion. Someone, he felt in desperation, someone must accept responsibility; the practical jokers, not himself or Genevieve. Even though she had played along. (The body had not resisted, but the eyes were empty, the smeared mouth open but without sound.)

Beimen looked in at the kraal and once again mounted Poon. He leaned down to the pricked ear: 'I'm sorry, Poon'; and rode toward the Van Onselens. Toward Oom Frik, Tant Das and Let with her purple face. If they were not responsible, who was? God? And if it was God, what was to be done? Live resignedly with your sin and your anguish? Fix your windmill and pray for rain?

The Van Onselen homestead was deserted; curtains drawn and doors locked. Nonetheless he continued to knock, walking from window to window. The panes on the western side were tepid beneath his fingers and suddenly he began to weep; he wanted people because he felt hopelessly lost.

Streepsak found him on the stoep bench. Legs apart he sat, head bowed, his huge body wracked with sobs.

'The master knows?'

'What should I know?'

'About the other little master, master Freddy.' Streepsak opened his mouth, showing the rotten stumps, opened it wide and slowly raised his hand and slowly crooked a finger.

'Huh?' Beimen asked stupidly.

And Streepsak repeated the slow gesture more with lasciviousness than with sympathy. Beimen stared with revulsion at the finger that was both finger and trigger. '*Kapukile!*' Streepsak cried at the end of his mime. 'He killed himself, blew his head off.'

'My God, my God,' moaned Beimen, but he did not cry. His earlier tears had dried on his cheeks in the south wind that had risen.

'And everyone has gone there?'

'The police he was here and the doctor. The old madam has gone to help . . .'

Streepsak couldn't remember the word and Beimen was grateful, he did not want to hear it. But on the road to the post-office-and-store where Freddy had worked he muttered continually: lay out the body, lay out, lay out. Only a few hours earlier, that body, the same body had lain under him, the flowered dress pushed up above the white buttocks, and he had emptied his rage and disappointment into that body.

Two weeks ago he had met Genevieve, Oom Frik's so-called niece from Kimberley. He had lost his heart to her. Everyone was giggling that night, but he had thought: It's because I am so much in love. Let them laugh: I have the feeling and they don't, and it is a good way to feel, for someone wants me. Someone who is beautiful as well. There were no lamps in the room that Saturday night, only candles. And not many of those. 'A lamp makes the room so warm,' was Tant Das's excuse, and he had accepted it because in that soft light he could come closer to Genevieve. But they were already close from the moment that Oom Frik had said: 'May I introduce you to my niece Fifi.' At that moment Toon Lourens with the long face had started giggling and Tant Das had said angrily: 'Behave yourself, Toon! Why are you being so silly?'

Later it had been ugly Let who had laughed in his face when she had come butting in with her everlasting orange syrup. He had been on the point of saying: 'Here is my heart. Take it. Trample on it, do what you will with it, for it will never again be mine.' That was just how he would have said it, but Let had buggered it up by coming in with her damned orange squash. There is a time and place to say something, and the time was that precise moment, and the place was the settee in old Frik van Onselen's front room. He had tried to say it later, with a kiss, when they said goodbye. And she had answered back as no woman had ever done with a mere kiss, saying clearly and without false modesty: 'Take my heart and do what you will.'

The following day he had even tried to write a letter, but the words became unwieldy when he tried to marshal them. On the Monday he was at Freddy's at the crack of dawn. In the little store, between the chintz and pungent tobacco, blue soap and coffee, he explained the love he felt and Freddy expressed it in beautiful, learned words. 'That's not what I said,' he taxed Freddy. 'But it's precisely what you think and feel, isn't it?' Freddy had replied teasingly. 'Write it down nicely while I go and make tea for us and call me if someone comes to collect post.'

It was wonderful to talk to Freddy about Genevieve. Freddy understood everything. He almost stopped longing for her when Freddy was with him; suddenly she seemed so close.

Poon stumbled and with a curse Beimen reined him in. It was now twilight and the light was false. A measureless sorrow possessed Beimen Botes. Why had he done that to Freddy? Because he wanted Genevieve back? To punish Freddy? But to punish him like that? With violence and humiliation?

He had ridden to Freddy's early that afternoon. Hoping that there would be an extra letter from Genevieve, one with a photo enclosed. But it was Genevieve herself who awaited him in Freddy's room. She was different in the daylight from what she had been by candlelight. Her mouth was messy, her bun crooked, her hands were male and her naked feet were big, with corns on them. He wanted to revenge himself on her: he wanted to take her.

Beimen spurred on his horse. It was the hour when bats flit and owls hoot. It was only when he came over the rise and saw the lights in the post office that he became calm.

He wanted to see Genevieve again before they fastened the lid over his face, to see her face, clean, without make-up and false hair. Then he recalled what Streepsak had said and halted his horse. Afraid of the house of the dead, even more afraid of the dead in his own house, he sat and felt the night sink into him like dew.

AND HATH LOVE 2

The Van Onselens drink their coffee at four o'clock on the stoep because it is cool there and there is a breeze. They sit next to one another, upright, on the bench: Oom Frik, skeletal and mischievous with a drooping moustache, next to him his corpulent wife, Tant Das, then their unmarried daughter, Let, who – although mature – has been passed by because of the birthmark that mars her face. She has inherited something of her father's sense of humour, but in her it has darkened into irony that from time to time sours into cynicism. About herself she often says: 'I should sell myself to a circus as a clown, I'm already made up.' And recently, when she repeated the observation again, it was touch-and-go whether Oom Frik said: 'Yes, by all means, it will bring in a little extra money.' The times were bad for the farmers at Die Hoek: the drought and depression. For Oom Frik it was better than for many others, especially beginners such as Beimen Botes and Toon Lourens – they were thoroughly choked in those days. For that reason he entertained them willingly, but he would not offer even one bale of lucerne from his stone barn, no matter what they were willing to pay.

The Van Onselens sat as if for their portrait, dead still as if they had forgotten about the cups in their hands. Above them hung a set of horns which Oom Frik's brother-in-law had brought from South West: kudu, gemsbok, eland.

They sat frozen, as if they were afraid the horns would fall on them.

It was Let who finally broke the silence. 'Shoo, but it's hot.'

Tant Das, annoyed, pulled her handkerchief out from between her breasts. It was damp with sweat and eau-de-Cologne. Let was young and thin and knew nothing yet about hot flushes.

'I wonder whether the fellows will come visiting again tonight. Old Streepsak says Beimen is having trouble with his windmill pump.'

'What, again?' asked Let.

'Yes,' sighed Oom Frik, 'mark my words, always in a drought when you need your hands for other problems.'

'Poor Beimen,' began Tant Das.

'He'll be all right,' Oom Frik cut her short, 'he's got character.'

Let took the cups away. 'He won't be all right,' she said loudly in the kitchen, 'because he hasn't got character.' Angrily she began to wash up.

For two years she had been darning and mending for him, without payment. Why did she do it? He never even looked at her. He couldn't look at her because of the stain on her face. He liked things to be whole and complete. He retreated from deformity or deviation. An animal had to be well-formed for him. Yet she continued to darn for him, to repair the holes and tears in his trousers and shirts that happened whenever he thoughtlessly stretched or bent too quickly. When nobody was near, she buried her face in his clothes, smelling them to seek out whether some trace of him lingered, sweat or the smell of tobacco, or something private, sweet or stinking, close, like the smell of old toadstools.

Let began drying the cups. One slipped from her hand, but she caught it in time. Let it break. Let something or somebody be broken. Beimen had no character and no money either. What did character matter if you had money? Her father had money, more than he cared to admit. They could go and farm Wolfiespoort, take over the mortgage from her father. Because Beimen was a hard worker. He had huge hands. And at night in the dark, when all cats are grey (even the piebald ones), he would not need to wince.

'Let, Le-e-t!' her father called from the stoep. 'Toon's coming. Bring something to drink.'

'Something' wasn't going to be coffee, Let decided angrily. It would be orange syrup. And if the water in the water-bag wasn't cold enough, her father and Toon could make some other arrangement. That they would do in any case, but later; Toon always brought something with him for her pa. They drank it secretly, in the stable or behind the quince hedge, and in their simplicity they thought that if they chewed peppermints neither she nor her mother would twig. Oh, they were a pair, her father and Toon Lourens; they laughed at each other's jokes over and over and over again and boasted about their knowledge of the world.

If anybody had knowledge about the world in that district, then it was Freddy McTavish, even if his sort of knowledge had no meaning in a godforsaken hole. He had taken over the post office and store, but only temporarily, everyone said; he was in the Stormberg for his health. He was from Cape Town and had travelled abroad, he understood people. Also women, although he wasn't really interested in them. He was like a brother to her. They talked about everything under the sun, the depression and poultry diseases. She showed him her embroidery and he advised her on the colours she should use. Sometimes he brought English books for her to read, but they were too full of difficult words and the print was too small. Now they lay on her bedside table on top of her hymn book.

'Let! Are you saddling horses?' Oom Frik yelled from the stoep.

'I'm coming!'

So Let played the role of Martha who served, a role that made her acceptable to everybody – even, from time to time, to Beimen Botes. She loaded her gaudy tray with multi-coloured glasses and a glass jug with pale orange syrup and a jug of water. As she walked, the beads on the doilies covering the jugs clinked against them; delicate music, like that from a music box.

She shook Toon Lourens's hand and said, 'Shoo, it's hot!'

'I wonder if Beimen will come tonight,' her father said, 'I understand he's having trouble with that windmill pump.'

'Oh, he'll come,' chuckled Toon Lourens. 'Because he's dying for company. He even rides over in the middle of the week to the post office just to talk to Freddy.'

'What could they have to talk about?' laughed Tant Das.

'Oh, lots of things,' said Toon. 'Freddy is writing down his stories.'

'What does Beimen know of stories?'

'Not those sort of stories, Oom Frik. Anecdotes about Die Hoek,' explained Toon.

'But I know those better than he does, and I can tell them better. Old Beimen is heavy of tongue.'

'So are you, sometimes,' Tant Das landed a blow below the belt. She nudged Let, who giggled behind her handkerchief.

'Come on, Toon,' said Oom Frik, taking offence, 'these women have nothing to say.'

Let took the glasses and jugs to the kitchen. She didn't feel like washing up yet and fetched her bonnet and apron.

'What? In this heat?' asked Tant Das in amazement.

'I'm going to look for eggs,' said Let stubbornly. 'There are some hideaway hens that have strayed away to lay under the karree bushes.'

'In this heat? What about the snakes?'

'Precisely because of the snakes. I don't want them eating up my profits. I'm not scared of snakes, I'll take a kierie with me.'

It was much too hot to collect eggs and Let knew it. The heat struck from all directions, from above as well as beating up from the earth. She could feel it through the soles of her shoes. But she needed to think, and for that she had to be alone.

Let took a round-about way to the stables; she held a few eggs cradled in her apron. She caught her father and Toon in the act, just as she knew she would. Hurriedly they tried to stash away the half-jack behind a tin of dubbin in the cupboard. But they were too late.

'Let, if you tell your mother . . .' said Oom Frik, half angrily as well as ashamed.

Let laughed. 'Pa knows that I'm a good sport, but then Pa must help me tonight. I have a plan for some fun. That's if Beimen and Freddy come over tonight, because I need them both.'

'Oh, they'll come,' said Toon with a spiteful laugh.

'Freddy as well?'

'Yes, because "Jonathan delighted much in David". Read your Bible.'

Let didn't actually like Toon Lourens, but for tonight he would be an ideal ally. He also had it in for Beimen for he and Beimen had been inseparable before Freddy came.

'I want us to make Freddy up like a girl. Then we'll introduce him to Beimen as Pa's niece from Kimberley. We'll call her Genevieve.'

'I don't know about that,' said Oom Frik. 'It's crazy, and Beimen would surely know at once.'

'Oh no, he won't! Not when I've finished with Freddy.'

'All right, then,' sighed Oom Frik.

'But Pa must suggest it to Freddy. He has a great deal of respect for Pa.'

'And what if he won't?'

'Oh, he will,' Let laughed with deadly certainty. 'Oh yes, he will.'

And she was right, for finally Freddy only had one reservation: his moustache.

'That's nothing,' said Oom Frik, who was beginning to enjoy the game. 'We'll shave it off and you can start growing it again from the beginning. But this time treat it with chicken shit.'

Let fetched the razor, the strop, the soap and water.

There was something deliberate in her movements; something masculine about the way she stropped the razor that surprised Oom Frik. He looked at Toon, but Toon simply sat smiling.

Freddy didn't seem too willing to allow Let to shave him, but Oom Frik reassured him: 'She shaves me regularly.'

It was soon apparent that Let knew what she was doing. There were no cuts, not a drop of blood. She shaved off Freddy's moustache and then she began shaving his cheeks. 'But I shaved this morning,' he protested through the mounds of foam, but Let went calmly ahead. 'I want your face to be as smooth as a baby's bottom,' she said.

After that she took him to the room, where she had laid out a dress, a blue one with daisies printed on it. Tant Das sat watching, bemused by Freddy's transformation. Her switch, from the days of her youth, blended well with his long blond hair, while Let's red earrings made his cherry lips look even more red. Even shoes weren't a problem, for Let had particularly large feet for a girl. Something strange happened in the process: Freddy was transformed from within. He laughed flirtatiously, his voice became slightly higher than usual, from sheer excitement. His gestures became feminine.

Let van Onselen had never laughed as she did that night, intensely and often. Sometimes she went to her room to smother her fits of laughter in her pillow; sometimes she went behind the *bakoond* to catch her breath.

With the prescience of an experienced woman she knew when Beimen would ask the fatal question. She saw it in his eyes when he danced so closely with Genevieve – pressing himself against her thighs – and he sang raucously:

> 'When I was a little calf
> I didn't get no milk.'

'Well, drink then!' Let thought with contempt. 'Drink until you shit.'

She waited in the passage with a tray and with perfect timing she intercepted his proposal. 'Here, you must be thirsty,' she giggled and offered orange syrup.

The Van Onselens knew nothing of the exchange of letters between Genevieve and Beimen. They first got to know about it when Freddy came one afternoon on his bicycle with his crazy request to borrow the Genevieve get-up. Of course they were furious. The whole scheme had been theirs, and now they were pushed aside and didn't have a share in the sports. But still they lent him the clothes.

As they watched Freddy ride away, Oom Frik said: 'I wonder if that boy is all right, he looks so pale.'

'It's because he's shaved off his moustache,' explained Tant Das. 'It makes him look pale.'

'There is something else,' Let agreed with her father, 'a restlessness.'

'Yes, that's it, yes,' agreed Oom Frik, 'a restlessness.'

'Now that you mention it,' said Tant Das, 'he trembled when he took the box from me. Yes, I remember it quite well, he trembled.'

Even years later the Van Onselens would recall this short exchange in the finest detail. People simply like to be considered prophetic.

The accident happened the following week. Sergeant Zietsman brought the tidings and Doctor Rowland was with him in the side-car. Both men, strong and hardened, looked ready to break.

'He did it with a revolver, Oom Frik, which he put into his mouth. His brains spilled out like kapok from a cushion. The worst is that he was wearing women's clothing. That's why we are here.'

Doctor Rowland took over from the sergeant. 'Would Tant Das please come and lay him out, please. It is tragic enough and one doesn't want gossip. He was such a dear boy.'

'I will go with you,' said Let. 'I can help.'

Doctor Rowland hesitated. 'Oom Frik . . .'

'Oh, Let is strong, doctor. And she and Freddy were like brother and sister.'

It was Let who took control. Tant Das was overcome by the shock. It was Let who gathered towels and soap and gauze and asked in a practical way, 'Shouldn't he have a shroud?' Without waiting for an answer she went to the camphor kist and fetched her father's.

Let looked stark, something to which the dark half of her face contributed greatly, but inwardly she was seething. While she worked, her hands now here and now there, she thought constantly: If only it was Beimen. If only it was Beimen Botes's body.

Translated by Ian Ferguson

ETIENNE VAN HEERDEN

Mad Dog

Jakadas Pool first noticed the rabid dog following their donkey cart on the ninth day of their trek over the Wapadsberg. He was sick to death of staring ahead over the dull grey backs of his two donkeys. The sight of their stupid heads working up and down against the vast nothingness of the plains made him wish that he was back in the valleys of Rooidraai, on a Sunday afternoon when he'd come up from the river, washed clean by the shining waters of the Great Fish, and his wife Kintie would rub Vaseline into his hair. Then the first and very best swig of the thick creamy corn beer from the six bowls standing before the house in the sunshine.

As soon as he saw the madness in the dog, he handed the reins to Kintie, thinking: We can't outspan today – not before we've shaken off that scrawny creature. The three children will just have to piss over the side of the cart as we go along. The dog had gained on them gradually, but it kept its distance at about fifty paces. It was a common shaggy-coated thing that could have come from any of the huts in the Wapadsberg. But the dog was mad. Jakadas saw that the minute he turned round the first time and spotted the dog with the foaming mouth, skew head and white showing in the eyes.

'Most likely bitten by a meerkat,' he told Kintie, unfastening his knobkerrie from the cart rail. He tipped the last of the paraffin into the lamp, turned the wick down as low as possible and lit it. He held his oldest child, Fielies, by the ankles while the skinny boy hung over the back of the cart and fastened the lamp to the rear axle so that it just cleared the ground.

'Right,' said Jakadas, once he'd helped his son pull himself back up on top of their piled-up possessions. 'The smell of paraffin will keep the animal off.' He took the reins back from Kintie and asked her to turn round, sitting with her back to the road ahead, so she could help the children keep an eye on the dog. They were to tell him if it came closer than fifty paces. He wasn't sure what he'd do then. Everyone in the Karoo knew about rabies: even if you were licked by a rabid cow, you got the fits, the fear of water and the foam at your mouth, the lonely wandering and then death, somewhere on the plains, where they had to burn your remains. A meerkat that came creeping up could bite the madness into you. Even if the bark of a rabid dog fell on your ear, said the old people, the germ would get into your head. There was only one thing to do with a mad beast on the farm: run and call the boss so that he could shoot it dead in its tracks.

If they could only find water, thought Jakadas: that would chase the dog away. They'd used the last of their water early that morning, long before the dog had picked up their track. Kintie was near her time and she was always thirsty. The waterbag, swinging from the axle under the cart, was dry; it wouldn't even help for her to hold it against her stomach for the moisture and coolness that might remain in the canvas. Fielies had felt it: bone dry.

He remembered clearly, with the swaying ears of the donkeys ahead of him and Kintie's back against his, how Uncle Danster had fallen foul of a rabid dog in the Camdeboo. Uncle Danster was resting under a thorn tree, minding his goats, when he noticed a draggle-tailed dog slinking up from the lonely plains. The dog was mad, he saw at once: the open mouth, the foaming saliva, the uneven gait. Uncle Danster just left his goats and ran for the nearest water – under a wind-pump about four hundred paces away. But before he was halfway there, the dog got him, just one nip on the shin, before it picked up the smell of water on the breeze and gave way, stagger-stagger off into the scrub.

Uncle Danster knew he had only three days left on the plains. He drove his goats into the fold, keeping a safe distance from them, bound up the gatepost securely with a thong and then, from the other side of the wind, shouted his last requests and wishes to his wife and children as they stared at him from the hut window.

For three days all the hut doors were kept shut while Uncle Danster wandered his last wanderings on this earth. The first night they could hear him crying like a jackal, by the second night he was so crazy he came and hammered on their doors. Inside everyone huddled together inhaling the smell of paraffin from the lamps. It wasn't until early morning that they heard him wandering off again – once he had torn all Granny Danster's laying hens to death with his teeth. When he left – Granny Danster always shuddered at this – they could hear his jaws snapping as the fever gripped him.

The third night, when everyone in the huts had run out of food, he came back and scuttled around the yard on all fours and the people knew: Uncle Danster had turned into a mad dog and for the rest of his life he would trail anyone who had done him wrong. The morning after the third night, Granny Danster knocked at all the huts. 'You can come out,' she said to the frightened faces at the opened top half of each door. 'The Karoo has taken Uncle Danster, God bless his poor wretched soul.'

He felt Kintie's back stir against his and then she spoke. He knew that movement of her body when she pulled her headscarf low over her brow to speak. 'It's your Uncle Danster,' she said. And in a little while, pulling down her headscarf again, 'What did you do to him, Jakadas?'

He shrugged and tried to joke. 'So I milked his goats in the donga.' But the hollow pit in his stomach also said: Uncle Danster had to choose *this* time – when they'd had trouble over rations at Rooidraai and were forced to leave the district – to pick on him for the sins of his childhood.

Sjambokking the donkeys to force them into a trot wouldn't help. They didn't have any strength left after nine hot days on the road. And the dog still seemed so lightfooted, even though its head hung so low. Luckily, Jakadas thought as he looked around, the children were asleep. Fielies lay with his one arm still hanging over the side – he'd been playing with a twig in the spokes of the wheel. The two girls lay in a heap behind the cooking grid and the food tins. Kintie had thrown a sack over their heads for shade.

He still remembered how the old people had followed Uncle Danster's tracks to find his corpse so they could cover it with thorn tree branches and set it alight. His tracks went in great circles over the plains, down into the dongas in the dry riverbeds, up against the foothills of the Sneeuberg, but always back to the closed doors of the little mission church under the pepper trees where Uncle Danster had scratched his first name – all he'd ever learned to write – in the dust.

It was the last lucid thing he ever did. The old people tracking him swore that eventually his spoor changed: the footprints round Granny Danster's fowl run were already half-man's, half-dog's, and those round the thresholds of the huts were a dog's.

And now, on the ninth day of their trek, Uncle Danster had to come back out of the past. Nine days – he could hardly believe it – he and Kintie and the children had already been on the road. At every turn-off with a farm sign they'd outspanned, hobbling the donkeys so they could graze on the government land on either side of the road. Further than that the donkeys were not allowed – the farmers were pretty quick to shoot a trek donkey. Once the tarpaulin was slung up for shade and there was enough wood to make a fire, he'd set off down the farm road after Kintie had read him the name of the farmer on the board. From some farmers a man simply wouldn't take a job if he could possibly help it. These were the sjambok farmers, who gave you nothing but salted fish, mealie meal and trouble.

He walked alone down the farm roads, and by the last gate, where the trees and flowerbeds began, the yard dogs had usually started to bark. Then, to show proper respect, you kept your distance, waiting until the boss or missus came out or asked one of the kitchen maids to find out what you wanted.

But there was no work anywhere. Everywhere, trek groups rested at the side of the road. The drought was taking its toll and the farmers laid workers off when there were too many hands and too little work. Then back to the trek at the road. While he was still a long way off, Kintie would stand watching him with one hand shading her eyes, and he would shake his head so she had time to cry her tears out before he got back. And when he got to her, down came the headscarf. 'Jakadas Pool, I didn't want to have the baby here on the side of the road, how will the child feel when he grows up and hears he came into this life on the side of the road like a piece of rubbish someone's thrown away?'

On the second day the two hens in the wire cage hanging beside the waterbag died at the same time, as if they'd been given a sign. That night they ate plump chicken, and again his thoughts went back to Rooidraai. If that boss Rooikoos had kept his promise to increase the rations, they'd still be there at the bend in the river with its red dongas full of dassie burrows. But when the boss came down on him in the rations store, hitting him so he staggered against the meal bags, in front of the other workers, and fell on to the concrete floor and had to stagger up and wipe the mealie meal from his cheek, he threw his tobacco and coffee and bokkems at the feet of the white man, walked home and said to Kintie: 'A man has to be able to hold up his head. Even though you can't raise your fists to a white man.'

His brother Seun had already done two of his three years for assault; it was actually against boss Rooikoos's cousin, Piet Donker-hoek, that he'd raised his fists. They said Piet Donkerhoek caught Seun drunk in the milking shed, singing as he milked with one of the cow's unfastened legs in the half-full milk bucket. They slugged it out right there in the milking shed, slipping in the cow dung and falling into the urine drain, and Piet Donkerhoek's pedigree cows wouldn't let their milk down again for a week. When the udders had swollen right up between the cows' hind legs and the milk had started to ooze from the teats, they were forced to call the vet. It cost Piet Donkerhoek a lot and he lost his quota at the cheese factory because he couldn't deliver milk for two weeks.

Seun's wife and children – she was a housemaid at the big house and the oldest son was Piet Donkerhoek's gate opener – were chased off the farm and the police beat Seun up behind the milking shed before they carted him off in their van. His wife and children lived next to the railway line for three months, stealing food at night from the rubbish bins at the guest-house down near the river.

'A person can't stand up to a white boss. You don't bite the hand that feeds you,' Kintie said when he came home the night of the blow. But he said, 'A man must be able to hold up his head.' They left that night, Kintie crying until they could no longer hear the barking of the Rooidraai dogs. Then she pulled her headscarf down on her brow and the bitter expression settled around her mouth.

They rode until late that night, with the stars open above them and the white road between the donkeys' heads. He used his whip because he wanted to put as much distance as possible between them and Rooidraai before daybreak. Rooikoos might come after him in his bakkie and make him work his month's notice before he left. At the turn-off to Graaff-Reinet he and Kintie argued for a long time. The moon was sinking and far away over the plains of prickly pear a jackal howled. She wanted to go straight on to Middelburg – she had family in the location there. He wanted to go over the Wapadsberg to Graaff-Reinet because he'd heard they had rain there. There would be work.

On the fourth day when they started up the first slopes of the Wapadsberg, Fielies got stomach fever from the dead coot they'd found at the roadside. It was only afterwards that they thought: the bird had been lying beside the road all day and no other animal had touched it. They should have realised, but they'd been hungry and pleased with the unexpected piece of meat and Kintie made a stew with some pig's-ear bulbs that she and the children dug up along the side of the road. Fielies was the only one who got sick and for two days his stomach spewed a yellow mess. The coot must have had DDT or jackal-poison in it.

'The child is half dead,' Kintie wailed. 'That bird was full of poison, the Lord help us.' She hugged her stomach as the crows circled above them and the donkeys moved even more slowly and wearily. Later he beat them raw, only letting up because they simply laid their ears down flat and farted in his face.

'The donkeys are giving in,' Kintie said.

'Mangy trash!'

'Don't hammer them, Jakadas, they are the Lord's creatures.'

He'd also heard that the Lord rode on a donkey, but not like these, not Karoo donkeys, that was for sure.

Kintie looked at him quietly, with her hand on her belly. 'I'm not getting enough healthy food.'

He pulled up, outspanned and went to sit under a tree to think – away from Kintie and the children. Going back was out of the question, the boss would have allowed another trek to come in by now. No, they had to go forward to where it had rained, wherever that was.

And, on the ninth day, suddenly: the dog. He had looked back at the road that tailed off behind them, sat like that for a while and then turned forward until something made him look back again. Suddenly, out of thin air, the dog was there. Whites showing in its eyes, muzzle low to the ground, foam dripping from its jaw. Right between the two wheel tracks, as though they were wires that it had to trot between.

'We can't get down until we reach water,' he told the children. 'If the dog smells water, he'll be off.'

'And if we don't find water, Pa?' Fielies looked up from his game with the wheel spokes. The girls were like their mother, sulky and quiet.

'We will get water. The springs have to come out somewhere. There was lightning in the mountains last night. That way.' He pointed with his whip.

'Don't lie to the children, Jakadas,' Kintie said. 'There was no lightning. I lay awake all night.'

'Under the tarpaulin, yes. I saw the veins of lightning on that side.' He pointed again. 'And this morning I smelt rain.'

'It's dew. You know you can smell dew when the veld is as dry as this. It isn't rain.' And down came the headscarf.

'We'll get water.' He returned to the front, away from the dog behind them, and poked the donkeys' arses with the butt of the whip. 'Get up, you rubbishes. Gee-yup, gee-yup!'

The day that Fielies made yellow puddles on the side of the road every couple of hundred paces, the shearers came past on their old bicycles. They stopped, leaning their bicycles against a telephone pole. Fielies lay sweating in the shade of the tarpaulin. Jakadas and the six men smoked together companionably. One of them was a Xhosa and there was also a yellow Bushman who had learnt to shear in Botswana. The Xhosa went to look for a fat-leafed plant in the veld and they crushed it up and mixed it with a little paraffin and dosed Fielies. He slept through until the next day and was better when he woke up. The world looks poor over Graaff-Reinet way, said the shearers. The fleeces had been soiled by dust storms and any sheep you turned on its back lay splay-legged from the worms. The farmers were paying badly – only sixpence a fleece now. A lot of farmers had bought electric shears, so one man did the work of a whole team in a day.

To console them, he took out the whetstone he had inherited from his father. It was kept in some damp rags near the waterbag. 'My pa was also a shearer, until the sinews in his hand were cut in a fight.' Wordlessly, they took out their shears and honed them while the coffee water hissed on the fire and two herons flew high above them. He pointed, 'Look, Kintie, there must be water.' She put her hand on her belly and watched the moisture from the whetstone dry grey on the shearers' fingers. The shearers gave him a little plug of chewing tobacco before they left, crouched low over their handlebars. They'd heard that a couple of farmers in Somerset East were looking for a gang of shearers. It was still four days' ride away, they had to push on.

'The world forgot about mercy a long time ago,' one said to Kintie. Jakadas and Kintie and the girls stood and watched the shearers pedalling off into the distance.

'You know how to shear sheep, Jakadas,' Kintie said that night.

'And a house? Are you and the children going to wait on the roadside while I go shearing from farm to farm? The police will pick you up, Kintie.'

'We could look for a house.'

'The farmers only give you a house if you give your hands; you know that, Kintie.'

'I can go and stay with my people in Middelburg.'

'They are already sleeping seven to a room. And you haven't got the right papers to stay in the location.'

The scarf over the eyes. How she had laughed, on Rooidraai, when he brought her a bowl of prickly pears from the plains.

And now the dog. Even at dusk, still: the dog. Kintie had to hang on to Fielies while he passed water as they rode. The dog trotted over the droplets in the sand, kept on coming as though he'd seen nothing, just the empty waterbag hanging from the axle.

Once, a long way ahead, they saw a cloud of dust moving towards them.

'A car!' shouted Kintie. 'A white man!'

They waited until the car came closer, and Kintie said, 'We must stop him.' She got up awkwardly, unsteady on her feet. 'He might have a gun.'

The dog raised its head at the drone of the engine; with ears pricked, it trotted to the side of the road, but didn't stop. Sunlight flashed on the windscreen as Jakadas stood up, waving his arms and Kintie lost her balance, collapsing back on to their things. The car was full of white people pointing at the donkey cart as they shot past. As the cloud of dust settled on them they all coughed and the children started to cry. When the dust had cleared they saw the dog, back in the middle of the road between the wheel tracks. 'It's your Uncle Danster,' whispered Kintie. 'He's staring into my eyes.'

The dog's eyes gleamed in the light of the lantern on the axle. Kintie broke off pieces of bread and held out the tin of dripping so he could smear his bread with it. 'He doesn't come closer even when he can smell food,' said Kintie. The smaller girl had started to cry in the early evening and although she was now half asleep she still moaned quietly if they went over a bump and the cart rattled. He ate with one hand, holding the reins with the other.

On the slope, the donkey on the left came to a halt, standing foursquare in its tracks. He laid into it with the whip, but neither donkey would budge. Behind them they could see the dog's eyes sink lower as it lay down on the ground. 'He's not coming any closer,' said Kintie. She put the food tin away in the trunk, its lid squeaking in the silence. It was dead quiet in the veld. Every creature knew – even the jackals and the crickets – that a mad dog was on the prowl, thought

Jakadas. Every living thing would wait until its tracks had crossed the mountain before venturing out. He got to work with his whip again and suddenly a huge owl whirred low over their heads.

'An owl in the road,' he said without looking at Kintie. She was superstitious about owls. The donkeys moved on again. The owl was probably sitting on the road eating a mouse. Was he imagining it, or could he hear the dog's pads on the gravel? Dew soaked into his clothes, chilling him. Kintie and the children had subsided under the blankets, she was keeping an eye on the dog as she lay there. He thought about Rooidraai: the moisture on the lower half of the door when he pushed it open to the fresh morning that lay mistily in the curves of the river. The white storks swooping in low over the lucerne fields, at the same time every morning, before the bees started buzzing among the blossoms and the heat pressed down on your shoulders with its heavy hand.

Rations were scarce, also spare money for clothes or shoes, and the master was mean and strict. But it was a nice farm. On Sundays the police searched the huts for stolen meat or tins of rendered-down fat. The world was hungry and the wandering people caught and killed the farmers' pedigree stock as though they were slaughter animals. Every Sunday the police van came bouncing over the stones and broken bottles and half bricks of the road to the compound, but the people had hidden it all away: a well-salted haunch of beef in the wreck of an old Ford, on top of the rotten tyre, under the mudguard. Once a whole carcass high in the wind-pump. 'You think the police don't look up,' said the constable – a brown man too, one of their own people – dragging his cousin Willempie away to the van.

As they drove off, cousin Willempie shouted through the wire mesh of the van just for good measure: 'You'd better set your hare-traps, cousin Jakadas, and tighten your belts on those stomachs!' And the meat in the wreck – the detectives were alerted by a swarm of bluebottles buzzing around the mudguard in the heat of the afternoon.

Otherwise, beyond the hunger for meat and the gagging on salted fish, they could eke out an existence at Rooidraai. The summer before, the boss had put a tap in near the huts so they could grow vegetables. After a month or two his patch of tattered mealies was all that was left standing in the dry wind that pushed across the flats from the east. The others' vegetables had shrivelled up, or died from the forgetfulness and neglect that comes with getting up before daybreak and returning home bone weary at sunset to bad-tempered wives and snotty-nosed children. On Saturdays and Sundays Sixpence and his gang fell into a drunken sleep in the vegetables, on the cool spinach and lettuces, until everything was flattened or pissed to death.

And when he said to boss Rooikoos, 'The rations are not enough for a man who works hard with his hands from early morning until late and for a woman and for three children . . .' the white man said: 'But it was good enough until now. What story is this again today?'

'Our food is finished, boss. And my wife is near her time, boss.'

'And it cost me a lot of money to put the tap in,' said Rooikoos's freckled face right up close to his, 'and all you do is let the brats leave the tap open. Look at that bloody enormous pool of water collecting around the tap, and nothing came of your vegetable gardens, even though I gave you seed and spades and everything.'

My vegetable garden is standing, boss, he wanted to say. But in the heat of the moment it slipped out: 'The people have lost heart, boss.'

'Why? Why? Because nothing is good enough for you any more? Because of the agitators who sneak off the trains at night and come sniffing about your huts?'

'Because of the life on the farm, boss.'

'You get houses, you get food, you get work, you get everything. Do you think I get anything for nothing? Where do I get a handout?' Boss Rooikoos in front of him: the red beard, the eyebrows starting to rust – as they always joked over their spades while he walked away from them. The freckles suddenly enlarged, the face was so close; he could smell the breath, he could smell meat on the breath, the fat rib chops that Jakadas himself had fetched from the meatroom for the kitchen maids to prepare.

'We are hungry, boss. Look how fat your children are.'

And then the flat-handed blow.

Kintie coming along with her heavy heart. Weeping, she'd loaded the cart and hoisted her heavy body up on to it. Sixpence had given her the tin of dripping – it was left over from the stolen sheep they'd come across in the lay-by near the station. 'Who is this ewe without a boss?' the men asked. 'Let's fix it up so our wives can laugh again with shining faces.'

When the railway police arrived, the last sinews had been devoured and the last hoof and tuft of wool burnt to cinders. The policeman looked at the children's bulging stomachs and at the toothless old people sleeping off the feast in the shade of the huts while bluebottles foraged round their mouths and they said, 'Scum of Rooidraai, we'll get you, just you wait. Let us rake out as much as one scrap of sheep's horn from your hearths, and every one of you will land up in front of the magistrate.' But everything was burnt away and human droppings are just human droppings – as the detectives realised when they went to investigate in the donga behind the aloes. The ewe disappeared into the hungry bellies of Rooidraai and came out the other end as nothing.

He smiled, and then noticed that Kintie was lying with the children. He looked back: there were the eyes, the eyes that would not leave them. Eyes he remembered from the dreams of his boyhood when Uncle Danster turned into a dog: you're sitting in the veld, completely comfortable, when suddenly a tame meerkat shows up and you think he'll run away when he sees a person, but as he gets closer, your second thought is that this must be a pet that's wandered away from its home, and before you have a chance to look it in the eye, it attacks you with foaming, gaping jaws, scrabbling claws, biting the madness into your flesh. And now: he pretended he couldn't hear Kintie crying from where she'd burrowed her head in between the children. Over the sound of the donkeys' hooves he could now clearly hear the crunch-crunch of the dog's paws.

'The owl,' Kintie said, sitting upright when he turned around again.

At daybreak, as the dog grew clearer in the dim light, they arrived at the top of the Wapadsberg. The winding pass slipped down and far on the empty plains they could see a mistiness collected. 'Dry mist,' he said to Kintie. They started to go down, he pulled both sets of reins in tight, the donkeys braked back in their bits, swaying their heads from side to side as though they were trying to see past the blinkers. The shaft lay high against their necks.

'There's a farmyard!' he shouted suddenly. The sun flashed on the roof of a house between tall trees. 'Kintie, get out the bread and the fat, we're going to that farm.'

Kintie was beside him, her eyes shining with excitement. 'The food is finished,' she said, but it didn't matter any more. Fielies started to cry when he heard and Kintie got nauseous and vomited over the side of the cart. He heard the retching of her empty stomach. He didn't look round: the dog would step over the stuff from her stomach without even sniffing at it, he knew.

Down on the flats they turned on to the farm road.

'Paradise Valley,' read Kintie.

'And the boss? And the boss?'

'The name isn't clear,' she answered. 'The paint's worn off.'

Slowly they rumbled up the farm road with its avenue of trees. The dog also took the turning at the signboard and followed them.

'Is that mongrel still coming?'

Her silence answered his question.

The farmyard gate was open so he needn't have sat and planned how he'd have to leap off to open it. The gardens were a bit neglected.

Jakadas looked round at the dog again. Kintie and the children were clustered round him now. He could feel her stomach pressing against his back. Bright sunflowers stood next to the road, some of them bent by the wind.

The doors of the wagon shed were open. It was empty. Kintie drew in her breath. 'There's no one here, Jakadas!' she grabbed hold of him, her fingers in his ribs. 'Oh, Lord, Jakadas, the owl warned us: the dog is going to get us right here.'

He had to think quickly. There wasn't a road round the house. There was space to turn the donkeys, but only the one road out. He looked round.

Fifty paces back, between the tracks, head hanging low: the dog.

'We're going into the house,' he said.

Kintie gasped. 'That's breaking in. The police . . .'

'Shut up, Kintie.' He slapped the children to make them stop their crying and aimed a slap at Kintie too. Then he looked back again. The dog was a good way back; foam flecked the red tongue and the teeth.

With two vicious cracks of the whip, he spurred the donkeys quickly up to the front door, throwing the reins to Kintie and leaping off. He looked back but couldn't see the dog, it must have been somewhere behind the cart and the donkeys. With his first kick the door creaked. It was made of tough wood. With the second Kintie started to cry. With the third the wood cracked around the lock. He shouldered it open. Kintie passed the children down, first Fielies, who was tossed head-over-heels into the house, then the two girls, then Kintie, heavy and clumsy in his arms and her breath sour from the vomiting on the mountain pass after they'd seen the farmhouse.

Just before he slammed the door shut and pushed a chest against it, his eyes searched for the dog but there was still no sign of it.

Nervously they looked round the dim house. The furniture was grand: copper ashtrays and vases, a big portrait over the fireplace, deep easy-chairs. He wiped his mouth with the back of his hand. A white man's house – he could smell it: floor polish and meat in the kitchen. Soap, fly spray. Thick carpets on the floor and, in front of the fireplace, a leopard skin with a stuffed head. Open mouth and glass eyes. He shuddered and looked out. The donkeys stood in their harness, grazing on the lawn, unaware of the dog and the cart that joggled comically with their movements. The dog lay in the middle of the yard, head on its paws, eyes fixed on the front door.

Kintie and the children went down the passage ahead of him. In the bedrooms beds were neatly made up. In the bathroom, with its snow-white black-lidded lavatory, the children sucked thirstily at the closed tap. When Kintie opened it, clear water splashed over their faces. Fielies stuck his head under the tap and laughed at the water that rinsed over his dusty neck and ran in a brown stream into the white bath.

Jakadas pushed the pantry door open. Thick, heavy biltong – choice cuts – hung from the ceiling. There was a half-opened sack of yellow-gold dried peaches. He took a handful and popped them into the children's cheeks. Kintie turned and stood before him with a tear-stained face. She looked down at the children and then back at him. 'Today we are stealing, Jakadas, in the eyes of the Lord.'

He found some kindling and a few pieces of firewood in the corner, stuck them into the stove and fetched a box of matches from the pantry. When the flames were roaring in the black stove, Kintie put a mug of coffee before him. He cut long strips of biltong. They stayed in the kitchen near all the food until they'd eaten their fill. It was late morning when Fielies fell asleep on a sofa in the living-room. Kintie let the two girls bath in the white bath. They soaked in water up to their shoulders, their small bodies brown against the white enamel. Jakadas's fingers caressed the smooth, glossy tiles.

Later, when the children were all asleep, he and Kintie went to the sitting-room at the front of the house.

'Where's your Uncle Danster?' she asked.

Jakadas looked outside.

'He's lying in the yard, watching the front door.'

Kintie looked at the portraits on the wall. 'Your uncle,' she said, 'did he have a reason to harm you?'

He shook his head. 'No.'

Kintie took his arm. 'Let's get some rest, Jakadas.'

They slept the whole afternoon and right through the night. When he woke up next morning and peered through the window of the front room, the dog was gone. He checked from the other windows but there was nothing to be seen. Then he filled a bucket of water and, while Kintie waited anxiously at the front door, he stepped out into the yard. He gripped the bucket tightly, ready to throw it.

He looked first at the place where the dog had lain. The gorged donkeys dozed in the shade of a gum tree in the garden. Donkeys' hoofprints and the marks of cartwheels were clear in the gravel, leading up to the front door and away again, through the yard gate. Their footprints – his and Kintie's and the children's – lay crookedly round the front door where they'd jumped off the car and rushed inside.

Jakadas went back to the house. Kintie opened up for him. 'The mad dog has gone,' he said. 'Probably to die out in the open.'

It wasn't until late that evening, when the children were asleep with full stomachs and he and she were sitting in the bath together and he was rubbing her round, swollen belly with white soap lather . . . it wasn't until then that he told her there were no dog tracks.

Translated by Catherine Knox

BARTHO SMIT

I Take Back My Country

I first met Silwane Nxumalo in front of the Johannesburg Art Gallery one afternoon. Hands tucked under his shabby raincoat, he stood on the steps of the imposing grey building studying the signboard advertising an exhibition of modern French art. I was mounting the steps when he turned and approached me.

'Excuse me, sir.' His voice was clear and courteous but he fidgeted self-consciously with his open raincoat. 'I would very much like to see those paintings, but they won't let me in.'

My interest was aroused immediately. I don't know quite why, but a black person who is an artist or who is interested in art always elicits my unreserved sympathy. I have often asked myself whether there can be any difference between a black and a white artist, but time and again, whenever I meet a black one, that inexplicable fellow-feeling wells up in me. Perhaps it was my conviction – which was also a profound fear – that the cultural future of this country lies locked in the hearts of the black millions and not in us.

'Just wait here a moment,' I told him.

I went in search of the curator: I had periodic dealings with him in the course of my work as art critic for a daily paper. It wasn't difficult to get permission for Silwane to accompany me to the exhibition.

When I went back to him, Silwane's face was alight with expectation.

'Come along,' I said.

His entire bearing spoke of his gratitude. He trailed along a little way behind me as we entered the spacious foyer. He was tentative, almost tip-toeing, as though he feared that the sound of his tread in the expansive space would attract the attention of the huge marble statues. The hall where the French works were on show was deserted. I left Silwane Nxumalo to his own devices and lost myself among the rather poor examples of the work of Braque, Derain, Utrillo, Matisse,

Picasso and dozens of others. It was only once I had been right round the exhibition that I recalled he was still there. He was standing before a Picasso etching, his face a dark silhouette against the white wall behind him. He looked deeply offended.

'Don't you like the exhibition?' I asked.

'It's beautiful,' he said, without conviction.

'Why don't you like it?'

He didn't answer at once. His gaze was still fixed on the etching. Then he said hesitantly, 'They paint only things made by man.'

My eye ran fleetingly down the ranks of canvases. That's true, I realised: only houses, lamp-posts and streets; no mountains or plains or trees. Our interest has focused increasingly inward on ourselves and our works; the vastness of nature has lost its importance in our lives. 'That's true,' I said thoughtfully. 'But still they are able to say things by means of these subjects. Look at that one.' I nodded at the Picasso etching, of an old-fashioned streetlamp with eyes and feet. He had called it 'The Owl'.

'We made that streetlight of iron and glass and flame with our own hands. It symbolises engineering and technology. But it's more than a streetlight, it's an owl too. You know about owls: they sit in the darkness and presage death . . .'

'They're powerful, I know, sir,' he said, but obviously wasn't even remotely convinced. We contemplated 'The Owl' in silence for a few moments. I was eaten up with curiosity about whether he painted too.

'What do you paint?' I asked finally. 'Nature? Mountains and trees and plains?' His eyes flew to my face as though he suspected I was mocking him. Then he answered with almost childlike pride, 'Yes, sir. The earth is a living thing, it breathes. But these things . . .' He cast a scornful glance at the Picasso.

'I'd like to see some of your paintings.'

'I'll bring them along one day, sir.' But something in his voice told me that he never would.

'No, I'd like to see them at your home. I'd like to see where you work.'

'I don't have a home.' He'd turned his face away from me. 'I live in a shack.'

'Where?'

'In Moroka.'

'I'll come and visit you tomorrow afternoon. Meet me at the police station at four.'

'OK, sir,' he agreed reluctantly. We left, he lagging behind me as he had done when we entered the gallery. He won't be there tomorrow, I thought.

Out in the street I asked him for his address and wrote it down. We had walked a little further when he stopped and said, 'I have to turn off here to catch my bus. Many thanks, sir.'

'Don't forget now: four tomorrow afternoon.'

'Fine, sir.'

He went down a narrow side street.

I followed him at a distance until he joined a long queue at a bus stop. The bus was full but everyone surged forward and forced a way in. Some people hung from the handrails at the door like crows on a branch. Silwane Nxumalo had melted back into the black multitude.

The stench was the first thing that struck me as I approached Moroka the next day. A heavy reek of breath and food and human excrement rose off that small patch of earth on which hundreds of thousands of people had been herded together. The air for miles around was thick with it, and I wondered fleetingly whether the pall of smoke hanging over the mean, cramped hovels was not simply a visible manifestation of the stink. But by the time I reached the police station I was already acclimatised and breathing freely again.

Silwane Nxumalo was waiting for me. I was struck by the sickly grey sheen on his face, and there was something in his eyes that had not been there the previous afternoon: a combination of bewilderment and rage which his glance conveyed as sympathy and hatred at the same time.

'Shall we drive or walk?' I asked, indicating my car.

'Would you mind if we walked, sir?'

'Not in the least.'

I locked the car and we made our way down an alley that snaked through a maze of shacks constructed from sacking, iron and mud. The place swarmed with noisy, playing children. Some were in tatters, others almost naked, and as we approached they fell silent, gaping at us with undisguised curiosity. A fire flickered before each shanty. Women were preparing evening meals, and the acrid smoke that engulfed everything had my eyes smarting.

Silwane Nxumalo came to a stop in front of one of the few dwellings made of corrugated iron. A neat fence surrounded the tiny plot. The roof had been patched together from odd-shaped scraps of iron; the low plank door was painted green and one of the panes in the tiny window had been replaced with cardboard. An old woman sat on the ground against the wall in the last of the afternoon sun. She was the same sickly colour as Silwane Nxumalo and her face was thin and so desiccated I imagined I could see her skull through the wrinkled skin.

Silwane Nxumalo pushed open the small gate and we entered. The old woman greeted me without moving. 'That's my mother,' Silwane told me as we went into the house and he closed the door behind us. In the dim light I made out a pair of narrow iron bedsteads, a small wooden table, three chairs and a kitchen dresser with cups and plates on its shelves. A tanned goatskin lay on the floor.

'This is my house,' he said with a touch of bitterness. 'Please take a seat, sir.'

I pulled one of the chairs away from the table and sat on it. Silwane opened a trunk in the corner, returning with a stack of painted canvases which he placed on the table.

'They aren't framed. I'll hold them in the light for you.'

He carefully raised the first up in front of him. It was an enormous landscape painted in wild colours with broad brush-strokes – a desolate expanse of plains with mountains in the background. There was an ungainly crudeness about it which I didn't like. As if he'd sensed my reaction, he immediately put it down and raised another canvas. This was the same: featureless plains and heavy, primitive mountain shapes. The third was no different. Compassion welled up in me and before he could put away the third canvas, I checked him with a gesture. As I studied it the strange reality of the landscape became familiar. The mountains receded, the plains opened out, gaining depth and dimension, and I sensed a pulse behind the images. Like a sleeping animal, Silwane Nxumalo's work stirred and came to life before my eyes. All at once I realised: this is Africa – rougher and far greater than the land I had known until now, throbbing with life under a scorching sun. Each tree and hill, each human form which appeared against the background of vast distances, each cloud was as heavy and cumbersome as an outgrowth of the earth itself. And now I understood what Silwane had meant the previous afternoon when he said: 'The land is alive; it breathes.'

Every now and then he would lift a new canvas into the light, but I hardly noticed. I was aware only of the vast land, alive within the four walls of a cramped tiny shanty: brown mountains basking in the summer sunshine like loaves of bread fresh from the oven, and grassy plains, white as a deathbed in winter. I glimpsed the inner soul of this country – a silent eternal emptiness.

'They're wonderful, Silwane,' I told him as he laid down the last canvas. 'You've captured the spirit of Africa.'

'I'm very pleased that you like them, sir,' he responded humbly.

'We must try to organise an exhibition for you.'

He glanced swiftly at me and then his eyes dropped. 'Thank you very much, sir. But I don't want an exhibition.'

'Why not?'

'I did these paintings for myself. For my people.'

'But do your people ever buy paintings?' I asked in surprise.

'No. But they will – one day.'

'But how do you make a living? Where do you get the money for paint and canvases?'

'I work as a gardener – one week a month.'

He started putting the canvases carefully back into the trunk. And as he bent over it, I tried to imagine him working with a pick and shovel. He was so thin!

They haunted me, those white plains and the ungainly mountains that had come to life that afternoon at Silwane's. The lingering impression was of ugliness, clumsiness, and still I couldn't shake it off.

I drove to Moroka again. Without a word, Silwane took his canvases out and held them up to the light. That day the plains were even more awesome than they'd been before; the mountains more clumsy, but also more overwhelming. And, after that second visit, the world around me began to take on the surreal quality of the canvases; I felt that, up until then, I had seen this country only through the eyes of a tourist. Silwane was out when I visited a third time. His mother was alone against the wall in the weak rays of the setting sun. As I pushed the gate open, she stood up with some difficulty.

'*Bayete*. He's not here, *nkosi*; but he should come back very soon.'

'May I wait for him?'

We stood in silence, watching two vultures hovering over the pall of smoke that screened countless shacks.

'Your son will be a great man one day.'

'He won't live to see that day, *nkosi*.' Her voice was calm, her eyes fixed on the wheeling vultures.

'How can you say that?'

'There is a large animal eating away within us.' Her gnarled hand had moved to her stomach. 'He will finish us off.'

'You talk in riddles.'

'You can't live very long if the male jackal never leaves his den, *nkosi*. The male jackal must go out for food.'

'I understand you now: Silwane doesn't bring food home.'

'When he was a child, I brought in the food. Now I am old. I am now the child, *nkosi*, but he never leaves the house.'

Suddenly one of the vultures soared up into the measureless heights of the sky, shrinking to a tiny black dot before disappearing completely. The old woman's eyes watered with her effort to keep the bird in focus.

'I no longer know Silwane,' she continued quietly. 'He is like that vulture: the food lies on the earth, but he seeks the heights.'

'He's doing important work.'

The glance she threw me had something of Silwane's shyness. 'Perhaps you are right, *nkosi*. I don't know. But it will not still the beast within us.'

'Does Silwane ever sell any of his paintings?' I felt desperately sorry for the old woman.

But she looked at me oddly, as though she pitied my stupidity.

'Your people might buy things like these, *nkosi*,' she answered almost indulgently. 'They have plenty of money. But what would our people do with them? Ah, here he is.'

Following her gaze, I made out Silwane's tall frame approaching though the early dusk.

'You must speak to him, *nkosi*,' she said with surprising urgency. 'He will listen to the authority of another man.'

'I'll have a word with him,' I promised quietly as the gate creaked open.

'The *nkosi* has been waiting for you the whole afternoon, my son,' she replied to his greeting.

'I see that he is here,' Silwane said. He held the door open for me. It was very gloomy inside. He put a match to the tin lamp on the table. A thin black trail of smoke rose from it and the flame chased shadows into corners, under the table and beds.

'I've finished a new painting,' Silwane said with an almost embarrassed smile. There was a strange expression on his face. His eyes were sunk so deep in their sockets they gleamed like an animal's; his cheekbones jutted gauntly and ash-grey flecks mottled the darker skin. I remembered the old woman's words about the gnawing beast, and for the first time I understood Silwane's sickly complexion.

'Show it to me,' I said.

'The light is bad.'

'That doesn't matter.'

He took a canvas from the trunk in the corner and held it up to the dull lamplight. Much was familiar – vast expanses of grassy plains and heavy mountains – but there was a new element too: part of Moroka in the foreground; untidy hovels, smoke, crowds of people. It lay like a rubbish-dump in an undefiled natural landscape.

And yet the sunlight which illuminated everything with unearthly clarity seemed to lift the human figures off the dump, identifying them with the landscape behind until they shone like stars in the dark waters of a swamp.

'This is one of your best,' I told him when he finally laid the canvas down.

'I'm pleased that you like it.'

'Now we really must organise an exhibition.'

He looked at me almost as though I was an enemy. 'No, sir.' His voice echoed the malevolence of his stare.

'Then you should at least sell one or two privately.'

'You want me to sell my country?'

'I sympathise with your feelings, Silwane. But there are other people who paint the land and they sell their work – even the greatest among them.'

'I'm not just painting the land.'

'Then what else are you doing?'

'I'm taking it back,' he said passionately. His anger was tangible, his eyes blazed.

'What do you mean?'

'You are forcing me to say things.'

'I am your friend,' I said encouragingly. 'You can tell me anything.'

'I am taking back the land you have grabbed from us. In the mornings I walk out of here, I take back a part of it and at night I bring it home. That's what I do.'

'But this country belongs to us all,' I said, somewhat disconcerted by this turn in the conversation.

'It belongs to us, but you are destroying it.'

'How are we destroying it?'

'You are destroying it with your cars and trains, you are destroying it with your houses. In a few years there won't be anywhere for trees to grow, for grass to send out green shoots, or for rivers to flow freely. We have already lost our freedom. You have imprisoned us in your mines and factories. You have cast us into slums.' He paced angrily from the table, stopping at the window behind me. I realised that all this had been bottled up inside him for far too long and that I'd better let him get it off his chest. 'This place,' he continued, 'and Alexandra and Orlando and Sophiatown – are these not the rubbish-dumps where you've thrown us in order to make more space for your houses, cars, trains and factories?'

'You came here from the countryside of your own free will,' I interjected.

'Because you forced us to live on farmlands and in villages that were far too small; because you shifted all the means of earning a living here. You knew very well that if you took the bones and buried them here, the dogs were sure to follow. And only now that we are here do we see that you buried the bones under concrete.'

'You have bones right here in your house, yet you refuse to eat them.'

'You can joke, but I warn you I'm not the only one who is taking this country back from under the white man's nose. Many others do the same.'

'How?'

'They slip quietly about you in the dark, stealing your property, raping your women, murdering. You think we don't know what we're about. But we know only too well we are making you afraid. We want you to become like small children in the darkness of this country . . .'

'But you won't live to see it happen.'

He turned to me questioningly.

'You are starving, Silwane, and hunger can become a killer illness.'
I got up to stand before him. Like a backwash, the gleam drained
from his eyes, leaving only a dull longing there. 'And it isn't only you,
but your mother as well. She fed you when you were young but now
that she's old, now that she has become the child, you don't feed her.'

He didn't answer but I could tell that my words had struck home.

'The hand that only takes empties itself, Silwane. To be full, the
hand must give.'

He looked up quickly, a new gleam in his eye. 'What did you give?'
he demanded in a gruff, barely audible voice. 'You took our whole
country, and what did you give besides starvation, gaols and the
anxiety of not knowing where we are free to move?'

'I am your friend, Silwane. Sell me one of your paintings so you can
eat and live.'

'And what kind of person are you to use a man's hunger in order to
take his country from him?' He spoke through tight lips.

'I'm not using your hunger.'

'You know I'm starving. You know a hungry man will sell even his
eyes for food. You know these things. But I recognise you for the
vulture you are. You're all vultures.' He was so angry words failed
him and he turned his back on me.

I went to the table to look at the painting of Moroka again. And
now I saw that centuries of hatred had been distilled in those simple
lines and surfaces. It was an apocalyptic vision.

'That's simply not true,' I answered calmly. 'You still have to learn
to know a friend when you see one.'

I took a five-pound note from my wallet.

It was a mistake. Silwane swung round like a wounded animal.

'I don't want your money.' He was shaking from head to foot.

'At least listen to me, Silwane . . .'

'I don't want your money!'

I dropped the note on the table and made for the door, but he was
quicker. 'I don't want it!' There were tears in his voice.

'Then throw it away,' I said resolutely, moving to the door again.
After that, the unexpected happened. He snatched up the canvas and
pressed it into my hands.

'Take it,' he said.

'But I don't want it, Silwane.'

'Then throw it away,' he repeated my own words. Large tears rolled down his cheeks as he ushered me gently out. 'But you mustn't come back. Don't ever come back again.'

He held the door open for me and I left without thanking him. I had nothing to say. A man had sold his eyes to me because he was starving.

Sorrow rose painfully in my throat.

The gate creaked shut and I stepped into the narrow, crooked alley.

Moroka was alive with muffled voices. The smouldering fires glared at me like red eyes through the smoke.

As silent and ghostly as a black moth in the darkness, a figure flitted past. And I was miserable, small and lonely in that world of shacks, a mouse trapped in a nightmare circus tent. I hurried along, stumbling over the soil of a country where I was just one of a few homeless and unwanted guests.

Translated by Catherine Knox and Martin Trump

CAN THEMBA

The Suit

Five-thirty in the morning, and the candlewick bedspread frowned as
the man under it stirred. He did not like to wake his wife lying by his
side – as yet – so he crawled up and out by careful peristalsis. But
before he tiptoed out of his room with shoes and socks under his arm,
he leaned over and peered at the sleeping serenity of his wife: to him a
daily matutinal miracle.

He grinned and yawned simultaneously, offering his wordless Te
Deum to whatever gods for the goodness of life; for the pure beauty of
his wife; for the strength surging through his willing body; for the
even, unperturbed rhythms of his passage through days and months
and years – it must be – to heaven.

Then he slipped soundlessly into the kitchen. He flipped aside the
curtain of the kitchen window, and saw outside a thin drizzle, the
type that can soak one to the skin, and that could go on for days and
days. He wondered, head aslant, why the rain in Sophiatown always
came in the morning when workers had to creep out of their burrows;
and then at how blistering heat waves came during the day when
messengers had to run errands all over; and then at how the rain
came back when workers knocked off and had to scurry home.

He smiled at the odd caprice of the heavens, and tossed his head at
the naughty incongruity, as if, 'Ai, but the gods!'

From behind the kitchen door, he removed an old rain cape,
peeling off in places, and swung it over his head. He dashed for the
lavatory, nearly slipping in a pool of muddy water, but he reached the
door. Aw, blast, someone had made it before him. Well, that is the
toll of staying in a yard where twenty . . . thirty other people have to
share the same lean-to. He was dancing and burning in that climactic
moment when trouser-fly will not come wide soon enough. He
stepped round the lavatory and watched the streamlets of rainwater
quickly wash away the jet of tension that spouted from him. That

infinite after-relief. Then he dashed back to his kitchen. He grabbed the old baby bath-tub hanging on a nail under the slight shelter of the gutterless roof-edge. He opened a large wooden box and quickly filled the bath-tub with coal. Then he inched his way back to the kitchen door and inside.

He was huh-huh-huhing one of those fugitive tunes that cannot be hidden, but often just occur and linger naggingly in the head. The fire he was making soon licked up cheerfully, in mood with his contentment.

He had a trick for these morning chores. While the fire in the old stove warmed up, the water kettle humming on it, he gathered and laid ready the things he would need for the day: briefcase and the files that go with it; the book that he was reading currently; the letters of his lawyer boss which he usually posted before he reached the office; his wife's and his own dry-cleaning slips for the Sixty-Minutes; his lunch tin solicitously prepared the night before by his attentive wife; and, today, the battered rain cape. By the time the kettle on the stove sang (before it actually boiled), he poured water from it into a wash basin, refilled and replaced it on the stove. Then he washed himself carefully: across the eyes, under, in and out the armpits, down the torso and in between the legs. This ritual was thorough, though no white man a-complaining of the smell of wogs knows anything about it. Then he dressed himself fastidiously. By this time he was ready to prepare breakfast.

Breakfast! How he enjoyed taking in a tray of warm breakfast to his wife, cuddled in bed. To appear there in his supremest immaculacy, tray in hand when his wife comes out of ether to behold him. These things we blacks want to do for our own . . . not fawningly for the whites for whom we bloody-well got to do it. He felt, he denied, that he was one of those who believed in putting his wife in her place even if she was a good wife. Not he.

Matilda, too, appreciated her husband's kindness, and only put her foot down when he offered to wash up also.

'Off with you,' she scolded him on his way.

At the bus-stop he was a little sorry to see that jovial old Maphikela was in a queue for a bus ahead of him. He would miss Maphikela's raucous laughter and uninhibited, bawdy conversations in fortissimo. Maphikela hailed him nevertheless. He thought he noticed hesitation in the old man, and a slight clouding of his countenance, but the old man shouted back at him, saying that he would wait for him at the terminus in town.

Philemon considered this morning trip to town with garrulous old Maphikela as his daily bulletin. All the township news was generously reported by loud-mouthed heralds, and spiritedly discussed by the bus at large. Of course, 'news' included views on bosses (scurrilous), the Government (rude), Ghana and Russia (idolatrous), America and the West (sympathetically ridiculing), and boxing (bloodthirsty). But it was always stimulating and surprisingly comprehensive for so short a trip. And there was no law of libel.

Maphikela was standing under one of those token bus-stop shelters that never keep out rain nor wind nor sun-heat. Philemon easily located him by his noisy ribbing of some office boys in their khaki-green uniforms. They walked together into town, but from Maphikela's suddenly subdued manner, Philemon gathered that there was something serious coming up. Maybe a loan.

Eventually, Maphikela came out with it.

'Son,' he said sadly, 'if I could've avoided this, believe you me I would, but my wife is nagging the spice out of my life for not talking to you about it.'

It just did not become blustering old Maphikela to sound so grave and Philemon took compassion upon him.

'Go ahead, dad,' he said generously. 'You know you can talk to me about anything.'

The old man gave a pathetic smile. 'We-e-e-ll, it's not really any of our business . . . er . . . but my wife felt . . . you see. Damn it all! I wish these women would not snoop around so much.' Then he rushed it. 'Anyway, it seems there's a young man who's going to visit your wife every morning . . . ah . . . for these last bloomin' three months. And that wife of mine swears by her heathen gods you don't know a thing about it.'

It was not quite like the explosion of a devastating bomb. It was more like the critical breakdown in an infinitely delicate piece of mechanism. From outside the machine just seemed to have gone dead. But deep in its innermost recesses, menacing electrical flashes were leaping from coil to coil, and hot, viscous molten metal was creeping upon the fuel tanks . . .

Philemon heard gears grinding and screaming in his head . . .

'Dad,' he said hoarsely, 'I . . . I have to go back home.'

He turned round and did not hear old Maphikela's anxious, 'Steady, son. Steady, son.'

The bus ride home was a torture of numb dread and suffocating despair. Though the bus was now emptier Philemon suffered crushing claustrophobia. There were immense washerwomen whose immense bundles of soiled laundry seemed to baulk and menace him. From those bundles crept miasmata of sweaty intimacies that sent nauseous waves up and down from his viscera. Then the wild swaying of the bus as it negotiated Mayfair Circle hurtled him sickeningly from side to side. Some of the younger women shrieked delightedly to the driver, '*Fuduga*! . . . Stir the pot!' as he swung his steering-wheel this way and that. Normally, the crazy tilting of the bus gave him a prickling exhilaration. But now . . .

He felt like getting out of there, screamingly, elbowing everything out of his way. He wished this insane trip were over, and then again, he recoiled at the thought of getting home. He made a tremendous resolve to gather in all the torn, tingling threads of his nerves contorting in the raw. By a merciless act of will, he kept them in subjugation as he stepped out of the bus back in the Victoria Road terminus, Sophiatown.

The calm he achieved was tense . . . but he could think now . . . he could take a decision . . .

With almost boyishly innocent urgency, he rushed through his kitchen into his bedroom. In the lightning flash that the eye can whip, he saw it all . . . the man beside his wife . . . the chestnut arm around her neck . . . the ruffled candlewick bedspread . . . the suit across the chair. But he affected not to see.

He opened the wardrobe door, and as he dug into it, he cheerfully spoke to his wife, 'Fancy, Tilly, I forgot to take my pass. I had already reached town, and was going to walk up to the office. If it hadn't been for wonderful old Mr Maphikela.'

A swooshing noise of violent retreat and the clap of his bedroom window stopped him. He came from behind the wardrobe door and looked out from the open window. A man clad only in vest and underpants was running down the street. Slowly, he turned round and contemplated . . . the suit.

Philemon lifted it gingerly under his arm and looked at the stark horror in Matilda's eyes. She was now sitting up in bed. Her mouth twitched, but her throat raised no words.

'Ha,' he said, 'I see we have a visitor,' indicating the blue suit. 'We really must show some of our hospitality. But first, I must phone my boss that I can't come to work today . . . mmmm–er, my wife's not well. Be back in a moment, then we can make arrangements.' He took the suit along.

When he returned he found Matilda weeping on the bed. He dropped the suit beside her, pulled up the chair, turned it round so that its back came in front of him, sat down, brought down his chin on to his folded arms before him, and waited for her.

After a while the convulsions of her shoulders ceased. She saw a smug man with an odd smile and meaningless inscrutability in his eyes. He spoke to her with very little noticeable emotion; if anything, with a flutter of humour.

'We have a visitor, Tilly.' His mouth curved ever so slightly. 'I'd like him to be treated with the greatest of consideration. He will eat every meal with us and share all we have. Since we have no spare room, he'd better sleep in here. But the point is, Tilly, that you will meticulously look after him. If he vanishes or anything else happens to him . . .' A shaft of evil shot from his eye . . . 'Matilda, I'll kill you.'

He rose from the chair and looked with incongruous supplication at her. He told her to put the fellow in the wardrobe for the time being. As she passed him to get the suit, he turned to go. She ducked frantically, and he stopped.

'You don't seem to understand me, Matilda. There's to be no violence in this house if you and I can help it. So, just look after that suit.' He went out.

He went out to the Sophiatown Post Office, which is placed on the exact line between Sophiatown and the white man's surly Westdene. He posted his boss's letters, and walked to the beerhall at the tail end of Western Native Township. He had never been inside it before, but somehow the thunderous din laved his bruised spirit. He stayed there all day.

He returned home for supper . . . and surprise. His dingy little home had been transformed, and the air of stern masculinity it had hitherto contained had been wiped away, to be replaced by anxious feminine touches here and there. There were even gay, colourful curtains swirling in the kitchen window. The old-fashioned coal stove gleamed in its blackness. A clean, chequered oil cloth on the table. Supper ready.

Then she appeared in the doorway of the bedroom. Heavens! here was the woman he had married; the young, fresh, cocoa-coloured maid who had sent rushes of emotion shuddering through him. And the dress she wore brought out all the girlishness of her, hidden so long beneath German print. But no hint of coquettishness, although she stood in the doorway and slid her arm up the jamb, and shyly slanted her head to the other shoulder. She smiled weakly.

'What makes a woman like this experiment with adultery?' he wondered.

Philemon closed his eyes and gripped the seat of his chair on both sides as some overwhelming, undisciplined force sought to catapult him towards her. For a moment some essence glowed fiercely within him, then sank back into itself and died . . .

He sighed and smiled sadly back at her, 'I'm hungry, Tilly.'

The spell snapped, and she was galvanised into action. She prepared his supper with dexterous hands that trembled a little only when they hesitated in mid-air. She took her seat opposite him, regarded him curiously, clasped her hands waiting for his prayer, but in her heart she murmured some other, much more urgent prayer of her own.

'Matilda!' he barked. 'Our visitor!' The sheer savagery with which he cracked at her jerked her up, but only when she saw the brute cruelty in his face did she run out of the room, toppling the chair behind her.

She returned with the suit on a hanger, and stood there quivering like a feather. She looked at him with helpless dismay. The demoniacal rage in his face was evaporating, but his heavy breathing still rocked his thorax above the table, to and fro.

'Put a chair, there.' He indicated with a languid gesture of his arm. She moved like a ghost as she drew a chair to the table.

'Now seat our friend at the table . . . no, no, not like that. Put him in front of the chair, and place him on the seat so that he becomes indeed the third person.'

Philemon went on relentlessly: 'Dish up for him. Generously. I imagine he hasn't had a morsel all day, the poor devil.'

Now, as consciousness and thought seeped back into her, her movements revolved so that always she faced this man who had changed so spectacularly. She started when he rose to open the window and let in some air.

She served the suit. The act was so ridiculous that she carried it out with a bitter sense of humiliation. He came back to sit down and plunge into his meal. No grace was said for the first time in this house. With his mouth full, he indicated by a toss of his head that she should sit down in her place. She did so. Glancing at her plate, the thought occurred to her that someone, after a long famine, was served a sumptuous supper, but as the food reached her mouth it turned to sawdust. Where had she heard it?

Matilda could not eat. She suddenly broke into tears.

Philemon took no notice of her weeping. After supper, he casually gathered the dishes and started washing up. He flung a dry cloth at her without saying a word. She rose and went to stand by his side drying up. But for their wordlessness, they seemed a very devoted couple.

After washing up, he took the suit and turned to her. 'That's how I want it every meal, every day.' Then he walked into the bedroom.

So it was. After that first breakdown, Matilda began to feel that her punishment was not too severe, considering the heinousness of the crime. She tried to put a joke into it, but by slow, unconscious degrees, the strain nibbled at her. Philemon did not harass her much more, so long as the ritual with the confounded suit was conscientiously followed.

Only once, he got one of his malevolent brainwaves. He got it into his head that 'our visitor' needed an outing. Accordingly the suit was taken to the dry cleaners during the week, and, come Sunday, they had to take it out for a walk. Both Philemon and Matilda dressed for the occasion. Matilda had to carry the suit on its hanger over her back and the three of them strolled leisurely along Ray Street. They passed the church crowd in front of the famous Anglican Mission of Christ the King. Though the worshippers saw nothing unusual in them, Matilda felt, searing through her, red-hot needles of embarrassment, and every needle-point was a public eye piercing into her degradation.

But Philemon walked casually on. He led her down Ray Street and turned into Main Road. He stopped often to look into shop windows or to greet a friend passing by. They went up Toby Street, turned into Edward Road, and back home. To Philemon the outing was free of incident, but to Matilda it was one long, excruciating incident.

At home, he grabbed a book on Abnormal Psychology, flung himself into a chair and calmly said to her, 'Give the old chap a rest, will you, Tilly?'

In the bedroom, Matilda said to herself that things could not go on like this. She thought of how she could bring the matter to a head with Philemon; have it out with him once and for all. But the memory of his face, that first day she had forgotten to entertain the suit, stayed her. She thought of running away, but where to? Home? What could she tell her old-fashioned mother had happened between Philemon and her? All right, run away clean then. She thought of many young married girls who were divorcees now, who had won their freedom.

What had happened to Staff Nurse Kakile? The woman drank heavily now, and when she got drunk, the boys of Sophiatown passed her around and called her the Cesspot.

Matilda shuddered.

An idea struck her. There were still decent, married women around Sophiatown. She remembered how after the private schools had been forced to close with the advent of Bantu Education, Father Harringay of the Anglican Mission had organised Cultural Clubs. One, she seemed to remember, was for married women. If only she could lose herself in some cultural activity, find absolution for her conscience in some doing good; that would blur her blasted home life, would restore her self-respect. After all, Philemon had not broadcast her disgrace abroad . . . nobody knew; not one of Sophiatown's slander-mongers suspected how vulnerable she was. She must go and see Mrs Montjane about joining a Cultural Club. She must ask Philemon now if she might . . . she must ask him nicely.

She got up and walked into the other room where Philemon was reading quietly. She dreaded disturbing him, did not know how to begin talking to him . . . they had talked so little for so long. She went and stood in front of him, looking silently upon his deep concentration. Presently, he looked up with a frown on his face.

Then she dared, 'Phil, I'd like to join one of those Cultural Clubs for married women. Would you mind?'

He wrinkled his nose and rubbed it between thumb and index finger as he considered the request. But he had caught the note of anxiety in her voice and thought he knew what it meant.

'Mmmm,' he said, nodding. 'I think that's a good idea. You can't be moping around all day. Yes, you may, Tilly.' Then he returned to his book.

The Cultural Club idea was wonderful. She found women like herself, with time (if not with tragedy) on their hands, engaged in wholesome, refreshing activities. The atmosphere was cheerful and cathartic. They learned things and they did things. They organised

fêtes, bazaars, youth activities, sport, music, self-help and community projects. She got involved in committees, meetings, debates,
conferences. It was for her a whole new venture into humancraft, and
her personality blossomed. Philemon gave her all the rein she
wanted.

Now, abiding by that silly ritual at home seemed a little thing . . . a
very little thing . . .

Then one day she decided to organise a little party for her friends
and their husbands. Philemon was very decent about it. He said it
was all right. He even gave her extra money for it. Of course, she
knew nothing of the strain he himself suffered from his mode of
castigation.

There was a week of hectic preparation. Philemon stepped out of
its cluttering way as best he could. So many things seemed to be
taking place simultaneously. New dresses were made. Cakes were
baked: three different orders of meat prepared; beef for the uninvited
chancers; mutton for the normal guests; turkey and chicken for the
inner pith of the club's core. To Philemon, it looked as if Matilda
planned to feed the multitude on the Mount with no aid of miracles.

On the Sunday of the party, Philemon saw Matilda's guests. He
was surprised by the handsome grace with which she received them.
There was a long table with enticing foods and flowers and serviettes.
Matilda placed all her guests round the table, and the party was
ready to begin in the mock-formal township fashion. Outside a steady
rumble of conversation went on where the human odds and ends of
every Sophiatown party had their 'share'.

Matilda caught the curious look on Philemon's face. He tried to
disguise his edict when he said, 'Er . . . the guest of honour.'

But Matilda took a chance. She begged, 'Just this once, Phil.'

He became livid. 'Matilda!' he shouted, 'Get our visitor!' Then
with incisive sarcasm, 'Or are you ashamed of him?'

She went ash-grey; but there was nothing for it but to fetch her
albatross. She came back and squeezed a chair into some corner, and
placed the suit on it. Then she slowly placed a plate of food before it.
For a while the guests were dumbfounded. Then curiosity flooded in.
They talked at the same time. 'What's the idea, Philemon?' . . . 'Why
must she serve a suit?' . . . 'What's happening?' Some just giggled in a
silly way. Philemon carelessly swung his head towards Matilda. 'You
better ask my wife. She knows the fellow best.'

All interest beamed upon poor Matilda. For a moment she could not speak, all enveloped in misery. Then she said, unconvincingly, 'It's just a game that my husband and I play at mealtime.' They roared with laughter. Philemon let her get away with it.

The party went on, and every time Philemon's glare sent Matilda scurrying to serve the suit each course; the guests were no-end amused by the persistent mock-seriousness with which this husband and wife played out their little game. Only, to Matilda, it was no joke; it was a hot poker down her throat. After the party, Philemon went off with one of the guests who had promised to show him a joint 'that sells genuine stuff, boy, genuine stuff'.

Reeling drunk, late that sabbath, he crashed through his kitchen door, onwards to his bedroom. Then he saw her.

They have a way of saying in the argot of Sophiatown, 'Cook out of the head!' signifying that someone was impacted with such violent shock that whatever whiffs of alcohol still wandered through his head were instantaneously evaporated and the man stood sober before stark reality.

There she lay, curled, as if just before she died she begged for a little love, implored some implacable lover to cuddle her a little . . . just this once . . . just this once more.

In screwish anguish, Philemon cried, 'Tilly!'

BHEKI MASEKO

Mamlambo

Mamlambo is a kind of snake that brings fortune to anyone who accommodates it. One's money or livestock multiplies incredibly.

This snake is available from traditional doctors who provide instructions regarding its exploitation. Certain necessities are to be sacrificed in order to maintain it. Sometimes you may have to sacrifice your own children, or go without a car or clothes. It all depends on the instructions of the doctor concerned.

The duties involved are so numerous that some people tend to forget some of them. A beast must be slaughtered from time to time. And failure to comply with the instructions results in disaster.

It is said that this monster can kill an entire family, always starting with the children and leaving its owner for last.

Getting rid of this fortune snake is not an easy task after one has had enough of luck and sacrificing. Some say a beast must be slaughtered. Then the entire carcass must be enfolded with the skin and thrown away. This is done in the presence of an indigenous doctor who performs the necessary ritual.

Another will come along, pick up a shiny object – and Mamlambo is his.

Many stories have been told about this monster. Here is one about how Sophie acquired Mamlambo and what happened to her.

Sophie Zikode was a young, ebony faced, beautiful woman with a beautiful body; neither slim nor fat.

She worked in a Johannesburg suburb and lived in the servants' quarters attached to the white family's house.

Before coming to work in the Golden City Sophie had never had a steady boyfriend. But one man remained her lover for longer than the others. His name was Elias Malinga from Ermelo. He was the first man she met in Johannesburg and the only man she truly loved.

So besotted was she with this man that she readily discarded any possessions or habits that Elias disliked. Elias was a married man and loved his wife and children who stayed in Ermelo. Sophie was aware that her lover had a family but this did not matter to her.

One day Sophie and Elias had a quarrel. Elias got up and walked out on her. A few days went by. A week. Sophie could bear it no longer. She phoned his place of employment and asked to speak to him. A friend came to the phone and told the distraught woman that Elias had had enough of her. She never heard from him again.

After Elias Sophie never again had a steady boyfriend. They all deserted her after two or three months. But this did not hurt the unfortunate woman. The only name that haunted her day and night was 'Elias'.

Since her love affair with Elias Sophie never really loved another man. All she wanted now was a husband she could be loyal to. But she could not find one.

Until Jonas came into her life.

Jonas was a tall, well-built Malawian. He was considerate and responsible. And this set him apart from the other men.

For the first time in her life a thought came to her mind. She must consult a traditional doctor for help. She wanted to keep Jonas forever. She must see Baba Majola.

One morning Sophie set off to see Baba Majola. He was a street cleaner. The old man listened sympathetically to her problem while he swept rubbish out of a gutter. He told her to return to him at 4 pm that afternoon. Sophie was there on time.

Baba Majola gave her a smelly, sticky concoction in a bottle. He advised her to rub her whole body with it before her boyfriend called on her. And to put it underneath her pillow when they slept together.

Sophie carried out the doctor's orders to the letter.

Sophie had prepared a meal for her and Jonas and they sat down to eat. Except for the ticking of the small clock on the table between them, they ate in complete silence. Jonas was usually cheerful and talkative and his unusual behaviour this evening disturbed Sophie. Did this have anything to do with Majola's potion? she wondered.

That night in bed Jonas was awakened by something peculiar under the pillow. It felt cold and smooth.

'Sophie,' he whispered in the dark, 'there's something under the pillow . . . what is it?'

'I don't know,' she replied sleepily. 'Switch on the light, let's have a look.'

Jonas fumbled for the switch.

'A snake!' Jonas cried.

The couple leapt out of bed and ran to the door. In their haste to get out they struggled to open the door. Jonas turned the key, yanked the door open and they both fled into the brightly lit street.

They ran to a neighbour's house and knocked on the door of the servant's room there. Sophie's friend Sheila opened up. Her eyes, bleary with sleep, widened when she saw her half-naked friends.

Quickly they told Sheila what had happened. She gave them both some clothes for the sake of warmth and decency. Sheila's own boyfriend had left a coat in her room and she gave this to Jonas. Then the threesome went back to Sophie's room.

Through the window they saw the snake lying contentedly on the bed. Sophie was scared, but Jonas could hardly speak!

Sophie could no longer keep her secret. Still shaking she turned to Jonas. She told him about the potion she had received from Baba Majola and how she had smeared it on her body before he arrived that night.

'I did it because I wanted to keep you forever,' she said tearfully.

Sophie and Jonas decided to visit a traditional doctor for advice. They chose a man who lived a few streets away. Sheila accompanied them.

They knocked and, after waiting a while, the doctor answered. He opened the door but no sooner had he done this than he slammed it shut again.

'Wait outside,' they heard him say, 'I sense something melancholy.'

Then they heard the muffled sounds of the doctor chanting in a strange language. The smell of burning muti reached their nostrils.

The indigenous doctor began to moan as if he were speaking to gods in a faraway land. Finally he opened the door and enquired what their problem was.

Sophie retold her story.

'Oh!' he shuddered. 'What you have in your room is Mamlambo.'

'No!' Sophie gasped. 'What have I done to deserve such punishment? What big sin have I committed to be punished in this manner!' Tears of despair rolled down her cheeks.

'Crying won't solve the problem, child,' said the doctor in broken Zulu. 'You have to get rid of the snake. I can help you if you co-operate. I'll give you a suitcase to take back to your room . . .'

'No, no, no,' Sophie shook her head vigorously, 'I cannot go back there!'

'The choice is yours, my girl. You either keep it or get rid of it. The sooner the better because if you don't it will be with you wherever you go. It is your snake now. The witchdoctor was tired of it so he transferred it to you. You are duty-bound to transfer it to someone else or keep it.'

'Transfer it to someone else?' Sophie saw no sense in this. 'Can't we simply throw it into the river?'

'That is not an option,' the doctor said, losing his patience with this unreasonable girl. 'Either you transfer it or you keep it. Do you want me to help or not?'

'Yes,' Sophie pleaded. She glanced at Sheila and the timid Jonas for approval.

The traditional doctor took a large suitcase from a wardrobe. He sprinkled some muti into the empty case and burnt it. Again he intoned the gods for what seemed like an eternity. Eventually he closed the case and handed it to the reluctant Sophie.

'Take this case to your room and put it next to your bed. The snake will roll itself into the case.'

Sophie looked at him doubtfully.

'It's your snake, it won't harm you,' the doctor assured her. 'After you have captured it go to a busy place and hand it to someone.'

'To whom?' Sophie asked.

'That is entirely up to you.'

They thanked the doctor and went back to Sophie's room. The snake was still there.

Sophie plucked up courage and tiptoed into the room. She opened the suitcase and placed it next to her bed.

Slowly, as if it were smelling something, the snake lifted its head. It slid into the case and gathered itself into a neat coil.

Sophie had an idea. It was almost 8 pm but Johannesburg Station would still be bustling with workers who, for one or other reason, were loath to leave the bright lights of the city. And those who were journeying to faraway cities. She would go immediately to seek out Mamlambo's new owner there!

Jonas and Sheila wished her well.

Sophie walked to the taxi rank impervious to the weight of the suitcase.

She did not want to do this to anyone but she had no option.

Remembering that taxis were scarce after 8.00 she quickened her pace. A few police cars patrolled the affluent suburb. Probably because of the high rate of housebreakings, she thought.

At the bus stop she stood, tense and determined to get rid of her unwanted luggage.

On the corner, about fifty metres away, the traffic light turned green and a patrol car slowly made its way down the road towards her. Should she drop the suitcase and run? But they had already seen her and she would not get far. How would she explain the contents of the case to the police? Would they believe her story? The news would spread like wildfire that she is a witch. What would Elias think of her?

There were two policemen in the van. The one in the passenger seat had already turned down his window when the van stopped.

'What are you doing here so late?' he demanded.

'I'm waiting for a taxi,' said Sophie. 'I'm going to the station.' She was surprised that her voice sounded so steady.

'We don't want to find you here when we come back,' warned the policeman eyeing the suitcase. The van pulled away slowly.

Sophie was relieved when a taxi arrived. The driver loaded the suitcase in the boot. He asked her why it was so heavy.

'Groceries,' she said.

There were two other passengers in the taxi who both got off before the taxi reached the city.

'Are you going to the station?' enquired the driver.

'No,' Sophie said, 'I'm going to the bus terminus.'

'I know you're going to the station and I'm taking you there,' the driver said.

'You can't take me to the station,' Sophie said, surprised by the man's familiarity. 'I'm going to the bus terminus in Main Street.'

The man ignored her and drove straight to the station, smiling smugly. At the station he got out of the car and removed the suitcase from the boot.

Sophie paid him and gestured that she wanted her suitcase. He ignored her.

'Which platform?' the man asked her. 'I want to take you there.'

'I don't want your help at all,' Sophie snapped. 'Give me my suitcase and leave me alone!' She was now very agitated.

The man ignored her desperate plea.

'You're going to the luggage office then,' he decided and proceeded towards the brightly lit office.

Sophie was in a quandary: Should she leave the suitcase with this man and vanish from the scene? Or should she wait and see what happens? What was this man up to? Did he know what was in the suitcase or was he simply suspicious? If she bolted now he would find her quite easily. If only she had brought someone with her.

Suddenly she was overwhelmed by anger. Something told her to take her suitcase from the man by force. He had no business to interfere in her affairs. She went into the office, pulled the suitcase from between the man's legs and stormed out.

Stiff-legged, Sophie walked towards the station platform feeling eyes following her. She zig-zagged through the crowds, deaf to the pandemonium of voices and music blaring from portable radios.

She hoped the man was not following her but did not dare look back to see.

'Hey you, girl! Where do you think you're going?' It was the voice of the taxi driver.

She stopped dead in her tracks but did not turn around. She felt a lump in her throat and tears began to roll down her cheeks. She shook with anger. Suddenly she turned around and screamed at the man.

'What do you want from me?'

His worn-out cap was tipped at an angle. His hands were stuck deep in his khaki coat pocket. With his eyebrows arched he smiled at Sophie coolly.

The man's arrogance angered her even more.

A crowd had begun to gather.

'You are running away and you are trying to erase traces,' the man said. From time to time he fingered his cap.

A policeman came forward.

'What's going on here?' he demanded.

'This man has been following me from the bus stop and won't leave me alone,' Sophie stammered tearfully.

'This woman is a liar,' said the man. 'She boarded my taxi and has been nervous all the way from Kensington. She's running away from something. She's a crook!' He turned to the crowd for approval.

'Liar!' Sophie screamed. 'I did not board your taxi and I don't know you. You followed me when I left the bus rank!'

'Let her open the case and let's see what's inside,' the man said. He walked towards the case.

The crowd broke into an excited murmur.

'All right, all right,' the policeman intervened. 'Quiet everybody. I do the talking now. Young man, do you know this woman?'

'I picked her up at Kens . . .'

'I said do you know her!'

'Yes, she was in my taxi . . .'

'Listen, young man,' said the policeman, getting impatient, 'I asked you a straightforward question and I want a straightforward answer. For the last time, do you know this woman?' He pointed emphatically at Sophie.

'No,' replied the man sheepishly. He adjusted his cap.

'Off you go then, before I arrest you for public disturbance.' He waved the man on. Then he turned to Sophie.

'My child,' the policeman said kindly, 'go where you are going. This rascal has no business to interfere in your affairs.'

Relieved, Sophie picked up her suitcase and thanked the policeman. She made her way towards Platform 14 as the policeman dispersed the crowd.

Platform 14. The old woman grew impatient. What's holding him? she wondered. Every second month she collected her pension. The taxi then dropped them on the platform and her son went to buy food for the train journey home. This ritual had been going on for years. Today though, her son was unusually long in coming back.

A young, pretty woman, suitcase in hand, came up to the bench where the old woman sat.

'Greetings, Gogo,' said the young woman, her smile producing dimples. She put the case down carefully.

'Greetings, my child,' said the old woman, regarding this lovely woman. A symbol of a lovely and respectable makoti, she thought.

'When is the Durban train departing? Sophie asked, looking at her watch.

'At ten o'clock, child.'

The conversation was very easy with the friendly old woman. As they spoke more and more people spilled on to the platform.

Then Sophie made her decision.

'Gogo, will you look after my luggage while I go to the shop? I won't be long.'

'Certainly, my child.'

Sophie pushed the suitcase nearer to the woman's own luggage.

She hurried away, along the platform and up a flight of stairs. When she reached the top she was panting.

To her surprise here was Elias shaking hands with another man! The two men chatted away excitedly like old friends who hadn't seen each other for a long time.

Sophie stood there confused. Elias's back was turned to her and the place was teeming with people. Quickly she regained her wits and mingled with the crowd. Without looking back she made her way through the busy arcade and into the street.

She was relieved when she reached her servant's room late that night. She was rid of Mamlambo. And she had come within a hair's breadth of meeting her ex-lover. Luckily he was too engrossed in chatting to his friend to see her.

And that infuriating taxi driver! What would he have done if she had accidentally gotten into his taxi on her way back home?

Something bothered Sophie. Who was the old woman? And why did she choose her as the snake's unfortunate new owner? Did she know this woman from some distant past? She searched her memory but came up with nothing.

Did she take the suitcase? Sophie wondered.

And Elias? What was he doing there? She suddenly felt a deep resentment for him. To do what he had done to her was so cruel! And how he had humiliated her when she phoned his work. Suddenly she grew angry for having allowed herself to be dominated by a love that brought no peace or happiness. And Jonas was there now giving all the love and kindness he possessed.

For the first time in her life Sophie fell in love with Jonas. But would he accept her after her foolish actions? If only he would ask her to marry him. She would not do it for the sake of getting married, she would agree because she truly loved him.

The next day Jonas and a Nyasa doctor visited Sophie. She told them about her adventures the night before, but Jonas seemed preoccupied. Finally he spoke.

'My father wants me back in Malawi because he can no longer handle the farm by himself.'

'Then you're leaving me,' Sophie moaned in despair.

'No,' Jonas smiled, 'I want you to come with me.'

The plane took off and the crowds waved cheerfully. Sophie felt that it was taking her away from the monster that had terrified her a few weeks ago.

The building below grew smaller as the plane made its ascent until all she saw was a vast blue sky underneath.

Where, in one of those houses, was Mamlambo? she wondered. She would never know that the evil snake had become the property of Elias Malinga. Yes, after Elias had chatted with his friend he went to his mother on the platform.

'Whose case is this, Mama?'

'A lovely young girl's. She asked me to look after it for her until she returns from the shop. But she's been gone a long time.'

'Well, if she doesn't come back, I'll take it.'

MANGO TSHABANGU

Thoughts in a Train

When we ride these things which cannot take us all, there is no doubt as to our inventiveness. We stand inside in grotesque positions – one foot in the air, our bodies twisted away from arms squeezing through other twisted bodies to find support somewhere. Sometimes it is on another person's shoulder, but it is stupid to complain so nobody does. It's as if some invisible sardine packer has been at work. We remain in that position for forty minutes or forty days. How far is Soweto from Johannesburg? It is forty minutes or forty days. No one knows exactly.

We remain in that position, our bodies sweating out the unfreedom of our souls, anticipating happiness in that unhappy architectural shame – the ghetto. Our eyes dart apprehensively, on the lookout for those of our brothers who have resorted to the insanity of crime to protest their insane conditions. For, indeed, if we were not scared of moral ridicule we would regard crime as a form of protest. Is not a man with a hungry stomach in the same position as a man whose land has been taken from him? What if he is a victim in both ways!

We remain in that position for forty minutes or forty days. No one knows exactly. We, the young, cling perilously to the outside of the coach walls. It sends the guts racing to the throat, yes, but to us it is bravery. We are not a helpless gutless lot whose lives have been patterned by suffering. The more daring among us dance like gods of fate on the rooftop. Sometimes there is death by electrocution but then it is just hard luck . . . He was a good man, Bayekile. It is not his fault that he did not live to face a stray bullet.

We remain in that position for forty minutes or forty days. No one knows exactly.

We move parallel to or hurtle past their trains. Most often my impression is that it is they who cruise past our hurtling train. Theirs is always almost empty. They'll sit comfortably on seats made for that purpose and keep their windows shut, even on hot days. And they sit there in their train watching us as one watches a play from a private box. We also stare back at them, but the sullen faces don't interest us much. Only the shut windows move our thinking.

On this day it was Msongi and Gezani who were most interested in the shut windows. You see, ever since they'd discovered Houghton golf course to be offering better tips in the caddy business, Msongi and Gezani found themselves walking through the rich suburbs of Johannesburg. Their experience was a strange one. There was something eerie in the surroundings. They always had fear, the like of which they'd never known. Surely it was not because of the numerous policemen who patrolled the streets and snarled in unison with their dogs at black boys moving through those gracious thoroughfares.

Msongi and Gezani were young no doubt, but bravery born of suffering knows no age nor danger nor pattern. Fear of snarling policemen was out for these two young black boys. Nevertheless, this overwhelming fear the like of which they'd never known was always all around them whenever they walked through the rich suburbs of Johannesburg. They could not even talk about it. Somehow, they were sure they both had this strange fear.

There was a time when they impulsively stood right in the middle of a street. They had hoped to break this fear the like of which they'd never known. But the attempt only lasted a few seconds and that was too short to be of any help. They both scurried off, hating themselves for lack of courage. They never spoke of it.

In search of the truth, Msongi became very observant. He'd been noticing the shut windows of *their* train every time he and Gezani happened to be in ours. On this day, it was a week since Msongi had decided to break the silence. Msongi's argument was that the fear was in the surroundings and not in them. The place was full of fear. Vicious fear which, although imprisoned in stone walls and electrified fences, swelled over and poured into the streets to oppress even the occasional passer-by. Msongi and Gezani were merely walking through this fear. It was like walking in darkness and feeling the darkness all around you. That does not mean you are darkness yourself. As soon as you come to a lit spot, the feeling of darkness dies. Why, as soon as they hit town proper, and mixed with the people, the fear the like of which they'd never known disappeared. No, Msongi was convinced it was not they who had fear. Fear flowed from somewhere, besmirching every part of them, leaving their souls trembling; but it was not they who were afraid.

They did not have stone walls or electrified fences in Soweto. They were not scared of their gold rings being snatched for they had none. They were not worried about their sisters being peeped at for their sisters could look after themselves. Oh, those diamond toothpicks could disappear you know . . . Those too, they did not have. They were not afraid of bleeding, for their streets ran red already. On this day Msongi stared at the shut windows. He looked at the pale sullen white faces and he knew why.

He felt tempted to throw something at them. Anything . . . an empty cigarette box, an orange peel, even a piece of paper; just to prove a point. At that moment, and as if instructed by Msongi himself, someone threw an empty beer bottle at the other train.

The confusion: they ran around climbing on to seats. They jumped into the air. They knocked against one another as they scrambled for the doors and windows. The already pale faces had no colour to change into. They could only be distorted as fear is capable of doing that as well. The shut windows were shattered wide open, as if to say danger cannot be imprisoned. The train passed swiftly by, disappearing with the drama of the fear the like of which Msongi and Gezani had never known.

DAN JACOBSON

The Zulu and the Zeide

Old man Grossman was worse than a nuisance. He was a source of constant anxiety and irritation; he was a menace to himself and to the passing motorists into whose path he would step, to the children in the streets whose games he would break up, sending them flying, to the householders who at night would approach him with clubs in their hands, fearing him a burglar; he was a butt and a jest to the African servants who would tease him on street corners.

It was impossible to keep him in the house. He would take any opportunity to slip out — a door left open meant that he was on the streets, a window unlatched was a challenge to his agility, a walk in the park was as much a game of hide-and-seek as a walk. The old man's health was good, physically; he was quite spry, and he could walk far, and he could jump and duck if he had to. All his physical activity was put to only one purpose: to running away. It was a passion for freedom that the old man might have been said to have, could anyone have seen what joy there could have been for him in wandering aimlessly about the streets, in sitting footsore on pavements, in entering other people's homes, in stumbling behind advertisement hoardings that fenced undeveloped building plots, in toiling up the stairs of fifteen-storey blocks of flats in which he had no business, in being brought home by large young policemen who winked at Harry Grossman, the old man's son, as they gently hauled his father out of their flying-squad cars.

'He's always been like this,' Harry would say, when people asked him about his father. And when they smiled and said: 'Always?' Harry would say, 'Always. I know what I'm talking about. He's my father, and I know what he's like. He gave my mother enough grey hairs before her time. All he knew was to run away.'

Harry's reward would come when the visitors would say: 'Well, at least you're being as dutiful to him as anyone can be.'

It was a reward that Harry always refused. 'Dutiful? What can you do? There's nothing else you can do.' Harry Grossman knew that there was nothing else he could do. Dutifulness had been his habit of life; it had had to be, having the sort of father he had, and the strain of duty had made him abrupt and begrudging. He even carried his thick, powerful shoulders curved inwards, to keep what he had to himself. He was a thick-set, bunch-faced man, with large bones, and short, jabbing gestures; he was in the prime of life, and he would point at the father from whom he had inherited his strength, and on whom the largeness of bone showed now only as so much extra leanness that the clothing had to cover, and say: 'You see him? Do you know what he once did? My poor mother saved enough money to send him from the old country to South Africa: she bought clothes for him, and a ticket, and she sent him to her brother, who was already here. He was going to make enough money to bring me out, and my mother and my brother, all of us. But on the boat from Bremen to London he met some other Jews who were going to South America, and they said to him: "Why are you going to South Africa? It's a wild country, the blacks there will eat you. Come to South America and you'll make a fortune." So in London he exchanges his ticket. And we don't hear from him for six months. Six months later he gets a friend to write to my mother asking her please to send him enough money to pay for his ticket back to the old country – he's dying in the Argentine, the Spaniards are killing him, he says, and he must come home. So my mother borrows from her brother to bring him back again. Instead of a fortune he brought her a new debt, and that was all.'

But Harry was dutiful, how dutiful his friends had reason to see again when they would urge him to try sending the old man to a home for the aged. 'No,' Harry would reply, his features moving heavily and reluctantly to a frown, a pout, as he showed how little the suggestion appealed to him. 'I don't like the idea. Maybe one day when he needs medical attention all the time I'll feel differently about it, but not now, not now. He wouldn't like it, he'd be unhappy. We'll look after him as long as we can. It's a job. It's something you've got to do.'

More eagerly Harry would go back to a recital of the old man's past. 'He couldn't even pay for his own passage out. I had to pay the loan back. We came out together – my mother wouldn't let him go by himself again, and I had to pay off her brother who advanced the money for us. I was a boy – what was I? – sixteen, seventeen, but I paid for his passage, and my own, and my mother's and then my brother's. It took me a long time, let me tell you. And then my troubles with him weren't over.' Harry even reproached his father for his myopia; he could clearly enough remember his chagrin when shortly after their arrival in South Africa, after it had become clear that Harry would be able to make his way in the world and be a support to the whole family, the old man – who at that time had not really been so old – had suddenly, almost dramatically, grown so short-sighted that he had been almost blind without the glasses which Harry had had to buy for him. And Harry could remember too how he had then made a practice of losing the glasses or breaking them with the greatest frequency, until it had been made clear to him that he was no longer expected to do any work. 'He doesn't do that any more. When he wants to run away now he sees to it that he's wearing his glasses. That's how he's always been. Sometimes he recognises me, at other times, when he doesn't want to, he just doesn't know who I am.'

What Harry said was true. Sometimes the old man would call out to his son, when he would see him at the end of a passage, 'Who are you?' Or he would come upon Harry in a room and demand of him, 'What do you want in my house?'

'Your house?' Harry would say, when he felt like teasing the old man. 'Your house?'

'Out of my house!' the old man would shout back.

'Your house? Do you call this your house?' Harry would reply, smiling at the old man's fury.

Harry was the only one in the house who talked to the old man, and then he did not so much talk to him, as talk of him to others. Harry's wife was a dim and silent woman, crowded out by her husband and the large-boned sons like himself that she had borne him, and she would gladly have seen the old man in an old-age home. But her husband had said no, so she put up with the old man, though for herself she could see no possible better end for him than a period of residence in a home for aged Jews which she had once visited, and which had impressed her most favourably with its glass and yellow brick, the noiseless rubber tiles in its corridors, its secluded grassed grounds, and the uniforms worn by the attendants to the establishment. But she put up with the old man; she did not talk to him. The grandchildren had nothing to do with their grandfather – they were busy at school, playing rugby and cricket, they could hardly speak Yiddish, and they were embarrassed by him in front of their friends; when the grandfather did take notice of them it was only to call them Boers and *goyim* and *shkolzim* in sudden quavering rages which did not disturb them at all.

The house itself – a big single-storied place of brick, with a corrugated iron roof above and a wide stoep all around – Harry Grossman had bought years before. In the continual rebuilding the suburb was undergoing it was beginning to look old fashioned. But it was solid and prosperous, and indoors curiously masculine in appearance, like the house of a widower. The furniture was of the heaviest African woods, dark, and built to last, the passages were lined with bare linoleum, and the few pictures on the walls, big brown and grey mezzotints in heavy frames, had not been looked at for years. The servants were both men, large ignored Zulus who did their work and kept up the brown gleam of the furniture.

It was from this house that old man Grossman tried to escape. He fled through the doors and the windows and into the wide sunlit streets of the town in Africa, where the blocks of flats were encroaching upon the single-storied houses behind their gardens. In these streets he wandered until he was found.

It was Johannes, one of the Zulu servants, who suggested a way of dealing with old man Grossman. He brought to the house one afternoon Paulus, whom he described as his 'brother'. Harry Grossman knew enough to know that 'brother' in this context could mean anything from the son of one's mother to a friend from a neighbouring kraal, but by the speech that Johannes made on Paulus' behalf he might indeed have been the latter's brother. Johannes had to speak for Paulus, for Paulus knew no English. Paulus was a 'raw boy', as raw as a boy could possibly come. He was a muscular, moustached and bearded African, with pendulous earlobes showing the slits in which the tribal plugs had once hung; on his feet he wore sandals the soles of which were cut from old motor car tyres, the thongs from red inner tubing. He wore neither hat nor socks, but he did have a pair of khaki shorts which were too small for him, and a shirt without any buttons; buttons would in any case have been of no use for the shirt could never have closed over his chest. He swelled magnificently out of his clothing, and above there was a head carried well back, so that his beard, which had been trained to grow in two sharp points from his chin, bristled ferociously forward under his melancholy and almost mandarin-like moustache. When he smiled, as he did once or twice during Johannes' speech, he showed his white, even teeth, but for the most part he stood looking rather shyly to the side of Harry Grossman's head, with his hands behind his back and his bare knees bent a little forward, as if to show how little he was asserting himself, no matter what his 'brother' might have been saying about him.

His expression did not change when Harry said that it seemed hopeless, that Paulus was too raw, and Johannes explained what the baas had just said. He nodded agreement when Johannes explained to him that the baas said that it was a pity that he knew no English. But whenever Harry looked at him, he smiled, not ingratiatingly, but simply smiling above his beard, as though saying: 'Try me'. Then he looked grave again as Johannes expatiated on his virtues. Johannes pleaded for his 'brother'. He said that the baas knew that he, Johannes, was a good boy. Would he, then, recommend to the baas a boy who was not a good boy too? The baas could see for himself, Johannes said, that Paulus was not one of these town boys, these street loafers: he was a good boy, come straight from the kraal. He was not a thief or a drinker. He was strong, he was a hard worker, he was clean, and he could be as gentle as a woman. If he, Johannes, were not telling the truth about all these things, then he deserved to be chased away. If Paulus failed in any single respect, then he, Johannes, would voluntarily leave the service of the baas, because he had said untrue things to the baas. But if the baas believed him, and gave Paulus his chance, then he, Johannes, would teach Paulus all the things of the house and the garden, so that Paulus would be useful to the baas in ways other than the particular task for which he was asking the baas to hire him. And, rather daringly, Johannes said that it did not matter so much if Paulus knew no English, because the old baas, the *oubaas*, knew no English either.

It was as something in the nature of a joke – almost a joke against his father – that Harry Grossman gave Paulus his chance. He was given a room in the servants' quarters in the backyard, into which he brought a tin trunk painted red and black, a roll of blankets, and a guitar with a picture of a cowboy on the back. He was given a houseboy's outfit of blue denim blouse and shorts, with red piping round the edges, into which he fitted, with his beard and his physique, like a king in exile in some pantomime. He was given his food three times a day, after the white people had eaten, a bar of soap every week, cast-off clothing at odd intervals, and the sum of one pound five shillings per week, five shillings of which he took, the rest being left at his request with the baas, as savings. He had a free afternoon once a week, and he was allowed to entertain not more than two friends at any one time in his room. In all the particulars that Johannes had enumerated, Johannes was proved reliable. Paulus was not one of these town boys, these street loafers. He did not steal or drink, he was clean and he was honest and hard-working. And he could be as gentle as a woman.

It took Paulus some time to settle down to his job; he had to conquer not only his own shyness and strangeness in the new house filled with strange people – let alone the city, which, since taking occupation of his room, he had hardly dared to enter – but also the hostility of old man Grossman, who took immediate fright at Paulus and redoubled his efforts to get away from the house upon Paulus' entry into it. As it happened, the first result of this persistence on the part of the old man was that Paulus was able to get the measure of the job, for he came to it with a willingness of spirit that the old man could not vanquish, but could only teach. Paulus had been given no instructions, he had merely been told to see that the old man did not get himself into trouble, and after a few days of bewilderment Paulus found his way. He simply went along with the old man.

At first he did so cautiously, following the old man at a distance, for he knew the other did not trust him. But later he was able to follow the old man openly; still later he was able to walk side by side with him, and the old man did not try to escape from him. When old man Grossman went out, Paulus went too, and there was no longer any need for the doors and windows to be watched, or the police to be telephoned. The young bearded Zulu and the old bearded Jew from Lithuania walked together in the streets of the town that was strange to them both; together they looked over the fences of the large gardens and into the shining foyers of the blocks of flats; together they stood on the pavements of the main arterial roads and watched the cars and trucks rush between the tall buildings; together they walked in the small, sandy parks, and when the old man was tired Paulus saw to it that he sat on a bench and rested. They could not sit on the bench together, for only whites were allowed to sit on the benches, but Paulus would squat on the ground at the old man's feet and wait until he judged the old man had rested long enough, before moving on again. Together they stared into the windows of the suburban shops, and though neither of them could read the signs outside the shops, the advertisements on billboards, the traffic signs at the side of the road, Paulus learned to wait for the traffic lights to change from red to green before crossing a street, and together they stared at the Coca-Cola girls and the advertisements for beer and the cinema posters. On a piece of cardboard which Paulus carried in the pocket of his blouse Harry had had one of his sons print the old man's name and address, and whenever Paulus was uncertain of the way home, he would approach an African or a friendly-looking white man and show him the card, and try his best to follow the instructions, or at least the gesticulations which were all of the answers of the white men that meant anything to him. But there were enough Africans to be found, usually, who were more sophisticated than himself, and though they teased him for his 'rawness' and for holding the sort of job he had, they helped him too. Neither Paulus nor old man Grossman were aware that when they crossed a street hand-in-hand, as they sometimes did when the traffic was particularly heavy, there were people who averted their eyes from the sight of this degradation, which could come upon a man when he was senile and dependent.

Paulus knew only Zulu, the old man knew only Yiddish, so there was no language in which they could talk to one another. But they talked all the same: they both commented on or complained to each other of the things they saw around them, and often they agreed with one another, smiling and nodding their heads and explaining again with their hands what each happened to be talking about. They both seemed to believe that they were talking about the same things, and often they undoubtedly were, when they lifted their heads sharply to see an aeroplane cross the blue sky between two buildings, or when they reached the top of a steep road and turned to look back the way they had come, and saw below them the clean impervious towers of the city thrust nakedly against the sky in brand-new piles of concrete and glass and facebrick. Then down they would go again, among the houses and the gardens where the beneficent climate encouraged both palms and oak trees to grow indiscriminately among each other – as they did in the garden of the house to which, in the evenings, Paulus and old man Grossman would eventually return.

In and about the house Paulus soon became as indispensable to the old man as he was on their expeditions out of it. Paulus dressed him and bathed him and trimmed his beard, and when the old man woke distressed in the middle of the night it would be for Paulus that he would call – '*Der schwarzer*', he would shout (for he never learned Paulus' name), '*vo's der schwarzer*' – and Paulus would change his sheets and pyjamas and put him back to bed again. '*Baas Zeide*,' Paulus called the old man, picking up the Yiddish word for grandfather from the children of the house.

That was something that Harry Grossman told everyone of. For Harry persisted in regarding the arrangement as a kind of joke, and the more the arrangement succeeded the more determinedly did he try to turn it into a joke not only against his father but against Paulus too. It had been a joke that his father should be looked after by a raw Zulu: it was going to be a joke that the Zulu was successful at it. '*Baas Zeide*! That's what *der schwarzer* calls him – have you ever heard the like of it? And you should see the two of them, walking about in the streets hand-in-hand like two schoolgirls. Two clever ones, *der schwarzer* and my father going for a promenade, and between them I tell you you wouldn't be able to find out what day of the week or what time of day it is.'

And when people said, 'Still that Paulus seems a very good boy,' Harry would reply:

'Why shouldn't he be? With all his knowledge, are there so many better jobs that he'd be able to find? He keeps the old man happy – very good, very nice, but don't forget that that's what he's paid to do. What does he know any better to do, a simple kaffir from the kraal? He knows he's got a good job, and he'd be a fool if he threw it away. Do you think,' Harry would say, and this too would insistently be part of the joke, 'if I had nothing else to do with my time I wouldn't be able to make the old man happy?' Harry would look about his sitting-room, where the floorboards bore the weight of his furniture, or when they sat on the stoep he would measure with his glance the spacious garden aloof from the street beyond the hedge. 'I've got other things to do. And I had other things to do, plenty of them, all my life, and not only for myself.' The thought of them would send him back to his joke. 'No, I think the old man has just about found his level in *der schwarzer* – and I don't think *der schwarzer* could cope with anything else.'

Harry teased the old man to his face too, about his 'black friend', and he would ask him what he would do if Paulus went away; once he jokingly threatened to send the Zulu away. But the old man didn't believe the threat, for Paulus was in his room at the time, and the old man simply left Harry and went straight to Paulus, and sat in the room with him. Harry did not follow him: he would never have gone into any of his servant's rooms, least of all that of Paulus. For though he made a joke of him to others, to Paulus himself he always spoke gruffly, unjokingly, with no patience. On that day he had merely shouted after the old man, 'Another time he won't be there.'

Yet it was strange to see how Harry Grossman would always be drawn to the room in which he knew his father and Paulus to be. Night after night he came into the old man's bedroom when Paulus was dressing or undressing the old man; almost as often Harry stood in the steamy, untidy bathroom when the old man was being bathed. At these times he hardly spoke, he offered no explanation of his presence. He stood dourly and silently in the room, in his customary powerful, begrudging stance, with one hand clasping the wrist of the other and both supporting his waist, and he watched Paulus at work. The backs of Paulus' hands were smooth and hairless, they were paler on the palms and at the finger-nails, and they worked deftly about the body of the old man, who was submissive under their ministrations. At first Paulus had sometimes smiled at Harry while he worked, with his straightforward, even smile in which there was no invitation to a complicity in patronage, but rather an encourage-ment to Harry to draw forward. After the first few evenings Paulus no longer smiled at his master, but he could not restrain himself, even under Harry's stare, from talking in a soft, continous flow of Zulu, to encourage the old man and to exhort him to be helpful and to express his pleasure in how well the work was going. When Paulus at last wiped the gleaming soapsuds from his hands he would occasionally, when the old man was tired, stoop low and with a laugh pick him up and carry him easily down the passage to his bedroom. Harry would follow; he would stand in the passage and watch the burdened, bare-footed Zulu until the door of his father's room closed behind them both.

Only once did Harry wait on such an evening for Paulus to re-appear from his father's room. Paulus had already come out, had passed him in the narrow passage, and had already subduedly said: 'Good night, baas,' before Harry called suddenly:

'Hey! Wait!'

'Baas,' Paulus said, turning his head. Then he came quickly to Harry. 'Baas,' he said again, puzzled to know why his baas, who so rarely spoke to him, should suddenly have called him like this, when his work was over.

Harry waited again before speaking, waited long enough for Paulus to say: 'Baas?' once more, to move a little closer, and to lift his head for a moment before lowering it respectfully.

'The *oubaas* was tired tonight,' Harry said. 'Where did you take him? What did you do with him?'

'Baas?'

'You heard what I said. What did you do with him that he looked so tired?'

'Baas – I – ' Paulus was flustered, and his hands beat in the air, but with care, so that he would not touch his baas. 'Please baas.' He brought both hands to his mouth, closing it forcibly. He flung his hands away. 'Johannes,' he said with relief, and he had already taken the first step down the passage to call his interpreter.

'No!' Harry called. 'You mean you don't understand what I say? I know you don't,' Harry shouted, though in fact he had forgotten until Paulus had reminded him. The sight of Paulus' puzzled and guilty face before him filled him with a lust to see this man, this nurse with the face and the figure of a warrior, look more puzzled and guilty yet; and Harry knew that it could so easily be done, it could be done simply by talking to him in the language he could not understand. 'You're a fool,' Harry said. 'You're like a child. You understand nothing, and it's just as well for you that you need nothing. You'll always be where you are, running to do what the white baas tells you to do. Look how you stand! Do you think I understood English when I came here?' Then with contempt, using one of the few Zulu words he knew: '*Hamba*! Go! Do you think I want to see you?

'*Au* baas!' Paulus exclaimed in distress. He could not remonstrate; he could only open his hands in a gesture to show that he understood neither the words Harry used, nor in what he had been remiss that Harry should have spoken in such angry tones to him. But Harry gestured him away, and had the satisfaction of seing Paulus shuffle off like a schoolboy.

Harry was the only person who knew that he and his father had quarrelled shortly before the accident that ended the old man's life. That was one story about his father he was never to repeat.

Late in the afternoon they quarrelled, after Harry had come back from the shop in which he made his living. He came back to find his father wandering about the house, shouting for *der schwarzer*, and his wife complaining that she had already told the old man at least five times that *der schwarzer* was not in the house: it was Paulus' afternoon off.

Harry went to his father, and he too told him, '*Der schwarzer*'s not here.' The old man turned away and continued going from room to room, peering in through the doors. '*Der schwarzer*'s not here,' Harry repeated 'What do you want him for?'

Still the old man ignored him. He went down the passage towards the bedrooms. 'What do you want?' Harry called after him.

The old man went into every bedroom, still shouting for *der schwarzer*. Only when he was in his own bare bedroom did he look at Harry. 'Where's *der schwarzer*?'

'I've told you ten times I don't know where he is. What do you want him for?'

'I want *der schwarzer*.'

'I know you want him. But he isn't here.'

'I want *der schwarzer*.'

'Do you think I haven't heard you? He isn't here.'

'Bring him to me,' the old man said.

'I can't bring him to you. I don't know where he is.' Harry steadied himself against his own anger. He said quietly: 'Tell me what you want. I'll do it for you. I'm here, I can do what *der schwarzer* can do for you.'

'Where's *der schwarzer*?'

'I've told you he isn't here,' Harry shouted. 'Why don't you tell me what you want? What's the matter with me – can't you tell me what you want?'

'I want *der schwarzer*.'

'Please,' Harry said. He threw out his arms towards his father, but the gesture was abrupt, almost as though he were thrusting him away. 'Why can't you ask me? You can ask me – haven't I done enough for you already? Do you want to go for a walk? – I'll take you for a walk. What do you want? Do you want – do you want – ?' Harry could not think what his father might want. 'I'll do it,' he said. 'You don't need *der schwarzer*.'

Then Harry saw that his father was weeping. His eyes were hidden behind the thick glasses that he had to wear: his glasses and beard made of his face a mask of age. But Harry knew when the old man was weeping – he had seen him crying too often before, when they had found him at the end of a street after he had wandered away, or even, years earlier, when he had lost another of the miserable jobs that seemed to be the only ones he could find in a country in which his son had, later, prospered.

'Father,' Harry asked, 'what have I done? Do you think I've sent *der schwarzer* away?' His father turned away, between the narrow bed and the narrow wardrobe. 'He's coming – ' Harry said, but he could not look at his father's back, at his hollowed neck, on which the hairs that Paulus had clipped glistened above the pale brown discolorations of age – Harry could not look at the neck turned stiffly away from him while he had to try to promise the return of the Zulu. He dropped his hands and walked out of the room.

No one knew how the old man managed to get out of the house and through the front gate without having been seen. But he did manage it, and in the road he was struck down by a man on a bicycle. It was enough. He died a few days later in the hospital.

Harry's wife wept, even the grandsons wept; Paulus wept. Harry himself was stony, and his bunched, protuberant features were immovable; they seemed locked upon the bones of his face. A few days after the funeral he called Paulus and Johannes into the kitchen and said to Johannes: 'Tell him he must go. His work is finished.'

Johannes translated for Paulus, and then, after Paulus had spoken, he turned to Harry. 'He says, yes baas.' Paulus kept his eyes on the ground; he did not look up even when Harry looked directly at him. Harry knew that this was not out of fear or shyness, but out of courtesy for his master's grief – which was what they could not but be talking of, when they talked of his work.

'Here's the pay.' Harry thrust a few notes towards Paulus, who took them in his cupped hands, and retreated.

Harry waited for them to go, but Paulus stayed in the room, and consulted with Johannes in a low voice. Johannes turned to his master. 'He says, baas, that the baas still has his savings.'

Harry had forgotten about Paulus' savings. He told Johannes that he had forgotten, and that he did not have enough money at the moment, but would bring the money the next day. Johannes translated and Paulus nodded gratefully. Both he and Johannes were subdued by the death there had been in the house.

Harry's dealings with Paulus were over. He took what was to have been his last look at Paulus, but this look stirred him once more against the Zulu. As harshly as he told Paulus that he had to go, so now, implacably, seeing Paulus in the mockery and simplicity of his houseboy's clothing, feeding his anger to the very end, Harry said: 'Ask him what he's been saving for. What's he going to do with the fortune he's made?'

Johannes spoke to Paulus and came back with a reply. 'He says, baas, that he is saving to bring his wife and children from Zululand to Johannesburg. He is saving, baas,' Johannes said, for Harry had not seemed to understand, 'to bring his family to this town also.'

The two Zulus were bewildered to know why it was then that Harry Grossman's clenched, fist-like features should have fallen from one another, or why he stared with such guilt and despair at Paulus, while he cried, 'What else could I have done? I did my best!' before the first tears came.

NADINE GORDIMER

Six Feet of the Country

My wife and I are not real farmers – not even Lerice, really. We bought our place, ten miles out of Johannesburg on one of the main roads, to change something in ourselves, I suppose; you seem to rattle about so much within a marriage like ours. You long to hear nothing but a deep satisfying silence when you sound a marriage. The farm hasn't managed that for us, of course, but it has done other things, unexpected, illogical. Lerice, who I thought would retire there in Chekhovian sadness for a month or two, and then leave the place to the servants while she tried yet again to get a part she wanted and become the actress she would like to be, has sunk into the business of running the farm with all the serious intensity with which she once imbued the shadows in a playwright's mind. I should have given it up long ago if it had not been for her. Her hands, once small and plain and well-kept – she was not the sort of actress who wears red paint and diamond rings – are hard as a dog's pads.

I, of course, am there only in the evenings and at weekends. I am a partner in a travel agency which is flourishing – needs to be, as I tell Lerice, in order to carry the farm. Still, though I know we can't afford it, and though the sweetish smell of the fowls Lerice breeds sickens me, so that I avoid going past their runs, the farm is beautiful in a way I had almost forgotten – especially on a Sunday morning when I get up and go out into the paddock and see not the palm trees and fishpond and imitation-stone bird bath of the suburbs but white ducks on the dam, the lucerne field brilliant as window-dresser's grass, and the little, stocky, mean-eyed bull, lustful but bored, having his face tenderly licked by one of his ladies. Lerice comes out with her hair uncombed, in her hand a stick dripping with cattle dip. She will stand and look dreamily for a moment, the way she would pretend to look sometimes in those plays. 'They'll mate tomorrow,' she will say. 'This is their second day. Look how she loves him, my little

Napoleon.' So that when people come to see us on Sunday afternoon, I am likely to hear myself saying as I pour out the drinks, 'When I drive back home from the city every day past those rows of suburban houses, I wonder how the devil we ever did stand it . . . Would you care to look around?' And there I am, taking some pretty girl and her young husband stumbling down to our river bank, the girl catching her stockings on the mealie-stooks and stepping over cow turds humming with jewel-green flies whils she says, ' . . . the *tensions* of the damned city. And you're near enough to get into town to a show, too! I think it's wonderful. Why, you've got it both ways!'

And for a moment I accept the triumph as if I *had* managed it – the impossibility that I've been trying for all my life: just as if the truth was that you could get it 'both ways', instead of finding yourself with not even one way or the other but a third, one you had not provided for at all.

But even in our saner moments, when I find Lerice's earthy enthusiasms just as irritating as I once found her histrionical ones, and she finds what she calls my 'jealousy' of her capacity for enthusiasm as big a proof of my inadequacy for her as a mate as ever it was, we do believe that we have at least honestly escaped those tensions peculiar to the city about which our visitors speak. When Johannesburg people speak of 'tension', they don't mean hurrying people in crowded streets, the struggle for money, or the general competitive character of city life. They mean the guns under the white men's pillows and the burglar bars on the white men's windows. They mean those strange moments on city pavements when a black man won't stand aside for a white man.

Out in the country even ten miles out, life is better than that. In the country, there is a lingering remnant of the pre-transitional stage; our relationship with the blacks is almost feudal. Wrong, I suppose, obsolete, but more comfortable all around. We have no burglar bars, no gun. Lerice's farm boys have their wives and their piccanins living with them on the land. They brew their sour beer without the fear of police raids. In fact, we've always rather prided ourselves that the poor devils have nothing much to fear, being with us; Lerice even keeps an eye on their children, with all the competence of a woman who has never had a child of her own, and she certainly doctors them all – children and adults – like babies whenever they happen to be sick.

It was because of this that we were not particularly startled one night last winter when the boy Albert came knocking at our window long after we had gone to bed. I wasn't in our bed but sleeping in the little dressing-room-cum-linen-room next door, because Lerice had annoyed me and I didn't want to find myself softening towards her simply because of the sweet smell of the talcum powder on her flesh after her bath. She came and woke me up. 'Albert says one of the boys is very sick,' she said. 'I think you'd better go down and see. He wouldn't get us up at this hour for nothing.'

'What time is it?'

'What does it matter?' Lerice is maddeningly logical.

I got up awkwardly as she watched me – how is it I always feel a fool when I have deserted her bed? After all, I know from the way she never looks at me when she talks to me at breakfast next day that she is hurt and humiliated at my not wanting her – and I went out, clumsy with sleep.

'Which of the boys is it?' I asked Albert as we followed the dance of my torch.

'He's too sick. Very sick,' he said.

'But who? Franz?' I remembered Franz had had a bad cough for the past week.

Albert did not answer; he had given me the path, and was walking along beside me in the tall dead grass. When the light of the torch caught his face, I saw that he looked acutely embarrassed. 'What's this all about?' I said.

He lowered his head under the glance of the light. 'It's not me, baas. I don't know. Petrus he send me.'

Irritated, I hurried him along to the huts. And there, on Petrus's iron bedstead, with its brick stilts, was a young man, dead. On his forehead there was still a light, cold sweat; his body was warm. The boys stood around as they do in the kitchen when it is discovered that someone has broken a dish – unco-operative, silent. Somebody's wife hung about in the shadows, her hands wrung together under her apron.

I had not seen a dead man since the war. This was very different. I felt like the others – extraneous, useless. 'What was the matter?' I asked.

The woman patted at her chest and shook her head to indicate the painful impossibility of breathing.

He must have died of penumonia.

I turned to Petrus. 'Who was this boy? What was he doing here?'

The light of a candle on the floor showed that Petrus was weeping. He followed me out the door.

When we were outside, in the dark, I waited for him to speak. But he didn't. 'Now, come on, Petrus, you must tell me who this boy was. Was he a friend of yours?'

'He's my brother, baas. He came from Rhodesia to look for work.'

The story startled Lerice and me a little. The young boy had walked down from Rhodesia to look for work in Johannesburg, had caught a chill from sleeping out along the way and had lain ill in his brother Petrus's hut since his arrival three days before. Our boys had been frightened to ask us for help for him because we had never been intended ever to know of his presence. Rhodesian natives are barred from entering the Union unless they have a permit; the young man was an illegal immigrant. No doubt our boys had managed the whole thing successfully several times before; a number of relatives must have walked the seven or eight hundred miles from poverty to the paradise of zoot suits, police raids and black slum townships that is their *Egoli*, City of Gold – the African name for Johannesburg. It was merely a matter of getting such a man to lie low on our farm until a job could be found with someone who would be glad to take the risk of prosecution for employing an illegal immigrant in exchange for the services of someone as yet untainted by the city.

Well, this was one who would never get up again.

'You would think they would have felt they could tell *us*,' said Lerice next morning. 'Once the man was ill. You would have thought at least – ' When she is getting intense over something, she has a way of standing in the middle of a room as people do when they are shortly to leave on a journey, looking searchingly about her at the most familiar objects as if she had never seen them before. I had noticed that in Petrus's presence in the kitchen, earlier, she had had the air of being almost offended with him, almost hurt.

In any case, I really haven't the time or inclination any more to go into everything in our life that I know Lerice, from those alarmed and pressing eyes of hers, would like us to go into. She is the kind of woman who doesn't mind if she looks plain, or odd; I don't suppose she would even care if she knew how strange she looks when her whole face is out of proportion with urgent uncertainty. I said, 'Now I'm the one who'll have to do all the dirty work, I suppose.'

She was still staring at me, trying me out with those eyes – wasting her time, if she only knew.

'I'll have to notify the health authorities,' I said calmly. 'They can't just cart him off and bury him. After all, we don't really know what he died of.'

She simply stood there, as if she had given up – simply ceased to see me at all.

I don't know when I've been so irritated. 'It might have been something contagious,' I said. 'God knows.' There was no answer.

I am not enamoured of holding conversations with myself. I went out to shout to one of the boys to open the garage and get the car ready for my morning drive to town.

As I had expected, it turned out to be quite a business. I had to notify the police as well as the health authorities, and answer a lot of tedious questions: How was it I was ignorant of the boy's presence? If I did not supervise my native quarters, how did I know that that sort of thing didn't go on all the time? And when I flared up and told them that so long as my natives did their work, I didn't think it my right or concern to poke my nose into their private lives, I got from the coarse, dull-witted police sergeant one of those looks that come not from any thinking process going on in the brain but from that faculty common to all who are possessed by the master-race theory – a look of insanely inane certainty. He grinned at me with a mixture of scorn and delight at my stupidity.

Then I had to explain to Petrus why the health authorities had to take away the body for a post-mortem – and, in fact, what a post-mortem was. When I telephoned the health department some days later to find out the result, I was told that the cause of death was, as we had thought, pneumonia, and that the body had been suitably disposed of. I went out to where Petrus was mixing a mash for the fowls and told him that it was all right, there would be no trouble; his brother had died from that pain in his chest. Petrus put down the paraffin tin and said, 'When can we go to fetch him, baas?'

'To fetch him?'

'Will the baas please ask them when we must come?'

I went back inside and called Lerice, all over the house. She came down the stairs from the spare bedrooms, and I said, '*Now* what am I going to do? When I told Petrus, he just asked calmly when they could go and fetch the body. They think they're going to bury him themselves.'

'Well, go back and tell him,' said Lerice. 'You must tell him. Why didn't you tell him then?'

When I found Petrus again, he looked up politely. 'Look, Petrus,' I said. 'You can't go to fetch your brother. They've done it already – they've *buried* him, you understand?'

'Where?' he said slowly, dully, as if he thought that perhaps he was getting this wrong.

'You see, he was a stranger. They knew he wasn't from here, and they didn't know he had some of his people here so they thought they must bury him.' It was difficult to make a pauper's grave sound like a privilege.

'Please, baas, the baas must ask them.' But he did not mean that he wanted to know the burial place. He simply ignored the incomprehensible machinery I told him had set to work on his dead brother; he wanted the brother back.

'But, Petrus,' I said, 'how can I? Your brother is buried already. I can't ask them now.'

'Oh, baas!' he said. He stood with his bran-smeared hands uncurled at his sides, one corner of his mouth twitching.

'Good God, Petrus, they won't listen to me! They can't, anyway. I'm sorry, but I can't do it. You understand?'

He just kept on looking at me, out of his knowledge that white men have everything, can do anything; if they don't, it is because they won't.

And then, at dinner, Lerice started. 'You could at least phone,' she said.

'Christ, what d'you think I am? Am I supposed to bring the dead back to life?'

But I could not exaggerate my way out of this ridiculous responsibility that had been thrust on me. 'Phone them up,' she went on. 'And at least you'll be able to tell him you've done it and they've explained that it's impossible.'

She disappeared somewhere into the kitchen quarters after coffee. A little later she came back to tell me, 'The old father's coming down from Rhodesia to be at the funeral. He's got a permit and he's already on his way.'

Unfortunately, it was not impossible to get the body back. The authorities said that it was somewhat irregular, but that since the hygiene conditions had been fulfilled, they could not refuse permission for exhumation. I found out that, with the undertaker's charges, it would cost twenty pounds. Ah, I thought, that settles it. On five pounds a month, Petrus won't have twenty pounds – and just as well, since it couldn't do the dead any good. Certainly I should not offer it to him myself. Twenty pounds – or anything else within reason, for that matter – I would have spent without grudging it on doctors or medicines that might have helped the boy when he was alive. Once he was dead, I had no intention of encouraging Petrus to throw away, on a gesture, more than he spent to clothe his whole family in a year.

When I told him, in the kitchen that night, he said, 'Twenty pounds?'

I said, 'Yes, that's right, twenty pounds.'

For a moment, I had the feeling, from the look on his face, that he was calculating. But when he spoke again I thought I must have imagined it. 'We must pay twenty pounds!' he said in the faraway voice in which a person speaks of something so unattainable it does not bear thinking about.

'All right, Petrus,' I said, and went back to the living-room.

The next morning before I went to town, Petrus asked to see me. 'Please, baas,' he said, awkwardly, handing me a bundle of notes. They're so seldom on the giving rather than the receiving side, poor devils, they don't really know how to hand money to a white man. There it was, the twenty pounds, in ones and halves, some creased and folded until they were soft as dirty rags, others smooth and fairly new – Franz's money, I suppose, and Albert's, and Dora the cook's, and Jacob the gardener's, and God knows who else's besides, from all the farms and smallholdings round about. I took it in irritation more than in astonishment, really – irritation at the waste, the uselessness of this sacrifice by people so poor. Just like the poor everywhere, I thought, who stint themselves the decencies of life in order to ensure themselves the decencies of death. So incomprehensible to people like Lerice and me, who regard life as something to be spent extravagantly and, if we think about death at all, regard it as the final bankruptcy.

The farm-hands don't work on Saturday afternoon anyway, so it was a good day for the funeral. Petrus and his father had borrowed our donkey-cart to fetch the coffin from the city, where, Petrus told Lerice on their return, everything was 'nice' – the coffin waiting for them, already sealed up to save them from what must have been a rather unpleasant sight after two weeks' interment. (It had taken all that time for the authorities and the undertaker to make the final arrangements for moving the body.) All morning, the coffin lay in Petrus's hut, awaiting the trip to the little old burial ground, just outside the eastern boundary of our farm, that was a relic of the days when this was a real farming district rather than a fashionable rural estate. It was pure chance that I happened to be down there near the fence when the procession came past; once again Lerice had forgotten her promise to me and had made the house uninhabitable on a Saturday afternoon. I had come home and been infuriated to find her in a pair of filthy old slacks and with her hair uncombed since the night before, having all the varnish scraped from the living-room floor, if you please. So I had taken my No. 8 iron and gone off to practise my approach shots. In my annoyance, I had forgotten about the funeral, and was reminded only when I saw the procession coming up the path along the outside of the fence towards me; from where I was standing, you can see the graves quite clearly, and that day the sun glinted on bits of broken pottery, a lopsided homemade cross, and jam-jars brown with rainwater and dead flowers.

I felt a little awkward, and did not know whether to go on hitting my golf ball or stop at least until the whole gathering was decently past. The donkey-cart creaks and screeches with every revolution of the wheels, and it came along in a slow, halting fashion somehow peculiarly suited to the two donkeys who drew it, their little potbellies rubbed and rough, their heads sunk between the shafts, and their ears flattened back with an air submissive and downcast; peculiarly suited, too, to the group of men and women who came along slowly behind. The patient ass. Watching, I thought, you can see now why the creature became a Biblical symbol. Then the procession drew level with me and stopped, so I had to put down my club. The coffin was taken down off the cart – it was a shiny, yellow-varnished wood, like cheap furniture – and the donkeys twitched their ears against the flies. Petrus, Franz, Albert and the old father from Rhodesia hoisted it on their shoulders and the procession moved on, on foot. It was really a very awkward moment. I stood there rather foolishly at the fence, quite still, and slowly they filed past, not looking up, the four men bent beneath the shiny wooden box, and the straggling troop of mourners. All of them were servants or neighbours' servants whom I knew as casual easygoing gossipers about our lands or kitchen. I heard the old man's breathing.

I had just bent to pick up my club again when there was a sort of jar in the flowing solemnity of their processional mood; I felt it at once, like a wave of heat along the air, or one of those sudden currents of cold catching at your legs in a placid stream. The old man's voice was muttering something; the people had stopped, confused, and they bumped into one another, some pressing to go on, others hissing them to be still. I could see that they were embarrassed, but they could not ignore the voice; it was much the way that the mumblings of a prophet, though not clear at first, arrest the mind. The corner of the coffin the old man carried was sagging at an angle; he seemed to be trying to get out from under the weight of it. Now Petrus expostulated with him.

The little boy who had been left to watch the donkeys dropped the reins and ran to see. I don't know why – unless it was for the same reason people crowd around someone who has fainted in a cinema – but I parted the wires of the fence and went through, after him.

Petrus lifted his eyes to me – to anybody – with distress and horror. The old man from Rhodesia had let go of the coffin entirely, and the three others, unable to support it on their own, had laid it on the ground, in the pathway. Already there was a film of dust lightly wavering up its shiny sides. I did not understand what the old man was saying; I hesitated to interfere. But now the whole seething group turned on my silence. The old man himself came over to me, with his hands outspread and shaking, and spoke directly to me, saying something that I could tell from the tone, without understanding the words, was shocking and extraordinary.

'What is it, Petrus? What's wrong?' I appealed.

Petrus threw up his hands, bowed his head in a series of hysterical shakes, then thrust his face up at me suddenly. 'He says, "My son was not so heavy".'

Silence. I could hear the old man breathing; he kept his mouth a little open, as old people do.

'My son was young and thin,' he said at last, in English.

Again silence. Then babble broke out. The old man thundered

against everybody; his teeth were yellowed and few, and he had one of those fine, grizzled, sweeping moustaches one doesn't often see nowadays, which must have been grown in emulation of early Empire-builders. It seemed to frame all his utterances with a special validity. He shocked the assembly; they thought he was mad, but they had to listen to him. With his own hands he began to prise the lid off the coffin and three of the men came forward to help him. Then he sat down on the ground; very old, very weak and unable to speak, he merely lifted a trembling hand towards what was there. He abdicated, he handed it over to them; he was no good any more.

They crowded round to look (and so did I), and now they forgot the nature of this surprise and the occasion of grief to which it belonged, and for a few minutes were carried up in the astonishment of the surprise itself. They gasped and flared noisily with excitement. I even noticed the little boy who had held the donkeys jumping up and down, almost weeping with rage because the backs of the grown-ups crowded him out of his view.

In the coffin was someone no one had seen before: a heavily built, rather light-skinned native with a neatly stitched scar on his forehead – perhaps from a blow in a brawl that had also dealt him some other, slower-working injury that had killed him.

I wrangled with the authorities for a week over that body. I had the feeling that they were shocked, in a laconic fashion, by their own mistake, but that in the confusion of their anonymous dead they were helpless to put it right. They said to me, 'We are trying to find out', and 'We are still making inquiries'. It was as if at any moment they might conduct me into their mortuary and say, 'There! Lift up the sheets; look for him – your poultry boy's brother. There are so many black faces – surely one will do?'

And every evening when I got home, Petrus was waiting in the kitchen. 'Well, they're trying. They're still looking. The baas is seeing to it for you, Petrus,' I would tell him. 'God, half the time I should be in the office I'm driving around the back end of the town chasing after this affair,' I added aside, to Lerice, one night.

She and Petrus both kept their eyes turned on me as I spoke, and, oddly, for those moments they looked exactly alike, though it sounds impossible: my wife, with her high, white forehead and her attenuated Englishwoman's body, and the poultry boy, with his horny bare feet below khaki trousers tied at the knee with string and the peculiar rankness of his nervous sweat coming from his skin.

'What makes you so indignant, so determined about this now?' said Lerice suddenly.

I stared at her. 'It's a matter of principle. Why should they get away with a swindle? It's time these officials had a jolt from someone who'll bother to take the trouble.'

She said, 'Oh.' And as Petrus slowly opened the kitchen door to leave, sensing that the talk had gone beyond him, she turned away, too.

I continued to pass on assurances to Petrus every evening, but although what I said was the same and the voice in which I said it was the same, every evening it sounded weaker. At last, it became clear that we would never get Petrus's brother back, because nobody really knew where he was. Somewhere in a graveyard as uniform as a housing scheme, somewhere under a number that didn't belong to him, or in the medical school, perhaps, laboriously reduced to layers of muscle and strings of nerve? Goodness knows. He had no identity in this world anyway.

It was only then, and in a voice of shame, that Petrus asked me to try and get the money back.

'From the way he asks, you'd think he was robbing his dead brother,' I said to Lerice later. But as I've said, Lerice had got so intense about this business that she couldn't even appreciate a little ironic smile.

I tried to get the money; Lerice tried. We both telephoned and wrote and argued, but nothing came of it. It appeared that the main expense had been the undertaker, and after all he had done his job. So the whole thing was a complete waste, even more of a waste for the poor devils than I had thought it would be.

The old man from Rhodesia was about Lerice's father's size, so she gave him one of her father's old suits, and he went back home rather better off, for the winter, than he had come.

AHMED ESSOP

The Hajji

When the telephone rang several times one evening and his wife did not attend to it as she usually did, Hajji Hassen, seated on a settee in the lounge, cross-legged and sipping tea, shouted: 'Salima, are you deaf?' And when he received no response from his wife and the jarring bell went on ringing, he shouted again: 'Salima, what's happened to you?'

The telephone stopped ringing. Hajji Hassen frowned in a contemplative manner, wondering where his wife was now. Since his return from Mecca after the pilgrimage, he had discovered novel inadequacies in her, or perhaps saw the old ones in a more revealing light. One of her salient inadequacies was never to be around when he wanted her. She was either across the road confabulating with her sister, or gossiping with the neighbours, or away on a shopping spree. And now, when the telephone had gone on assaulting his ears, she was not in the house. He took another sip of the strongly spiced tea to stifle the irritation within him.

When he heard the kitchen door open he knew that Salima had entered. The telephone burst out again in a metallic shrill and the Hajji shouted for his wife. She hurried to the phone.

'Hullo . . . Yes . . . Hassen . . . Speak to him? . . . Who speaking? . . . Caterine? . . . Who Caterine? . . . Au-right . . . I call him.'

She put the receiver down gingerly and informed her husband in Gujarati that a woman named 'Caterine' wanted to speak to him. The name evoked no immediate association in his memory. He descended from the settee and squeezing his feet into a pair of crimson sandals, went to the telephone.

'Hullo . . . Who? . . . Catherine? . . . No, I don't know you . . . Yes . . . Yes . . . Oh . . . now I remember . . . Yes . . .'

He listened intently to the voice, urgent, supplicating. Then he gave his answer:

'I am afraid I can't help him. Let the Christians bury him. His last wish means nothing to me . . . Madam, it's impossible . . . No . . . Let him die . . . Brother? Pig! Bastard!' He banged the receiver on to the telephone in explosive annoyance.

'O Allah!' Salima exclaimed. 'What words! What is this all about?'

He did not answer but returned to the settee, and she quietly went to the bedroom.

Salima went to bed and it was almost midnight when her husband came into the room. His earlier vexation had now given place to gloom. He told her of his brother Karim who lay dying in Hillbrow. Karim had cut himself off from his family and friends ten years ago; he had crossed the colour line (his fair complexion and grey eyes serving as passports) and gone to cohabit with a white woman. And now that he was on the verge of death he wished to return to the world he had forsaken and to be buried under Moslem funeral rites and in a Moslem cemetery.

Hajji Hassen had, of course, rejected the plea, and for good reason. When his brother had crossed the colour line, he had severed his family ties. The Hajji at that time had felt excoriating humiliation. By going over to the white Herrenvolk, his brother had trampled on something that was vitally part of him, his dignity and self-respect. But the rejection of his brother's plea involved a straining of the heartstrings and the Hajji did not feel happy. He had recently sought God's pardon for his sins in Mecca, and now this business of his brother's final earthly wish and his own intransigence was in some way staining his spirit.

The next day Hassen rose at five to go to the mosque. When he stepped out of his house in Newtown the street lights were beginning to pale and clusters of houses to assume definition. The atmosphere was fresh and heady, and he took a few deep breaths. The first trams were beginning to pass through Bree Street and were clanging along like decrepit yet burning spectres towards the Johannesburg City Hall. Here and there a figure moved along hurriedly. The Hindu fruit and vegetable hawkers were starting up their old trucks in the yards, preparing to go out for the day to sell to suburban housewives.

When he reached the mosque the Somali muezzin in the ivory-domed minaret began to intone the call for prayers. After prayers, he remained behind to read the Koran in the company of two other men. When he had done the sun was shining brilliantly in the courtyard on to the flowers and the fountain with its goldfish.

Outside the house he saw a car. Salima opened the door and whispered, 'Caterine'. For a moment he felt irritated, but realising that he might as well face her he stepped boldly into the lounge.

Catherine was a small woman with firm fleshy legs. She was seated cross-legged on the settee, smoking a cigarette. Her face was almost boyish, a look that partly originated in her auburn hair which was cut very short, and partly in the smallness of her head. Her eyebrows, firmly pencilled, accentuated the grey-green glitter of her eyes. She was dressed in a dark grey costume.

He nodded his head at her to signify that he knew who she was. Over the telephone he had spoken with aggressive authority. Now, in the presence of the woman herself, he felt a weakening of his masculine fibre.

'You must, Mr Hassen, come to see your brother.'

'I am afraid I am unable to help,' he said in a tentative tone. He felt uncomfortable; there was something so positive and intrepid about her appearance.

'He wants to see you. It's his final wish.'

'I have not seen him for ten years.'

'Time can't wipe out the fact that he's your brother.'

'He is a white. We live in different worlds.'

'But you must see him.'

There was a moment of strained silence.

'Please understand that he's not to blame for having broken with you. I am to blame. I got him to break with you. Really you must blame me, not Karim.'

Hassen found himself unable to say anything. The thought that she could in some way have been responsible for his brother's rejection of him had never occurred to him. He looked at his feet in awkward silence. He could only state in a lazily recalcitrant tone: 'It is not easy for me to see him.'

'Please come Mr Hassen, for my sake, please. I'll never be able to bear it if Karim dies unhappily. Can't you find it in your heart to forgive him, and to forgive me?'

He could not look at her. A sob escaped from her, and he heard her opening her handbag for a handkerchief.

'He's dying. He wants to see you for the last time.'

Hassen softened. He was overcome by the argument that she had been responsible for taking Karim away. He could hardly look on her responsibility as being in any way culpable. She was a woman.

'If you remember the days of your youth, the time you spent together with Karim before I came to separate him from you, it will be easier for you to pardon him.'

Hassen was silent.

'Please understand that I am not a racialist. You know the conditions in this country.'

He thought for a moment and then said: 'I will go with you.'

He excused himself and went to his room to change. After a while they set off for Hillbrow in her car.

He sat beside her. The closeness of her presence, the perfume she exuded stirred currents of feeling within him. He glanced at her several times, watched the deft movements of her hands and legs as she controlled the car. Her powdered profile, the outline taut with a resolute quality, aroused his imagination. There was something so businesslike in her attitude and bearing, so involved in reality (at the back of his mind there was Salima, flaccid, cow-like and inadequate) that he could hardly refrain from expressing his admiration.

'You must understand that I'm only going to see my brother because you have come to me. For no one else would I have changed my mind.'

'Yes, I understand. I'm very grateful.'

'My friends and relatives are going to accuse me of softness, of weakness.'

'Don't think of them now. You have decided to be kind to me.'

The realism and the common sense of the woman's words! He was overwhelmed by her.

The car stopped at the entrance of a building in Hillbrow. They took the lift. On the second floor three white youths entered and were surprised at seeing Hassen. There was a separate lift for non-whites. They squeezed themselves into a corner, one actually turning his head away with a grunt of disgust. The lift reached the fifth floor too soon for Hassen to give a thought to the attitude of the three white boys. Catherine led him to apartment 65.

He stepped into the lounge. Everything seemed to be carefully arranged. There was her personal touch about the furniture, the ornaments, the paintings. She went to the bedroom, then returned and asked him in.

Karim lay in bed, pale, emaciated, his eyes closed. For a moment

Hassen failed to recognise him: ten years divided them. Catherine placed a chair next to the bed for him. He looked at his brother and again saw, through ravages of illness, the familiar features. She sat on the bed and rubbed Karim's hands to wake him. After a while he began to show signs of consciousness. She called him tenderly by his name. When he opened his eyes he did not recognise the man beside him, but by degrees, after she had repeated Hassen's name several times, he seemed to understand. He stretched out a hand and Hassen took it, moist and repellent. Nausea swept over him, but he could not withdraw his hand as his brother clutched it firmly.

'Brother Hassen, please take me away from here.'

Hassen's agreement brought a smile to his lips.

Catherine suggested that she drive Hassen back to Newtown where he could make preparations to transfer Karim to his home.

'No, you stay here. I will take a taxi.' And he left the apartment.

In the corridor he pressed the button for the lift. He watched the indicator numbers succeeding each other rapidly, then stop at five. The doors opened – and there they were again, the three white youths. He hesitated. The boys looked at him tauntingly. Then suddenly they burst into deliberately brutish laughter.

'Come into the parlour,' one of them said.

'Come into the Indian parlour,' another said in a cloyingly mocking voice.

Hassen looked at them, annoyed, hurt. Then something snapped within him and he stood there, transfixed. They laughed at him in a raucous chorus as the lift doors shut.

He remained immobile, his dignity clawed. Was there anything so vile in him that the youths found it necessary to maul that recess of self-respect within him? 'They are whites,' he said to himself in bitter justification of their attitude.

He would take the stairs and walk down the five floors. As he descended he thought of Karim. Because of him he had come there and because of him he had been insulted. The enormity of the insult bridged the gap of ten years when Karim had spurned him, and diminished his being. Now he was diminished again.

He was hardly aware that he had gone down five floors when he reached ground level. He stood still, expecting to see the three youths again. But the foyer was empty and he could see the reassuring activity of street life through the glass panels. He quickly walked out as though he would regain in the hubbub of the street something of his assaulted dignity.

He walked on, structures of concrete and glass on either side of him, and it did not even occur to him to take a taxi. It was in Hillbrow that Karim had lived with the white woman and forgotten the existence of his brother; and now that he was dying he had sent for him. For ten years Karim had lived without him. O Karim! The thought of the youth he had loved so much during the days they had been together at the Islamic Institute, a religious seminary though it was governed like a penitentiary, brought the tears to his eyes and he stopped against a shop window and wept. A few pedestrians looked at him. When the shopkeeper came outside to see the weeping man, Hassen, ashamed of himself, wiped his eyes and walked on.

He regretted his pliability in the presence of the white woman. She had come unexpectedly and had disarmed him with her presence and subtle talk. A painful lump rose in his throat as he set his heart against forgiving Karim. If his brother had had no personal dignity in sheltering behind his white skin, trying to be what he was not, he was not going to allow his own moral worth to be depreciated in any way.

When he reached central Johannesburg he went to the station and took the train. In the coach with the blacks he felt at ease and regained his self-possession. He was among familiar faces, among people who respected him. He felt as though he had been spirited away by a perfumed well-made wax doll, but had managed with a prodigious effort to shake her off.

When he reached home Salima asked him what had been decided and he answered curtly, 'Nothing.' But feeling elated after his escape from Hillbrow he added condescendingly, 'Karim left of his own accord. We should have nothing to do with him.'

Salima was puzzled, but she went on preparing supper.

Catherine received no word from Hassen and she phoned him. She was stunned when he said: 'I'm sorry but I am unable to offer any help.'

'But . . .'

'I regret it. I made a mistake. Please make some other arrangements. Goodbye.'

With an effort of will he banished Karim from his mind. Finding his composure again he enjoyed his evening meal, read the paper and then retired to bed. Next morning he went to mosque as usual, but when he returned home he found Catherine there again. Angry that she should have come, he blurted out: 'Listen to me, Catherine. I can't forgive him. For ten years he didn't care about me, whether I was alive or dead. Karim means nothing to me now.'

'Why have you changed your mind? Do you find it so difficult to forgive him?'

'Don't talk to me of forgiveness. What forgiveness, when he threw me aside and chose to go with you? Let his white friends see to him, let Hillbrow see to him.'

'Please, please, Mr Hassen, I beg you . . .'

'No, don't come here with your begging. Please go away.'

He opened the door and went out. Catherine burst into tears. Salima comforted her as best she could.

'Don't cry Caterine. All men hard. Dey don't understand.'

'What shall I do now?' Catherine said in a defeated tone. She was an alien in the world of the non-whites. 'Is there no one who can help me?'

'Yes, Mr Mia help you,' replied Salima.

In her eagerness to find some help, she hastily moved to the door. Salima followed her and from the porch of her home directed her to Mr Mia's. He lived in a flat on the first floor of an old building. She knocked and waited in trepidation.

Mr Mia opened the door, smiled affably and asked her in.

'Come inside, lady; sit down . . . Fatima,' he called to his daughter, 'bring some tea.'

Mr Mia was a man in his fifties, his bronze complexion partly covered by a neatly trimmed beard. He was a well-known figure in the Indian community. Catherine told him of Karim and her abortive appeal to his brother. Mr Mia asked one or two questions, pondered for a while and then said: 'Don't worry, my good woman. I'll speak to Hassen. I'll never allow a Muslim brother to be abandoned.'

Catherine began to weep.

'Here, drink some tea and you'll feel better.' He poured tea. Before Catherine left he promised that he would phone her that evening and told her to get in touch with him immediately should Karim's condition deteriorate.

Mr Mia, in the company of the priest of the Newtown mosque, went to Hassen's house that evening. They found several relatives of Hassen's seated in the lounge (Salima had spread the word of Karim's illness). But Hassen refused to listen to their pleas that Karim should be brought to Newtown.

'Listen to me Hajji,' Mr Mia said. 'Your brother can't be allowed to die among the Christians.'

'For ten years he has been among them.'

'That means nothing. He's still a Muslim.'

The priest now gave his opinion. Although Karim had left the community, he was still a Muslim. He had never rejected the religion and espoused Christianity, and in the absence of any evidence to the contrary it had to be accepted that he was a Muslim brother.

'But for ten years he has lived in sin in Hillbrow.'

'If he has lived in sin that is not for us to judge.'

'Hajji, what sort of a man are you? Have you no feeling for your brother?' Mr Mia asked.

'Don't talk to me about feeling. What feeling had he for me when he went to live among the whites, when he turned his back on me?'

'Hajji, can't you forgive him? You were recently in Mecca.'

This hurt Hassen and he winced. Salima came to his rescue with refreshments for the guests.

The ritual of tea-drinking established a mood of conviviality and Karim was forgotten for a while. After tea they again tried to press Hassen into forgiving his brother, but he remained adamant. He could not now face Catherine without looking ridiculous. Besides he felt integrated now; he would resist anything that negated him.

Mr Mia and the priest departed. They decided to raise the matter with the congregation in the mosque. But they failed to move Hassen. Actually his resistance grew in inverse ratio as more people came to learn of the dying Karim and Hassen's refusal to forgive him. By giving in he would be displaying mental dithering of the worst kind, as though he were a man without an inner fibre, decision and firmness of will.

Mr Mia next summoned a meeting of various religious dignitaries and received their mandate to transfer Karim to Newtown without his brother's consent. Karim's relatives would be asked to care for him, but if they refused Mr Mia would take charge.

The relatives, not wanting to offend Hassen and also feeling that Karim was not their responsibility, refused.

Mr Mia phoned Catherine and informed her of what had been decided. She agreed that it was best for Karim to be amongst his people during his last days. So Karim was brought to Newtown in an ambulance hired from a private nursing home and housed in a little room in a quiet yard behind the mosque.

The arrival of Karim placed Hassen in a difficult situation and he bitterly regretted his decision not to accept him into his own home. He first heard of his brother's arrival during the morning prayers when the priest offered a special prayer for the recovery of the sick man. Hassen found himself in the curious position of being forced to pray for his brother. After prayers several people went to see the sick man, others went up to Mr Mia to offer help. Hassen felt out of place and as soon as the opportunity presented itself he slipped out of the mosque.

In a mood of intense bitterness, scorn for himself, hatred of those who had decided to become his brother's keepers, infinite hatred for Karim, Hassen went home. Salima sensed her husband's mood and did not say a word to him.

In his room he debated with himself. In what way should he conduct himself so that his dignity remained intact? How was he to face the congregation, the people in the streets, his neighbours? Everyone would soon know of Karim and smile at him half sadly, half ironically, for having placed himself in such a ridiculous position. Should he now forgive the dying man and transfer him to his home? People would laugh at him, snigger at his cowardice, and Mr Mia perhaps even deny him the privilege: Karim was now *his* responsibility. And what would Catherine think of him? Should he go away somewhere (on the pretext of a holiday) to Cape Town, to Durban? But no, there was the stigma of being called a renegade. And besides, Karim might take months to die, he might not die at all.

'O Karim, why did you have to do this to me?' he said, moving towards the window and drumming at the pane nervously. It galled him that a weak, dying man could bring such pain to him. An adversary could be faced, one could either vanquish him or be vanquished, with one's dignity unravished, but with Karim what could he do?

He paced his room. He looked at his watch; the time for afternoon prayers was approaching. Should he expose himself to the congregation? 'O Karim! Karim!' he cried, holding on to the burglar-proof bar of his bedroom window. Was it for this that he had made the pilgrimage – to cleanse his soul in order to return into the penumbra of sin? If only Karim would die he would be relieved of his agony. But what if he lingered on? What if he recovered? Were not prayers being said for him? He went to the door and shouted in a raucous voice: 'Salima!'

But Salima was not in the house. He shouted again and again, and his voice echoed hollowly in the rooms. He rushed into the lounge, into the kitchen, he flung the door open and looked into the yard.

He drew the curtains and lay on his bed in the dark. Then he heard the patter of feet in the house. He jumped up and shouted for his wife. She came hurriedly.

'Salima, Salima, go to Karim, he is in a room in the mosque yard. See how he is, see if he is getting better. Quickly!'

Salima went out. But instead of going to the mosque, she entered her neighbour's house. She had already spent several hours sitting beside Karim. Mr Mia had been there as well as Catherine – who had wept.

After a while she returned from her neighbour. When she opened the door her husband ran to her. 'How is he? Is he very ill? Tell me quickly!'

'He is very ill. Why don't you go and see him?'

Suddenly, involuntarily, Hassen struck his wife in the face.

'Tell me, is he dead? Is he dead?' he screamed.

Salima cowered in fear. She had never seen her husband in this raging temper. What had taken possession of the man? She retired quickly to the kitchen. Hassen locked himself in the bedroom.

During the evening he heard voices. Salima came to tell him that several people, led by Mr Mia, wanted to speak to him urgently. His first impulse was to tell them to leave immediately; he was not prepared to meet them. But he had been wrestling with himself for so many hours that he welcomed a moment when he could be in the company of others. He stepped boldly into the lounge.

'Hajji Hassen,' Mr Mia began, 'please listen to us. Your brother has not long to live. The doctor has seen him. He may not outlive the night.'

'I can do nothing about that,' Hassen replied, in an audacious matter-of-fact tone that surprised him and shocked the group of people.

'That is in Allah's hand,' said the merchant Gardee. 'In our hands lie forgiveness and love. Come with us now and see him for the last time.'

'I cannot see him.'

'Añd what will it cost you?' asked the priest who wore a long black cloak that fell about his sandalled feet.

'It will cost me my dignity and my manhood.'

'My dear Hajji, what dignity and what manhood? What can you lose by speaking a few kind words to him on his death-bed? He was only a young man when he left.'

'I will do anything, but going to Karim is impossible.'

'But Allah is pleased by forgiveness,' said the merchant.

'I am sorry, but in my case the circumstances are different. I am indifferent to him and therefore there is no necessity for me to forgive him.'

'Hajji,' said Mr Mia, 'you are only indulging in glib talk and you know it. Karim is your responsibility, whatever his crime.'

'Gentlemen, please leave me alone.'

And they left. Hassen locked himself in his bedroom and began to pace the narrow space between bed, cupboard and wall. Suddenly, uncontrollably, a surge of grief for his dying brother welled up within him.

'Brother! Brother!' he cried, kneeling on the carpet beside his bed and smothering his face in the quilt. His memory unfolded a time when Karim had been ill at the Islamic Institute and he had cared for him and nursed him back to health. How much he had loved the handsome youth!

At about four in the morning he heard an urgent rapping. He left his room to open the front door.

'Brother Karim dead,' said Mustapha, the Somali muezzin of the mosque, and he cupped his hands and said a prayer in Arabic. He wore a black cloak and a white skull-cap. When he had done he turned and walked away.

Hassen closed the door and went out into the street. For a moment his release into the street gave him a feeling of sinister jubilation, and he laughed hysterically as he turned the corner and stood next to Jamal's fruit shop. Then he walked on. He wanted to get away as far as he could from Mr Mia and the priest who would be calling upon him to prepare for the funeral. That was no business of his. They had brought Karim to Newtown and they should see to him.

He went up Lovers' Walk and at the entrance of Orient House he saw the night-watchman sitting beside a brazier. He hastened up to him, warmed his hands by the fire, but he did this more as a gesture of fraternisation as it was not cold, and he said a few words facetiously. Then he walked on.

His morbid joy was ephemeral, for the problem of facing the congregation at the mosque began to trouble him. What opinion would they have of him when he returned? Would they not say: he hated his brother so much that he forsook his prayers, but now that his brother is no longer alive he returns. What a man! What a Muslim!

When he reached Vinod's Photographic Studio he pressed his forehead agains the neon-lit glass showcase and began to weep.

A car passed by filling the air with nauseous gas. He wiped his eyes, and looked for a moment at the photographs in the showcase; the relaxed, happy, anonymous faces stared at him, faces whose momentary expressions were trapped in film. Then he walked on. He passed a few shops and then reached Broadway Cinema where he stopped to look at the lurid posters. There were heroes, lusty, intrepid, blasting it out with guns; women in various stages of undress; horrid monsters from another planet plundering a city; Dracula.

Then he was among the quiet houses and an avenue of trees rustled softly. He stopped under a tree and leaned against the trunk. He envied the slumbering people in the houses around him, their freedom from the emotions that jarred him. He would not return home until the funeral of his brother was over.

When he reached the Main Reef Road the east was brightening up. The lights along the road seemed to be part of the general haze. The buildings on either side of him were beginning to thin and on his left he saw the ghostly mountains of mine sand. Dawn broke over the city and when he looked back he saw the silhouettes of tall buildings bruising the sky. Cars and trucks were now rushing past him.

He walked for several miles and then branched off on to a gravel road and continued for a mile. When he reached a clump of blue-gum trees he sat down on a rock in the shade of the trees. From where he sat he could see a constant stream of traffic flowing along the highway. He had a stick in his hand which he had picked up along the road, and with it he prodded a crevice in the rock. The action, subtly, touched a chord in his memory and he was sitting on a rock with Karim beside him. The rock was near a river that flowed a mile away from the Islamic Institute. It was a Sunday. He had a stick in his hand and he prodded at a crevice and the weather-worn rock flaked off and Karim was gathering the flakes.

'Karim! Karim!' he cried, prostrating himself on the rock, pushing his fingers into the hard roughness, unable to bear the death of that beautiful youth.

He jumped off the rock and began to run. He would return to Karim. A fervent longing to embrace his brother came over him, to touch that dear form before the soil claimed him. He ran until he was tired, then walked at a rapid pace. His whole existence precipitated itself into one motive, one desire, to embrace his brother in a final act of love.

His heart beating wildly, his hair dishevelled, he reached the highway and walked on as fast as he could. He longed to ask for a lift from a passing motorist but could not find the courage to look back and signal. Cars flashed past him, trucks roared in pain.

When he reached the outskirts of Johannesburg it was nearing ten o'clock. He hurried along, now and then breaking into a run. Once he tripped over a cable and fell. He tore his trousers in the fall and found his hands were bleeding. But he was hardly conscious of himself, wrapped up in his one purpose.

He reached Lovers' Walk, where cars growled around him angrily; he passed Broadway Cinema, rushed towards Orient House, turned the corner at Jamal's fruit shop. And stopped.

The green hearse, with the crescent moon and stars emblem, passed by; then several cars with mourners followed, bearded men, men with white skull-caps on their heads, looking rigidly ahead, like a procession of puppets, indifferent to his fate. No one saw him.

BESSIE HEAD

The Prisoner Who Wore Glasses

Scarcely a breath of wind disturbed the stillness of the day and the long rows of cabbages were bright green in the sunlight. Large white clouds drifted slowly across the deep blue sky. Now and then they obscured the sun and caused a chill on the backs of the prisoners who had to work all day long in the cabbage field. This trick the clouds were playing with the sun eventually caused one of the prisoners who wore glasses to stop work, straighten up and peer short-sightedly at them. He was a thin little fellow with a hollowed-out chest and comic knobbly knees. He also had a lot of fanciful ideas because he smiled at the clouds.

'Perhaps they want me to send a message to the children,' he thought, tenderly, noting that the clouds were drifting in the direction of his home some hundred miles away. But before he could frame the message, the warder in charge of his work span shouted: 'Hey, what do you think you're doing, Brille?'

The prisoner swung round, blinking rapidly, yet at the same time sizing up the enemy. He was a new warder, named Jacobus Stephanus Hannetjie. His eyes were the colour of the sky but they were frightening. A simple, primitive, brutal soul gazed out of them. The prisoner bent down quickly and a message was quietly passed down the line: 'We're in for trouble this time, comrades.'

'Why?' rippled back up the line.

'Because he's not human,' the reply rippled down and yet only the crunching of the spades as they turned over the earth disturbed the stillness.

This particular work span was known as Span One. It was composed of ten men and they were all political prisoners. They were grouped together for convenience as it was one of the prison regulations that no black warder should be in charge of a political prisoner lest this prisoner convert him to his view. It never seemed to occur to the authorities that this very reasoning was the strength of Span One and a clue to the strange terror they aroused in the warders. As political prisoners they were unlike the other prisoners in the sense that they felt no guilt nor were they outcasts of society. All guilty men instinctively cower, which was why it was the kind of prison where men got knocked out cold with a blow at the back of the head from an iron bar. Up until the arrival of Warder Hannetjie, no warder had dared beat any member of Span One and no warder had lasted more than a week with them. The battle was entirely psychological. Span One was assertive and it was beyond the scope of white warders to handle assertive black men. Thus, Span One had got out of control. They were the best thieves and liars in the camp. They lived all day on raw cabbages. They chatted and smoked tobacco. And since they moved, thought and acted as one, they had perfected every technique of group concealment.

Trouble began that very day between Span One and Warder Hannetjie. It was because of the short-sightedness of Brille. That was the nickname he was given in prison and is the Afrikaans word for someone who wears glasses. Brille could never judge the approach of the prison gates and on several occasions he had munched on cabbages and dropped them almost at the feet of the warder and all previous warders had overlooked this. Not so Warder Hannetjie.

'Who dropped the cabbage?' he thundered.

Brille stepped out of line.

'I did,' he said meekly.

'All right,' said Hannetjie. 'The whole Span goes three meals off.'

'But I told you I did it,' Brille protested.

The blood rushed to Warder Hannetjie's face.

'Look 'ere,' he said. 'I don't take orders from a kaffir. I don't know what kind of kaffir you think you are. Why don't you say Baas. I'm your Baas. Why don't you say Baas, hey?'

Brille blinked his eyes rapidly but by contrast his voice was strangely calm.

'I'm twenty years older than you,' he said. It was the first thing that came to mind but the comrades seemed to think it a huge joke. A titter swept up the line. The next thing Warder Hannetjie whipped out a knobkerrie and gave Brille several blows about the head. What surprised his comrades was the speed with which Brille had removed his glasses or else they would have been smashed to pieces on the ground.

That evening in the cell Brille was very apologetic.

'I'm sorry, comrades,' he said. 'I've put you into a hell of a mess.'

'Never mind, brother,' they said. 'What happens to one of us, happens to all.'

'I'll try to make up for it, comrades,' he said. 'I'll steal something so that you don't go hungry.'

Privately, Brille was very philosophical about his head wounds. It was the first time an act of violence had been perpetrated against him but he had long been a witness of extreme, almost unbelievable human brutality. He had twelve children and his mind travelled back that evening through the sixteen years of bedlam in which he had lived. It had all happened in a small drab little three-bedroomed house in a small drab little street in the Eastern Cape, and the children kept coming year after year because neither he nor Martha ever managed the contraceptives the right way, and a teacher's salary never allowed moving to a bigger house, and he was always taking exams to improve his salary only to have it all eaten up by hungry mouths. Everything was pretty horrible, especially the way the children fought. They'd get hold of each other's heads and give them a good bashing against the wall. Martha gave up somewhere along the line so they worked out a thing between them. The bashings, biting and blood were to operate in full swing until he came home. He was to be the bogey-man and when it worked he never failed to have a sense of godhead at the way in which his presence could change savages into fairly reasonable human beings.

Yet somehow it was this chaos and mismanagement at the centre of his life that drove him into politics. It was really an ordered beautiful world with just a few basic slogans to learn along with the rights of mankind. At one stage, before things became very bad, there were conferences to attend, all very far away from home.

'Let's face it,' he thought ruefully. 'I'm only learning right now what it means to be a politician. All this while I've been running away from Martha and the kids.'

And the pain in his head brought a hard lump to his throat. That was what the children did to each other daily and Martha wasn't managing and if Warder Hannetjie had not interrupted him that morning he would have sent the following message: 'Be good comrades, my children. Co-operate, then life will run smoothly.'

The next day Warder Hannetjie caught this old man of twelve children stealing grapes from the farm shed. They were an enormous quantity of grapes in a ten-gallon tin and for this misdeed the old man spent a week in the isolation cell. In fact, Span One as a whole was in constant trouble. Warder Hannetjie seemed to have eyes at the back of his head. He uncovered the trick about the cabbages, how they were split in two with the spade and immediately covered with earth and then unearthed again and eaten with split-second timing. He found out how tobacco smoke was beaten into the ground and he found out how conversations were whispered down the wind.

For about two weeks Span One lived in acute misery. The cabbages, tobacco and conversations had been the pivot of jail life to them. Then one evening they noticed that their good old comrade who wore the glasses was looking rather pleased with himself. He pulled out a four-ounce packet of tobacco by way of explanation and the comrades fell upon it with great greed. Brille merely smiled. After all, he was the father of many children. But when the last shred had disappeared, it occurred to the comrades that they ought to be puzzled. Someone said: 'I say, brother. We're watched like hawks these days. Where did you get the tobacco?'

'Hannetjie gave it to me,' said Brille.

There was a long silence. Into it dropped a quiet bomb-shell.

'I saw Hannetjie in the shed today,' and the failing eyesight blinked rapidly. 'I caught him in the act of stealing five bags of fertiliser and he bribed me to keep my mouth shut.'

There was another long silence.

'Prison is an evil life,' Brille continued, apparently discussing some irrelevant matter. 'It makes a man contemplate all kinds of evil deeds.'

He held out his hand and closed it.

'You know, comrades,' he said. 'I've got Hannetjie. I'll betray him tomorrow.'

Everyone began talking at once.

'Forget it, brother. You'll get shot.'

Brille laughed.

'I won't,' he said. 'That is what I mean about evil. I am a father of children and I saw today that Hannetjie is just a child and stupidly truthful. I'm going to punish him severely because we need a good warder.'

The following day, with Brille as witness, Hannetjie confessed to the theft of the fertiliser and was fined a large sum of money. From then on Span One did very much as they pleased while Warder

Hannetjie stood by and said nothing. But it was Brille who carried this to extremes. One day, at the close of work Warder Hannetjie said: 'Brille, pick up my jacket and carry it back to the camp.'

'But nothing in the regulations says I'm your servant, Hannetjie,' Brille replied coolly.

'I've told you not to call me Hannetjie. You must say Baas,' but Warder Hannetjie's voice lacked conviction. In turn, Brille squinted up at him.

'I'll tell you something about this Baas business, Hannetjie,' he said. 'One of these days we are going to run the country. You are going to clean my car. Now, I have a fifteen-year-old son and I'd die of shame if you had to tell him that I ever called you Baas.'

Warder Hannetjie went red in the face and picked up his coat.

On another occasion Brille was seen to be walking about the prison yard, openly smoking tobacco. On being taken before the prison commander he claimed to have received the tobacco from Warder Hannetjie. Throughout the tirade from his chief, Warder Hannetjie failed to defend himself but his nerve broke completely. He called Brille to one side.

'Brille,' he said. 'This thing between you and me must end. You may not know it but I have a wife and children and you're driving me to suicide.'

'Why don't you like your own medicine, Hannetjie?' Brille asked quietly.

'I can give you anything you want,' Warder Hannetjie said in desperation.

'It's not only me but the whole of Span One,' said Brille, cunningly. 'The whole of Span One wants something from you.'

Warder Hannetjie brightened with relief.

'I think I can manage if it's tobacco you want,' he said.

Brille looked at him, for the first time struck with pity, and guilt.

He wondered if he had carried the whole business too far. The man was really a child.

'It's not tobacco we want, but you,' he said. 'We want you on our side. We want a good warder because without a good warder we won't be able to manage the long stretch ahead.'

Warder Hannetjie interpreted this request in his own fashion and his interpretation of what was good and human often left the prisoners of Span One speechless with surprise. He had a way of slipping off his revolver and picking up a spade and digging alongside

Span One. He had a way of producing unheard of luxuries like boiled eggs from his farm nearby and things like cigarettes, and Span One responded nobly and got the reputation of being the best work span in the camp. And it wasn't only take from their side. They were awfully good at stealing certain commodities like fertiliser which were needed on the farm of Warder Hannetjie.

CHRISTOPHER HOPE

Learning to Fly

AN AFRICAN FAIRY TALE

Long ago, in the final days of the old regime, there was a colonel who held an important job in the State Security Police and his name was Rocco du Preez. Colonel du Preez was in charge of the interrogation of political suspects and because of his effect on the prisoners of the old regime he became widely known in the country as 'Window-jumpin' ' du Preez. After mentioning his name it was customary to add 'thank God', because he was a strong man and in the dying days of the old regime everyone agreed that we needed a strong man. Now Colonel du Preez acquired his rather strange nickname not because he did any window jumping himself but rather because he had been the first to draw attention to this phenomenon which affected so many of the prisoners who were brought before him.

The offices of State Security were situated on the thirteenth floor of a handsome and tall modern block in the centre of town. Their high windows looked down on to a little dead end street far below. Once this street had been choked with traffic and bustling with thriving shops. Then one day the first jumper landed on the roof of a car parked in the street, and after that it was shut to traffic and turned into a pedestrian shopping mall. The street was filled in and covered over with crazy paving and one or two benches set up for weary shoppers. However, the jumpings increased and became a spate: sometimes one or two a week and several nasty accidents on the ground began to frighten off the shoppers.

Whenever a jump had taken place the whole area was cordoned off to allow in the emergency services; the police, the undertaker's men, the municipal workers brought in to hose down the area of impact which was often surprisingly large. The jumpings were bad for business and the shopkeepers grew desperate. The authorities were sympathetic and erected covered walkways running the length of the street leaving only the central area of crazy paving and the benches, on which no one had ever been known to sit, exposed to the heavens; the walkways protected by their overhead concrete parapets were guaranteed safe against any and all flying objects. But still trade dwindled and one by one the shops closed and the street slowly died and came to be known by the locals, who gave it a wide berth, as the 'landing field'.

As everyone knows, window jumpings increased apace over the years and being well placed to study them probably led Colonel Rocco du Preez to his celebrated thesis afterwards included in the manual of psychology used by recruits at the Police College and known as Du Preez's Law. It states that all men, when brought to the brink, will contrive to find a way out if the least chance is afforded them and the choice of the means is always directly related to the racial characteristics of the individual in question. Some of Du Preez's remarks on the subject have come down to us, though these are almost certainly apocryphal, as are so many of the tales of the final days of the old regime. 'Considering your average white man,' Du Preez is supposed to have said, 'my experience is that he prefers hanging – whether by pyjama cord, belt, strips of blanket; providing he finds the handy protuberance, the cell bars, say, or up-ended bedstead he needs, you'll barely have turned your back and he'll be up there swinging from the light cord or other chosen noose. Your white man in his last throes has a wonderful sense of rhythm – believe me, whatever you may have heard to the contrary – I've seen several whites about to cough it and all of them have been wonderful dancers. Your Indian, now, he's something else, a slippery customer who prefers smooth surfaces. I've known Asians to slip and crack their skulls in a shower cubicle so narrow you'd have sworn a man couldn't turn in it. This innate slitheriness is probably what makes them good businessmen. Now, your Coloured, per contra, is more clumsy a character altogether. His hidden talent lies in his amazing lack of co-ordination. Even the most sober rogue can appear hopelessly drunk to the untrained eye. On the surface of things it might seem that you can do nothing with him: he has no taste for the knotted strip of blanket or the convenient bootlace; a soapy bathroom floor leaves him unmoved – yet show him a short, steep flight of steps and he instinctively knows what to do. When it comes to Africans I have found that they, perverse as always, choose another way out.

They are given to window jumping. This phenomenon has been very widespread in the past few years. Personally, I suspect its roots go back a long way, back to their superstitions – i.e. to their regard for black magic and witchcraft. Everyone knows that in extreme instances your average blackie will believe anything: that his witchdoctors will turn the white man's bullets to water; or, if he jumps out of a window thirteen stories above *terra firma* he will miraculously find himself able to fly. Nothing will stop him once his mind's made up. I've seen up to six Bantu jump from a high window on one day. Though the first landed on his head and the others saw the result they were not deterred. It's as if despite the evidence of their senses they believed that if only they could practise enough they would one day manage to take off.'

'Window-jumpin' ' du Preez worked in an office sparsely furnished with an old desk, a chair, a strip of green, government-issue carpet, a very large steel cabinet marked 'Secret' and a bare, fluorescent light in the ceiling. Poor though the furnishings were, the room was made light and cheerful by the large windows behind his desk and nobody remembers being aware of the meanness of the furnishings when Colonel du Preez was present in the room. When he sat down in his leather swivel chair behind his desk, witnesses reported that he seemed to fill up the room, to make it habitable, even genial. His reddish hair and green eyes were somehow enough to colour the room and make it complete. The eyes had a peculiarly steady glint to them. This was his one peculiarity. When thinking hard about something he had the nervous habit of twirling a lock of the reddish hair, a copper colour with gingery lights, in the words of a witness, around a finger. It was his only nervous habit. Since these were often the last words ever spoken by very brave men, we have to wonder at their ability to register details so sharply under terrible conditions; for it is these details that provide us with a glimpse of the man Du Preez, as no photographs have come down to us.

It was to this office that three plainclothes men one day brought a new prisoner. The charge-sheet was singularly bare; it read simply, Mphahlele . . . Jake. 'Possession of explosives'. Obviously they had got very little out of him. The men left closing the door softly, almost reverently, behind them.

The prisoner wore an old black coat, ragged grey flannels and a black beret tilted at an angle which gave him an odd, jaunty, rather continental look, made all the more incongruous by the fact that his hands were manacled behind him. Du Preez reached up with his desk ruler and knocked off the beret revealing a bald head gleaming in the overhead fluorescent light. It would have been shaved and polished Du Preez guessed, by one of the wandering barbers who traditionally gathered on Sundays down by the municipal lake, setting up three-legged stools and basins of water and hanging towels and leather strops for their cutthroat razors from the lower branches of a convenient tree and draping their customers in large red and white check cloths, giving them little hand mirrors so that they could look on while the barbers scraped, snipped, polished and gossiped away the sunny afternoon by the water's edge beneath the tall bluegums. Clearly Mphahlele belonged to the old school of whom there were fewer each year as the fashion for Afro-wigs and strange woollen bangs took increasing hold among younger blacks. Du Preez couldn't help warming to this just a little. After all, he was one of the old school himself in the new age of trimmers and ameliorists. Mphahlele was tall, as tall as Du Preez and, he reckoned, about the same age – though it was always difficult to tell with Africans. A knife scar ran from his right eye down to his collar, the flesh fused in a livid welt as if a tiny mole had burrowed under the black skin pushing up a furrow behind it. His nose had been broken, too, probably as the result of the same township fracas, and had mended badly turning to the left and then sharply to the right as if unable to make up its mind. The man was obviously a brawler. Mphahlele's dark brown eyes were remarkably calm – almost to the point of arrogance Du Preez thought for an instant, before dismissing the absurd notion with a tiny smile. It shocked to see an answering smile on the prisoner's lips. However he was too old a hand to let this show.

'Where are the explosives?'

'I have no explosives,' Mphahlele answered. 'Also, I will tell you nothing.'

He spoke quietly but Du Preez thought he detected a most unjustifiable calm amounting to confidence, or worse, to insolence, and he noted how he talked with special care. It was another insight. On his pad he wrote the letters M.K. The prisoner's diction and accent betrayed him: Mission Kaffir. Raised at one of the stations by a foolish clergy as though he was one day going to be a white man. Of course, the word 'kaffir' was not a word in official use any longer. Like other names at that time growing less acceptable as descriptions of Africans: 'native', 'coon' and even 'bantu', the word had given way to softer names in an attempt to respond to the disaffection springing up among people. But Du Preez, as he told himself, was too old a dog to learn new tricks. Besides, he was not interested in learning to be more 'responsive'. He did not belong to the ameliorists. His job was to control disaffection and where necessary to put it down with proper force. And anyway, his notes were strictly for his own reference, private reminders of his first impressions of a prisoner, useful when, and if, a second interview took place. The number of people he saw was growing daily and he could not expect to keep track of them all in his head.

Du Preez left his desk and slowly circled the prisoner. 'Your comrade who placed the bomb in the shopping centre was a bungler. There was great damage. Many people were killed. Women and children among them. But he wasn't quick enough, your friend. The blast caught him too. Before he died he gave us your name. The paraffin tests show you handled explosives recently. I want the location of the cache. I want the make-up of your cell with names and addresses as well as anythintg else you might want to tell me.'

'If the bomb did its business then the man was no bungler,' Mphahlele said.

'The murder of women and children – no bungle?'

Mphahlele shrugged. 'Casualties of war.'

Du Preez circled him and stopped beside his right ear. 'I don't call the death of children war. I call it barbarism.'

'Our children have been dying for years but we have never called it barbarism. Now we are learning. You and I know what we mean. I'm your prisoner of war. You will do whatever you can to get me to tell you things you want to know. Then you will get rid of me. But I will tell you nothing. So why don't you finish with me now? Save time.' His brown eyes rested briefly and calmly on Du Preez's empty chair, and then swept the room as if the man had said all he had to say and was now more interested in getting to know that terrible office.

A muscle in Du Preez's cheek rippled and it took him a moment longer than he would have liked to bring his face back to a decent composure. Then he crossed to the big steel cabinet and opened it. Inside was the terrible, tangled paraphernalia of persuasion, the electric generator, the leads and electrodes, the salt water for sharpening contact and the thick leather straps necessary for restraining the shocked and writhing victim. At the sight of this he scored a point; he thought he detected a momentary pause, a faltering in the steady brown eyes taking stock of his office, and he pressed home the advantage. 'It's very seldom that people fail to talk to me after this treatment.' He held up the electrodes, 'The pain is intense.'

In fact, as we know now, the apparatus in the cabinet was not that actually used on prisoners – indeed, one can see the same equipment on permanent exhibition in the National Museum of the Revolution. But Du Preez, in fact, kept it for effect. The real thing was administered by a special team in a soundproof room on one of the lower floors. But the mere sight of the equipment, whose reputation was huge among the townships and shanty towns, was often enough to have the effect of loosening stubborn tongues. However, Mphahlele looked at the tangle of wires and straps as if he wanted to include them in his inventory of the room and his expression suggested not fear but rather – and this Du Preez found positively alarming – a hint of approval. There was nothing more to be said. He went back to his desk, pressed the buzzer and the plainclothes men came in and took Mphahlele downstairs.

Over the next twenty-four hours 'Window-Jumpin'' du Preez puzzled over his new prisoner. It was a long time before he put his finger on some of the qualities distinguishing this man from others he'd worked with under similar circumstances. Clearly, Mphahlele was not frightened. But then other men had been brave too – for a while. It was not only bravery, one had to add to it the strange fact that this man quite clearly did not hate him. That was quite alarming: Mphahlele had treated him as if they were truly equals. There was an effrontery about this he found maddening and the more he thought about it, the more he raged inside. He walked over to the windows behind his desk and looked down to the dead little square with its empty benches and its crazy paving which, with its haphazard joins where the stones were cemented one to the next into nonsensical, snaking patterns, looked from the height of the thirteenth storey as if a giant had brought his foot down hard and the earth had shivered into a thousand pieces. He was getting angry. Worse, he was letting his anger cloud his judgement. Worse still, he didn't care.

Mphahlele was in a bad way when they brought him back to Du Preez. His face was so bruised that the old knife scar was barely visible, his lower lip was bleeding copiously and he swayed when the policemen let him go and might have fallen had he not grabbed the edge of the desk and hung there swaying. In answer to Du Preez's silent question the interrogators shook their heads. 'Nothing. He never said *nothing*.'

Mphahlele had travelled far in the regions of pain and it had changed him greatly. It might have been another man who clung to Du Preez's desk with his breath coming in rusty pants; his throat was choked with phlegm or blood he did not have the strength to cough away. He was bent and old and clearly on his last legs. One eye was puffed up in a great swelling shot with green and purple bruises, but the other, he noticed with a renewed spurt of anger, though it had trouble focusing, showed the same old haughty gleam when he spoke to the man.

'Have you any more to tell me about your war?'

Mphahlele gathered himslf with a great effort, his one good eye flickering wildly with the strain. He licked the blood off his lips and wiped it from his chin. 'We will win,' he said, 'soon.'

Du Preez dismissed the interrogators with a sharp nod and they left his presence by backing away to the door, full of awe at his control. When the door closed behind them he stood up and regarded the swaying figure with its flickering eye. 'You are like children,' he said bitterly, 'and there is nothing we can do for you.'

'Yes,' said Mphahlele, 'we are your children. We owe you everything.'

Du Preez stared at him. But there was not a trace of irony to be detected. The madman was quite plainly sincere in what he said and Du Preez found that insufferable. He moved to the windows and opened them. It was now that, so the stories go, he made his fateful remark. 'Well, if you won't talk, then I suppose you had better learn to fly.'

What happened next is not clear except in broad outline even today, the records of the old regime which were to have been made public have unaccountably been reclassified as secret, but we can make an informed guess. Legend then says that Du Preez recounted for his prisoner his 'theory of desperate solutions' and that, exhausted though he was, Mphahlele showed quickening interest in the way out chosen by white men – that is to say, dancing. We know this is true because Du Preez told the policemen waiting outside the door when he joined them in order to allow Mphahlele to do what he had to do. After waiting a full minute, Du Preez entered his office again closing the door behind him, alone, as had become customary in such cases, his colleagues respecting his need for a few moments of privacy before moving on to the next case. Seconds later these colleagues heard a most terrible cry. When they rushed into the room they found it was empty.

Now we are out on a limb. We have no more facts to go on. All is buried in obscurity or say, rather, it is buried with Du Preez who plunged from his window down to the landing field at the most terrible speed, landing on his head. Jake Mphahlele has never spoken of his escape from Colonel 'Window-Jumpin' ' du Preez. All we have are the stories. Some firmly believe to this day that it was done by a special magic and Mphahlele had actually learnt to fly and that the colonel on looking out of his window, was so jealous at seeing a black man swooping in the heavens that he had plunged after him on the supposition, regarded as axiomatic in the days of the old regime, that anything a black man could do, a white man could do ten times better. Others, more sceptical, said that the prisoner had hidden himself in the steel cabinet with the torture equipment and emerged to push Du Preez to hell and then escaped in the confusion you will get in a hive if you kill the queen bee. All that is known for sure is that Du Preez lay on the landing field like wet clothes fallen from a washing line, terribly twisted and leaking everywhere. And that in the early days of the new regime Jake Mphahlele was appointed chief investigating officer in charge of the interrogation of suspects and that his work with political prisoners, especially white prisoners, was soon so widely respected that he won rapid promotion to the rank of colonel and became known throughout the country as Colonel Jake 'Dancin' ' Mphahlele, and after his name it was customary to add 'thank God', because he was a strong man and in the early days of the new regime everyone agreed we needed a strong man.

CHRISTOPHER HOPE, 1976

ALAN PATON

Life for a Life

The doctor had closed up the ugly hole in Flip's skull so that his widow, and her brothers and sisters, and their wives and husbands and children, and Flip's own brothers and sisters and their wives and husbands and children, could come and stand for a minute and look down on the hard stony face of the master of Kroon, one of the richest farmers of the whole Karroo. The cars kept coming and going, the police, the doctor, the newspapermen, the neighbours from near and far.

All the white women were in the house, and all the white men outside. An event like this, the violent death of one of themselves, drew them together in an instant, so that all the world might see that they were one, and that they would not rest till justice had been done. It was this standing there, this drawing together, that kept the brown people in their small stone houses, talking in low voices; and their fear communicated itself to their children, so that there was no need to silence them. Now and then one of them would leave the houses to relieve his needs in the bushes, but otherwise there was no movement on this side of the valley. Each family sat in its house, at a little distance from each front door, watching with anxious fascination the goings and the comings of the white people standing in front of the big house.

Then the white predikant came from Poort, you could tell him by the black hat and the black clothes. He shook hands with Big Baas Flip's sons, and said words of comfort to them. Then all the men followed him into the house, and after a while the sound of the slow determined singing was carried across the valley, to the small stone houses on the other side, to Enoch Maarman, head shepherd of Kroon, and his wife Sara, sitting just inside the door of their own house. Maarman's anxiety showed itself in the movements of his face and hands, and his wife knew of his condition but kept her face averted from it. Guilt lay heavily upon them both, because they had hated Big Baas Flip, not with clenched fists and bared teeth, but, as befitted people in their station, with salutes and deference.

Sara suddenly sat erect.

'They are coming,' she said.

They watched the four men leave the big stone house, and take the path that led to the small stone houses, and both could feel the fear rising in them. Their guilt weighed down on them all the more heavily because they felt no grief. They felt all the more afraid because the show of grief might have softened the harshness of the approaching ordeal. Someone must pay for so terrible a crime, and if not the one who did it, then who better than the one who could not grieve? That morning Maarman had stood hat in hand before Baas Gysbert, who was Big Baas Flip's eldest son, and had said to him, 'My people are sorry to hear of this terrible thing.' And Baas Gysbert had given him the terrible answer, 'That could be so.'

Then Sara said to him, 'Robbertse is one.'

He nodded. He knew that Robbertse was one, the big detective with the temper that got out of hand, so that reddish foam would come out of his mouth, and he would hold a man by the throat till one of his colleagues would shout at him to let the man go. Sara's father, who was one of the wisest men in all the district of Poort, said that he could never be sure whether Robbertse was mad or only pretending to be, but that it didn't really matter, because whichever it was, it was dangerous.

Maarman and his wife stood up when two of the detectives came to the door of the small stone house. One was Robbertse, but both were big men and confident. They wore smart sports jackets and grey flannels, and grey felt hats on their heads. They came in and kept their hats on their heads, looking round the small house with the air of masters. They spoke to each other as though there were nobody standing there waiting to be spoken to.

Then Robbertse said, 'You are Enoch Maarman?'

'Yes, baas.'

'The head shepherd?'

'Yes, baas.'

'Who are the other shepherds?'

Enoch gave him the names, and Robbertse sat down on one of the chairs, and wrote the names in his book. Then he tilted his hat back on his head and said, 'Has any of these men ever been in jail?'

Enoch moistened his lips. He wanted to say that the detective could easily find it out for himself, that he was the head shepherd and would answer any question about the farm or the work. But he said instead, 'I don't know, baas.'

'You don't know Kleinbooi was in jail at Christmas?'

'Yes, I know that, baas.'

Suddenly, Robbertse was on his feet, and his head almost touching the ceiling, and his body almost filling the small room, and he was shouting in a tremendous voice, 'Then why did you lie?'

Sara had shrunk back into the wall, and was looking at Robbertse out of terrified eyes, but Enoch did not move though he was deathly afraid.

He answered, 'I didn't mean to lie, baas. Kleinbooi was in jail for drink, not killing.'

Robbertse said, 'Killing? Why do you mention killing?'

Then when Enoch did not answer, the detective suddenly lifted his hand so that Enoch started back and knocked over the other chair. Down on his knees, and shielding his head with one hand, he set the chair straight again, saying, 'Baas, we know that you are here because the master was killed.'

But Robbertse's lifting his hand had been intended only to remove his hat from his head, and now with a grin he put his hat on the table.

'Why fall down,' he asked, 'because I take off my hat? I like to take off my hat in another man's house.'

He smiled at Sara, and looking at the chair now set upright, said to her, 'You can sit.'

When she made no attempt to sit on it, the smile left his face, and he said to her coldly and menacingly, 'You can sit.'

When she had sat down, he said to Maarman, 'Don't knock over any more chairs. For if one gets broken, you'll tell the magistrate I broke it, won't you? That I lifted it up and threatened you?'

'No, baas.'

Robbertse sat down again, and studied his book as though something were written there, not the names of shepherds. Then he said suddenly, out of nothing, 'You hated him, didn't you?'

And Enoch answered, 'No, baas.'

'Where's your son Johannes?'

'In Cape Town, baas.'

'Why didn't he become a shepherd?'

'I wouldn't let him, baas.'

'You sent him to the white university?'

'Yes, baas.'

'So that he could play the white baas?'

'No, baas.'

'Why does he never come to see you?'

'The Big Baas would not let him, baas.'

'Because he wouldn't become a shepherd?'

'Yes, baas.'

'So you hated him, didn't you?'

'No, baas.'

Robbertse looked at him with contempt.

'A man keeps your own son away from your door, because you want a better life for him, and you don't hate him? God, what are you made of?'

He continued to look at Maarman with contempt, then shrugged his shoulders as though it were a bad business; then he suddenly grew intimate, confidential, even friendly.

'Maarman, I have news for you, you may think it good, you may think it bad. But you have a right to know it, seeing it is about your son.'

The shepherd was suddenly filled with a new apprehension. Robbertse was preparing some new blow. That was the kind of man he was, he hated to see any coloured man holding his head up, he hated to see any coloured man anywhere but on his knees or his stomach.

'Your son,' said Robbertse, genially, 'you thought he was in Cape Town, didn't you?'

'Yes, baas.'

'Well, he isn't,' said Robbertse, 'he's here in Poort, he was seen there yesterday.'

He let it sink in, then he said to Maarman, 'He hated Big Baas Flip, didn't he?'

Maarman cried out, 'No, baas.'

For the second time Robbertse was on his feet, filling the room with his size, and his madness.

'He didn't hate him?' he shouted. 'God Almighty, Big Baas Flip wouldn't let him come to his own home, and see his own father and mother, but he didn't hate him. And you didn't hate him either, you creeping yellow bastard, what are you all made of?'

He looked at the shepherd out of his mad red eyes. Then with contempt he said again, 'You creeping yellow hottentot bastard.'

'Baas,' said Maarman.

'What?'

'Baas, the baas can ask me what he likes, and I shall try to answer him, but I ask the baas not to insult me in my own house, before my own wife.'

Robbertse appeared delighted, charmed. Some other man might have been outraged that a coloured man should so advise him, but he was able to admire such manly pride.

'Insult you?' he said. 'Didn't you see me take off my hat when I came into this house?'

He turned to Sara and asked her, 'Didn't you see me take off my hat when I came into this house?'

'Yes, baas.'

'Did you think I was insulting your husband?'

'No, baas.'

Robbertse smiled at her ingratiatingly. 'I only called him a creeping yellow hottentot bastard,' he said.

The cruel words destroyed the sense of piquancy for him, and now he was truly outraged. He took a step towards the shepherd, and his colleague, the other detective, the silent one, suddenly shouted at him, 'Robbertse!'

Robbertse stopped. He looked vacantly at Maarman. 'Was someone calling me?' he asked. 'Did you hear a voice calling me?'

Maarman was terrified, fascinated, he could see the red foam. He was at a loss, not knowing whether this was madness, or madness affecting to be madness, or what it was.

'The other baas was calling you, baas.'

Then it was suddenly all over. Robbertse sat down again on the chair to ask more questions.

'You knew there was money stolen?'

'Yes, baas.'

'Who told you?'

'Mimi, the girl who works at the house.'

'You knew the money was in an iron safe, and they took it away?'

'Yes, baas.'

'Where would they take it to?'

'I don't know, baas.'

'Where would you have taken it, if you had stolen it?'

But Maarman didn't answer.

'You won't answer, eh?'

All three of them watched Robbertse anxiously, lest the storm should return. But he smiled benevolently at Maarman, as though he knew that even a coloured man must have pride, as though he thought all the better of him for it, and said, 'All right, I won't ask that question. But I want you to think of the places where that safe could be. It must have been carried by at least two men, perhaps more. And they couldn't have got it off the farm in the time. So it's still on the farm. Now all I want you to do is to think where it could be. No one knows this farm better than you.'

'I'll think, baas.'

The other detective suddenly said, 'The lieutenant's come.' The two of them stood just inside the door, looking over to the house on the other side of the valley. Then suddenly Robbertse rounded on Maarman, and catching him by the back of the neck, forced him to the door, so that he could look too.

'You see that,' he said. 'They want to know who killed Big Baas Flip, and they want to know soon. Do you see them?'

'Yes, baas.'

'And you see that lieutenant. He rides round in a Chrysler, and by God, he wants to know too. And by God he'll ride me if I don't find out.'

He pulled the shepherd back into the room, and put on his hat and went out, followed by the other.

'Don't think you've seen the last of me,' he said to Maarman. 'You've got to show me where your friends hid that safe.'

Then he and his companion joined the other two detectives, and all four of them turned back towards the big house. They talked animatedly, and more than once all of them stood for a moment while one of them made some point or put forward some theory. No one would have known that one of them was mad.

Twelve hours since they had taken her husband away. Twelve hours since the mad detective had come for him, with those red tormented eyes, as though the lieutenant were riding him too hard. He had grinned at her husband. 'Come and we'll look for the safe,' he said.

The sun was sinking in the sky, over the hills of Kroon. It was not time to be looking for a safe.

She did not sleep that night. Her neighbours had come to sit with her, till midnight, till two o'clock, till four o'clock, but there was no sign. Why did he not come back? Were they still searching at this hour of the morning? Then the sun was rising, over the hills of Kroon.

On the other side of the valley the big house was awake, for this was the day that Big Baas Flip would be laid to rest, under the cypress trees of the graveyard in the stones. Leaderless, the shepherds had gone to Baas Gysbert to be given the day's work; and Hendrik Baadjies, second shepherd, told Baas Gysbert that the police had taken Enoch Maarman at sunset, and now at dawn he had not yet returned, and that his wife was anxious. Would Baas Gysbert not please strike the telephone, not much only a little, not for long only a short time, to ask what had become of his father's head shepherd?

And Baas Gysbert replied in a voice trembling with passion, 'Do you not know it was my father who was killed?'

So Hendrik Baadjies touched his hat, and said, 'Pardon me, baas, that I asked.'

Then he went to stand with the other shepherds, a man shamed standing with other shamed men, who must teach their children to know for ever their station.

Fifteen hours. But she would not eat. Her neighbours brought food, but she would not. She could see the red foam at the corners of the mouth, and see the tremendous form and hear the tremendous voice that filled her house, with anger, and with feigned politeness, and with contempt, and with cruel smiling. Because one was a shepherd, because one had no certitude of home or work or life or favour, because one's back had to be bent though one's soul would be upright, because one had to speak the smiling craven words under any injustice, because one had to bear as a brand this dark sun-warmed colour of the skin, as good surely as any other, because of these things, this mad policeman could strike down, and hold by the neck, and call a creeping yellow hottentot bastard, a man who had never hurt another in his long gentle life, a man who like the great Christ was a lover of sheep and of little children, and had been a good husband and father except for those occasional outbursts that any sensible woman will pass over, outbursts of the imprisoned manhood that has got tired of the chains that keep it down on its knees. Yes this mad policeman could take off his hat mockingly in one's house, and ask a dozen questions that he, for all that he was as big as a mountain, would never have dared to ask a white person.

But the anger went from her suddenly, leaving her spent, leaving her again full of anxiety for the safety of her husband, and for the safety of her son who had chosen to come to Poort at this dangerous hour. Just as a person sits in the cold, and by keeping motionless enjoys some illusion of warmth, so she sat inwardly motionless, lest by some interior movement she would disturb the numbness of her mind, and feel the pain of her condition. However she was not allowed to remain so, for at eleven o'clock a message came from Hendrik Baadjies to say that it was certain that neither detective nor head shepherd was on the farm of Kroon. Then at noon a boy brought her a message that her brother Solomon Koopman had come with a taxi to the gate of the farm, and that she should come at once to him there, because he did not wish to come to her house. She tied a doek round her head, and as soon as she saw her brother, she cried to him, 'Are they safe?' When he looked mystified, she said, 'My man and my child,' and her brother told her it must have been Robbertse's joke, that her son was safe in Cape Town and had not been in Poort at all. He was glad to be able to tell her this piece of news, for his other news was terrible, that Enoch her husband was dead. He had always been a little afraid of his sister, who had brought up the family when their mother had died, so he did not know how to comfort her. But she wept only a little, like one who is used to such events, and must not grieve but must prepare for the next.

Then she said, 'How did he die?' So he told her the story that the police had told him of Enoch's death, how that the night was dark, and how they had gone searching down by the river, and how Enoch had slipped on one of the big stones there and had fallen on his head, and how they had not hesitated but had rushed him to Poort, but he had died in the car.

What can one say to a story like that? So they said nothing. He was ashamed to tell it, but he had to tell it so, because he had a butcher's licence in Poort, and he could not afford to doubt the police.

'This happened in the dark,' Sara said. 'Why do they let me know now?'

Alas, they could not give her her husband's body, it was buried already! Alas, she would know what it was like in the summer, how death began to smell because of the heat, that was why they had buried it! Alas, they wouldn't have done it had they only known who he was, and that his home was so near, at the well-known farm of Kroon!

Couldn't the body be lifted again, and be taken to Kroon, to be buried there in the hills where Enoch Maarman had worked so faithfully for nearly fifty years, tending the sheep of Big Baas Flip? Alas, no it couldn't be, for it is one thing to bury a man, and quite another thing to take him up again! To bury a man one only needs a doctor, and even that not always, but to take him up again you would have to go to Cape Town and get the permission of the Minister himself. And they do not permit that lightly, to disturb a man's bones when once he has been laid to rest in the earth.

Solomon Koopman would have gone away, with a smile on his lips, and cold hate in his heart. But she would not. For this surely was one thing that was her own, the body of the man she had lived with for so many years. She wanted the young white policeman behind the desk to show her the certificate of her husband's death, and she wanted to know by whose orders he had been buried, and who had hurried his body into the earth, so that she could tell for herself whether it was possible that such a person had not known that this was the body of Enoch Maarman, head shepherd of the farm of Kroon, who had that very night been in the company of Detective Robbertse.

She put these questions, through her brother Solomon Koopman, who had a butcher's licence, and framed the questions apologetically, because he knew that they implied that something was very wrong somewhere, that something was being hidden. But although he put the questions as nicely as possible, he could see that the policeman behind the desk was becoming impatient with this importunity, and was beginning to think that grief was no excuse for this cross-examination of authority. Other policemen came in too, and listened to the questions of this woman who would not go away, and one of them said to the young constable behind the desk, 'Show her the death certificate.'

There it was, 'Death due to sub-cranial bleeding.'

'He fell on his head,' explained the older policeman, 'and the blood inside finished him.'

'I ask to see Detective Robbertse,' she said.

The policemen smiled and looked at each other, not in any flagrant way, just knowingly.

'You can't see him,' said the older policeman. 'He went away on holiday this very morning.'

'Why does he go on holiday,' she asked, 'when he is working on this case?'

The policemen began to look at her impatiently. She was going too far, even though her husband was dead. Her own brother was growing restless, and he said to her, 'Sister, let us go.'

Her tears were coming now, made to flow by sorrow and anger. The policemen were uneasy, and drifted away, leaving only the young constable at the desk.

'What happened?' she asked. 'How did my husband die? Why is Detective Robbertse not here to answer my questions?'

The young policeman said to her angrily, 'We don't answer such questions here. If you want to ask such questions, get a lawyer.'

'Good,' she said. 'I shall get a lawyer.'

She and her brother turned to leave, but the older policeman was there at the door, polite and reasonable.

'Why isn't your sister sensible?' he asked Solomon Koopman. 'A lawyer will only stir up trouble between the police and the people.'

Koopman looked from the policeman to his sister, for he feared them both.

'Ask him,' Sara said to her brother, 'if it is not sensible to want to know about one's husband's death.'

'Tell her,' said the policeman to Koopman, 'that it was an accident.'

'He knows who I am,' Sara said. 'Why did he allow my husband to be buried here when he knew that he lived at Kroon?'

Her voice was rising, and to compensate for it, the policeman's voice grew lower and lower.

'I did not have him buried,' he said desperately. 'It was an order from a high person.'

Outside in the street, Koopman said to his sister miserably, 'Sister,

I beg you, do not get a lawyer. For if you do, I shall lose the licence, and who will help you to keep your son at the university?'

Sara Maarman got back to her house as the sun was sinking over the hills of Kroon, twenty-four hours from the time that her husband had left with Detective Robbertse to look for the safe. She lit the lamp and sat down, too weary to think of food. While she sat there, Hendrik Baadjies knocked at the door and came in and brought her the sympathy of all the brown people on the farm of Kroon. Then he stood before her, twisting his hat in his hand almost as though she were a white woman. He brought a message from Baas Gysbert, who now needed a new shepherd and needed Enoch Maarman's house for him to live in. She would be given three days to pack all her possessions, and the loan of the cart and donkeys to take them and herself to Poort.

'Is three days enough?' asked Baadjies. 'For if it is not, I could ask for more.'

'Three days is enough,' she said.

When Baadjies had gone, she thought to herself, three days is three days too many, to go on living in this land of stone, three days before she could leave it all for the Cape, where her son lived, where people lived, so he told her, softer and sweeter lives.

ZOË WICOMB

A Trip to the Gifberge

You've always loved your father better.

That will be her opening line.

The chair she sits in is a curious affair, crude like a crate with armrests. A crate for a large tough-skinned vegetable like hubbard squash which is of course not soft as its name suggests.

I move towards her to adjust the goatskin karos around her shoulders. It has slipped in her attempt to rise out of the chair. I brace myself against the roar of distaste but no, perhaps her chest is too tight to give the words their necessary weight. No, she would rather remove herself from my viperous presence. But the chair is too low and the gnarled hands spread out on the armrests cannot provide enough leverage for the body to rise with dignity. ('She doesn't want to see you,' Aunty Cissie said, biting her lip.)

Her own words are a synchronic feat of syllables and exhalations to produce a halting hiss. 'Take it away. I'll suffocate with heat. You've tried to kill me enough times.' I drop the goatskin on to the ground before realising that it goes on the back of the chair.

I have never thought it unreasonable that she should not want to see me. It is my insistence which is unreasonable. But why, if she is hot, does she sit here in the last of the sun? Her chair stands a good twenty yards from the house, beyond the semi-circle of the grass broom's vigorous expressionistic strokes. From where I stand, having made the predicted entrance through the back gate, she is a painterly arrangement alone on the plain. Her house is on the very edge of the location. Behind her the Matsikamma Range is interrupted by two swollen peaks so that her head rests in the cleavage.

Her chair is uncomfortable without the karos. The wood must cut into the small of her back and she is forced to lean forward, to wriggle. Our eyes meet for a second, accidentally, but she shuts hers instantly so that I hold in my vision the eyes of decades ago. Then they flashed coal-black, the surrounding skin taut across the high cheekbones. Narrow, narrow slits which she forced wide open and like a startled rabbit stared entranced into a mirror as she pushed a wave into the oiled black hair.

'If only,' she lamented, 'if only my eyes were wider I would be quite nice, really nice,' and with a snigger, 'a princess.'

Then she turned on me. 'Poor child. What can a girl do without good looks? Who'll marry you? We'll have to put a peg on your nose.'

And the pearled half moon of her brown fingertip flashed as she stroked appreciatively the curious high bridge of her own nose. Those were the days of the monthly hairwash in the old house. The kitchen humming with pots of water nudging each other on the stove, and afterwards the terrible torments of the comb as she hacked with explorer's determination the path through the tangled undergrowth, set on the discovery of silken tresses. Her own sleek black waves dried admirably, falling into place. Mother.

Now it is thin, scraped back into a limp plait pinned into a bun. Her shirt is the fashionable cut of this season's muttonleg sleeve and I remember that her favourite garments are saved in a mothballed box. Now and then she would bring something to light, just as fashion tiptoeing out of a dusty cupboard would crack her whip after bowing humbly to the original. How long has she been sitting here in her shirt and ill-matched skirt and the nimbus of anger?

She coughs. With her eyes still closed she says, 'There's Jantjie Bêrend in an enamel jug on the stove. Bring me a cup.'

Not a please and certainly no thank you to follow. The daughter must be reminded of her duty. This is her victory: speaking first, issuing a command.

I hold down the matted Jantjie Bêrend with a fork and pour out the yellowish brew. I do not anticipate the hand thrust out to take the drink so that I come too close and the liquid lurches into the saucer. The dry red earth laps up the offering of spilled infusion which turns into a patch of fresh blood.

'Clumsy like your father. He of course never learned to drink from a cup. Always poured it into a saucer, that's why the Shentons all have lower lips like spouts. From slurping their drinks from saucers. Boerjongens, all of them. My Oupa swore that the English potteries cast their cups with saucers attached so they didn't have to listen to Boers slurping their coffee. Oh, he knew a thing or two, my Oupa. Then your Oupa Shenton had the cheek to call me a Griqua meid.'

Her mouth purses as she hauls up the old grievances for which I have no new palliatives. Instead I pick up the bunch of proteas that I had dropped with my rucksack against the wall. I hand the flowers to her and wonder how I hid my revulsion when Aunt Cissie presented them to me at the airport.

'Welcome home to South Africa.' And in my arms the national blooms rested fondly while she turned to the others, the semi-circle of relatives moving closer. 'From all of us. You see everybody's here to meet the naughty girl.'

'And Eddie,' I exclaimed awkwardly as I recognised the youngest uncle now pot-bellied and grey.

'Ag no man, you didn't play marbles together. Don't come here with disrespectful foreign ways. It's your Uncle Eddie,' Aunt Cissie reprimanded. 'And Eddie,' she added, 'you must find all the children. They'll be running all over the place like chickens.'

'Can the new Auntie ride in our car?' asked a little girl tugging at Aunt Cissie's skirt.

'No man, don't be so stupid, she's riding with me and then we all come to my house for something nice to eat. Did your Mammie bring some roeties?'

I rubbed the little girl's head but a tough protea had pierced the cellophane and scratched her cheek which she rubbed self-pityingly.

'Come get your baggage now,' and as we waited Aunt Cissie explained. 'Your mother's a funny old girl, you know. She just wouldn't come to the airport and I explained to her the whole family must be there. Doesn't want to have anything to do with us now, don't ask me why, jus turned against us jus like that. Doesn't talk, not that she ever said much, but she said, right there at your father's funeral – pity you couldn't get here in time – well, she said, "Now you can all leave me alone", and when Boeta Danie said, "Ag man sister you musn't talk so, we've all had grief and the Good Lord knows who to take and who to leave", well you wouldn't guess what she said' . . . and Aunt Cissie's eyes roved incredulously about my person as if a good look would offer an explanation . . . 'she said plainly, jus like that, "Danie", jus dropped the Boeta there and then in front of everybody, she said . . . and I don't know how to say it because I've always had a tender place in my heart for your mother, such a lovely shy girl she was . . .'

'Really?' I interrupted. I could not imagine her being described as shy.

'Oh yes, quite shy, a real lady. I remember when your father wrote home to ask for permission to marry, we were so worried. A Griqua girl, you know, and it was such a surprise when he brought your mother, such nice English she spoke and good features and a nice figure also.'

Again her eyes took in my figure so that she was moved to add in parenthesis, 'I'll get you a nice step-in. We get good ones here with the long leg, you know, gives you a nice firm hip-line. You must look after yourself man; you won't get a husband if you let yourself go like this.'

Distracted from her story she leaned over to examine the large ornate label of a bag bobbing by on the moving belt.

'That's not mine,' I said.

'I know. I can mos see it says Mev. H.J. Groenewald,' she retorted. Then, appreciatively as she allowed the bag to carry drunkenly along. 'But that's now something else hey. Very nice. There's nothing wrong in admiring something nice man. I'm not shy and there's no Apartheid at the airport. You spend all that time overseas and you still afraid of Boers.' She shook her head reproachfully.

'I must go to the lavatory,' I announced.

'OK. I'll go with hey.'

And from the next closet her words rose above the sound of abundant pee gushing against the enamel of the bowl, drowning my own failure to produce even a trickle.

'I made a nice pot of beans and samp, not grand of course but something to remind you you're home. Stamp-en-stoot we used to call it on the farm', and her clear nostalgic laughter vibrated against the bowl.

'Yes,' I shouted, 'funny, but I could actually smell beans and samp hovering just above the petrol fumes in the streets of London.'

I thought of how you walk along worrying about being late, or early, or wondering where to have lunch, when your nose twitches with a teasing smell and you're transported to a place so specific and the power of the smell summons the light of that day when the folds of a dress draped the brick wall and your hands twisted anxiously, Is she my friend, truly my friend?

While Aunt Cissie chattered about how vile London was, a terrible place where people slept under the arches in newspapers and brushed the pigeonshit off their brows in the mornings. Funny how Europeans could sink so low. And the Coloured people from the West Indies just fighting on the streets, killing each other and still wearing their doekies from back home. Really, as if there weren't hairdressers in

London. She had seen it all on TV. Through the door I watched the patent-leather shoes shift under the heaving and struggling of flesh packed into corsets.

'Do they show the riots here in South Africa on TV?'

'Ag, don't you start with politics now,' she laughed, 'but I got a new TV you know.'

We opened our doors simultaneously and with the aid of flushing water she drew me back, 'Yes, your father's funeral was a business.'

'What did Mamma say?'

'Man, you mustn't take notice of what she says. I always say that half the time people don't know what they talking about and blood is thicker than water so you jus do your duty hey.'

'Of course Auntie. Doing my duty is precisely why I'm here.' It is not often that I can afford the luxury of telling my family the truth.

'But what did she say?' I persisted.

'She said she didn't want to see you. That you've caused her enough trouble and you shouldn't bother to go up to Namaqualand to see her. And I said, "Yes Hannah it's no way for a daughter to behave but her place is with you now." ' Biting her lip she added. 'You mustn't take any notice. I wasn't going to say any of this to you, but seeing that you asked . . . Don't worry man, I'm going with you. We'll drive up tomorrow.'

'I meant what did she say to Uncle Danie?'

'Oh, she said to him, "Danie", just like that, dropped the Boeta right there in the graveyard in front of everyone, she said, "He's dead now and I'm not your sister so I hope you Shentons will leave me alone." Man, a person don't know what to do.'

Aunt Cissie frowned.

'She was always so nice with us you know, such a sweet person, I jus don't understand, unless . . .' and she tapped her temple, 'unless your father's death jus went to her head. Yes,' she sighed, as I lifted my rucksack from the luggage belt, 'it never rains but pours; still, every cloud has a silver lining', and so she dipped liberally into her sack of homilies and sowed them across the arc of attentive relatives.

'It's in the ears of the young,' she concluded, 'that these thoughts must sprout.'

She has never seemed more in control that at this moment when she stares deep into the fluffy centres of the proteas on her lap. Then she takes the flowers still in their cellophane wrapping and leans them heads down like a broom against the chair. She allows her hand to fly to the small of her back where the wood cuts.

'Shall I get you a comfortable chair? There's a wicker one by the stove which won't cut into your back like this.'

Her eyes rest on the eaves of the house where a swallow circles anxiously.

'It won't of course look as good here in the red sand amongst the thornbushes,' I persist.

A curt 'No.' But then the loose skin around her eyes creases into lines of suppressed laughter and she levers herself expertly out of the chair.

'No, it won't, but it's getting cool and we should go inside. The chair goes on the stoep', and her overseer's finger points to the place next to a tub of geraniums. The chair is heavy. It is impossible to carry it without bruising the shins. I struggle along to the unpolished square of red stoep that clearly indicates the permanence of its place, and marvel at the extravagance of her gesture.

She moves busily about the kitchen, bringing from the pantry and out of the oven pots in advanced stages of preparation. Only the peas remain to be shelled but I am not allowed to help.

'So they were all at the airport hey?'

'Not all, I suppose; really I don't know who some of them are. Neighbours for all I know,' I reply guardedly.

'No you wouldn't after all these years. I don't suppose you know the young ones at all; but then they probably weren't there. Have better things to do than hang about airports. Your Aunty Cissie wouldn't have said anything about them . . . Hetty and Cheryl and Willie's Clint. They'll be at the political meetings, all UDF people. Playing with fire, that's what they're doing. Don't care a damn about the expensive education their parents have sacrificed for.'

Her words are the ghostly echo of years ago when I stuffed my plaits into my ears and the sour guilt rose dyspeptically in my throat. I swallow, and pressing my back against the cupboard for support I sneer. 'Such a poor investment children are. No returns, no compound interest, not a cent's worth of gratitude. You'd think gratitude were inversely proportionate to the sacrifice of parents. I can't imagine why people have children.'

She turns from the stove, her hands gripping the handles of a pot, and says slowly, at one with the steam pumping out the truth.

'My mother said it was a mistake when I brought you up to speak English. Said people spoke English just to be disrespectful to their elders, to You and Your them about. And that is precisely what you do. Now you use the very language against me that I've stubbed my tongue on trying to teach you. No respect! Use your English as a catapult!'

I fear for her wrists but she places the pot back on the stove and keeps her back turned. I will not be drawn into further battle. For years we have shunted between understanding and failure and I the Caliban will always be at fault. While she stirs ponderously, I say, 'My stories are going to be published next month. As a book I mean.'

She sinks into the wicker chair, her face red with steam and rage.

'Stories,' she shouts, 'you call them stories? I wouldn't spend a second gossiping about things like that. Dreary little things in which nothing happens, except . . . except . . .' and it is the unspeakable which makes her shut her eyes for a moment. Then more calmly, 'Cheryl sent me the magazine from Joburg, two, three of them. A disgrace. I'm only grateful that it's not a Cape Town book. Not that one could trust Cheryl to keep anything to herself.'

'But they're only stories. Made up. Everyone knows it's not real, not the truth.'

'But you've used the real. If I can recognise places and people, so can others, and if you want to play around like that why don't you have the courage to tell the whole truth? Ask me for stories with neat endings and you won't have to invent my death. What do you know about things, about people, this place where you were born? About your ancestors who roamed these hills? You left. Remember?' She drops her head and her voice is barely audible.

'To write from under your mother's skirts, to shout at the world that it's all right to kill God's unborn child! You've killed me over and over so it was quite unnecessary to invent my death. Do people ever do anything decent with their education?'

Slumped in her chair she ignores the smell of burning food so that I rescue the potatoes and baste the meat.

'We must eat,' she sighs. 'Tomorrow will be exhausting. What did you have at Cissie's last night?'

'Bobotie and sweet potato and stamp-en-stoot. They were trying to watch the television at the same time so I had the watermelon virtually to myself.'

She jumps up to take the wooden spoon from me. We eat in silence the mutton and sousboontjies until she says that she managed to save some prickly pears. I cannot tell whether her voice is tinged with bitterness or pride at her resourcefulness. She has slowed down the ripening by shading the fruit with castor-oil leaves, floppy hats on the warts of great bristling blades. The flesh is nevertheless the colour of burnt earth, a searing sweetness that melts immediately so that the pips are left swirling like gravel in my mouth. I have forgotten how to peel the fruit without perforating my fingers with invisible thorns.

Mamma watches me eat, her own knife and fork long since resting sedately on the plate of opaque white glass. Her finger taps the posy of pink roses on the clean rim and I am reminded of the modesty of her portion.

'Tomorrow,' she announces, 'we'll go on a trip to the Gifberge.'

I swallow the mouthful of pips and she says anxiously, 'You can drive, can't you?' Her eyes are fixed on me, ready to counter the lie that will attempt to thwart her and I think wearily of the long flight, the terrible drive from Cape Town in the heat.

'Can't we go on Thursday? I'd like to spend a whole day in the house with the blinds drawn against the sun, reading *The Cape Times*.'

'Plenty of time for that. No, we must go tomorrow. Your father promised, for years he promised, but I suppose he was scared of the pass. Men can't admit that sort of thing, scared of driving in the mountains, but he wouldn't teach me to drive. Always said my chest wasn't good enough. As if you need good lungs to drive.'

'And in this heat?'

'Don't be silly, child, it's autumn and in the mountains it'll be cool. Come,' she says, taking my arm, and from the stoep traces with her finger the line along the Matsikamma Range until the first deep fold. 'Just there you see, where the mountains step back a bit, just there in that kloof the road goes up.'

Maskam's friendly slope stops halfway, then the flat top rises perpendicularly into a violet sky. I cannot imagine little men hanging pegged and roped to its sheer sides.

'They say there are proteas on the mountain.'

'No,' I counter, 'it's too dry. You only find proteas in the Cape Peninsula.'

'Nonsense,' she says scornfully, 'you don't know everything about this place.'

'Ag, I don't care about this country; I hate it.'

Sent to bed, I draw the curtains against huge stars burning into the night.

'Don't turn your light on, there'll be mosquitoes tonight,' she advises.

My dreams are of a wintry English garden where a sprinkling of snow lies like insecticide over the stubbles of dead shrub. I watch a flashing of red through the wooden fence as my neighbour moves along her washing line pegging out the nappies. I want to call to her that it's snowing, that she's wasting her time, but the slats of wood fit closely together and I cannot catch at the red of her skirt. I comfort myself with the thought that it might not be snowing in her garden.

Curtains rattle and part and I am lost, hopelessly tossed in a sharp first light that washes me across the bed to where the smell of coffee anchors me to the spectre of Mamma in a pale dressing gown from the past. Cream, once primrose seersucker, and I put out my hand to clutch at the fabric but fold it over a saucer-sized biscuit instead. Her voice prises open the sleep seal of my eyes.

'We'll go soon and have a late breakfast on the mountain. Have another biscuit,' she insists.

At Van Rhynsdorp we stop at the store and she exclaims appreciatively at the improved window dressing. The wooden shelves in the window have freshly been covered with various bits of patterned Fablon on which oil lamps, toys and crockery are carefully arranged. On the floor of blue linoleum a huge doll with blonde curls and purple eyes grimaces through the faded yellow cellophane of her box. We are the only customers.

Old Mr Friedland appears not to know who she is. He leans back from the counter, his left thumb hooked in the broad braces while the right hand pats with inexplicable pride the large protruding stomach. His eyes land stealthily, repeatedly, on the wobbly topmost button of his trousers as if to catch the moment when the belly will burst into liberty.

She has filled her basket with muddy tomatoes and takes a cheese from the counter.

'Mr Friedland,' she says in someone else's voice, 'I've got the sheepskins for Mr Friedland in the bakkie. Do . . . er . . . does Mr Friedland want them?'

'Sheepskins?'

His right hand shoots up to fondle his glossy black plumage and at that moment, as anyone could have predicted, at that very moment of neglect, the trouser button twists off and shoots into a tower of tomato cans.

'Shenton's sheepskins.' She identifies herself under cover of the rattling button.

The corvine beak peck-pecks before the words tumble out hastily, 'Yes, yes, they say old Shenton's dead hey? Hardworking chap that!' And he shouts into a doorway. 'Tell the boy to get the skins from the blue bakkie outside.'

I beat the man in the white polystyrene hat to it and stumble in with the stiff salted skins which I dump at his fussy directions. The skin mingles with the blue mottled soap to produce an evil smell. Mr Friedland tots up the goods in exchange and I ask for a pencil to make up the outstanding six cents.

'Ugh,' I grunt, as she shuffles excitedly on the already hot plastic seat, her body straining forward to the lure of the mountain. 'How can you bear it?'

'What, what?' She resents being dragged away from her outing. 'Old Friedland you mean? There are some things you just have to do whether you like it or not. But those people have nothing to do with us. Nothing at all. It will be nice and cool in the mountains.'

As we leave the tarred road we roll up the windows against the dust. The road winds perilously as we ascend and I think sympathetically of Father's alleged fear. In an elbow of the road we look down on to a dwarfed homestead on the plain with a small painted blue pond and a willow lurid against the grey of the veld. Here against the black rock the bushes grow tall, verdant, and we stop in the shadow of a cliff. She bends over the bright feathery foliage to check, yes it is ysterbos, an infallible remedy for kidney disorders, and for something else, but she can't remember other than that the old people treasured their bunches of dried ysterbos.

'So close to home,' she sighs, 'and it is quite another world, a darker, greener world. Look water!' And we look up into the shaded slope. A fine thread of water trickles down its ancient worn path, down the layered rock. Towards the bottom it spreads and seeps and feeds woman-high reeds where strange red birds dart and rustle.

The road levels off for a mile or so but there are outcroppings of rock all around us.

'Here we must be closer to heaven,' she says. 'Father would've loved it here. What a pity he didn't make it.'

I fail to summon his face flushed with pleasure; it is the stern Sunday face of the deacon that passes before me. She laughs.

'Of course he would only think of the sheep, of how many he could keep on an acre of this green veld.'

We spread out our food on a ledge and rinse the tomatoes in a stone basin. The flask of coffee has been sweetened with condensed milk and the Van Rhynsdorp bread is crumbly with whole grains of wheat. Mamma apologises for no longer baking her own. I notice for the first time a slight limp as she walks, the hips working unevenly against a face of youthful eagerness as we wander off.

'And here,' I concede, 'are the proteas.'

Busy bushes, almost trees, that plump out from the base. We look at the familiar tall chalice of leathery pink and as we move around the bush, deciding, for we must decide now whether the chalice is more attractive than the clenched fist of the imbricated bud, a large whirring insect performs its aerobatics in the branches, distracting, so that we linger and don't know. Then the helicopter leads us further, to the next bush where another type beckons. These are white protea torches glowing out of their silver-leafed branches. The flowers are open, the petals separated to the mould of a cupped hand so that the feathery parts quiver to the light.

'I wonder why the Boers chose the protea as national flower,' I muse, and find myself humming mockingly:

> *Suikerbossie'k wil jou hê,*
> *Wat sal jou Mamma daarvan sê . . .*

She harmonises in a quavering voice.

'Do you remember,' she says, 'how we sang? All the hymns and carols and songs on winter evenings. You never could harmonise.' Then generously she adds. 'Of course there was no one else to sing soprano.'

'I do, I do.'

We laugh at how we held concerts, the three of us practising for weeks as if there would be an audience. The mere idea of public performance turns the tugging condition of loneliness into an exquisite terror. One night at the power of her command the empty room would become a packed auditorium of rustles and whispers. And around the pan of glowing embers the terror thawed as I opened my mouth to sing. With a bow she would offer around the bowl of raisins and walnuts to an audience still sizzling with admiration.

'And now,' she says, 'I suppose you actually go to concerts and theatres?'

'Yes. Sometimes.'

'I can't imagine you in lace and feathers eating walnuts and raisins in the interval. And your hair? What do you do with that bush?'

'Some perfectly sensible people,' I reply, 'pay pounds to turn their sleek hair into precisely such a bushy tangle.'

'But you won't exchange your boskop for all the daisies in Namaqualand! Is that sensible too? And you say you're happy with your hair? Always? Are you really?

'I think we ought to go. The sun's getting too hot for me.'

'Down there the earth is baking at ninety degrees. You won't find anywhere cooler than here in the mountains.'

We drive in silence along the last of the incline until we reach what must be the top of the Gifberge. The road is flanked by cultivated fields and a column of smoke betrays a hidden farmhouse.

'So they grow things on the mountain?'

'Hmm,' she says pensively, 'someone once told me it was fertile up here, but I had no idea of the farm!'

The bleached mealie stalks have been stripped of their cobs and in spite of the rows lean arthritically in the various directions that pickers have elbowed them. On the other side a crop of pumpkins lies scattered like stones, the foliage long since shrivelled to dust. But the fields stop abruptly where the veld resumes. Here the bushes are shorter and less green than in the pass. The road carries on for two miles until we reach a fence. The gate before us is extravagantly barred; I count thirteen padlocks.

'What a pity,' she says in a restrained voice, 'that we can't get to the edge. We should be able to look down on to the plain, at the strip of irrigated vines along the canal, and the white dorp and even our houses on the hill.'

I do not mind. It is mid-afternoon and the sun is fierce and I am not allowed to complain about the heat. But her face crumples. For her the trip is spoiled. Here, yards from the very edge, the place of her imagination has still not materialised. Nothing will do but the complete reversal of the image of herself in the wicker chair staring into the unattainable blue of the mountain. And now, for one brief moment, to look down from these very heights at the cars crawling along the dust roads, at the diminished people, at where her chair sits empty on the arid plain of Klein Namaqualand.

Oh, she ought to have known; at her age ought not to expect the unattainable ever to be anything other than itself. Her disappointment is unnerving. Like a tigress she paces along the cleared length of fence. She cannot believe its power when the bushes disregard it with such ease. Oblivious roots trespass with impunity and push up their stems on the other side. Branches weave decoratively through the diamond mesh of the wire.

'Why are you so impatient?' she complains. 'Let's have an apple then you won't feel you're wasting your time. You're on holiday, remember.'

I am ashamed of my irritation. In England I have learnt to cringe at the thought of wandering about, hanging about idly. Loitering even on this side of the fence makes me feel like a trespasser. If someone were to question my right to be here . . . I shudder.

She examines the padlocks in turn, as if there were a possibility of picking the locks.

'You could climb over, easy,' she says.

'But I've no desire to.'

'Really? You don't?' She is genuinely surprised that our wishes do not coincide.

'I think I saw an old hut on our way up,' she says as we drive back through the valley. We go slow until she points, there, there, and we stop. It is further from the road than it seems and her steps are so slow that I take her arm. Her fluttering breath alarms me.

It is probably an abandoned shepherd's hut. The reed roof, now reclaimed by birds, has parted in places to let in shafts of light. On the outside the raw brick has been nibbled at by wind and rain so that the pattern of rectangles is no longer discernible. But the building does provide shelter from the sun. Inside, a bush flourishes in the earth floor.

'Is it ghanna?' I ask.

'No, but it's related, I think. Look, the branches are a paler grey, almost feathery. It's Hotnos-kooigoed.'

'You mean Khoi-Khoi-kooigoed.'

'Really, is that the educated name for them? It sounds right doesn't it?' And she repeats Khoi-Khoi-kooigoed, relishing the alliteration.

'No, it's just what they called themselves.'

'Let's try it,' she says, and stumbles out to where the bushes grow in abundance. They lift easily out of the ground and she packs the uprooted bushes with the one indoors to form a cushion. She lies down carefully and mutters about the heat, the fence, the long long day and I watch her slipping off to sleep. On the shaded side of the hut I pack a few of the bushes together and sink my head into the softness. The heat has drawn out the thymish balm that settles soothingly about my head. I drift into a drugged sleep.

Later I am woken by the sun creeping round on to my legs. Mamma starts out of her sleep when I enter the hut with the remaining coffee.

'You must take up a little white protea bush for my garden,' she says as we walk back to the bakkie.

'If you must,' I retort. 'And then you can hoist the South African flag and sing "Die Stem".'

'Don't be silly; it's not the same thing at all. You who're so clever ought to know that proteas belong to the veld. Only fools and cowards would hand them over to the Boers. Those who put their stamp on things may see in it their own histories and hopes. But a bush is a bush; it doesn't become what people think they inject into it. We know who lived in these mountains when the Europeans were still shivering in their own country. What they think of the veld and its flowers is of no interest to me.'

As we drive back we watch an orange sun plummet behind the hills. Mamma's limp is pronounced as she gets out of the bakkie and hobbles in to put on the kettle. We are hungry. We had not expected to be out all day. The journey has tired her more than she will admit.

I watch the stars in an ink-blue sky. The Milky Way is a smudged white on the dark canvas; the Three Kings flicker, but the Southern Cross drills her four points into the night. I find the long axis and extend it two and a half times, then drop a perpendicular, down on to the tip of the Gifberge, down on to the lights of the Soeterus Winery. Due South.

When I take Mamma a cup of cocoa, I say, 'I wouldn't be surprised if I came back to live in Cape Town again.'

'Is it?' Her eyes nevertheless glow with interest.

'Oh, you won't approve of me here either. Wasted education, playing with dynamite and all that.'

'Ag man, I'm too old to worry about you. But with something to do here at home perhaps you won't need to make up those terrible stories hey?'

NOTES ON CONTRIBUTORS

AUCAMP, HENNIE Born in 1934 in Dordrecht, Eastern Cape, and studied at Stellenbosch University, where he is now head of the Department of Education. One of the most consummate exponents of the short story form in Afrikaans, his central prediliction is the 'private ache', almost always attenuated by humour. A collection of stories, *House Visits*, was published in English in 1983; 'For Four Voices' appeared in *Volmink* (Full Mink) (1981). Aucamp has also published two collections of essays on short fiction, and in recent years has written several texts for cabaret.

BOETIE, DUGMORE Born in 1926 in Sophiatown, a black township outside Johannesburg. He lost a leg in the Western Desert during the Second World War, after which his jobs ranged from circus elephants' foot-washer to jazz guitarist. He also admitted to seventeen criminal convictions. His one book, the autobiographically-based *Familiarity is the Kingdom of the Lost* (1969) was midwived and edited by the theatre director and writer Barney Simon. Various sections of this book first appeared as short stories, some in the seminal South African literary journal *The Classic*, and the one reprinted here, also entitled 'Familiarity is the Kingdom of the Lost', in the October 1966 issue of *London Magazine*. Boetie died in 1966.

BOSMAN, HERMAN CHARLES Born in 1905 of an Afrikaans-speaking family in Kuils River, outside Cape Town. He obtained a teaching diploma in 1925, and took up an appointment as a schoolmaster in the Groot Marico District of the Western Transvaal. Here, in the space of six months, he collected together the material for 160 short stories and other pieces (in English) which were to make the district famous and Bosman one of South Africa's most widely read writers. In his chequered existence, he served four years of a life sentence for the murder of his step-brother, lived out much of the 1930s in Britain, was repatriated to South Africa during the Second World War, and worked as a journalist and literary editor, turning out interviews, art criticism, reviews and talk-of-the-town columns, as well as a play and poetry. A first novel, *Jacaranda in the Night* (1947) was followed by a collection of short stories, *Mafeking Road* (1947) and *Cold Stone Jug* (1949), an account of his prison experience. Bosman died in 1951; posthumously published were a novel, *Willemsdorp* (1977), collections of poems, essays, sketches, and three collections of short stories, including *A Bekkersdal Marathon* (1971) whose title story (first published in 1951) is reprinted here.

BREYTENBACH, BREYTEN Born in 1939 in Bonnievale, Cape Province. A writer of poetry and prose as well as a painter, he has lived much of his life in Paris since 1961. In work marked by widely differing philosophical and artistic currents such as Buddhism and Surrealism, he has continuously explored themes of love and pain in a landscape as personal as it is permeated by the realities of South Africa. In 1975 he entered the country illegally for political purposes, was arrested and sentenced to nine years' imprisonment, of which he served seven. It is from a book of short stories largely shaped by this experience, *Mouroir* (1984), that 'The Double Dying of an Ordinary Criminal' is taken. Breytenbach, who writes in both Afrikaans and English, has been a strong reference point for South African, and more particularly, Afrikaans writers over the past three decades. He has published one other collection of short stories, *Katastrofes* (Castastrophes) (1964), fourteen volumes of poetry, short prose pieces, novels, essays and three autobiographical accounts of his travels and prison experience in South Africa: *A Season in Paradise* (1976); *The True Confessions of an Albino Terrorist* (1984); and *Return to Paradise* (1993).

COPE, JACK Born in 1913 in Mooi River, Natal. His access to the world of the Zulus from an early age is reflected in such books as *The Rain Maker* (1972), one of eight novels, and *The Tame Ox* (1960), the first of three collections of short stories and source of 'Flight from Love'. Cope also published two volumes of poetry. He is of importance in the world of South African letters not only as a writer but also as an editor, notably, between 1960 and 1980, of the long-lasting English/Afrikaans journal *Contrast*. He was co-editor with Uys Krige of *The Penguin Book of South African Verse*, the first extensive anthology to bring together South African poetry in many languages. In 1980 he moved to England, and in 1982, published a commentary on dissident Afrikaans writers, *The Adversary Within*. He died in 1991.

ESSOP, AHMED Born in 1931 near Surat, in India, he went to South Africa in 1934 with his family, studied at the University of South Africa, and has worked both as a teacher and in the business world. He has published two novels, *The Visitation* (1980) and *The Emperor* (1984). 'The Hajji' is taken from *The Hajji and Other Stories* (1978), while *Noorjehan and Other Stories* appeared in 1990. He writes particularly of the Indian community of South Africa, often directing the sharp wink of the satirist at the deviousness and hypocrisy of human doings.

GORDIMER, NADINE Born in 1923 in Springs, Transvaal, she studied at the University of the Witwatersrand. Beginning in 1953 with *The Lying Days*, she has written ten novels, amongst them *A Guest of Honour* (1970), *The Conservationist* (1974) and *Burger's Daughter* (1979), alternating these with nine collections of short stories. *Six Feet of the Country*, of which the title story is included here, was published in 1956. Taken together, much of her fiction maps out the uneasy shifts in South African society over four decades. Her focus moves from the erosive comforts of white suburbia to those questions of political guilt and engagement which have led to several of her books being banned at various times in South Africa. She is the author of two books of critical essays, *The Black Interpreters* (1973) and *The Essential Gesture* (1988), and has written the texts of two books of photographs by David Goldblatt. Her long list of literary awards in both South Africa and abroad was crowned by the Nobel Prize for Literature in 1991.

HAVEMANN, ERNST Born in 1918 in Zululand, Natal, where he grew up on a farm speaking both Afrikaans and Zulu. He studied at Natal University, served in Libya and Egypt during the Second World War and worked in African administration for both the South African Railways and the Province of Natal before practising as a mining engineer. In the 1970s he emigrated to British Colombia, Canada, where he has written a number of spare, precise stories (in English), ranging in subject matter from border war and tribal history to the human cruelty of an animal lover. 'Bloodsong' appeared in his one book to date, *Bloodsong and Other Stories of South Africa* (1987).

HEAD, BESSIE Born in 1937 in Pietermaritzburg, Natal. She trained as a teacher, worked as a journalist for the magazine *The Golden City Post*, and then left for a teaching post in Botswana, living there from 1964 until her death in 1986. Her work, much of it written in and concerning life in Botswana, includes the novels *When Rain Clouds Gather* (1968), *Maru* (1971) and *A Question of Power* (1973). There are also various autobiographical texts, documentary writings on Botswana – among them a living momento to her adopted village, *Serowe: Village of the Rain Wind* (1981) – and two collections of short stories. 'The Prisoner Who Wore Glasses', originally published in 1973, appeared in the second of these,

Tales of Tenderness and Power (1989). Bessie Head's South African stories often have a political focus; the work rooted in Botswana explores exile and madness; elsewhere, it integrates the tales of people steeped in tribal lore in the midst of the twentieth century.

HOPE, CHRISTOPHER Born in 1944 in Johannesburg, he grew up in Pretoria and studied at the universities of the Witwatersrand and Natal. He has worked as an underwriter, copywriter, teacher and journalist both in South Africa and England, where he settled in 1975. He has published four collections of poems, beginning in 1971. His first novel, *A Separate Development*, published in 1980 and temporarily banned, has been followed by more than half a dozen more, including *Kruger's Alp* (1984) and *Black Swan* (1987). Some of his short stories, including 'Learning to Fly', were published in *Private Parts and Other Tales* (1981). His fiction moves beyond the traditional mould of liberal realism, into black humour and bizarre feats of the imagination. His more recent work, no longer set in South Africa, portrays a Europe where Africans appear as exiles and exotic visitors. One of his returns to South Africa was recorded in the autobiographical *White Boy Running* (1988).

JACOBSON, DAN Born in 1929 in Johannesburg, he grew up in Kimberley, which, along with the surrounding Karroo, provides the landscape for much of his South African writing. He settled in London in 1954 and has taught literature at several universities in the United States and Britain, including University College, London, from which he recently retired. He has published six books of short stories since 1958, as well as the selection *Through the Wilderness* (1973). The collection to which 'The Zulu and the Zeide' gave its title was published in 1959. There are also nine novels and novellas including *The Trap* (1955), *A Dance in the Sun* (1956), *The Price of Diamonds* (1959), *The Rape of Tamar* (1970), and *The Confessions of Josef Baisz* (1977). His South African fiction roves from inter-racial love to illicit diamond buying, sometimes touching on the questions of being 'demi-European' and Jewish at the foot of Africa; in his post-South African work, the focus on Jewishness sharpens. He has written five books of non-fiction, including the essays in *Time of Arrival* (1963) and *Time and Time Again* (1985).

MASEKO, BHEKI Born in 1951 in Botha's Pass, near Newcastle, Natal, he grew up in Soweto, and left school to work first as a truck driver, later in a laboratory at the Chamber of Mines. He is currently studying at the University of South Africa. 'Malambo' is included in his one book to date, *Malambo and Other Stories* (1991). It was first published in 1982 in *Staffrider* – a magazine to which he has contributed several stories, and which came to the fore after 1976, marking a resurgence of popular black writing. Maseko is one of a small but growing number of township story-tellers who have chosen the written page as a medium.

MULLER, ELISE Born in 1919 in Ceres, Cape Province, where her father was a clergyman, she studied at the Paarl College of Education and then at the University of Stellenbosch, but had to abandon her studies because of ill health. She published seven novels and novellas, beginning with *Ek, 'n Samaritaanse Vrou* (I, a Samaritan Woman) in 1943. She is however best known for the intensity of her short stories, most of them set among poor, rural Afrikaaners, and focused on that pivotal moment when a character is forced to some deeper understanding of reality. 'Night at the Ford', originally published in 1947, appeared in the collection *Die Vrou op die Skuit* (The Woman on the Boat) (1956). Further short stories were included in *Verhale en Essays 1942–1981* (Stories and Essays 1942–1981) which appeared posthumously in 1989, following her death in 1985.

NDEBELE, NJABULO Born in 1948 in Western Native Township, Johannesburg, he grew up 50km away in Charterston location, the setting for many of his stories. He holds degrees from the Universities of Botswana, Cambridge and Denver, and was Pro-Vice Chancellor of the University of Lesotho until 1991, when, after a long absence, he returned to South Africa to become head of the Department of African Literature at the University of the Witwatersrand. He is at present Principal and Vice-Chancellor of the University of the North. Once prominent in the Black Consciousness movement and now head of the Congress of South African Writers, Ndebele began his writing life as a poet. He is now best known for his stories (*Fools*, from which 'The Prophetess' is taken, was first published in 1983), and his theoretical essays, some of them assembled in *Rediscovery of the Ordinary* (1991). Together, this work steers away from the description of suffering, inspired instead by the complexity and resilience of black everyday life. Ndebele's depth of analysis and craftsmanship make him one of the central figures in South African writing today.

PATON, ALAN Born in 1903 in Pietermaritzburg, Natal, he qualified as a teacher and taught in Ixopo (also in Natal), setting for the opening scene of *Cry, the Beloved Country* (1948). Paton then became principal of Diepkloof Reformatory for black children and adolescents, his experience there over thirteen years informing several of his writings. Apart from three novels, the other two being *Too Late the Phalarope* (1953) and *Ah, But Your Hand is Beautiful* (1981), he published biographies, collections of shorter writings, a book of religious meditation, and several autobiographical works. A volume of his short stores, *Debbie Go Home* (1961) includes 'Life for a Life', while other short stories appeared in *Knocking on the Door* (1975). Paton was President of the South African Liberal Party from 1958 until it was disbanded in 1968 following legislation against racially mixed political organisations. His extended political essay, *Hope for South Africa*, was published in 1958. He died in 1988.

SMIT, BARTHO Born in Klerskraal, near Potchefstroom, in the Transvaal in 1924, he studied at the University of Pretoria, worked as a journalist, editor and theatre critic before leaving for Europe in 1952. There he immersed himself in theatre, and returned home to become one of the most important dramatists writing in Afrikaans. Beginning with *Moeder Hanna* (Mother Hanna) (1959), he wrote a string of plays, the last of which was *Die Keiser* (The Kaiser) (1977). He translated into Afrikaans such playwrights as Molière, Strindberg, Durrenmatt and Ionesco. Smit, who also worked as a publisher, edited three journals closely associated with the Afrikaans protest movement known as the Sestigers. He wrote few short stories. 'I Take Back My Country', originally published in 1951, appeared in the anthology *Bolder* (Bollard) (1973), edited by Hennie Aucamp, whose work also features in this volume. Smit died in 1986.

THEMBA, CAN Born in Marabastad, Pretoria in 1924, he studied at Fort Hare University and went on to work as a teacher and journalist. He became editor of the magazine *Africa*, and then associate editor of *Drum*, a journalistic kaleidoscope of black urban culture in the 1950s. Later, he taught at high schools in South Africa and Swaziland, where he lived from 1963 until his death in 1968. His work, banned for many years in South Africa, consisted of impressionistic journalism, 'opinion pieces' and a handful of short stories, all with the same ebullience and backwash of despair. It was collected together in *The Will to Die* (1972) – in which 'The Suit' is to be found – and *The World of Can Themba* (1985), edited by Essop Patel.

TSHABANGU, MANGO Born in 1949 near Bushbuckridge in the North Eastern Transvaal. He went to school in Soweto, has worked as a laboratory assistant, contributed to the *Sunday Times* and *World* news-papers, and is at present a communications manager. He has also been involved in theatre, and was co-editor of the theatre review *S'ketch*. His short stories have appeared in *Donga* and *Staffrider*, thus participating in the revival of black South African writing in the years following 1976.

'Thoughts in a Train' first appeared in the anthology *Forced Landing* (1980), edited by Mothobi Mutloatse.

VAN HEERDEN, ETIENNE Born in 1954 in Johannesburg, he grew up in the Great Fish River Valley where his father was a sheep farmer. He studied at Stellenbosch University, worked for a firm of attorneys before lecturing in Afrikaans at both the University of Zululand and Rhodes University, Grahamstown. He has written four novels, including *Toorberg*, translated from the Afrikaans as *Ancestral Voices* (1989); two volumes of poetry, and scenarios for cabaret. Two collections of short stories have appeared in Afrikaans; 'Mad Dog' is taken from the second of these, *Lieg fabriek* (Lie Factory) (1988). A selection of his stories has been published in English under the title *Mad Dog and Other Stories* (1992). Van Heerden's fictional themes range from race and ancestry in South Africa's rural heartland, to border wars and military repression in the country over the past decades.

VLADISLAVIĆ, IVAN Born in 1957 in Pretoria, he studied at the University of the Witwatersrand, and works as a freelance editor. He was closely associated with *Staffrider* magazine, and co-edited, with Andries Oliphant, the anthology *Ten Years of Staffrider* (1988). He has published a book of short stories, *Missing Persons* (1989), which depicts a series of estranged people in the recognisable yet dream-changed world of apartheid. Vladislavić's novel *The Folly* appeared in 1993. 'The Brothers' was included in the anthology *Soho Square V* (1992), edited by Steven Kromberg and James Ogude.

WICOMB, ZOË Born in 1948 near Van Rhynsdorp in the Cape Province. She studied at the University of the Western Cape and then at Reading and Strathclyde Universities in Great Britain, where she later taught English at institutions of further and higher education. In 1991 she returned to South Africa to teach at the University of the Western Cape. Actively involved in questions of contemporary South African society and literature, she is on the editorial board of *The Southern African Review of Books*. Her one published book to date is a collection of sequential short stories, *You Can't Get Lost in Cape Town* (1987), rare for the acerbic freshness of its language and unrelenting description of a coloured girl's initiation into adulthood. 'A Trip to the Gifberge' is the final story in this book.